Everstille

A Novel

Susan M. Szurek

Book One of the Everstille Stories

Chapbook Press

Schuler Books
2660 28th Street SE
Grand Rapids, MI 49512
(616) 942-7330
www.schulerbooks.com

Everstille, A Novel

ISBN 13: 9781948237451

Library of Congress Control Number: 2020907677

Part of the chapter "Business of the Day" was published as a short story in *Imagine That! 2013*, an ArtPrize Literature Contest Anthology.

The cover picture is from the set of Mary Mabel Shutes (1892-1984)

Printed in the United States by Chapbook Press.

For my sisters,

Kathy and Anita

The characters in this novel are not real, nor are they

based on any living or dead people.

However, they have been living in my head for years.

First

Mitchell's Emporium and Dry Goods

Upon pushing open the substantially built entry door, the bell would tinkle, alerting everyone inside to the fact that another customer had arrived. It was only six or seven steps across the creaking wooden floor until the large glass divided case filled with an assortment of candy was reached. The wonderous array was overwhelming. Chocolate in all shapes: stars, malted milk balls, caramels, bridge mix, and large bars of pure unadulterated sugar; soft chewies which stayed on teeth until pried off with a finger; orange and sour cherry slices, peppermint slices, and perfectly formed raspberry bites; chewing gum: Juicy Fruit and Cloves and Beechies Peppermint, tiny multi-colored shards, and jaw breakers which needed to be sucked until the center collapsed; Boston Baked Beans, and giant swirled rainbow decorated lollipops, and Tootsie rolls, both tiny and enormous, all just needing the point of a small finger and a few pennies to loose them from the glass cage.

Over to the left of the candy territory were tables filled with indispensable kitchen items: potato mashers and cookie presses, white metal canisters and lemon colored breadboxes, strainer sieves, and all the accountments needed for canning vegetables and fruits when summer ended and their ripeness demanded use. Iron trivets, food mills, pastry cutters, hand mixers, slicers, molds of all sizes and types scattered along the tables and piled on the shelves. All important. All crucial. All with the prices marked clearly at the bottom.

The measuring table, counter, and shelves directly across the way connected sewers and quilters and embroiderers with their necessities. Threads, buttons, snaps, collar stays, pins, seam rippers, rick-rack, floss of all weights and colors, scissors of all sizes including the brand-new pinking shears, all for purchase. Bolts of cloth: linens and cottons, patterned and plain, and even silks and wools, cozied up to each other. Thick Butterick and McCall pattern books, available for perusal and stacked up underneath the measuring table, were leaning precariously to one side.

Pots, pans, and larger items were stored along the back. Step down three stairs into a room traditionally called the *Men's Corner* to select any number of smaller tools hung on the walls, just in case one was needed and Jensen's Hardware and Agriculture Needs down one street and over two more, seemed too far away. Hoes and shovels, rakes and planers, hand saws, pliers, hand drills and more could be acquired here.

A large table loaded with odds and ends: some binoculars, a butterfly kite kit, a rather tarnished silver hand mirror, a pair of swan planters that had been ordered and never picked up, whisk brooms, and an assemblage of wicker fly swatters which proved popular in the summer months, was entertaining to look through. Additional items continually enhanced the collection.

Mitchell's Store had almost anything anyone needed. For decades, traveling salesmen assisted the proprietor in fulfilling the needs of the townspeople in Everstille. Michael Mitchell was the third generation to run the establishment and had many thoughts about how to improve and structure the store. In this endeavor, he was grateful for the advice and help of his wife, Mary, who had the inventiveness and vision to reorganize efficiently and restock attractively. At her suggestion, one of the first changes he undertook was to remove the ancient, faded, and splintered wooden sign which hung crookedly on the hooks outside the substantial entry door. He hired a proficient and professional sign painter from Chicago to stencil, paint, and outline in gold leaf across the new window he had installed, a sign which read:

Mitchell's Emporium and Dry Goods

The Mitchells

Mary Mitchell was admired by the town and loved by her family who accepted her gentle and firm sovereignty. Certain neighbors and close friends were delighted to receive invitations to her Sunday suppers where they admired the dining room table decorated with seasonal plants and the pink flowered china set Mary's parents gave the Mitchells on their wedding day, and enjoyed the delicious menu created by Mary and prepared by Tillie. Mrs. Mitchell arranged lavish formal parties as well as casual get-togethers for her groups of friends. Summer picnics convened on the vast and carefully manicured Mitchell lawn. She was repeatedly designated Rachel Circle's chairwoman of the Methodist Episcopal Church. Her personal responsibilities were not overlooked despite her social activities, and she assisted her children, Nathan and Viola, with their school lessons when they were young, and encouraged her husband, whenever he was available, to act as tutor when those lessons became more intricate. When, in due course, her children did not need her constant supervision, Mr. Mitchell appreciated his wife's periodic assistance at the Emporium and valued her advice about which items to acquire and how to display them, thus encouraging their purchase. She was considerate to her housekeeper-cook, Tillie, and did not interfere with her cooking and cleaning decisions. Mary Mitchell was committed to life.

Michael Mitchell was the proprietor of Mitchell's Emporium. He spent his days at the store which had been in his family for three generations, and he needed Mary's sense of sociability to keep him centered and to prevent him from becoming a social recluse. He was a man with high standards and expectations. Not everyone lived up to his ethics and work principles, and he had difficulty finding the right people to employ. He had begun to train his own son at age ten, but Nathan fared no better than past employees. Now, Nathan was close to sixteen and, unfortunately, did not have the ambition or the sense his father thought he should have had by this time, even though he had tried to instill in his son worthy work habits by requiring him to work at the store after school on Friday and Saturday, the busiest times of the week. After all, the store would one day belong to Nathan. Perhaps it was fortunate that Mr. Mitchell never knew that the store would not survive Nathan's management.

One late afternoon, Michael Mitchell, sweeping the back area of his Emporium, put down the broom, straightened his back, and stretched his arms. He glanced at the clock and realized that it was almost time for the children. Several them regularly came after school to choose orange slices or chocolate malted balls or impossibly colored bits of chewing gum from the candy counter. Mary Mitchell had the patience to wait on them; he did not, and today, his sighs were audible as the children slowly completed their penny purchases. His wife had left a little after one o'clock because she was ill again. The idea that she could be seriously ill did not enter his thinking.

He closed the Emporium earlier than usual, and in the near dusk, walked down Main Street to his home. Mary was on his mind, and he wanted to check on her. She had been suffering from stomach pains, indigestion, and a cough for some time now. The teas and home remedies Tillie had fashioned eased but did not eradicate the problems. He saw Doctor Evans' car parked in front of his house, and he hurried up the front stairs where he was met by Tillie who said, "I was just gonna call for you to come home. Doc Evans is in the bedroom with Mrs. Mitchell. She just isn't feelin' good."

Mr. Mitchell took the stairs two at a time and upon entering the bedroom was relieved to see his wife sitting up and chatting with the doctor. He went over and kissed Mary's cheek in greeting and turned to Doctor Evans and raised his eyebrows in question.

"Well," said Doctor Evans, "I will not make a diagnosis just yet. There are tests to be done. It might be a gall bladder issue, and I have advised Mary about her diet and activity. I also spoke to Tillie about what and how she should be cooking for her. We'll take a wait and see approach to this, and I'll watch over her. Mary, you understand what to do? Good. Michael, will you walk me out?"

The two men left as Mary settled back against the pillowed headboard and smiled weakly as Tillie, who had been lurking outside the bedroom to hear the diagnosis, enveloped her with the hand embroidered coverlet.

The two men walked out to the front and away from Tillie's ears, and Doctor Evans turned and spoke, "Michael, I will not mince words. I suspect Mary has something called *acute cholecystitis,* a severe gall bladder problem. Tests are needed, and there is a possibility of surgery although it is a dangerous operation and rarely done. We'll hold off for a while and see how she responds to some common sense changes in her diet. I also left some drops for her cough and will check on her in a couple days. Call if you need me sooner."

The men shook hands, and Mr. Mitchell watched him drive away. He went back to the house and up to the bedroom, and seeing that Mary had fallen asleep, he quietly closed the door and went into the kitchen for a cup of coffee.

Doctor Evans was correct about Mary's condition. She did have severe gall bladder trouble, and while her jaundiced aspect and indigestion concerned him, he might have paid more attention to her cough which, to be fair to him, did not appear to be the major issue. Regrettably, it was. Mary Mitchell died of a particularly virulent form of pneumonia within ten days. Doctor Evans was a pallbearer at her funeral and never forgave himself for his oversight.

The funeral was an earnest affair. Rituals and traditions were observed, and afterwards, the Rachel Circle held a lovely repast luncheon in the church basement. Tillie made several of her famous blueberry pies, and Mr. Mitchell and the children were consoled by friends, and neighbors, and church members for the better part of the day. The inundation of casseroles and cakes delivered to the Mitchell home ensured that Tillie did no additional cooking for well over a week. Mitchell's Emporium was shuttered for fourteen days, and when it did open, at first for shortened hours, a melancholy and quiet period was observed by all who came to shop the shelves and scrutinize the new widower. Even the school children who eventually returned with their pennies, pointed to their chocolate stars and peppermint candies, and in subdued voices, whispered their thanks.

Mr. Mitchell mourned for the remainder of his life and took to visiting Mary's grave at North Cemetery on Sunday afternoons. Nathan offered to quit high school and help full time at the Emporium, but to both his and his father's relief, that idea was rejected. Instead, Mr. Mitchell hired a temporary part-time clerk who proved adept at urging the townswomen to purchase supplementary sewing materials, and even more adept at pocketing just enough cash to make it seem like an accounting error. Thirteen-year-old Viola became weepy and withdrawn, but Tillie guided and watched her until the stinging pain became an aching discomfort.

The Mitchell family endured. They continued neighborhood friendships, and in time, with Tillie's encouragement, served Sunday suppers to invited guests again although never with the elegance Mary Mitchell had provided. Her death, like all deaths, slowly faded to a fragile, lingering despondency. The Mitchells moved ahead with their lives, and eventually and occasionally, the family, collectively and individually, experienced something akin to happiness.

Matilda Joan Harper (Schmidt) Smith

Help comes in many forms. For the Mitchell family, that form was Tillie Smith. Tillie had been housekeeper and cook on a part-time basis from the time Nathan was born, but when Viola came along, Tillie agreed to work additional days. She had her own system of cleaning and cooking, and Mary Mitchell did not interfere with her ideas which was the perfect way for them to get along. The two women formed a strong partnership, and when Mary Mitchell died, Tillie honestly grieved.

Tillie nursed Mary Mitchell through her brief, vicious illness, remaining at Mary's bedside while she struggled to take her final shallow, shattering breaths. After her death, when Michael Mitchell fell apart and could not budge from his chair to reopen the Emporium, Tillie allowed him time to grieve before persuading him to resume work. He operated shorter hours at first, as Tillie suggested, and she offered to organize the store shelves as his wife used to do. Mary's son, Nathan, isolated himself because that was how he dealt with his sorrow. Tillie comforted him by talking about his mother and how she would have expected him to maintain his activities and interests, and how she wanted him to continue to assist his father at the Emporium. The daughter, Viola, being so young, needed the most help. Death was incomprehensible to her. Tillie babied her for a while, eventually encouraging her to become independent, to help her father at his business, to endure the loss of her mother.

Matilda Joan Harper (Schmidt) Smith was Tillie's full name although no one knew it. She was born near Chicago, Illinois, met her husband, Herman Schmidt, married him, and eventually moved to Everstille to live with his mother who was suffering from a multiplicity of diseases. Soon after the move, Tillie and Herman became parents of a healthy boy, and shortly after that, old Mrs. Schmidt died. Then both Herman and the baby developed a terrible cold which progressed to a horrendous cough, then an atrocious bout with pneumonia, and then a ghastly death. Within two months, Tillie had three graves to attend at North Cemetery and was alone in a shambling cottage towards the furthest edge of the town. With the help of kind neighbors, she moved to a rented apartment close to the main streets of Everstille and began a series of part-time jobs to support herself. She also changed the spelling of her last name to the easier *Smith* and set herself the task of living.

Tillie found jobs cleaning houses for some women at the Methodist Episcopal Church where the Mitchell's attended Sunday services. She baked pies and delivered them every Wednesday and Saturday morning to Peterson's Bakery which was right next to Mitchell's Emporium and Dry Goods. This was how she met Michael Mitchell. When the Mitchells welcomed baby Nathan to the family, Mary Mitchell realized that caring for the baby, cooking, cleaning, and keeping up with her church and social activities was overwhelming, so Tillie was hired. She stayed through the deaths of both Mitchells, the marriages of both their children, and, in turn, helped both Nathan and Viola with their families. She never let on to any of them that from the first time she saw Michael Mitchell, she loved him.

Michael Mitchell was not particularly handsome, although he was noteworthy. He was not talkative but rather reticent. He was polite, his manners were faultless, his etiquette unimpeachable, his work ethic admirable. Tillie never could determine exactly what it was about him that attracted her devotion. He treated her respectfully and gave no inkling that he saw her as anything but a kind and helpful individual, someone to whom he owed the same esteem as he would any other person. Maybe it was his greenish eyes, the small dimple in his cheek when he smiled, the tiny crooked little finger on his left hand that he had broken as a boy, his graying dark hair that had a slight curl, the way he stretched his arms towards the sun when he was tired, or the one ear lobe that was slightly longer than the other. Tillie noted it all. She was discreet with her admiration and regard and never, in any way, disclosed her feelings. She was deferential, and while she treasured being in his company, did not unnecessarily seek it out. She knew her feelings were indefensible, and she felt guilty. She tried not to think about him as she lay in her uneven bed in her rented apartment at night, as she helped Mary Mitchell set and decorate the family dining table for Sunday suppers, as she walked his children home from school and made sure they enjoyed a snack, as she ironed with utter precision and folded with loving care, his clothing. Tillie rationalized her love for Michael Mitchell by accepting it.

Tillie thought of herself as plain and ordinary. She was not educated beyond the sixth grade because that was when her father had disappeared and she, as the oldest, needed to stop squandering her time in a classroom, start to work, and bring in some money to help support her younger brothers. At least that is what Tillie's mother said. So, Tillie, at age twelve, was taken on as a maid's assistant and acquired knowledge and methods of cleaning, cooking, sewing, and organizing that would serve her well at the Mitchell's. She never minded the hard work. the long hours, and the modicum of wages earned. If she were not pretty and educated, she might as well be handy and serviceable. And when she met Herman Schmidt, he took note of her practicalities.

Tillie and Herman married on a Wednesday and moved into her mother's already crowded apartment on Thursday taking over the smallest back room. While Tillie's brothers grew, moved on with their lives. and out of the apartment, she and Herman stayed. They were saving for a down payment on their own place, but after a couple of years, Herman's mother became ill, and they moved to Everstille. Had he not been his mother's only living child, they might not have done so. Tillie knew she was pregnant when they moved and thought a small town could be advantageous when raising the large family she expected. Then Herman and the baby died. And the Mitchell family became Tillie's.

Tillie and Mary Mitchell were friendly but not friends. Mary Mitchell was benevolent and considerate but aware of their many distinctions. After all, she was attractive, educated, and schooled; she expected to marry successfully. Her family was disheartened by her choice of businessman husband, but she revived their spirits by becoming the town of Everstille's leading female citizen. Church activities, social gatherings, charity work, and, of course, her family obligations would have been unmanageable were it not for Tillie's service and support. And Tillie's service and support, her succor and sustenance, her encouragement and comfort were provided for the rest of her life to the Mitchell family because she loved Michael Mitchell and the dimple in his cheek and his crooked little finger and that long earlobe.

Nathan

Sometimes children are a disappointment which was how Michael Mitchell felt about his firstborn, Nathan. Of course, not at the beginning when he felt the exhilaration of becoming a father, of seeing his eyes and nose reproduced in a small being, of knowing that he was its creator. The congratulations from others, the slaps on the back from his friends, the cigars he handed out were all symbols of belonging to that special club called *Fatherhood.* And it continued to be thrilling and invigorating right up until that time, some weeks later, when Nathan became a fussy, colicky baby who cried through the night and made his wife tired and unhappy and kept Michael from getting the sleep he need-ed to continue to run his business. Ephemeral were the congratulations, the slaps, the cigars. Everlasting was the crying child who looked like him and stole his sleep.

On an early Wednesday morning, a tired Michael Mitchell moved towards his Emporium and noticed a woman walking to the bak-ery next door. He nodded his head to her and suddenly it registered with him that this was the same woman who regularly cleaned his house.

"Good morning, Mrs. Smith," and Michael was delighted he remembered her name given his exhausted state. "I want to tell you that your pies are delicious, and I regularly purchase one for our Sunday sup-pers. I especially like your blueberry pie."

Tillie Smith stared at him and felt her heart speed up and her face flush. "Thank you," was all she thought to say and continued to walk her pies towards the bakery.

Michael moved forward and held the bakery door for her and had a thought. "Mrs. Smith, my wife and I have a three-month old son, and we are in need of some additional help. Would you know someone who would be willing to give us a few days a week? If she knew about babies, that would be extraordinarily helpful."

Tillie swallowed hard as she thought of her child in North Cem-etery. Here was a chance to gain additional cash in a difficult time, and she had the knowledge. A small voice in the back of Tillie's mind whis-pered: *I would do anything you asked.* Out loud, Tillie responded that she was available if they wanted her for more than a biweekly cleaning, she knew something about babies, and she would be happy to help. A deal was struck.

Tillie was able to settle Nathan down probably because she was not an anxious, apprehensive, sleep-deprived parent. She helped with cleaning, cooking, and the baby, three mornings a week and on alternate Sundays when the Mitchells gave their Sunday suppers. Tillie received fair payment for these duties and was also able, at times, to be near Mr. Mitchell. The Mitchells were able to get some sleep, and Mary began to feel normal again since she was able to meet with her friends and resume her social activities. Michael was grateful to have their baby, albeit intermittently, silenced

Nathan recognized, adored, and wanted his mother. He held out his arms when he saw her and became both excited and contented when she held him. He gooed and cooed and smiled at Mary Mitchell. He turned his head away and fussed when his father came close to him. This was not unusual behavior from young children, but Michael felt rejected and refused. He was busy six days a week for ten hours a day and felt drained when he came home. He asked about Nathan and sometimes saw him, and while Nathan grew to know him as *Dada*, that special bond Michael thought all fathers and sons naturally had was absent. His own father had died when Michael was quite young, and he did not realize that special bonds do not just occur but are created through diligent presence.

Nathan walked and talked and ran and hopped and jumped and did all things children did at the correct age children did them. But Michael did not find these actions remarkable. He expected more. He was not sure exactly what he wanted, what Nathan should be able to do, what a three-year old was capable of, but a disenchantment with his son began. And persisted.

Nathan was a normal child who continued to grow in the normal ways. He was a mediocre student and a conventionally behaved boy. He had some friends, and while he was not overly popular, he received invitations to more parties and activities than he could attend, although this was probably due to his parents' business and social connections. His best friend was Edna Johnson, the little girl who lived across the street and three houses down, but with this too, Michael was dissatisfied. His son should be playing with the other boys in the neighborhood and not this little girl. Nathan should be throwing a ball and chasing after snakes and fishing in the pond. And occasionally Nathan did these things. With Edna.

One Saturday morning, when Nathan was ten, his father woke him early and brought him to the Emporium. "This is the family business," Michael explained to a disinterested and sleepy child, "and you need to understand what it is I do and how you are expected to help out. One day, you will take over this store and run it, so you must begin to work at it now. Start by taking the broom and sweeping the back room. I'll look in in you shortly to see how things are going."

Nathan, unhappy about spending a Saturday morning doing what was boring and unnecessary work, slowly made his way to the back, took the broom, and began to do the task in a typically average, ten-year old boy way. Michael sighed as he watched his son swish the broom around the floor without necessarily removing any of the obvious dirt. The next job, dusting the countertops, was performed in the same joyless manner. After three hours of tedious work, Nathan was turned loose with the reminder that every Saturday he would be expected to put in his time at the apprenticeship. "Yes, Sir," said Nathan, and went home to play with Edna.

For years, on Saturday mornings and Friday afternoons, Nathan and his father worked together. Michael taught and retaught Nathan how to order, receive, stock, organize, clean, and sell. But Nathan frustrated his father by his pedestrian and mistake-ridden approaches to ordering, receiving, stocking, organizing, cleaning, and selling. Attempting to escape what seemed like an eternal chore, Nathan, after high school graduation, talked his father into sending him to college. He managed to gain acceptance to Purdue University where he assumed he could effortlessly obtain instruction in something stimulating, but Nathan was disillusioned. He also continued to displease his father. Nathan spent one semi-successful year studying pharmaceutical science before giving up and coming home to work full time with his father in the Emporium. He did his best to understand the business, but he never enjoyed or valued the work he considered tedious and boring.

Some years the Emporium did well; often it did not due partly to the difficult times and partly to Mr. Mitchell's continual extension of credit to the townspeople of Everstille. When Michael died unexpectedly of a heart attack and the business came to Nathan to handle by himself, the sheer responsibility and massiveness of doing what he never wanted to do exhausted him. After years of ineffective management and lost profits, Nathan and his wife, Edna, made the decision to sell the Emporium.

Had Michael been alive, he might have been comforted that the new owners decided to keep the name, and *Mitchell's Emporium and Dry Goods* continued to do business in the town. In actuality, it was deemed, by the new owners, too expensive to change the expertly gold leaf outlined and stenciled name on the front window.

Nathan and Edna

Nathan hesitated when it came to introducing the worm to the hook. He made a face and threw the wiggly creature on the ground, then looked over to Edna who had no trouble sticking the pointed end directly through the middle of her worm so that both ends hung down evenly.

"Nathan, just do it like this," and Edna held out the example close to his face, "and do it quickly. It is not hard if you push down fast on the hook."

"I can't," Nathan looked at the worm which was attempting to relocate itself to the safety of a grassy area, "Can you do it for me? I promise I will do it next time."

Edna sighed and caught the moving thing and expertly pressed the sharpness into the middle. She handed his pole to Nathan, and they moved to the edge of the pond where there were few fish, but where it was still amusing to sit and throw the line into the murkiness, and talk about nothing, and wait in the sunshine.

Edna was fearless. At least it seemed that way to Nathan. The two friends spent as much time together as possible, and Nathan never resented the directions and instructions Edna gave to him. He had trouble making decisions and completing tasks, but Edna could always find ways to encourage him. Other children saw Edna as dictatorial and domineering, but Nathan did not. To him she had superlative ideas and plans, and he knew she would assist him with any of his struggles. He would take her suggestions and turn them around in his mind until they became his plans. Edna never seemed to mind.

The person who did mind all the time the two spent together was Nathan's father. Michael Mitchell lectured his son, during those infrequent times he spent with him, about the activities that he should be undertaking, and the boys with whom he should be associating. And then, a brief interruption in the friends' closeness would transpire during which Nathan simply waved to Edna as she waited for him across their street, and he joined the neighborhood boys in their doings. These separations were never lengthy. Soon, he and Edna would be back together at the pond, or in her backyard swinging from the tire, or sitting on a porch as he listened to her. Edna never minded these brief splits. She was as self-assured and confident as a child could be.

When Nathan and Viola were older, they were each allowed to

invite a friend to the Sunday suppers held at the Mitchell house. Viola alternated inviting her friends, not wishing to hurt any of their feelings. The only person Nathan ever invited was Edna. They would sit together at the dining room table talking quietly and ignoring the rest of the company. Mrs. Mitchell did not find this problematic, but Nathan's father found reason for concern.

"Honestly," said Michael Mitchell to his wife, "why is it that Nathan cannot ask one of the boys in the neighborhood? There is Jonathan down the street, and Ira Meager who is in his class. I know he spends some time with them. It just appears strange for Nathan to spend so much time with Edna. It seems as though they are courting, and that is ridiculous at their age!"

"Leave him be," answered his wife, "they are young and Nathan seems happy, and Edna is a good influence on him. Courting! You fret too much about Nathan." And that would be the end of the discussion until the next Sunday supper when Edna would again be Nathan's choice as guest. Eventually they were courting, and, had Mary Mitchell lived, she would have approved of it.

Nathan was a grade ahead of Edna in school, but they usually walked to and from classes together, talking about their day and planning for their evening.

"I hate working at the store," Nathan complained to Edna during a walk home. "My father complains about everything I do and the way I do it. I have been there for years, and even when I do exactly as he has taught me, I still mess it up. I just can't seem to do things good enough for him."

"I know you work at it and have never wanted to," commiserated Edna, "Have you thought about doing something besides working at the Emporium? You mentioned going to Purdue to study a science course."

"Maybe. I guess that might be something I could do. I know I am not that great at school, and it would mean being away from you, but I could start to think about it and talk to Pa. Do you think I could do it? What kind of science should I do?" And with Edna's eager help, and his father's reluctant money, Nathan decided on a course in pharmaceutical science. To everyone's surprise, Nathan was accepted at Purdue University the year after high school graduation.

College classes like Physics, Dispensing Laboratory, Botany, Pharmaceutical Latin were much more difficult than high school, and

Nathan did not do well. Not having Edna to encourage and sustain him was intolerable. After a stressful year, continual lecturing letters from his father, and a warning or two from the Dean of Students, Nathan decided that Purdue was not for him. He may not have enjoyed working at the Emporium, but it was something he comprehended. The summer after his year away, and after many lengthy discussions between Nathan and his father, it was decided that Nathan would stay home and work full time at the Emporium. And Nathan and Edna got married.

At the beginning of that fall, on an ideal autumn day with the sun blazing and multi-colored mums in full bloom, a perfectly lovely wedding was conducted at the Methodist Episcopal Church. There was a bitter-sweetness to the service and an emptiness in the pew where Mary Mitchell would have been. But Tillie had labored with Edna's mother, Millie, and between them the wedding was almost as enchanting as Mary Mitchell would have wanted. Afterwards, a reception was held in the spacious Mitchell yard. The bride was glowing, and the groom blissful. Michael Mitchell and Edna's parents, Millie and Ed, discussed the fact that this day had been ordained since their children were infants. All the neighbors agreed. Jonathan from down the street and Ira Merger who had been in Nathan's class were his groomsmen; Viola and Edna's best friend, Catherine were the bridesmaids.

The newlywed couple spent the weekend at the Grand Oakerton Hotel in South Bend, and then came home to their house just down the street from their families. The first year's rent was a wedding gift given jointly by their parents. Edna, self-assuredly and competently kept a perfectly clean and splendidly decorated house, planted an amazing vegetable and flower garden at the side of the rented property, and learned to cook delicious and nutritious meals. Nathan kissed his wife each morning and went to work at the Emporium, joylessly ordering, receiving, stocking, organizing, cleaning, and selling under the watchful eye and in the disgruntled presence of his father.

Viola

Sometimes children are not a disappointment. When Viola was born, her parents were delighted with the sweet-tempered, cooing little girl who was so very different than their son had been. No crying, colicky infant this one. Mary and Michael were both charmed by their delightful daughter, but Michael was bewitched by her dark, curly hair and greenish eyes which were so like his. She held onto her father's finger when he touched the center of her tiny, perfect hand, and when he spoke, she turned her head towards his voice and beamed. She gurgled. She laughed. The same dimple that was Michael's was present in her cheek as he held and rocked his daughter. Viola completed their family…four corners, a quadrilateral ensemble, a square set.

The Mitchells were a bit concerned about Nathan accepting a little sister because he had been the only child for three years. But he did not mind having another being in the house. In fact, in his three-year old mind, Nathan welcomed Viola because she was a distraction. His father did not seem to be as crabby around him when his sister was present. Nathan could divert attention from his misdeeds by saying to his father, "Papa, come and see Viola. She smiled at me today." And his father would always be willing to go. Nathan liked his sister. She was happy and pleasant and not a bother. She grew up babied and spoiled by her parents, and her brother, and Tillie. She was gentle and kindhearted, giving and thoughtful, considerate and charitable. These qualities formed her character. And her faults.

Her mother taught her to embroider, and Viola, ever anxious to please, practiced and became expert at French knots and satin stitches. She embroidered table runners, and napkins, and handkerchiefs and placed them in the solid oak chest her father presented to her one Christmas, having ordered it from the Emporium's catalog. She attempted to teach her friends the craft and was patient with them as they struggled to complete the simplest running stitch. Viola embroidered handkerchiefs for her mother's birthday and Tillie's birthday which happened to be only days apart. And when her mother died, she placed in her coffin a beautifully created handkerchief with a black blanket stitch border and her mother's initials in one corner. And hers in the opposite. She had stayed up for two nights to achieve the offering, and after the funeral, was ill for the better part of a week. Doctor Evans stayed with Viola most of that time fearing that she would follow her mother into the family plot at North Cemetery. He was determined not to lose another Mitchell and sighed with relief when she recovered.

After Mary Mitchell's death, the family struggled with the arduous task of remaining upright. Michael Mitchell threw himself into his work once Tillie convinced him to do so; Nathan threw himself into his room coming out only when cajoled; Viola threw herself into Tillie's apron on a daily basis, weeping and whimpering for her dead mother, and Tillie wiped away Viola's tears on the bullion knotted rose handkerchief.

Slowly the family came back together. Michael Mitchell continued to mourn and went every Sunday, weather permitting, to place whatever flowers were available on Mary's grave, and to tell her about the Emporium's newest delivery, and how Tillie was able to help out even though she never did shelve the items quite the expert way Mary had. He found these visits sustained him through the interminable week and the empty evenings. Nathan spent time with Edna who was agreeably disposed to comfort him. He had offered to quit school to work full time with his father but was secretly relieved when his offer was refused. Viola finished the napkins she had started with her mother's help. She asked Tillie to wash, starch, and iron them, after which she placed them in tissue paper, and then into her solid oak chest. She took her needles and floss, her hoops and scissors, her patterns and papers, organized them carefully, and placed them beneath the starched, ironed, and tissued napkins embroidered with chain stitches and feather stitches and the lovely Pekinese stitch which had two colors and all together, created a threaded garden of daisies and roses and tulips. Viola did not embroider again for many years.

The following summer after his wife's death, Michael went to Tillie to ask her advice.

"Tillie, do you think we should have a Sunday supper again? I would like to invite Doctor Evans and a few of our friends who have been so thoughtful and helpful this past year. Do you suppose it would be proper to do so? The children could each invite a friend, and we could arrange the dining table with some flowers from the backyard. I want to do what is correct, but I don't want to be viewed as being improper or hasty in my mourning."

Tillie looked at his greenish eyes and curling dark hair which, she noted, had turned a bit grayer over the past year. "I believe that would be fine, Mr. Mitchell. How many people would you like me to plan for?"

And with this settled, the Sunday suppers were reinstated. They were never held as often nor did they have the splendor that Mary

Mitchell's suppers had, but friends and neighbors were gladdened to see that life was going to continue. For that initial supper, Viola asked her friend, Sarah, and Nathan and Edna sat side by side with their hands often touching.

Michael was working long hours at the Emporium and while Tillie always left him a dinner plate warming in the oven, she thought he seemed a bit thin. After school, when Viola was available, Tillie began sending her to the Emporium with a carefully wrapped sandwich for him. During one visit, Viola picked up some kitchen gadgets that had recently been delivered and asked her father where he was going to display them.

"I don't know, Viola. I was never creative with those things, and your mother usually knew where best to place them. What do you think?"

Viola looked around and then said, "They would look fine in the front display window. I think I have an idea about this. Let me show you." She moved a chair to the front and in a few minutes the items were arranged in an imaginative and pleasing manner.

Michael looked at her and said, "You appear to have your mother's talent. That is perfect. Thank you, Viola."

Until that day, Viola had not shown interest in the Emporium, but a comparison to her mother was the inducement she needed. She felt flattered and grateful and useful. As she scrutinized the store, she saw the unpacked boxes that Nathan had not touched and the dusty counters he had never gotten around to cleaning, and without asking or being told, she began to work. Soon she was moving, and decorating, and placing items where they would be noticed. When new items arrived, she would arrive to the store after school, her father's sandwich in her hand, and spend her time arranging them. She leaned over her father's shoulder as he did his paperwork and asked pertinent questions and understood his often-confusing answers. In the succeeding years, Viola, without any fanfare or pomp, began ordering, receiving, stocking, organizing, cleaning, and selling in the Emporium, and she found a joy in it that Nathan never had.

Miss Viola Mitchell

"Miss Mitchell, where do you want these boxes put? There ain't much room in the back, but I can put them on top of the boxes already back there."

Viola looked up from the table where she was rearranging the new wooden sock darners, thimbles, and needle packets, and said, "That's fine, Frankie. I will get to those later."

Viola had hired Frankie part-time, but he seemed to need continual direction, and she hoped hiring him had not been a mistake. Since high school graduation the previous year, she had worked alongside Nathan giving their father some rest. Michael Mitchell had suffered some fainting spells, and Doctor Evans warned him that the long hours he had kept for years were catching up with him, and he needed to relax. The truth was, Nathan was not as good at managing the Emporium as Viola had become over the years, and only if she were there, was Michael willing to curtail his work and responsibilities. He waited until Viola had finished her education and was able to help Nathan full time. He had worried that Nathan would resent his sister working with him, but there had been no sign of that.

The truth was, Nathan was happy for Viola to take over as much as she wanted. He was prompt every morning, careful when completing his paperwork, and helpful in the store when there were enough customers to warrant his presence which was rarely the case. He was also prompt in leaving at close of day, careful not to ask for additional paperwork and helpful when Viola asked for his assistance, although only after the second or third request. Nathan depended on and appreciated his sister. He benefitted by her ability to establish a smoothly running business because that thwarted his father's criticism.

Viola was aware of this, but concern and worry about her father, and kindness and compassion for her brother kept her from mentioning it. Nathan was content to have Viola do the arranging and paperwork, and she felt useful. She enjoyed working. There was comfort in organizing and arranging and deciding. Because she was an efficient manager and had learned to deal effectively with the salesmen who regularly visited, her father had left much of the ordering of new stock to her. While her friends found husbands and began families, she found new stock and began systematizing it.

Viola would not have been able to work at the store had it not
been for Tillie who was at home managing the house, cooking, cleaning,
and completing the duties which traditionally would have been Viola's.
Tillie had become indispensable in the years since Mary Mitchell's death.
She was a surrogate mother to Mary's children and a support to Mary's
husband. Tillie's ardor for Michael Mitchell had not faded but had subtly
changed into feelings of dedication and watchfulness. She maintained
her own small apartment and developed her own set of friends. She even
sometimes entertained a not quite platonic relationship with Joseph, the
butcher at Clampet's Grocery Store and Meat Market. But she never
desired to remarry and only intermittently, while lying in her uneven bed,
did she ruminate about running her finger along the crevice in Michael
Mitchell's cheek caused by his dimple. Besides, Joseph was the source
of the sizeable, succulent chickens she sometimes roasted for the Sunday
suppers still periodically held at the Mitchell house.

It was at a preparation for one of these suppers that Tillie questioned Viola about Ted, a high school friend she had sometimes invited.

"Viola, will you be asking Ted to Sunday supper? I need to
know to make plenty of that potato casserole he likes."

Viola had just come home from the Emporium and was taking
off her jacket. She came into the kitchen and commented, "I had not
considered it. I think he is traveling with his brother right now. I suppose I can check to see if he'll be around," and she headed towards her
bedroom. She turned back and spoke to Tillie again saying, "On second
thought, I invited Sarah and her boyfriend, and with Nathan and Edna
and her parents, we will have a full table. Maybe next month."

Tillie shrugged. She liked Ted. She thought he and Viola well
matched.

Viola's thoughts were with the Emporium. She had recently
expanded the dry goods area and was thinking about ordering additional
sewing items. Some of the townswomen had asked for certain patterns
and colors of threads and buttons, and she had to place an order to Fred,
their usual salesman, for some sewing machine parts. She had made a
list in her head but needed to write it down before she forgot. The day
had been difficult. Her father and Nathan had argued about something,
and Frankie had not shown up for work, so she was not able to complete
the new display in the window she had planned. Perhaps next week she
could get to it. She knew tomorrow, Saturday, would be their busiest
day, and she and Nathan and their father would all need to assist customers. She just hoped Frankie would be there.

Frankie was not there. The Saturday was just as busy as she thought it would be, and while that was good for their business, it was an exhausting day. Nathan and their father had put aside their disagreement, and the three of them worked until late afternoon when most customers were gone.

"Go home, Pa," said Viola as she saw her father sink into a chair in the back. "Nathan and I will finish up and sweep and close. Few people will come in now, and we can manage. Besides, Tillie is getting ready for tomorrow's supper, and I know she baked pies. I guess she would allow you a piece if you wanted." Viola smiled at her father and he smiled back.

"Well, I think I will go if you two are going to be fine. A short rest before dinner is a good idea." Michael put on his hat and picked up the paper he had not read and walked home to Tillie's pie. Viola watched him as he went out the door and down the street.

***

Sunday was a bright day and Viola slept in, skipping services at the Methodist Episcopal Church. She looked forward to a relaxing time with friends and family. In the afternoon, she went to the backyard to gather flowers for the dining table. She clipped dahlias and arranged them in her mother's favorite vase and helped Tillie set the table and organize the dishes.

Her father came downstairs, and they sat on the front porch waiting for friends and family to arrive. When everyone was there, Tillie and Viola brought in the roasted chicken and side dishes.

"By the way, Viola," started Nathan, "a large box came in yesterday, and it was addressed to you. I didn't open it, but put it in the back room of the Emporium. Maybe it's those sewing notions you ordered, but I did not recognize the company it came from,"

"Oh good," Viola answered, "No, I think those are the new work smocks I ordered for myself and for you and Pa. They were a good price, and the aprons I have been wearing have not been large enough to cover my skirts. I've ruined more than I care to think about. I'll look at them tomorrow. I believe you will like yours. I ordered black ones for the two of you."

"Did you get black ones for yourself?" asked Michael Mitchell.

"No," said Viola, smiling, "mine are pink."

John Joshua Jasper

He was born with charm and charisma. He acquired cruelty and callousness. Eventually, there were only remnants of the former. It was uncertain whether this was due to an accumulating general unhappiness, increasing gin consumption, intensifying headaches, or a combination. John Joshua Jasper's early life and upbringing helped to create his character. He was born to older parents as a surprise after they thought no children would be theirs. His mother's happiness was short-lived as she died of a blend of age, poor health, and ever worse medical care when John was barely a year old. His father passed the child around to various indifferent family members to raise. It was an uneven childhood at best, but John thrived. When he had his own children...twin boys... he took little interest in their upbringing thus completing the circle of deficient parenting.

John's ready smile and handsome face got him pretty much whatever he wanted. He learned at an early age to pretend agreeability, pleasantness, and interest in others. His schoolteachers never caught him doing the cruel things schoolmates knew he did. Earnest performance convinced them of his innocence. He avoided hard work and created believable excuses when chores or homework were incomplete. Their apathetic sympathy coupled with John's posture and bearing, fooled the general community into believing he was knowledgeable and trustworthy, and so he managed to find success at the expense of others.

Due to several converging circumstances, including the death of his father, the negligence of his extended family, and a vanished interest in academia, John entered the work world early. At fourteen, he was a part-time gas jockey at the town's only station, the Kleanmotor Service Station. He pumped gas, cleaned windshields, and topped off oil in the automobiles that veered off the highway and into the town. His manners and smiles earned him tips, especially from the traveling salesmen who came to sell their merchandise in the town that, like most of the Midwest, was growing and expanding and needing all manner of modern conveniences.

By age sixteen, John worked full-time having gained enough expertise and knowledge to make small repairs. He acquired familiarity with road maps and could inform lost travelers where to go and, if they wished, where in the town to get a meal or a bed. John generated a cash understanding with the businesses in town who supplied those meals and beds. By age seventeen, he owned his own automobile, had mentally absorbed the road maps, and was biding time until he was old enough to leave and become one of those thriving salesmen he admired.

John was fascinated by the stories they told and titillated by the tales they whispered. He befriended the men and flattered them by asking questions and listening to their answers. He used his cash to buy some of their products. He spent time with them at the town's main hotel, anxious to know more about life on the road, and by doing this, gained their trust and learned their dodges. He examined their sample cases and echoed their style of speech. By the time he was eighteen, he was knowledgeable about planning sales routes, making sales reports, and writing receipts. The following year, Henry Wilson wanted to retire and was willing to take nineteen-year-old John on as his replacement.

Luggage, sample cases, and bags were piled into the automobile. A new route taking them through three states had been generated, and for a year they traveled together. Henry taught John how to sell to both business owners and housewives. With one, you handed over the pen to close the deal. With the other, you handed over flattery and fawning. He taught him how to place orders and which companies were sloppy about calculating delivered items. Henry knew the shipping clerks who would happily overlook a double shipment for a small monetary induce-ment. There was a method of handling sales reports and receipts which garnered a larger commission for the salesman. Henry knew all the strategies; soon John knew them too. He ingratiated himself into Henry's reality, and Henry thought of John as progeny to whom he could leave his knowledge. It was not just his knowledge he was leaving to John who would siphon off the dollars and change Henry was careless about on the nights after the two of them stopped for a meal and a few drinks at the local public house.

Sales terms and pitches, transactions and dealings, networks and connections were not the only things Henry taught John. In the seedier areas of the towns and cities they visited, there were pleasurable amuse-ments to be had. But one needed to be careful. Careful with both physi-cal hygiene, and the choice of residence in which to spend an hour or so. Henry taught John where to find the various enterprises, how to deal with the authorities who worked the doors, and the difference between the independent and ringer establishments.

"Stick to the ringers. The girls there get checked and are sani-tary. They ain't so likely to rob you, even though they cost more. Mon-days are slow days for 'em, and afternoons are best," and Henry winked and grinned.

John was young and charming and amiable, and he never had a difficult time obtaining his cravings. Even if he had to pay a bit more, his unusual requests were granted. He was curious about nonstandard practices and often would choose an older and more experienced woman who was inspired by his youth and comeliness. He learned to reimburse these women for their efforts, and they learned to keep quiet about his selective tastes.

And so, his education continued through the states. One morning after a grand night, Henry Wilson could not be roused, and when John, after emptying Henry's pockets of ready cash, contacted the local undertaker, he felt almost sad. However, the sample cases and bags fit more conveniently in the automobile with just one person. With no real reason to remain, he drove to Jim's Standard Station, put gas in the auto, air in the tires, and when the gas jockey topped off the oil, he flipped him a tip, nodded his head and drove off, excited to get to the next village, next town, next city.

Driving and selling, meeting other salesmen, collecting his pay, and spending it on diversions seemed to be the life he was always meant to lead. John periodically passed his home town but never stopped. There was nothing for him there; no family he wanted to see, and he could not indulge in his preferred pleasures in a place he was known.

***

For the next couple years, John enjoyed being a nomad. He traveled through the states discovering the villages where the housemakers welcomed both him and his sewing notion samples, the towns where he made his best sales, and the cities where the prettiest and cleanest women resided. He honed his skills and determined through trial and error which items sold best. The sample cases were constantly rearranged to include objects women coveted: linen swiss embroidered collars, rose appliques, eyelet lace, sequins, and trim. These articles opened many doors to him, and if the man of the house happened to be around, the case which displayed several small tools and clocks was shown. Chewing gum was gifted to children, although John considered this item a loss because he chewed so much of it himself. Businesses in the towns ordered the pots and pans and larger household gadgets which he kept stored in the more spacious automobile he had recently acquired. And John kept a supply of pens to hand to owners of the businesses with whom he signed contracts. Thank you, Henry.

***

Summer came, and John wanted to expand his sales area. He drove north in Indiana and entered a new, unexplored county. Fresh territory was always a challenge, but his confidence and assuredness were high, and he turned off the highway and down the road towards the town of Everstille.

John pulled the car over and got out on Main Street. He stretched his arms, rolled his neck and shoulders, and reached into the passenger seat to pull out his suit coat and put it on. As he shook out the wrinkles, his eye caught the swish of pink and he turned to watch as an attractive, dark-haired woman arranged items in a store's display window. John Jasper unconsciously nodded and swiped his hand through his hair. He spit his gum out on the street, straightened his tie, and placed his hat at a rakish angle on his head where the headache which had begun was promptly forgotten.

He bent to pick up his suitcase filled with wares, and with charm and charisma in tow, sauntered across Main Street, down towards the establishment which had stenciled in gold-leaf across its window:

Mitchell's Emporium and Dry Goods

Then

Plans

"John, would you like another piece of Tillie's pie?" Viola motioned to Tillie who had just come into the dining room with the coffee pot. "Perhaps you would like to try some of the sour cherry. She is such an expert baker, and we all love her desserts!"

John leaned back patting his stomach and declared, "No, thanks, but that was a great meal! I couldn't eat another bite right now. Traveling like I do, I get a taste of all sorts of pies, but Tillie, that was a special one!" and he turned to Tillie and smiled.

Tillie gave John Jasper a grimace that passed for a smile and continued to offer coffee to the family gathered around the dining table. Viola whispered *Thank you* with a smile, but Tillie ignored her. Since John had become a regular guest at the family's evening dinners, Tillie's attitude had become fractious. She could not help it. There was something about the man she had just served coffee to that provoked her. He had some manners, a carefully managed wardrobe, a handsome face, and seemed solicitous enough to Viola, but Tillie did not like or trust him. There was a disturbing quality to John Jasper that Tillie sensed but could not define. She wondered why Viola had taken to this man when Ted was a perfectly fine fellow. After all, Tillie knew Ted and his family. He and Viola grew up together. They went to the same church and had friends in common. This man was not Ted. But there was nothing Tillie could do. She just hoped this spell John seems to have cast over Viola would not last.

"This was a fine meal, and I thank you for inviting me. Mr. Mitchell and Nathan, if you would like, I could bring in my sample cases and show you the new items. I don't want to rush anyone, but I need to get to my next town by tomorrow afternoon, and I would hate for you to miss out. These new items are pretty popular, and there's already a back order for some of them. Miss Viola. you might be interested in seeing the new sewing notions. They're good sellers."

John understood the family hierarchy. He noted Nathan's disinterest in business matters and Viola's attentiveness to the same. He had observed Mr. Mitchell's dependence on his daughter and his confidence in her opinions and knew not to exclude her. Besides, she was attractive, and, although female, had a decent grasp of business. Quite a nice business. The Emporium was a large building filled with an accumulation of saleable items available to a growing customer base. That business needed someone who really knew how to advertise and move the stock; someone who understood sales techniques; someone who knew what the customer wanted or did not want but could be pressed into wanting. It was clear to John that the Mitchell men did not understand dealings and transactions the way he did. It was evident they were simple, unambitious, and frankly, old man Mitchell did not look well. A plan was forming in John's mind.

He excused himself and went to his car to get the cases while Mr. Mitchell and Nathan moved into the parlor to await the presentation of the newest gadgets. Nathan helped his father to his chair, and Viola helped Tillie clear up the dinner dishes. As they put away the leftovers and piled the plates on the counter near the sink, Tillie thought, *Maybe I should say something now.*

"That John Jasper," Tillie casually remarked, "he has sure been here for quite a few meals. For a traveling salesman, he does a whole lot of traveling to this town!" and she gave Viola a meaningful look.

"Stop it, Tillie. John is just a nice man who has some interesting stories to tell. Anyway, you know I am busy helping Nathan and Pa at the store and don't have a lot of time to meet new people. He has plenty of kitchen and sewing items to show us, and I want to see what those new things are. One of the ways to gain more business is to bring in new stock. You know that." She looked out of the window and remarked, "John is coming back now. Leave those pots soak, Tillie. I will wash them later once business is done and he has gone. Now, go on home and rest."

Viola gave Tillie a quick hug and left the kitchen to join the men in the parlor. Scowling, Tillie scoured the pots with steady annoyance.

John entered the parlor and explained the new items, giving them to the Mitchells to examine. Samples were handed back and forth, inspected, and discussed. The green-handled potato masher, and the tall wooden knife holder, the fruit-juice extractor, and the red-handled copper pot cleaner were great additions to any kitchen, according to John, and he made sure Viola kept a few sample items for Tillie's use. Viola admired the unusual buttons and thimbles and flowered appliques. She was pleased with the selection, but concerned that Everstille townswomen would not be willing to spend a bit extra for such fine adornments. The Mitchells discussed this; they did some figuring; they debated what would be best to order, and finally, made their decisions. After the contract for the kitchen gadgets and sewing notions was signed, John shook hands with all of them, holding Viola's for just a bit longer and smiling into her eyes. He handed Michael Mitchell the pen.

"Thank you, sir. I know these things will sell well. I should be back with them in two weeks, and I'll plan on seeing all of you then. Thanks again for such a grand meal. I need to get going, but, Miss Viola, why don't you walk me out to my automobile?"

John packed up the samples and closed the cases. He put his new tweed coat on and picked up his hat. He said his goodnights again to the men standing in the shade of the darkening parlor, and he walked with Viola outside to his car. He placed the cases carefully in the back and reached into the passenger side, bringing out a package and handing it to Viola. She opened it and took out a multi-colored iridescent carnival glass vase.

"I know you always decorate the dining table with flowers and always use the same vase, so I thought you might like something different. I do appreciate the food and your kindness to me. Thank Tillie again for the great meal. It was way better than some of those diners I eat at."

Viola looked at the shimmering vase judging it tawdry and loud, but she received few gifts and was gratified that he had thought of her. She would not denigrate the present by explaining that the vase she used was her mother's, so she simply smiled and said, "Thank you, John. This will be lovely on the table, and I will be sure to fill it with flowers the next time you are here. I am glad you were able to have dinner with us, and I'll be on the lookout for you in a couple of weeks. Have a safe trip now."

John smiled and nodded and placed his hat on his head. He opened the driver's side door and got in the car and started it. When he got to the corner, he stopped and leaning out of the open window, waved again to Viola who was standing at the curb in front of her house still watching him. *Well*, he thought, *that's a good sign.*

He drove through the town, passing Mitchell's Emporium and Dry Goods on Main Street and slowed down to take a good look at it. He turned the corner and drove around the block and then back to Main Street to see the building once more. Not bad. He began to ponder things. Maybe it was time for him to settle down. Maybe a permanent home should be his next move. Viola would make an acceptable wife. Besides, those Mitchell men were lame-brained business men, and old man Mitchell was on his last legs. Why should marriage keep him from enjoying any of his other distractions? Traveling and business trips were necessary. He would often be out of town.

As he drove, John deliberated and reflected and considered. He glanced over to the empty passenger seat and realized he had to get a gift for that girl... Molly? *Better stop and get another one. I promised to bring her something.* And as thoughts, iridescent and gleaming as the carnival glass vase swirled in his head, John turned the corner driving out of Everstille and on to the next village, the next town, the next city.

Cottonwood Fluff

Grief is a strange creature. It can be instant or gradual, but when it arrives, like the cottonwood fluff that floats in the air and sticks to hair and clothing, it is difficult to shake. When picking it off, soft malleability clings to fingers, and for just an instant, the temptation to grab and hold on becomes engulfing.

Tillie took a deep breath and rolled over again trying to find some comfort in her bed, but she knew the morning light would find her still seeking. Giving in to awareness, she got up, turned on the lamp and took the sweater from the bottom of the bed where she had thrown it last night. She located the sleeves for her arms, then reached under the bed for slippers. The coffeepot was washed and rinsed and ready, but she did not want anything yet. Her stomach ached from crying, her eyes swelled, her head throbbed. She hardly knew what to do, so she sat in her one comfortable chair, staring out of her one window, and watched as the gray gloom began to brighten into light. She yearned for rain and prayed the sun to stay hidden. It did not seem judicious for it to shine on the day Michael Mitchell was to be buried.

Doctor Evans had monitored his health for years and had cautioned him to ease up, but after those fainting spells had dissipated, Michael claimed he was just fine, and he continued to work long hours at the Emporium. He was needed there; Edna and Nathan recently welcomed a baby girl, and the new father was taking some time off from work to help Edna. At least, that was his excuse. Viola's recent marriage to John Jasper had her setting up house in their rented apartment, and although she helped when she could, John was peculiar about his wife working. Especially working at the Emporium. Viola could be found there on a regular basis when John was traveling, but she stayed home when he was there. Currently, he was there.

Three nights ago, Michael was closing the Emporium. When he did not come home for dinner, Tillie, as she often did, prepared his dinner, covered it, put it in the oven to keep warm. Then she left. The next morning when the dinner was still there, uneaten, and cold, and Michael Mitchell was not to be seen, she picked up the telephone and called the Emporium, but there was no answer.

She rushed to the store, found the substantial entry door unlocked, and Michael Mitchell sprawled on the floor next to the candy counter with the large bag of bridge mix he was using to refill the depleted stock, spread about him. Peanuts, raisins, macadamia nuts, nougat, and licorice pieces were kicked out of the way and thrown to the side as Tillie knelt beside him without any expectation that he would open his eyes. And in that intimate moment, before Tillie picked up the telephone to call the family and the doctor and leaned out the substantial entry door to scream for help, she stopped, and for the first and only time ever, kissed the chilled cheek which contained the dimple she had so wanted to touch.

***

The service was set for eleven at the church, and Tillie wanted to get there early and deliver the repast luncheon pies she had baked the last two days. Blueberry is Michael's favorite. *Was*, she reminded herself. She cleaned up, holding a cold cloth to her face, attempting to relieve the swelling of her eyes and the bright spots on her cheeks. Pulling her hair back into a rigid knot at the nape of her neck, she secured it with the long pins she had purchased, using her discount, at the Emporium. Her black cloche hat and sensible long black coat, both of which she had worn for years, were given a careful brushing. They might be a bit warm for this time of year, but warmth was welcome. Michael would never be warm again. His dinner would never be waiting, warmed in the oven. The sun would not shine down on his curling, mostly gray hair, touching it with warm caresses and spreading its passion along his face as he stretched his arms up and glanced skyward. No longer would the dimple in his cheek warm Tillie in the corner of her soul that belonged only to him. Warm thoughts entered Tillie's mind and left, becoming tepid, then turning chill.

The church began to fill up well before the time of the service. Family, friends, neighbors, businessmen, townspeople, even small children, the ones who pointed fingers at their sugary penny purchases, were there. The Mitchell family filled the front pew, and Viola turned to see Tillie come up from the church basement where she had left Michael's pies, and into the church sanctuary. She walked over to her, linked her arm through Tillie's, and brought her to the front pew to sit next to the family. "You are part of our family," she whispered to Tillie who could not answer or look at her, but twisted in her hands the bullion knotted rose handkerchief Viola had embroidered for her.

Tillie could not remember the service later. Prayers were spoken, hymns were sung, and eulogies were pronounced. The minister talked about Michael Mitchell's wonderful qualities as a father and friend and citizen of Everstille. There was weeping from many, and some sobbing was heard, but Tillie did not realize it was coming from her. The new Mitchell grandchild slept through the entire lengthy observance, and everyone commented later, at the luncheon in the church basement, while taking small polite bites of blueberry pie, how wonderful the child was, and how proud both Mary and Michael Mitchell would have been, if only…

After all was done, after the last of the Rachel Circle had left, after luncheon leftovers had been wrapped and divided up among the Mitchell clan, after the sun, which did have the audacity to shine that day, began to finally disappear, Viola and her new husband, John, drove Tillie home to her small rented apartment. Viola walked Tillie to the door and hugged her and said appropriate things, but Tillie could not concentrate on mere words. She hugged Viola with fond firmness. Plans were made to meet at the Mitchell home in two days. There were things to decide and spaces to clean. Clothing to distribute and knick-knacks to allot. The Emporium would remain closed for a week or so, while the family made decisions, and the Last Will and Testament that Michael Mitchell had the law firm of Granger and Wicks draw up, was read. Death keeps the living busy for a while.

Tillie closed and locked her door. She put away her black cloche hat, hung up her long, sensible black coat, and put on the sweater she had thrown on her one comfortable chair earlier that day. She started the water for coffee, and took the long pins from her hair placing them back in the small hairpin holder she had purchased at the Emporium using her discount. She braided her hair, pulling it over one shoulder. The water was boiling, but she turned it off having decided that she did not want coffee after all, and with a sigh that she was not even aware of, lowered herself into the chair.

The sun was gone, and with it, whatever heat had been tendered was rescinded. Tillie pulled her sweater close around her. She did not think she could sleep. She sat in the chair, staring out of her one window, looking at the clouds which were closing in and covering the sky. Finally, appropriately, it was going to rain. She waited to close her eyes until the rain fell, producing jeweled murmurs. There was no bed for Tillie that night. She fell asleep in her one comfortable chair, wrapped in her sweater, dreaming about a crooked little finger, and greenish eyes, and a dimple.

Marriage

The first time he hit her, she was not expecting it and gave a small gasp in surprise. She raised her hand to her face and felt the heat. She had never been stuck before. Certainly not by her parents. Nathan may have gently pinched her cheek, and Tillie only needed to glare at her to ensure she stop whatever nonsense she was generating. Once or twice she had heard about a physical fight between some of the boys at her school although she had not been there to see and could not quite picture what that would be like. Her life, up until this moment, had been entirely violence free. Viola, astonishment and shock on her face, regarded John who turned and walked outside, slamming the back door as he left.

John had hit other women, but he had paid for that pleasure. Of course his wife deserved it, but this had been done in anger and not as a prelude to gratification. Yet, the act had brought an enjoyment of sorts, a sense of power, of strength. And that, John decided, had been lacking in his marriage. He lit a cigarette and inhaled deeply and reviewed the act. He might be sorry later. He thought he probably should and would apologize and considered going back in, but just for the moment, wanted to savor the deed. He walked out to the wooded area and stared into the darkness of the trees.

***

Viola had not been prepared for marriage. Her mother died when she was thirteen, and her father had not thought to ask any female relatives to advise Viola in this area. The thought never occurred to Viola either, so she prepared for married life by embroidering table napkins, and painting delicately on china plates, and placing all into her solid oak chest. When Tillie left on infrequent trips to visit her relatives near Chicago, Viola practiced the rudiments of cooking on her father and brother with minor successes. She and some of her girlfriends would hold discussions about expectations and secrets of married life in their pink and green wallpapered bedrooms, but none of the other girls were any more knowledgeable than Viola. Their talks ended with giggling and blushing. And so, on her wedding night in the Bridal Suite of the Grand Oakerton Hotel in South Bend, Viola became a wife.

John Jasper was what could be called an experienced man. He had cultivated certain discriminations and definite habits through his experiences. In his courting of Viola, he confessed his love to her in sweet and innocent terms, but in his innermost self, he knew otherwise. The hope of eventually obtaining Mitchell's Emporium and Dry Goods for himself (or his wife's, it was all the same) loomed large in his plans, and having a sweet young wife to direct what he was sure would be a gentlemanly home and hearth was reason enough to propose.

John was also disappointed by both the wedding night and the eventual marriage prospects. Because he did not acquire the Emporium as he thought he would, he needed to continue his job as a traveling salesman. That turned out to be a boon for them both. John could indulge his tastes and return to his married life with some of his anger dissipated. And Viola only had to suffer the indignities of the kind of martial relations John expected periodically. And there were some happy times. Few, but then, was life meant to be happy?

After Michael Mitchell's funeral, when the Last Will and Testament was read to the gathered family by Mr. Richard Wicks of the law firm Granger and Wicks, Viola received a small monetary inheritance. Apparently, there were major bills to settle, and, according to tradition, Nathan, the only son, was given the ownership and directorship of what was left of the family business.

When the small house, once owned by the Pinkertons, on Smokehouse Road, a few miles west of town came up for sale, John and Viola used the meager inheritance she received as down payment on it, and they moved in. Viola tried her best to make it lovely and livable. She decorated the walls with the china plates she had painted as a girl. She placed her mother's delicate lace shawl across the old horsehair sofa left with the house. She used her mother's pink floral formal china creamer and sugar bowl to decorate the nicked and scratched kitchen table that she spent many hours buffing and shining. The carnival glass vase John had once given her adorned the top of the old upright she had been willed and had moved from her childhood home into her new parlor.

Distance and tradition kept Viola tethered to her new house. She missed being at the Emporium, and whenever possible, would get a ride into town and check out what Nathan was doing. She would arrange the front window display with new items and ensure the candy counter had the requisite amount of sweets. But her new husband resented her interest and involvement at the store. He thought the marriage would bring the dowry of the Mitchell Emporium to him, but that did not occur, and he, with considerable yelling and base language, eventually forbade her to do any work at the Emporium or give any help to Nathan. There were always ways around things. When John traveled, Nathan would drive out to the house and drop off paperwork to Viola who surreptitiously and competently, completed it.

Viola spent her time cleaning and dusting and polishing. Her friends lived in town, and she rarely saw them. The closest neighbors to John and Viola were the Rivens family who were busy working their farm. One day, Jena Rivens, in the spirit of welcoming, drove over to visit Viola and bring her some tomatoes she had just canned. John was traveling, and Viola was alone and sweeping the porch, but when Jena drove up, she was pleased and invited her in for some coffee. She proudly filled the pink floral creamer with milk and placed it on the table, and they sat down.

"I see you have a piano here. Do you play much?" and Jena sipped at the too strong and somewhat bitter coffee.

"I took lessons for a few years and played for the children's choir at church, but now I just pick away sometimes, especially when John is not home. He says my playing starts his head aching and he does not want to hear it," and Viola gave a little nervous laugh.

"Oh, I am sure you play well. My youngest, Anne, has always wanted to play, but there has been little time to teach her. Our piano at home has not been touched in years and it needs tuning," and Jena's thoughts trailed off. She looked at the painted plates hanging on the wall and commented on their loveliness, and the women finished their coffee in silence.

Viola saw her first guest out of the house and waved as Jena drove off. She washed and dried the cups and swept the kitchen, shaking out the rag rugs and polishing the already clean kitchen table. The day seemed sunnier, and she decided to use some of the gifted tomatoes in the new stew recipe Tillie had written out for her. John was due to return from his sales trip the following day, and a nice dinner would be a pleasant homecoming. After making herself something for dinner and cleaning the kitchen once again, she sat down at the piano and entertained herself until the darkness brought out the crickets.

The next morning, she was up early working at the dinner, sweeping the constantly swept house, and greeted John with a smile and kiss on his cheek as he walked in. But the trip had not been successful, and John, even after having stopped for a drink or two, was still in a bad mood when he came home, and the stew was not appetizing, and Viola spilled some coffee on John, and then there were harsh words said, and then the slapping commenced.

***

Viola went to the sink and ran some cold water on a cloth which she then held to her face. She was not sure what to think or to do. She looked outside the back-kitchen window and saw John standing by the wooded area near the house. He did not appear ready to come inside, so she went back to the kitchen. The dishes were washed, the table wiped, the floor swept. Viola rocked on the creaky rocking chair for a while, and then the darkness told her to get ready for bed.

She changed her clothes, hanging up the blue flowered dress she had especially chosen for the dinner, carefully washed her still sore face, brushed her teeth, and then her hair. She crawled into the bed on her side, and pulled the new quilt that the Rachel Circle had made for her wedding, up to her chin. She turned on her side and started to drift off. In a while there was a familiar heaviness beside her, and John's arm inched around her.

"Sorry," he whispered into her ear, "I won't do that again."

Promises. Broken promises.

Enceinte

When Viola found herself in the family way, she was shocked. She knew it was likely to happen, but did not expect it so soon after the wedding. She and John had been married just over a year when she began to gag at the smell of John's aftershave. Her stomach heaved when she made the morning coffee. She needed to take a long nap after lunch because she simply could not stay awake. She made an appointment with Doctor Evans who verified the miracle and gave her some sound medical advice about eating and sleeping and breathing. Her brother and sister-in-law were delighted for her and excited for their daughter, Edie, who would soon have a cousin. Tillie planned to make Viola's favorite casseroles since she knew the new mother would be too tired and busy to cook. Her friends, herded together by Sarah, were making plans to shower her with lovely handmade baby items. The Rachel Circle relived their own birth stories at their teas, and mourned the fact that Mary Mitchell, and now Michael Mitchell, would never know the joys of their grandchildren. John was somewhat pleased and was even somewhat kind to her throughout the entire pregnancy.

After the first few months when the sickness left her, Viola began to prepare. She went to the back room where her solid oak chest was located, unlocked, and opened it, shifted the embroidered napkins and table runners, and removed her embroidery tools. With the floss and needles, the hoops and scissors, the papers, and patterns, she resurrected her needlework. Smiling and humming, she sat on the creaky rocking chair creating small baby bibs with yellow daisies and petite rabbits flouncing along the edges. There was a feeling, a certainty she would have a little girl, and she goaded John into painting the second bedroom a particularly lovely shade of pale pink. Viola envisioned her daughter's dark ringleted hair brushed with adoring care, and her flawless small hands with pearly nails at the tips tenderly washed and dried. She wondered if her mother's name, Mary, should be her daughter's first or middle name, and she considered planting daisies in the plot next to the house so that when they bloomed in the summer, she and her little girl could make daisy crowns and wear them in the sunshine.

Viola was not prepared for the agony of the birthing process. No one mentioned to her that there would be so much blood and other bodily fluids present. or that the tearing and ripping and pulling would be so unpleasant. Throughout eighteen hours of agony, Viola writhed and struggled and vomited. She cried out for her mother and came close to cursing her husband who had decided that the best place for him to be was somewhere else. Tillie's reassuring presence and helpful advice was neither particularly reassuring or helpful. Doctor Evans, speaking in his most professional tone, assured Viola that things were moving along at the usual pace, and she was being a trooper, and she should try to breathe as she had been instructed to practice. All in all, it was a difficult, frightening birth, only diminished in danger by the fact that the major partaker in it was so young and healthy. It ended with a startling outcome. Doctor Evans had not suspected it; Tillie was astonished; and Viola was stunned at the birth of twins and saddened that they were both boys.

Once the shock was over and Doctor Evans had sponged and clipped and sewed what he needed to, and Tillie had made a soothing chamomile tea, and the new father had glanced down at the twin red faces and proclaimed them *fine,* and the new mother had rested, it was time to name the miracles. Their father seemed uninterested in having anything to do with the boys except perhaps, the creating of them, so Viola named the older one, the one with the brown splotch on his neck under his right ear, *Michael* which was her father's name and the younger one *Mitchell* which was her maiden name. They both received the same middle name: *John,* which cemented their parentage. The babies were swaddled snugly in two of the blankets Viola had received from the shower that Sarah and some of her other friends had given her and which had been held in the church basement and presided over by the Rachel Circle. The twin boys were placed side by side, together, in the small cradle her sister-in-law had specially ordered for her from the Emporium's catalog. John, after placing a chaste kiss on his wife's ashen brow, left to celebrate his new status at Mazie's, bringing with him the cigars he had picked up on his last sales trip. He would not be seen again for three days.

***

A scraggly John turned up three days later, and after dutifully holding each of the boys at the insistence of his wife, cleaned himself up, packed his car with all his sample cases, and took off for an extended sales trip. Tillie stayed with Viola for the first six weeks after the twins' birth. She made Viola's favorite meals and encouraged her to eat and woke up with Viola during those two A.M. feedings even though all she could do was to hold one of the screaming babies while Viola nursed the other. Viola had a difficult time nursing the babies at first, and if it had not been for the help of Tillie and Jena Rivens, she would have been up that creek without a paddle, an adage John often liked to use. Except, of course, John called the creek something vulgar.

Once Viola figured out how to feed and clean and bathe and change and play with her sons, she began to enjoy the tasks. There was the matter of obtaining two of everything because since only one had been expected there was a dearth of diapers and baby clothing and blankets and bibs. A second shower was organized. This time, only Sarah and Edna and Tillie came to Viola's house bearing the additional gifts that friends and the Rachel Circle had quickly created. A second cradle was ordered and sent special delivery and received just in time. The twins were growing and expanding, and they needed their own spaces to sleep and stretch and move. Eventually, the second bedroom was repainted blue by Nathan with the reluctant help of John, so that the boys could sleep and grow and play in the appropriate hue.

The boys learned to crawl and walk and talk in that house. Viola taught them their colors and numbers and, when John was not around, played the old upright and sang songs and simple hymns with them. They grew up toddling around the house and went up and down the back stairs and the front porch. The shed in the back contained any number of cats who had more kittens who grew into cats having more kittens, and the boys chased them around the shed and periodically snuck a favorite one into their beds at night until their father threatened to drown all the kittens if they did not stop.

As they grew older, they built forts in the wooded area behind their house and found all manner of interesting things to collect and examine. In the winter they had snowballs fights and made snowmen and slid downhill on the sleds specially ordered for them from the Emporium's catalog. In the summer they made matchbox houses for the crickets they caught, and slept outside in a makeshift tent when the night weather made sleeping indoors an oppressive undertaking. Mike and Mitch enjoyed their childhood and flowered in the total love of their mother, and their Uncle Nathan and Aunt Edna, and their cousin, Edie, and, of course, Tillie, and hardly ever realized that their father, who was usually traveling on sales trips, was even part of their family.

Gossip

While Viola strove to make a decent life for herself and her boys and, when he was home, her husband, Nathan and Edna worked at their family life in the Mitchell house which they moved into after Michael Mitchell's death. Tillie was convinced to give up her rented apartment and live with them to help raise their daughter Edith while they operated the Emporium. It took some persuading on Edna's part to get Tillie to move, but Edna could be persuasive.

The first project undertaken by Edna and Tillie was a schedule for the family. During the mornings, Tillie would clean and straighten while Edna played with her daughter and dealt with social commitments and activities; after lunch, when Edie took her nap, she would work at the Emporium while Tillie made the evening meal and watched Edie. Edna came home in the late afternoon and completed the social commitments and activities she had begun in the morning, and guided her daughter as she played. Tillie and Edna would sit down one evening each week and plan the next week's meals, and draw up a shopping list, and organize social commitments and activities. Tillie was given time off whenever she needed it, but generally Thursday nights and alternate Saturdays were hers to meet with her group of friends and sometimes visit with Joseph, the butcher at the meat market at Clampet's Grocery Store. On those days, Edna would serve up the leftovers from the previous night's meal. Nathan was at the Emporium six days of the week. He would also be wherever he was told to be by Edna. Or by Tillie. Things generally worked out.

Once a month, after dinner, Edna and Nathan would sit together in what Nathan called the *Library* and attempt to straighten out the receipts, and complete the ordering, and monitor the stock, and generally work at straightening out the *books*. The paperwork was not a pleasant task, and neither one of them enjoyed it or was proficient at it. Viola used to facilitate this task when she was able, but now, with the twins, and because of John's attitude, something Edna just did not understand, she no longer did. Nathan and Edna were on their own and struggled to do together what Viola so easily executed alone.

On one of those evenings, they proceeded to their library where Pearl S. Buck, F. Scott Fitzgerald, and Hemingway books, still unread, snuggled together comfortably on a bookshelf behind the rarely used desk where a desk lamp, a leather letter holder, and a telephone were displayed. Edna sat in the desk chair while Nathan pulled up another chair beside her. They spread the papers out and began to look at the numbers before them. They added and subtracted and multiplied and divided.

"I think you added this column of numbers incorrectly," Edna remarked to Nathan during this session. "Look, you forgot to double this item, and I am sure we received two boxes of them."

Nathan looked at his math. No, the column was not right, but as he examined it, there were additional errors that Edna had not even found.

"Let's begin again, Dear. You are correct about that, but look at this. I think we should just put this aside for now and try to figure out the invoices for the month. Where did you put them?"

And the evening would continue in this manner until they finally came to a sort of reasonably although not quite right but close enough completion of the task, and piled up the papers, invoices, letters, balance sheets, and calculations, and tied them together, putting a piece of paper on the top with the month and year. They both initialed it, and it was completed. Done for another month. The following day, Nathan would take the pile with him to the Emporium and file them with the others, in the warped green file cabinet which was under the stairs, next to the *Men's Corner*. It was getting full. Soon some of the paper piles would need to be packed away in a cardboard box and placed, with the other cardboard boxes, in the attic of the Emporium's building.

***

The Emporium was not doing well. Yes, times had been hard, and Nathan and Edna, but especially Nathan, continued to give credit out to the townspeople just as Michael Mitchell and his father before him had done. But customers' monthly statements were not paid in full, and the Mitchells continued to extend credit. And they continued to purchase stock. The Emporium had always offered the newest items and gadgets. People loved to look and to buy, or at least buy on credit. There was no lack of customers, or lookers, at the Emporium. After all, the town of Everstille was growing and expanding. Additional houses were being built, and there was talk of enlarging the library, and perhaps taking over the empty warehouse and making it into a separate high school. No one was sure how this would be accomplished since there was little money anywhere, but talk was cheap. It was gratifying to plan at the City Council business meetings. Money might be in short supply, but ideas were flowing.

As an Everstille businessman, Nathan came to these council meetings every month as his civic duty. It was also the one night a month he was allowed autonomy. Edna and Tillie did not mind his attending these meetings as long as he returned bearing any town talk that was important or interesting. It was not gossip when discussed by men.

Nathan closed the Emporium early, and dinner was served punctually, and he would eat quickly, putting on a fresh shirt, and making sure his shoes were shined and his hat brushed. It was important for him to look good and to be prompt to the meetings which, unless there was an unusual situation, finished within an hour. Then the councilmen and business men and other men who were as civic minded as Nathan would proceed to Mazie's across the way and into the back room for some of Mazie's baked apple pudding or her rice pudding if it was not apple season, and partake in a bit of drink, all legal once again.

One early fall evening, when the sun had not quite vanished, and the civic-minded men going to Mazie's could smell the delicious aroma of the baked apple pudding awaiting their arrival, Nathan, upon leaving the meeting, strolled over with Jim Banter, his friend and the owner of Banter's Drug Store and Pharmacy, and they discussed nothing of importance. Nathan was feeling content because the previous evening, when Edna and he had completed their monthly accounting tasks, the books had appeared to balance correctly for the first time in a long while. He was glad to walk and talk with another successful businessman even though he was not really listening to what Jim had to say until he heard a familiar name.

"Wait, Jim, would you repeat that?"

"Well, I ain't one to pass on untrue talk, but I heard this from more than one person. I know your brother-in-law does traveling for his job, and it seems that there was some trouble with him at a particular kind of establishment…you know the kind I mean… and he was kicked out and the local police called. I guess he was drunk and causing a ruckus, and he was told not to come back to that town with his wares anymore." Jim Banter shifted his eyes around to make sure none of the other civic minded citizens were hearing what he was telling Nathan.

"Are you sure about this?"

"Yessirreebob, I am. Like I said, more than one person told it to me, one of 'em being the sheriff, and he heard it from another sheriff, and, well, you know… they all spread the news…" and Jim trailed off because having passed on this information, he had lost interest in it, and the aroma from the apples was getting stronger.

Nathan mulled this over as he entered Mazie's. This was upsetting. He did not know whether he should tell either Edna or Tillie, especially because neither one of the women liked John. He was quiet the remainder of the evening and had some difficulty finishing his second dish of baked apple pudding. In fact, Nathan, after shaking the hands of the citizens and businessmen and council men, was one of the first to leave. He walked home slowly hoping his wife and Tillie would both be in bed by the time he got there.

He walked in and saw Edna sitting in the parlor glancing through a magazine. She looked up and smiled and asked, "Good night tonight?"

Nathan looked at her and looked around and asked in a whisper, "Where is Tillie? Has she gone to her room yet?"

"She said she was tired and went to bed early. She's going to get up early tomorrow morning to start some bread. Why? What is it? What's wrong?" Edna could always sense things.

Nathan sighed and said, "I did hear something tonight that was pretty upsetting, but I am not sure Tillie should be told. We should keep this between ourselves."

He sat next to his wife, and she put her magazine down, and in quiet voices, for the better part of two hours, they talked, and deliberated, and wondered, and worried, and the contentment they had both felt due to the successful accounting episode from the previous night dissipated into the air like the smell of Mazie's baked apple pudding.

John's Indiscretions

Jim Banter had heard correctly. However, he had not heard everything. Yes, John was asked to leave a certain type of establishment, and the local police were involved, and he was told not return to that town with his wares. That part was correct. The part that Jim did not know was that this was not the first establishment of that kind, nor the first involvement of the local police, nor the first time he was asked to leave a town and not return. John Jasper had created a reputation for himself, and it was not an honorable one.

Disappointments dogged John. Before he married Viola, he was carefree and enjoying life as a man was meant to do. He cherished his nomadic existence, and if something did not work out in one place with one woman, he simply moved on. In marrying Viola, John was convinced the Emporium would come with the marriage, but it did not, and then old man Mitchell died and left it to that bumbling brother-in-law of his before John could even prove his worth. Nathan, with Edna standing behind him, arms folded, even had the audacity to tell him that since he already had a job, he should just keep it because there was not enough work to have him employed in the store. John knew he could have made a real go of that place, and he also was pretty sure that Nathan was screwing it all up. Nathan even had Viola…his wife!...working to keep the books, but John had put a stop to that. And then those boys came along and there was no time for Viola to do anything else. At least those kids were good for something.

Traveling was a fine job although it was hard work. Most men were happy to come home, and rest, and see their families in between jaunts. John was not. He felt despondent when at the house. Those boys cried as babies, and yelled as they grew older, and they made his head ache. The two of them ran around constantly and messed things up, and then they expected him to play with them and bothered him to throw a ball or go fishing or read to them. He came home and was tired and just wanted to relax and catch up on sleep and maybe get some decent moonshine from the men he knew had the good stuff. Sure, it was legal again, but there was nothing quite as strong and with a kick like the stuff he could find in the back woods. When he had the cash. No credit given. Not anymore. Viola seemed to take up all the cash he had for those kids, and for the house, and it was a never-ending cycle of misery. He deserved some relaxation, and if the only place he could get it was in those ringer establishments, well then that seemed only reasonable and right. A man deserved some fun.

But now John had been refused entry to three of them in three different towns. He had to widen his sales territory and find new places, and that took time, and the only good thing about it was that he was gone from Viola and the kids for lengthier periods. Unfortunately, the word spread, so he needed to work quickly. He also owed some of the Moonshiners money and needed to arrange his travels around their woods. He had every intention of paying them, but he needed to earn more, sell more, get some big contracts. It was always something. Always something.

John was on the road again. He had to expand further south and west, and he knew he was inching into someone else's territory, but that could not be helped. He was even considering adding on another state. Maybe Kentucky or even Tennessee, although that was really stretching things. He drove along the route he had mapped out and was grateful the weather was not as warm as it had been yesterday. He was getting hungry and maybe a bit thirsty, and decided to take a lunch break. Later, he would check out a place of pleasure he had not yet visited but had heard about. He glanced at the map, taking the next left, driving on for close to ten miles before he began to see signs of civilization. All this monotonous farmland made driving more difficult and tiring.

Easing onto what was the main road in the town he was looking for, he saw a lunch wagon dining car with a tall red and yellow sign proclaiming SAM'S that looked promising, so he pulled in, stopped the car, and got out to stretch. Entering the eatery, he sat down at one of the rounded stools at the counter and saw the handprinted sign announcing:

Today's Feature Luncheon 25c

Cubed Minute Steak, Gravy, Buttered Beets, French Fried Potatoes,

Hot Roll and Butter

He called to the waitress headed his way. "Got some of that special left?" and when she nodded, said, "I'll take one with some coffee."

John relaxed while he waited and looked around. No, he did not recognize anyone, but the three men who sat at the counter engaged in various degrees of eating were obviously fellow salesmen. He nodded to the man closest to him who was finishing up some pie and asked, "Any luck today?"

Swallowing the last bite and washing it down with tepid coffee, the man answered, "Some, but it ain't like it used to be. You would think that with what looks like a war comin' more people would want to stock up on the necessaries, but that don't seem to be the case."

The waitress dropped off John's lunch before him, and he began to eat before answering. "You think there's gonna be another war?" and John loaded up his fork with bites of potato and beets. "Seems to me times are gettin' better."

"Well," said his lunch companion, "guess that depends on what you're sellin'. Good luck, Mister. I gotta get on the road again." And he left.

John nodded and finished eating in silence, watching as the other two men paid their tabs, nodded to him as they passed by and left. There was silence in the place. It let John consider what he was going to do with the remainder of his day. It was not going to be selling. He knew he could not ask the waitress about the place he wanted to visit and just hoped the directions he had received were accurate. He took his time eating a piece of blueberry pie thinking it was not as good as Tillie's, then paid for the meal, threw a generous nickel tip under the plate, and left.

John strode out to his car, leaned against it, and pulled out a cigarette. He glanced at the sky. Looked like it might rain. He might as well get going and hope to find this place. Taking a long drag, he threw the cigarette to the side, walked to the wooded area behind the wagon, and looked around to make sure there was no one there before he unzipped, relieved himself, and zipped back up. He sighed. Life had not been so easy lately, and he deserved some fun. Reaching into his pants pocket and pulling out his wallet, he counted and checked his cash. Always a smart thing to know what cash you had on you when going into a place, especially a new place. Some of the girls there might not be so honest.

Walking to the car, he got in, drove out, and proceeded down the road. Reaching the main street, he noted the signs and small buildings housing idle businesses. *Typical town*, he thought, *nothing special*. He continued driving slowly through town, and about a mile past the end of the main street, over to his left, he saw it.

The building was set back by itself away from the road. There was a light on at the front and a gristly looking man, probably the bouncer, sat in the doorway, chewing on an unlit cigar, leaning back on a stool, and looking out over the area. John pulled next to the only other car that was there, ran his hand through his hair, put his hat on pulling it down a bit in front of his face, and stepped out of the car. *Great*, he thought, *this is a Monday afternoon. I should have my pick.* He ambled up the walkway towards the door with a grin on his face.

Green Milk Glass

"Stop It! Stop the damn running!" John had no patience with his boys. He was just awake and sitting at the kitchen table when Mike and Mitch slammed the back door, ran through the house, and out the front in the way that only five-year olds can. Viola, taking advantage of an early summer morning breeze, was in the back hanging up sheets to dry and did not hear him. Had she, she would have asked him to be careful of his language, and then an argument would have launched, so it was fortunate she was in the back. It was also possible she had heard him and chose to ignore it. Arguments often lead to physical confrontations, and Viola was just healed from the last one.

John was home from a three-week extended trip which was mildly successful. He had been able to obtain several new customers because he had added miles and miles of territory. He was also able to visit a couple of his favorite spots and see a few of his preferred companions, and had found a fresh location to visit. All in all, it had not been a bad time. Now he needed to relax and do some planning and organizing and make a short trip to pick up some new samples, and visit the Emporium because they owed him an order. It was the least Nathan could do. John hoped Edna would not be there when he visited.

Viola came into the kitchen and saw that her husband was awake. She gave him a tired smile and asked, "Would you like breakfast? There are some eggs, and I baked bread yesterday."

"Sure, and I need coffee. Is there milk?"

"Yes, there's milk."

Viola readied the eggs and bread, placing them on the counter next to the stove. She put the water on to boil and reached into the ice box for the milk. She washed and dried her pink flowered creamer, filled it with milk, placing it on the table for John's use, then busied herself making his breakfast. She had just picked up his plate filled with eggs and carefully cut fresh bread and had turned to place it down before him when one of the twins crashed into the house and ran into the kitchen.

"Ma, come out here and look at the cat we found. We think it might have some kittens soon. Its stomach is awful big," and Mike ran over and pulled on his mother's hand which caused her to let go of the full plate which was located directly over John's lap.

In slow motion, the plate flipped and spread its contents on John's chest and lap and soaked his pajamas while a look of dismay spread itself over Viola's face, and Mike's lips spread apart into a smile, and then a laugh, and just as quickly as he saw anger spread itself over the face of his currently-at-home father, readjusted themselves into a perfect circle. For an instant, nobody moved, and then John stood and two things happened simultaneously. Mike turned, ran through the kitchen, out the front door, and down the porch while the pink flowered creamer that Viola's mother had received as part of the wedding gift from her parents, spread its milk through the air as it followed Mike across the kitchen and splattered against the door breaking into three pieces.

"No!" howled Viola.

She looked at John who looked back at her unsure for a second as to whether he had thrown the creamer or if it had somehow flung itself through the air.

"Those brats! Look at what they did!" John was unsure which one of the boys had created the problem, so he just lumped them both together. "If you had more control of them, this wouldn't happen"

He shook the remains of the eggs and toast from his pajamas onto the floor, stormed off to clean himself, and then find one or both twins and deliver the punishment one or both deserved.

Viola rushed over to the broken creamer as though hurrying to gather the pieces would render it whole. She bent down and cradled them against her, too distraught to cry, and brought them back to the kitchen. She carefully washed and dried the pieces and looked in the kitchen drawers for a proper coffer in which to place them. An old apron she rarely wore but which was clean, was removed from the drawer. Tenderly, the pieces were positioned in the middle, and wrapped in their shroud. She deliberated a few minutes deciding what to do, and then protectively clasping the packet to her chest, she went to the back room, walking as if in a religious procession, and unlocked her solid oak chest. Moving the embroidered napkins and handkerchiefs and table runners out of the way, she nestled the apron embracing the ruined creamer in the bottom, then covered it with the linens. She pulled down the lid and locked the chest: a rolling of the stone to seal the tomb. She sat for some minutes rethinking the incident, too angry and upset to weep. Tears would come later.

Returning to the kitchen, she cleaned up the eggs and toast and spilled milk. She threw the broken plate away, and polished, and scoured, and swept. She scrubbed, and swabbed, and mopped, eliminating any hint of the incident. She looked around the room and spied the creamer's matching pink flowered sugar bowl, and her breath caught. Viola picked up the bowl holding it close for a moment before she lovingly washed and dried it, retraced her steps to the back room where she unlocked, uncovered, and buried the bowl with its mate. *Requiescat in pace.*

The rest of the day passed solemnly. The boys knew their terrain and secreted themselves away until it was dark, and only then returned, peeking into the window to find their mother alone. They ate a quiet dinner and were sent to bed. Their father searched for them for a while, but gave up and took off in his car to find some liquid restorative. He was gone until the following night and upon his return was in no shape to deliver required castigation.

Viola sat on the porch in the dark after the boys were in bed. Fire flies swirled around, and the crescent moon gave partial light as she wiped the wet from her face. She remained outside until the dampness was dried by an amiable night breeze and then, she moved into the bedroom. Not bothering to get ready for bed, she merely lay down on her side, pulled the quilt up to her chin. With a troubled sigh, she closed her eyes and after a while, fell into a restless sleep.

***

A few weeks later, John steered into his driveway returning from another long voyage. He removed his sample cases from the car, brought them into the house, and placed them by the front door. Walking into the kitchen where Viola was shredding cabbage, he came over to the counter, kissed her cheek, and placed a package next to the cabbage. He went back out to the car to get the remainder of his bags and his suitcase.

Viola looked at the package, wiped her hands on her apron and opened it. Staring at her from the wrappings was a sugar and creamer set. The set was fashioned from thick milk glass, and the color was a dull, sluggish, cloudy, lackluster green. Viola took the set over to the sink where she washed and dried it. She then brought the bowl and creamer to the excessively polished kitchen table, placing them in the exact middle. She stood back and examined them.

John came into the kitchen, saw them, and with a smile inquired, "Do you like them? They are the newest thing. Been selling a lot of them lately."

Viola looked reflectively at John and replied, "Yes, they look perfect there."

She returned to her cabbage whose color, in contrast to the new sugar bowl and creamer, appeared light, and lively, and likeable.

Giving Thanks

"Stop that kicking," John muttered to Mitch or was he Mike? He was never sure unless he saw the brown spot on the kid's neck, and because both boys were seated to his right, and he could not see it, he just directed a general command to the both. "Eat your food and behave," and Mitch/Mike put a spoonful of the potatoes he had been sculpting into a mountain into his mouth. It was Thanksgiving Day.

The Mitchell family, all of them, and Doctor Evans, gathered at Nathan and Edna's home to join in the annual celebration of Thanksgiving and to partake of the first enormous meal of the day which Edna had been planning and Tillie had been cooking for a week. The earlier dinner included the children and was eaten at two in the afternoon. Afterwards, Mike and Mitch and Edie would be excused to play outside if the weather permitted or inside playing Monopoly in the front parlor, if it did not, while the men would partake of liquid refreshments and discuss world affairs in Nathan's library. The women would clear and clean and ready the second meal of the day which would feed additional guests: extended family, neighbors, and friends, and would commence by six in the evening.

This second feast had started as an extension of Mary and Michael Mitchell's Sunday suppers. Neighbors would bring a dish to share at a time when holiday meals were not much different than regular simple suppers, and the Mitchell children felt duty bound to continue it in their names. This second meal was an informal affair with the participants serving themselves from the vast array of food set out in the kitchen and dining room, and finding seats wherever they could throughout the house. The festivities usually concluded around ten at night, and when the guests left, Tillie and Edna and Viola would spend another two hours or so cleaning up while the children and the men of the family, and usually Doctor Evans, found their ways to a bed or sofa and promptly fell asleep. While cleaning and organizing, Tillie and Edna and Viola allowed themselves a glass or two of wine as a reward for another holiday expertly completed.

This day proceeded as planned, and as the first dinner concluded and the children ran outside, because for some reason the weather was cooperating and there was some sunshine and warmth. The women began their clearing and cleaning and readying, and the men moved off to the library.

Doctor Evans claimed the one club chair and eased himself down with a sigh. John sat in a chair in front of the makeshift bar Nathan set up on the desk. With practiced flourishes, Nathan worked his magic with the bottles and glasses and bar accountment and offered a martini wineglass to Doctor Evans and another to his brother-in-law. "Here," Nathan extended his full hands, "I have perfected the gin martini, and I think you will agree."

Doctor Evan took it, sipped, and nodded his approval. John took a great swallow downing half the glass and smiled.

"Yep, this is good. Better than the hooch I get on the road. Not bad, Nate." With a few gulps, he finished the drink and held the glass out to Nathan. "Fill 'er up."

"Easy now," cautioned Doctor Evans as he carefully took another small sip of his own drink. "This stuff can mangle the insides and tangle the outsides. I have seen it too often."

John gave a disbelieving laugh.

"Maybe others, but not me. I have always been able to handle the stuff. Just keep 'em comin', Nate. I need some relaxation. It has been rough being home all this week. Those boys of mine have been totally wild, and I need to unwind. There is a big trip coming up next week, and I am tired with the planning I've had to do. I'll be doing a whole bunch of driving then, so relaxation is what I need now. Say, Nate, have you seen the new stuff from the Elgin Watch Company? There are some dandy alarm clocks that I know will go over big at the Emporium."

And John launched into an involved sales description of the new clocks which, as Doctor Evans slowly finished his gin martini and rested his head on the back of the chair, promptly put him to sleep.

Nathan saw that the good doctor was not listening because little snores were softly escaping from his mouth, so he took advantage of a lull in the alarm clock description and decided that this might be a good time to bring up a prickly subject. One that Edna had encouraged him to discuss with John. Edna's encouragements were directives.

"Listen, John, there is something I need to talk to you about. And I don't really want to because I think that what a man does is generally his own business, but you are married to my sister, and I am concerned." Nathan took another sip of his own martini.

John observed Nathan. "So? Speak up, I can take it!" and a slightly drunken snort was discharged from his lips at the same time a snore escaped from Doctor Evans' and their duet would have made Nathan giggle had he not been so nervous.

"John, there has been talk by some of the men in town about an incident that you were involved in a while back. It took place at a…well, at a sort of …a place that…well, a disreputable kind of business and you were said to be…well…drunk…and…and the police were called…and… well…there is…"

Nathan trailed off and looked at John who had gone completely silent and serious and looked back at him with a penetrating stare. This was a pregnant moment, and both men knew exactly what the incident was, and where it had happened, and what was involved, and John's glare dared Nathan to go ahead and fill in the details. Nathan would not. He could not.

"John, it's just that Viola has always been so kind and considerate and lately, she seems so unhappy, and we, that is, Edna and I worry about her and the twins and …" Nathan ceased talking. This was going nowhere, and he wished Edna had not insisted, no, had not demanded that he bring this up. He was not even certain Jim Banter had the thing right. He should have kept his mouth shut and not said anything to Edna, and then he would not be involved in this inconveniency.

John looked at Nathan and said in a low voice, a forceful voice, a passionate voice, "Listen, Nate, whatever you heard didn't happen. Not the way you heard it. And I really don't appreciate you stickin' your nose where it really don't belong. I can handle myself and I'm takin' care of Viola and them kids, and that's the end of that. Do you read me?"

Nathan sighed and nodded his head. "All right, John, but you know that kind of talk gets around these small towns, and it wouldn't be good for Viola or the boys to hear about it. I just needed to say something." The two men fell silent thinking their separate thoughts.

Apparently, the sudden silence was what woke Doctor Evans who gave a big yawn and looked around and saw both men looking at him.

"Well," he started, "I guess that drink was stronger for my system than I thought. Nathan, you do make a mighty tasty drink, but I wonder if there is another piece of pumpkin pie, I could talk Tillie out of. Excuse me while I check on that."

And he got up from the club chair, stretched, and walked towards the door. "Care to join me? After all, there is quite a bit we must be thankful for, and Tillie's pie is certainly one of those things."

Nathan looked at John and motioned to the door. "John, care for more pie?"

John stared at Nathan for a moment before saying, "No, don't think so. Not right now. In fact, I think I might go out to the back for a smoke. I'll be back in shortly."

Nathan followed Doctor Evans to the kitchen. John grabbed his hat and coat and left for the back door. When John reached the farthest tree back by some bushes at the end of the Mitchell's yard, he stopped. He took a cigarette from his pocket and struck a match. He inhaled deeply and coughed out the smoke. Reaching into his coat pocket, he removed a flask, uncapped it, and took a long swig. This was the stuff. Strong and powerful. He took another long pull and put the almost empty flask back into his pocket.

He leaned against the tree and finished the smoke, flicking the end of the cigarette into the bare bushes. He unwrapped a piece of Wrigley's and started to chew while mulling over the conversation in the library. Thinking about what Nathan had said. Or almost said. *The fool couldn't even get out the words.* John speculated that he needed to be more careful in his doings. *Damn.* He rubbed his head where an ache was beginning and then spit the gum out. John pulled his coat tighter around himself. The weather was changing. *Maybe I can get Nathan to write an order for some of those clocks*, he mused, *and maybe another one of them martinis too. Now that would be something to be thankful for*! John glanced up at the darkening sky and strode back into the house.

Winter

The coal was delivered, and the coal stoker was working. The fire place in the parlor was blazing brightly, and the wood was stacked high. The heavy winter drapes hung in front of each window, and seasonal quilts and extra blankets were on all the beds. Long underwear was out of drawers and on bodies, and wool coats, scarves, hats, gloves, and boots were readied on the hooks by the back door, although not even the twins wanted to go outside. Long sleeved woolen shirts and corduroy pants were worn. Winter had settled in the Midwest with a harshness and savageness that had not been felt for years. Schools closed, snowdrifts created minor mountains surrounding houses, farmers worried that their livestock would freeze, and ice hung down from everything possible creating lovely and dangerous spiky prongs. The shed behind the Jasper house was frozen shut, and the back and front steps contained icy stretches that challenged the balance of all who dared to enter or leave. Everyone who was wise simply stayed in, and waited, and hoped for a break in the frigidity that was this early February, but John Jasper was out traveling.

He had planned this trip for well after the winter season thinking he could still get a head start on the other salesmen who normally took additional time at home and waited out the weather, especially when it was this ruthless. However, a combination of anxious itchiness to get out of the house and a grim and relentless series of arguments with Viola created the impetus for this early trip. Besides, there was that guilty feeling which came over him when he saw Viola's face. Their last fray ended up becoming substantially more physical than any other had before.

It was, of course, Viola's fault. She complained about the amount of alcohol John was drinking, and the quantity of money used for the purchase of it, and the supposed bad influence it all might have on the twins. Her exasperating badgering along with the boys who were bothersome and aggravating with their raucous playing, and constant talking, and blaring noise-making, created a maddening tension. John's head thudded. The only surprise is that it had not happened earlier.

That evening, once the boys were finally in bed and covered under a stack of quilts and blankets, John sat down on the horsehair sofa with his map, planning his travels. He had a bottle of the gin he had just bought placed by his right foot, and he would reach down and refill his glass every so often. Viola was cleaning the kitchen, polishing the table, and readying the vegetables for the following day's supper. When done, she came into the parlor holding a book she had been trying to start since Christmas. Perhaps tonight she would be able to begin. She sat in the chair, book lighted by the floor lamp, and opened to chapter one. She glanced at John who was refilling his glass and simply had to say something.

"Really, John, is that another new bottle? You just started one a day or two ago. It's no wonder you are always complaining about how your head aches. I wish you would stop."

John looked at her with annoyance. "What do you care how much I drink? It's really none of your business. Haven't I kept you and them boys warm and cozy in this house with my hard work? This is about the only relaxation I get, so you can just shut up about it." John followed this observation with a draining of his glass, then bent down to refill it.

"I am only worried about you and your health. Doctor Evans said you are causing yourself harm by all the drinking you do."

"What are you talking about? You're going to that old fraud and discussing me? You better not be. You shut your mouth about me to him or to anyone else. Who else you talkin' to?" At this point, John pushed the map he was looking at over to the side and moved forward on the sofa steadying his feet as if to get up.

"John, I am not talking about you to anyone. I just happened to see Doctor Evans a week or two ago when I was in town, and he asked how you were doing. I did not talk to anyone else. I am worried about you too. You have changed over the past years since we got married. You are different. You never used to be like this."

"Like what? I am tired of your constant complaining and griping and moaning about my *changes*. Talk about change! Ever since them boys were born, it's like I don't even count. You complain about me. You complain about my relaxation. You jump down my throat every time I want to spend a few of my hard-earned bucks on some decent liquor. I am sick and tired of this!"

This time John got up and walked towards Viola, and without considering any consequences, took the book from her hands and threw it against the fireplace where it careened off the mantle and landed in the pile of wood below.

"Stop it, John. You have no right to act like this!"

Viola knew where this was headed, so she attempted to get up and move away, but it was too late. John felt rage building up, and the power from it surged from his aching head, down through his neck and his right shoulder, and out of his right fist which connected with Viola's face just as she started to get up. It knocked her back down into the chair which then knocked over the floor lamp.

Now, normally, when these clashes happened, John stopped at this point. However, for some reason he later tried to deduce but could not determine, he did not. He pulled Viola up out of the chair and hit her again. And once more. And as she crumpled to the floor, he pulled her up by the shoulder of her dress which promptly tore, and slapped her, sending the blood which was dripping down her face to the wall where, later that night, before the twins woke in the morning to see it and ask about it, Viola cleaned it up. Then John ceased. He grabbed the bottle of gin, took the crumpled map, stomped out through the kitchen into their bedroom, and jerked the door closed behind him.

Viola sat on the floor wiping tears and blood from her face. She had a difficult time even thinking about what to do, so she just sat until her head cleared enough and her eyesight straightened out, and the pain from moving lessened, and she could pull herself up into the chair behind her. She sat there nauseous. After a time, she walked to the kitchen, and holding on to the shining table, got out a clean cloth which she wet and patted gently on her face. She continued until the wet cloth was scarlet, and then she squeezed out the blood and ran the cloth under cold water until only the lightest pink showed. She filled a glass with some water, swished it in her mouth, and spit it out. She then attempted to sip some through her sore mouth. She sat at the table not thinking but listening to the working of the furnace and the beating sound of the outside ice and snow, and the vague movements she could hear from the bedroom.

It took an hour for her to organize her thoughts, and because her eye hurt even more when she cried, she finally stopped. She went back to the parlor, straightened up the lamp and chair, cleaned the flecks of blood from the wall, and picked up her book from the woodpile, gently setting it on the chair. The fire was dying, and she added wood to it. She placed the wool blanket that decorated the back of the sofa over her shoulders, and fitting her frame onto the cushions, she fell into a fretful semi- doze.

The following morning before the sky was completely light, Viola woke to a burned down fire and the sound of an automobile's reluctant activation. She sat up and recognized the anger stored just behind her blackened eye and split lips and bruised face. She slowly moved to the edge of the sofa to stand up, and nudging the heavy winter drapes aside, looked out the window just in time to see John, having finally urged his vehicle to start, drive away. *Good riddance* she thought, and went to her bedroom to change and clean up before the twins got out of bed.

She stared into the mirror over the dresser, and had it not been so painful, would have rubbed her swollen eyes in disbelief. As rapidly as she could, she cleaned up, dressed, and allowed her dark hair to hang down hoping to partly screen her bruises. The furnace was producing heat, but to add additional warmth to the indifferent chill of the house, she went to the parlor to refill and restart the fire.

In the kitchen, she began to prepare pancakes, the twins' favorite, and as she started the stove, she quickly fashioned a story. A few minutes later, the boys smelled the cooking breakfast and bounded out of their room ready to greet the day. They stopped in shock as Viola turned to say as merrily as she could, "Pancakes today! Doesn't that sound great? Help me by getting your plates and forks and sitting down, please."

Mitch looked at her and asked, "Ma, what happened to your face?"

Viola reached over and smoothed his unblemished skin and said, "Well, you know how icy it is, and when you were in bed, I went out to gather some more wood for the fireplace, and I slipped on the back steps. It really looks worse than it is. I will be fine. Sit down and let's eat." Viola smiled and felt the ache.

Mitch nodded, completely accepted the story, pulled out the chair, and sat down. Mike stared at Viola for a while and then came over and hugged her. He looked at her bruised face and blackened eye and said, "I hope you get well soon, Ma." Mike, being the realist, was harder to convince. Viola patted his back and looked into his eyes.

"I am sure I will." She sat down with the boys to eat breakfast although every bite was agonizing, and she struggled to keep the pancakes and maple syrup down.

***

During a late night two weeks later, with faint bruises still blurring and shadowing her face, Viola sat in the kitchen sipping tea and reading her book. It was almost eleven o'clock, and she wanted to complete chapter four before heading to bed. A sudden thud outside on the front porch startled her, and she jerked. Someone or something was there. She pulled her robe closed, eased her way to the parlor, and peered out the window. John's car was parked crookedly on the driveway with the driver's door left wide open. He had been gone for these last fourteen days, but apparently, he was now home. Viola waited to hear him come into the house, but there was no movement. She waited another few minutes and then heard some low whimpering sounds, so she unlocked the front door and stepped out.

There sprawled on the subzero icy porch, face down, lay John. The smell of gin surrounded him. He was passed out cold. Viola walking carefully on the frozen porch, went over and tried to move him, but she was not strong enough to lift him up. He was alive because the frosty air which rose from his face let her know that. She called, "John," and shook him, but there was no response. The air was arctic and hostile, and she was freezing without a coat, so she went into the house and closed the front door.

She walked to the parlor and stood close to the fireplace, arranging a few more logs on the flame. She thought about her options. There were two. She could try to pull him in, or she could leave him out on the porch to freeze. She was certain death would happen. It was bitter winter, and he was drunk, and no one would blame her when the terrible accident was discovered. Doctor Evans knew about his drinking, and her brother knew about it, and probably everyone else in the town did too. The funeral would be a simple affair, and she would somehow survive and the boys might even be better off without such an example. It was the boys about whom she was concerned. What if for some reason one of them got up during the night and found him? How could she explain things to them? What a terrible experience for them!

She thought and considered. She raised her hand to the side of her face where it still hurt when touched. She thought of the other times this had happened. The drunk man collapsed on the icy porch was not the John she had married, the sweet and kind person who had courted her and convinced her that their life together would be wonderful. He was not the man who had made her laugh and brought her trinkets from his trips. She did not know that man; that person who lay in the ice barely breathing, so drunk she could not wake him. The late February freeze was killing him as she stood in front of the fireplace warming her hands and battered face.

***

The following morning with the grey sky filled with clouds, and the snow delicately, silently falling, John woke on the parlor floor in front of the dying fire, covered with the wool blanket from the sofa. He sat up and leaned his head back to the cushion and tried to remember. Where was his hat? He still had his coat and shoes on. He vaguely remembered drinking and driving and cold and ... his head pulsed, and he rubbed his forehead, and stretched his neck which was stiff. He slowly eased himself upwards on top of the sofa cushions, and sat straight until the vertigo passed, and he regained his balance. Then he smelled the coffee and heard the chattering of his sons. With his coat on and the wool blanket still wrapped around his shoulders, he walked into the kitchen, towards the coffee and the warmth.

Conversations

"Tillie, did you see where Nathan put today's newspaper? I wanted to check out our advertisement in it. It cost money, and I want to see that they got it right this time. Why pay for their mistakes?"

"Here it is, Edna. He left it on the chair when he went to the Emporium. Are you going to walk Edie to school this morning, or should I? I don't mind walking her because I can stop at Clampet's for some hamburger meat, and I need to check those chicken prices too."

"And say *hello* to a certain butcher, I suppose? Be careful with the chicken. Those prices are still pretty high, and Nathan and I talked about cutting down on the grocery bill."

"Stop that. You know Joseph and I are just friends. And, I know, I won't overspend. So, should I walk Edie?"

"Yes, thanks, Tillie. I wanted to get the Emporium a bit early today. Fred is coming in with the sewing machine parts we ordered for Mrs. Anderson, and I just don't think Nathan knows that. We need to check and see if the parts are the correct ones. Also, John is coming in, and if I am not there, Nathan will order more than we can sell again. Somehow John Jasper can talk Nathan into about anything, and we just need to be more careful with his orders, family or not. Come on, Edie, Tillie is ready to walk you to school. There you are. Now be good and please listen to Miss Willard's instructions today. Here, give me a kiss. I will see you later. Thanks, Tillie."

***

"…and these are the absolute best ones the market has to offer. I'm losing money when I offer them at this price, but you being family and all, I'm more than willing to do that. So, Nate, what do you think? Hows about signing this contract now? I can get the new stock to you in about ten days. I'm leaving on a short trip tomorrow or the next day to fill some other orders and pick up some supplies and new samples. Here, just put your signature there, and I'll be out of your hair. Use my pen."

"Well, John, I don't know. Edna is coming in early this morning, and I did tell her you were going to be here. She said wanted to see the new stuff, so I should probably wait for her."

"Come on, Nate, you are the owner here. Be a man, and make

some decisions for yourself. I mean, Edna is fine working with you and helping and all, but, don't let her wear the pants in your house. It ain't good for the relationship if that happens! Know what I mean?"

"John, I just have to wait. The last time I ordered, there was way too much stock and frankly, it did not sell like you said it would. In fact, there's still a whole bunch of it left in those boxes at the back. I just better wait and see...oh, here she is now. Morning, Dear. John is just showing me these new doodads for the kitchen and some sewing notions. Come and tell us what you think."

"Morning Nathan. Hello, John. Let's see what there is. Nathan, why don't you go and help Mr. Beacon over there? I believe he is look-ing at some of those tools in the back. Once I look at John's samples, we can make a decision. Mr. Beacon, Nathan will be right over! So, John, what have you been showing my husband? I am not so sure we can place too large an order this month because we just did not sell all the stock we ordered from you the last time, but you can certainly show me what you have. Well, this is new..."

***

"Hello there... good morning, Tillie. You look especially nice today. Always happy to see you. Hope the family is well. What can I get for you today?"

"Hello, Joseph. We're fine. Today I need two pounds of that hamburger meat. Don't give me too much fat. And how much are those chickens you brag about? And don't go overcharging the Mitchells for things. Just because they own that store don't mean they are rich."

"Why, Tillie, you know I always give you the best buy possi-ble. The hamburger meat is twelve cents a pound, but there is a special today, and you can get it for only eleven cents when you buy at least two pounds. Now, them chickens ain't so nice lately, but on your way out, check out aisle two where something new came in...called *SPAM*. Didn't taste it yet myself, you know, but you might be interested. And, say, hows about seein' that movie at the Bijou on Saturday night? It's the Three Stooges' new one, and we always have a laugh at them. What do you think? Might be fun."

"Well, just the two pounds of the hamburger then. And, I'll let you know about the movie, but it does sound good. We do get a laugh at those goofy guys! Now what is SPAM?"

***

"Morning, Mr. Beacon. Glad to see you. Can I help you find something?"

"Morning, Nathan. Well, I am makin' something for the missus, and I need a new hand saw and since my rheumatism's been acting up, I just need to pick one up here and not go walkin' over to Jensen's. You ain't gonna charge me more than he would, now, would you? Lookee here...that one is about the right size for my needs. See it over there? No, behind the other one. Yes, that one."

"Let me get that for you Mr. Beacon. And, of course, Mitchell's Emporium will not charge more than Mr. Jensen would. We merchants have a code, you know. Here you go. Looks like it is a perfect fit. What do you think? Is there something else you need?"

"Nope. This'll do. That's all for today, Nathan."

"Fine. Then, let's go to the front counter, and I can take care of this for you. Careful with these floorboards. So, did you hear about that Hindenburg disaster? What do you think about that?"

"Fools...all of 'em...makes no sense to try to fly such a thing. Foolish people! Thanks, Nathan. Go ahead now, and add this to my credit. Got to get home and start this project the missus wants done. Hindenburg...nonsense."

***

"Excuse me, John. Let me take care of this quickly, and I'll be right back. Hello Fred. So glad to see you. Yes, these are the parts Mrs. Anderson needs to fix her sewing machine. She has been anxious to complete some projects and will be happy you were able to get this to us so quickly. How has your wife been feeling? That's good. Now, just go over to the counter and John can help you with the invoice. John? Please take care of Fred. Thanks. That's fine, Fred. We will see you in a month or so. Now, John, Let's look at those sewing items again. By the way, how is Viola? We haven't seen her in town on a couple of weeks. I heard she is a bit under the weather."

"Viola is fine. She was feelin' poorly, but Doc Evans came out to check on her, and she is better now. I suspect she'll be in town soon. Now, Edna, are you sure about those lace collars? They are all the rage in Chicago, and all the women there are sportin' 'em. Look at how great they look! Those there sequins sure sparkle on the edges. They will fancy up the plainest dress, and I know you they will sell. You can charge a pretty penny for 'em too. Maybe Nate should take another look at 'em. Sometimes a man's opinion is good to have. Should we call him over?"

"No, John, I believe this order will be all. Come on over to the counter and let's take care of the paperwork. Nathan can sign below where I initialed it."

***

"Did Mr. Beacon get what he needed?"

"Yes, he wanted that handsaw. And he got it from us instead of Jensen, so I guess that's good for us."

"Did he pay you for it?"

"He said to put it on his credit line, so I did. Yes, Edna, I know we talked about this, but how could I demand blood from a turnip? They're no better off than others in the town. And, you know the Beacons have been coming to us since he and my father were young. There is something to be said for loyalty."

"Loyalty, my foot, Nathan. We are behind in all the contracts and bills, and you just need to be sterner with the customers. It's a good thing I cut back on that order from John. You would have let him talk you into getting way more stock than we need. He sure is some salesman, family or not. Did you clear things up with Fred and those parts he dropped off?"

"Yes, I did. And they were not cheap. I paid him the whole bill so that's done. I hope Mrs. Anderson will be in soon to pick them up."

"I believe she will be here this afternoon. Now, don't overcharge her, Nathan, but you know we need to cover the costs and made something on it, and I won't be here to see the transaction through. Make sure she pays cash, or at least pays for those parts. And if she gets additional things, ask for the cash payment on those too. Are you going to be able to handle it?"

"Of course. What am I...a pushover?"

***

"...and, Mrs. Anderson, will there be anything else?"

"Just those parts. And, oh, I think I need that red rick-rack back there. And maybe that packet of needles. No, not that one, the larger one in the back. That's the one. I am keen to finish those projects I started, but I had to wait for the parts to get in. Thanks so much for getting them. I know I can count on you to get my materials."

"There you are, all packed and ready for you. Are you sure this is everything?"

"That is perfect. Thank you, Nathan. I always enjoy shopping here. Please tell Viola I said hello, and make sure you add these purchases to my credit. Have a wonderful evening."

Gardening

It was a warm spring Saturday. The twins were playing in the yard, and Viola was feeling hopeful and even happy and not just because her husband was away on a sales trip. She had decided to plant some flowers and a few vegetables, and Jena Rivens was going to visit and advise her about the process. The breakfast dishes were washed and put away; the checkers game the boys had been playing while they ate their oatmeal was back in the bedroom, and the kitchen was swept. Viola retrieved the sugar cookies she had baked and hidden from her boys and placed them on the table next to the green milk glass creamer and sugar bowl, and she filled the coffee pot with water. She took off her flower-embroidered apron and hung it on the hook next to the tall cabinet. She walked to the front yard pleased to enjoy the sun and wait for her guest.

There were some other children in the yard with her boys who saw her and waved and yelled. "Ma, look at this cat from the shed," and one of them picked up the obviously pregnant animal who then yowled in anger.

"Put the cat down. She does not want to be held right now."

Mitch ran up to the porch and asked, "Is she gonna have more kittens? Can we keep them? Will Pa let us? He won't drown them, will he? She is just a real nice cat, and kittens are really cute."

"Well, we will see. But leave her alone for now. Who are your friends?"

"Oh, this is Hattie and her sister Rebecca. They live over at the place across the way. And Ma, can we give one of the kittens to them? They said their Ma don't care, and this cat is gonna have a whole lot just like the last cat."

"Well, we will see once they are born. In a week or so we can check on her. In the meanwhile, if you and Mike want to help, you can get that old saucer out in the back and fill it up with some water for her. Put it in the shed where she will probably want to stay."

Mitch ran back to Mike with the message, and all four of the children ran to the back to complete the task. Viola smiled as she watched, and then her smile grew as Jena drove up in her old truck.

"Hello there!" called Jena from the truck's open window. "So good to see you. And your boys are getting so big. I remember when mine were that age. I see there are a couple of the Wells girls here too." She pulled into the driveway and got out, slamming the door hard and then opening it and slamming it again. "Door just won't shut unless you really mean it!"

"Yes, they are all excited about one of the cats having more kittens. I am so glad you could come, Jena. This weather is finally turning decent, and I'm anxious to get some advice about a garden. I don't know much about planting, and am grateful for whatever help you can give me. Come on into the house. I baked some cookies yesterday from the recipe Tillie gave me and will put on a fresh pot of coffee. I believe my coffee making has improved."

They walked through the parlor and into the sun-flooded kitchen where Viola started the coffee. Sitting at the table, they began to talk about plants and vegetables with Viola taking notes as Jena explained. A plan for a small garden was made, and Viola asked about growing some of her favorite vegetables. Tomatoes, peppers, and maybe some snap peas would be a good start. They created a list of necessary supplies to get from the Emporium, and Jena agreed that some flowers would be a nice addition to the plot. The coffee was ready, the cookies tasted, and the two women conversed comfortably. Jena noticed the new telephone installed in the kitchen, and they talked about all the new telephone poles going up around town.

"We don't get many calls out here, but my brother thought it would be a good idea just in case something happened when John was traveling. Of course, John had quite a bit to say about the cost, and he and Nathan ended up squabbling over it, but I guess that's family for you." Viola gave a nervous laugh. "Actually, it did come in handy when Doctor Evans had to be called last month." Viola stopped here not meaning to say that.

"Did something happen to one of the boys? There is always trouble young'uns can get into. I remember mine." Jena looked at Viola's face and realized what was meant and what happened.

"Oh, Vi, I didn't know. Are you feeling fine now? When you are young as you are, those sometimes occur. I lost one between my second and third child. I'm glad the telephone was here for that emergency." Jena reached over and patted Viola's hand, and they sat silent for a moment, each remembering what might have been.

Viola got up and poured more coffee for them both. She gave a slight smile and said, "Doctor Evans was understanding and helpful. I'm feeling fine now, and you're right, the telephone did come in handy. John has not complained about it since. Do you think snapdragons would be a good start for the flowers? My mother grew them, and I remember playing with them when I was a little girl."

"Actually, I think those would be a good..." and Jena was interrupted here by a barrage of little feet marching into the kitchen.

"Ma, can we have some water? All of us are real thirsty. We gave the cats some of the water, and they're in the shed." Mike pointed out the back door just in case his mother forgot where the shed was located. Then as he turned, he saw the cookies on the table. "Did you bake those for us? We're all hungry too."

The children were sent to the bathroom to wash hands, while Viola got out some juice glasses and filled them with lemonade and placed a plate of four cookies on the back steps. Ablutions completed, the small hands and feet were sent out the door, each carefully holding a partially filled juice glass of lemonade and one cookie each. They munched away happily, and Viola sat back down at the table.

Jena lowered her voice. "The Wells girls are a bit like the stray cats. Once you feed them, they will stay. There are so many of them, I believe about ten, and Mr. Wells just disappears for months at a time. Supposedly he is out working, but I don't know how Mrs. Wells copes. I know that they have some money coming in from somewhere, but I don't know how much. They have a large vegetable truck patch, and it probably helps some, but it's a rough go for that large of a family. The church brings a box of food to them during the holidays, but it is hard scrabble the rest of the time."

The talk stopped when the smallest Wells girl came in with her empty glass and said, "Thanks, Ma'am. That sure was good. We don't get cookies like that, and I sure think you are a good cooker." She smiled and her lean little face became almost pretty.

"You are quite welcome." Viola smiled back. "Wait, your pretty red ribbon needs to be retied. Come here and let me do it." The little girl walked over and stood still while Viola retied the ribbon for her.

"Thank you. This is my bestest ribbon and my favorite color."

"Well, it is lovely and looks just fine in your hair," Jena told her, and as she left to join the others, the two women looked at each other.

"I need to get going, Viola. I told my husband that I wouldn't be too long, and I need to get supper started. I am teaching Anne, how to bake, and I told her we would make a pie this afternoon. Thanks for the cookies and coffee, and by the way, you are getting better at making it!"

Viola laughed. "Thanks. I think so too. I really appreciate your help. I may even use the telephone today and ask my brother Nathan to put in an order for the things on the list. I am anxious to start the planting and think I might work at turning over the soil today since it's soft from the rain."

They walked out the front door, and Jena climbed into her truck. After slamming the truck door a couple of times, she got it to close and backed out of the driveway giving a wave. Viola watched until the truck was out of sight and then walked around to the back. She saw the boys digging in the ground but the Wells girls weren't around.

"Is your company gone?" she asked.

"They had to get home," answered Mike. "Ma, we are going to build a city for the bugs we catch to live in."

"How about if you both help me do something else for now? I could use some strong arms for the garden I want to start. We need to dig up some of the ground and break the big clods of dirt down. Can you do that?"

"Sure," was the answer.

The boys left their pieces of cardboard and cans and ran over to their mother, each grabbing one of her hands. They walked together towards the tool shed and swung their interlocked hands back and forth, back and forth, back and forth.

Sugar Cookies

The vegetable patch and flower garden were flourishing. Every other day, Viola walked through it and pulled out weeds and took comfort in the noticeable growth of the tomatoes, and peppers, and snap peas. She collected the ripe and ready vegetables to use for meals, and planned that next season, she would expand the garden planting carrots, and onions, and maybe even a row of sweet corn. The snapdragons and zinnias were lovely, and she considered planting her mother's favorite dahlias the following year. Jena had been a great help to her, explaining when to plant and harvest her crop, and warned her about the poisonous weeds that looked like flowers, telling her to pluck out and burn Lily of the Valley and Hemlock, no matter how lovely they seemed. Viola had not done that yet because those wild flowers added charm to the rest, but she was careful about them.

School was out, and the twins were having an idyllic summer playing in the yard and the back wooded area. They were excited about another cat having kittens and were busy collecting various bugs and making a *bug-city* for them out of old tin cans, empty matchboxes, and bits of cardboard. They lounged in the grass on their backs, watching the clouds and naming the animals they resembled. Every so often, one or two or three of the Wells children would wander over from their sprawling, messy homestead, and romp with the boys, and run around the yard playing Tag and Hide-and-Go-Seek. They had a Ring Toss game and some tops and marbles and a wooden wagon to pull each other, and whichever cat would allow it, around the yard. They constructed a tent and slept in it whenever possible, and made up scary stories to startle each other, and generally just had fun. Viola enjoyed watching them play, and in cooler weather, she would bake a batch of sugar cookies from Tillie's recipe and bring them out to treat her boys and whatever other children were in the yard.

The proverbial fly in the ointment was John. When he was away on his sales trips, both the boys and Viola were comfortable and relaxed. Viola knew these trips included drinking and suspected there were additional activities, but she could not control that, and she tried not to think about it. When the trips were successful and lucrative, John came home in a good mood and, for a while, was amiable. He would not drink, and there would be no arguments followed by the usual physical eruptions. But after a few days at home, flareups occurred. His head would ache. Viola's cooking became unappetizing. The clamor from the twins was unendurable. The costs of running the household escalated, and money matters became increasingly challenging. John's travel maps and sales notebook would vanish when he needed them. Someone misplaced his new hat. The weather was miserably hot. Or cold. Or rainy. And then he needed a drink.

But John had taken advantage of the decent seasonal weather and the new tires he had recently purchased, and spent a large portion of the summer gone. His most recent trip had taken him into newly acquired territory, but he was due to return within a day or two. Viola was preparing to welcome him back and hoping this trip had been the successful. She washed the windows and scrubbed the floors, dusted, swept, and even laundered the floral summer curtains in their bedroom, giving the room a clean freshness. The vegetable patch was weeded, and flowers from her own garden placed in the iridescent glass vase John had once given her, and then positioned on the kitchen table next to the green milk glass creamer and sugar bowl.

Despite the summer heat, Viola baked the bread she knew John liked and had a casserole ready with a side of fresh snap peas she had cultivated herself. She even managed to get the boys in from outdoors, and got them to straighten their room, take a bath, comb their hair, and managed to dress them in clean clothes which fit. They grew so quickly. Viola put on her pretty summer dress, the one with the violet flowers and lace around the sleeves, and brushed her dark hair until it was shiny. The house, the boys, the meal, and Viola were as perfect as she could make them. The table was set, and the boys sat reading a book together when John pulled into the driveway, walked through the front door, and arrived in the parlor to be greeted by his family.

He was not smiling. The trip had not gone well. He had not made the sales he thought he would, had not been able to visit the places he wanted, and there was yet another town which let him know, in no uncertain terms, that he would not be welcomed back. His head had started to ache, his stomach was upset, and he was forced to change a tire... one of the new ones...not once but twice in the sun while it beat down around his neck leaving a sunburn as a reminder of its power. John had stopped to have a few drinks before coming home. And he had picked up a bottle of the gin he liked...damn the price...for consolation.

But the boys did not know this. "Pa!" they yelled, and dropped the book and flew at him ready for a hug. They reached around his legs and both talked at once trying to explain about the cat, and the expected kittens, and the *bug-city,* and asking if he could fix the wooden wagon because one of the slats had come off. And while he did not slap them away like the bothersome creatures they were, he did push them to the side, and one of them fell and started to cry.

"Damn it, Viola! It's hot, and I'm tired. You would think these kids would be under control! Is there any ice?" Without waiting for an answer, he marched past Viola standing in her pretty summer dress with the violet flowers and lace around the sleeves and her shiny brushed hair, and strode into the kitchen.

"No, John, there is no ice, but lemonade is in the ice-box and dinner is ready. Why don't we sit down and have a nice meal? I made the bread you like, and there are sugar cookies for dessert." Viola called the boys to the kitchen and wiped the tears from the one who was crying, and tried to settle all down for a pleasant family dinner.

The dinner wasn't pleasant. John mixed the gin in the lemonade and helped himself to the casserole and bread, ignoring the snap peas, but just pushed it around on his plate, and left most uneaten. The boys were not hungry but were sullen and silent, and there were some tears that would just not dry up. Viola tried to get everyone to eat and enjoy the meal she had prepared. She talked about the fresh snap peas which had grown right outside their house, and attempted to bribe the boys into trying them with the promise of freshly baked cookies for dessert. She endeavored to hold a conversation, but it was one-sided. John filled and refilled his glass, and finally got up from the table and retired to the parlor to sulk and finish the bottle of gin. Viola remained in the kitchen with the boys where she encouraged them to take a few more bites.

It was already dusk, so Viola excused the twins from the table and told them to get ready for bed, but they begged to spend the night outside in their tent. Faces washed and teeth brushed, they scooted out the back door and made themselves comfortable. Their mother tucked them in, brought cookies to make up for the wretched dinner, and she hugged and kissed them. Viola went back into the parlor and stood before John. She told him that he had no right to behave so badly, and she had tried to make his homecoming happy, and if he thought drinking his problems away would solve them, he was sadly mistaken. She went to the kitchen and cleaned, and wiped, and scoured, and went to bed. Later, John made it clear to Viola that it was, as usual, her fault.

The next few days, Viola kept to herself. She did not join Jena and some of the other neighboring women for a planned get-together. She used cool cloths to soothe her face and lavender oil for the bruises.

She stayed quiet and maintained a wifely aspect, and spent time weeding her garden and sitting in the shade of the backyard tree while John sat in the house complaining about the heat, the boys, and his terrible marriage. As she sat in a chair out in the yard, she looked at the garden growth and eyed the mixture of wicked weeds and fearsome flowers. And Viola thought and considered.

She planned a trip to town. She decided, so she told John, that she and the boys needed to visit with family for a while. After all, their Uncle Nathan, Aunt Edna, and cousin Edie rarely saw them. And didn't John agree that family was important? These comments initiated a passing argument. John was not happy being in the house with no one to look after him, and he let Viola know about his discontent. But Viola and the boys would go for the visit anyway. Nathan had agreed to drive out to pick them up, and they would only be gone a week.

Viola prepared for the trip by packing clothes and toys, and even took some placemats to embroider while she visited her family in town. Before they left, she was kind and understanding to John. She fulfilled her marital duties. She prepared, with special care, various dishes. His preferred dishes. She made sure there was plenty of food in the cupboard and the icebox. There were even the favorite sugar cookies made especially for John. Viola was careful to hide them away from the boys. They would not be safe for them to eat.

Nathan drove out to the Jasper house one evening after closing the Emporium. He pulled into the driveway and greeted Viola and the boys who were waiting for him. They placed their bags in his car and waved good-by to John who stood on the front porch smoking a cigarette. It was still late summer, and the heat had not subsided, but Viola wore a long-sleeved, high-necked dress. She took her best cardigan. It would be better to be a bit warm than to face any questions.

John Jasper was alone. He was not happy. He banged through the front screen door, stomped through the house, and swore at his absent family. He ground out his cigarette in the English ivy Viola had placed in the center of the kitchen table, and knocked over the green creamer which, due to its thickness, only chipped. He had not eaten yet that day and was hungry. He looked through the icebox and the cabinet and saw the sugar cookies Viola had carefully wrapped and placed at the front of the middle shelf. They looked good. *At least she does this right*, John thought, and took them out. They were tasty.

Tillie's Thoughts

Edie's Thoughts

Viola just looks too thin and I am worried about her health but those boys seem fine. I will try to fatten her up a bit since she will be here for a week. She used to like that potato and hamburger meat casserole I make and I will need to see Joseph for some more of that hamburger meat. And while I am there I will check on those chicken prices. I am never sure which of them boys is Mike and which one is Mitch but I think, no I am sure Mike is the one with the brown spot on his neck and if only the Mitchells were still alive they would make Viola move back with them I am sure of that. That no-good husband of hers is rotten. There are those rumors around town and even Joseph asked me about something and it was pretty bad because he could not even finish what it was about but I'm not stupid and I could sure figure it out and that just makes me sick. He don't deserve such a nice girl as Viola is and no matter how

I will need to hide my diary so those boys don't get it. In fact I think I will take it with me in this room and I don't know why I have to sleep in this old room because I have to let those icky boys have mine for the week they are here and I am almost two years older than them and they better stay out of all my things and Janet Lynn says boys are really awful and she should know because she has three older brothers and since she is my best friend she knows a lot and that is why when we get older we are going to leave this town and go somewhere really great maybe Chicago or even New York although I would like to go to Hollywood because Janet Lynn says I have a real talent as an actress because of how good I was in the church Christmas pageant when I was an angel and I made my wings look like they were flying. And now that those boys are here and I am supposed to be nice to them and take them to our store and the park over by nicey-nice he is to me I know what he is. But those two boys can use a strong hand and he's not even around enough to do something with them. I think there is a reason Viola is wearing that long-sleeved dress in this hot weather and I bet I know why and I will find out. I could just kick myself for not saying something to Mr. M. when he was alive and that John was smelling around Viola and pretending to just be interested in the Emporium just because she was workin' there but I know he was hoping to get his hands on some of that business for himself and I have had my problems with Edna, but she is smart enough to know that that John is not to be trusted and even though I do love Nathan, he just does not have the real sense Edna has and she can see through John like I do but I can't say much and at least Edna has stopped Nathan from ordering so much because he just can't seem to say NO and there is just too much piled in the back room at the Emporium and it is just not selling like John said it would and

the school to play and it is too strange to call the one Mitchell when that is my last name and I know Michael was my grandpa's name although I never remember what he was like being that he died when I was just a baby and I only saw that photograph that my Pa has of him the one that is on the desk in the library. But Janet Lynn said I do bear a resemble to him. I am going to check my real bedroom every day and see if those boys broke anything and if they did I will throw a real fit and I don't care if they are my cousins and twins. And I can't really tell who is who except the one I think it is Mitch is nice and that Mike is the one who threw that bug at me that time and they better not bring bugs into my real bedroom. I wonder if their Pa is coming because he is not so nice and does not talk and once he and my Ma were fighting about something about our store and I could not hear it all because Tillie told me to stop listening in on grown folks' conversations so I could not hear all of it but it was about our store being his too just

I am hopin' that while she is here for a while Viola can help those two straighten out the books and get the bills in order. At least she will be here for some time and maybe she will talk to me or Edna even though Viola has kept too much to herself since they moved out to that house. If Edie don't behave this time I will need to speak with her and get her straightened out. She was so bad when Edna moved her to that little unused bedroom and it is only for a week. Them two boys better not mess up her room I know she will have a fit. She just listens to that Janet Lynn friend of hers and those two are thick as thieves and that other little girl is just spoiled because she is the youngest girl although Edie being the one and only has been spoiled too I guess. Well here is Viola and the boys comin' back from the store with bags of candy! I think this week will be a good time for us all.

because he is married to Aunt Viola and then Tillie saw me. But Janet Lynn said she heard her parent talk too and they said that my Uncle John was not such a good man and that Aunt Viola would be better off without him being that he is gone so much of the time anyway but I think that might be a good thing. And I know that when those boys go to our store Pa would probably give them some of our candy for free and that is not fair because I can only get some if Ma is not there because she says it will spoil my appetite and it does not. Janet Lynn thinks because the store belongs to us that I should be able to get any candy I want any time. And I do think she is right about that but then she is almost five months older than me and knows more. I just hope Tillie does not make that old potato and hamburger meat casserole. I think this week will be a bad time for us all.

A Sunny Day

Sick. And angry. John had been sick for the better part of four days. He was angry for all that time. His sickness was due to something he had eaten. He was sure of that. Probably the various foods that Viola had left for him. Certainly the cookies. Perhaps he should not have eaten all of them, but they were sugar cookies. His favorite. Were. Not now. He dragged himself out of the bed and over to the kitchen sink where he gulped some lukewarm water from a Mason jar and then poured the remainder over his head. He threw the jar across the kitchen into the wall where the one unbroken hand-painted plate hung as decoration. It broke. He left the remnants on the floor. His wife could clean it all up when she returned with his boys. They should be here anyway. They should not have left. He should be tended. Taken care of. Fed and pampered. His house. His castle.

Still feeling sick and the anger barely abated, he went out to the back porch and sat for a while on the steps in the sun. It warmed his head and back, but did not make him feel better. He was not aware of the time, but since the sun was bright, he assumed it was early afternoon. Three days. At least three more until his family returned home. Until he was supposed to drive to his brother-in-law's and pick them up. Then he had to see Nathan's wife. Edna did not like him. He did not like Edna. Oh, she pretended to be nice, but he knew better. She was the real reason he did not own part of the Emporium. He could have talked that sop of a brother-in-law into at least part ownership. Now it was difficult enough to get a decent order from them. That Edna had to approve of everything. John spit into the dirt at the side of the porch and then stared into the dark wooded area behind his house.

Paperwork, planning, and mapping needed to be completed for his sales job. The kitchen pump needed work. The car's tires needed air. Things needed to be completed, but his head hurt badly. A drink of gin or that strong Moonshine would help, but he still owed for his last jars and didn't have ready cash. This was not the first time he found himself in this position, and he was sure no kindness would be extended to him. This day might as well be rainy and dreary. One of the cats squeezed from behind the shed door and made the unfortunate decision to amble near John. He shoved it away none too gently with his foot and swore at the creature. *Lucky*, he thought, *I could easily kick you into those damn woods and never think twice about it.*

He took the old, rickety outdoors chair and moved it to the shade. Thinking nothing positive, John wondered if there was anything decent to eat, not that he was that hungry. Later, he would clean up and go into town to Mazie's and order some dinner. He was not about to cook for himself. He guessed he would take his meals there the next few days. Maybe even pick up a bottle of gin in town. His credit was good.

A movement caught his attention, and he turned his head. A child was walking towards him. It was a little girl; one of those Wells kids. There were so many of them. She was wearing a blue floral sundress that was too large for her thin body, and a red ribbon hung down loosely from her uncombed, wispy hair. She crouched down to pet the cat he had pushed away, and then she looked around as if expecting to see someone greet her. After a short time, she stood up and seeing John in the chair, walked toward him.

He said, "Hi, little girl. You looking for my boys?"

"Yes," and she nodded, ribbon fluttering aside her hair.

"Well," he said, "my wife and them went to visit her brother. No one is here but me."

She turned as if to go back but he said, "I seen you and my boys play. You like to play in those back woods, don't you?"

She nodded her head and smiled a shy smile.

"There are some low trees we sometimes climb into. And some ditches we can hide in, and once we found us a dead squirrel, but it was spoiled, so I couldn't take it home to Ma for a stew."

John smiled a knowing smile and narrowed his eyes and then said, "Do you want me to play with you since the boys ain't here? I know where there's some good stuff in the woods to play with. Afterwards, there's some cookies my wife made you could have."

The girl lowered her eyes to consider this, and then the cat came towards her, and she bent down again, but the cat ran off this time. She thought about those cookies…those good ones like the last time. "Sure," she said, "I guess that would be fine."

"Wait here then," said John, "I need to put this chair back."

Tidying up done, John and the girl walked to the wooded area. They entered through the lowered branches and walked back where the trees canopied over their heads blocking out most of the light. They were quiet as they walked. John periodically bent down to pick up a stone or a feather and held it out to the girl who would nod her head and sometimes say, "That's real nice."

As they continued their journey, John ventured deeper into the woods than even he had ever been. Once he reached over and stroked her hair gently saying, "You sure are a nice little thing." The girl glanced at him and offered a slight grimace. They continued to walk deeper into the woods.

Far into the darkened place, the remote area where there was such scant light that the green was insignificant and the gloom was encompassing, they came across a small stream, and John saw that the girl was preparing to jump over it.

"Wait," he cautioned, "don't try to jump. The stream is bigger than you, and you'll get wet. I can pick you up and take you across."

He reached down, and pulled her into his arms, and held her tightly as he walked through the wetness. Once they were clear of the stream, she squirmed and tried to get free.

"Thanks, but I can walk now," she told him and pushed her lean hands and arms against his sizeable shoulders.

She touched one bare foot down on the ground and was almost loose, but John just grinned and grabbed her up again. "Where are you going, you nice little thing? I got more things to show you. And they ain't just feathers."

The girl might have gotten freed, but she was too slight, and he was too strong. And it was too dark. And the wooded area was close and silent.

***

Sometime later, John walked out of dark into the sunshine which still poured over the yard and the house. He placed his hands on his hips and stretched his back. He brushed off the leaves and small twigs from his hair and clothing and stooped to wipe off the mud from his hands on the tall green grass. He picked up a strong stick and scraped off the mud and leaves caked along the sides of his shoes and his pants. A small red ribbon hung out of his pocket, and he shoved it back in, then looked all around and saw there was no one anywhere. No one.

Walking towards the house, he realized he was thirsty and hungry, but other than that, he felt better than he had in at least four days. *Time to clean up* he thought. Mazie's food sounded just fine. So did some gin, and he knew his credit would be good too. He didn't even bother to kick the cat off the steps as he sauntered into his house.

Family Time

"Ma, what is this?" whispered Mitch to Viola as he pushed the potato and hamburger meat casserole around on his plate. "You never made anything like this."

"This is one of my favorite dinners, and Tillie made it especially for me. It's just potatoes and some meat and seasonings. You have had all this before, just not like this. Now, if you want some of her cherry pie, you will need to eat some casserole. You too, Mike." Mike was doing no better with his dinner.

The boys, bribed by the thought of the pie, slowly ate a few bites, and drank their milk. Across the table, Edie was repositioning the food on her plate. She had her elbow propped on the table with her head resting in it and was playing with the casserole. The difference was she had been tormented with the meal in the past and knew what to expect. She sipped at her milk and ate some bread, and pretended to take bites.

The adults seemed to enjoy the casserole. Or at least Viola did. She even had a small second helping, something that made Tillie smile. Tillie happily served Viola again and said quietly to her, "It's good to see you eat. You need some weight on those bones. And you are gonna get an extra big slice of the pie too. And eat it all!" Tillie squeezed Viola's shoulder making her wince. That bruise had not yet disappeared.

"Viola, when we are done, would you mind going over the books with Edna and me tonight? You have such a knack for figuring it all out, and we would sure appreciate it."

"Of course, Nate, I would be glad to. I know I haven't helped you with any of the paperwork in a while. I am sorry about it, but you know how John feels about that."

"Yes, well…we would like your help, thanks. Also, we thought that later this week we would invite Doctor Evans and your old friend Ted and his wife over for dinner. You could catch up with things and relax. I know that living out west you don't get much time to do that. Have you given any thought to learning to drive? That way you would not be stuck out there all the time. Maybe we could look into getting an old jalopy for you to drive. Wouldn't you be a sight?"

The adults laughed at the picture of Viola propelling that around, but Edna wondered why her husband would offer such a thing when expenses were so high. Where would that money come from?

Dinner over and dessert happily eaten, the children went to play in the yard until the dark drove them in. The women helped Tillie clear the table, and then told her to rest while they did the dishes. Nathan proceeded to the library to sort and stack the receipts, and stock lists, and letters, and all the month's paperwork he hoped Viola would be able to plod through and complete. He sighed in relief thinking that at least this month it would be calculated correctly. Perhaps she would even find some extra cash to pay the contracts he had signed and were due soon. He readied paper and pencils next to the telephone and turned the desk lamp on. Then he sat in the club chair and waited for his sister and wife to complete their kitchen work and come in. No sense in starting without Viola.

***

Outside as the sky darkened, Mike and Mitch were throwing a ball back and forth while Edie and her friend, Janet Lynn from two doors down, watched. The girls had no desire to join in, and anyway, the boys did not want them to. Edie and Janet Lynn talked quietly to each other so the twins did not hear their discussion.

"So they got candy from your store? So unfair! You and I rarely get any. Your mother would be upset if she knew, don't you think? I know, what about this plan? Tomorrow we could walk your cousins to the store before your mother gets there and ask your father for some more candy. We could tell the twins to say they dropped theirs and could not eat it. Don't you think he would let us have some too if your cousins get more?"

Janet Lynn always had plans like this. It was one of the reasons Edie liked spending so much time with her. It was one of the reasons Tillie did not like Edie spending so much time with her.

"Well, maybe we could do that. I don't know what Ma plans to do with Aunt Viola tomorrow, but if we do it sort of early, like right after breakfast, maybe it would work. You have the best ideas, Janet Lynn! Let's try that. If it doesn't work, then, oh well." Edie smiled.

They continued watching the boys until light totally vanished from the sky, and fire flies swam in the air. There was a call from the house two doors down, and Janet Lynn sighed and grudgingly headed home. Edie waved to her friend and continued sitting in the grass watching her cousins, but it was too dark to see the ball, and after several misses, the three cousins also decided the day was officially done.

As they came in through the back door, their mothers were turning out the kitchen lights and heading to the library. Edna turned and said to Viola, "Go on into the library, and you and Nathan can get started. I will get these three settled and be right there. Come on upstairs, boys, I will show you where you are to sleep."

Viola kissed her sons goodnight, and the three children trudged up the stairs after Edna.

As Viola entered the library, she saw Nathan almost asleep in the chair and the various piles of papers on the desk. "Well," she remarked, "I see I have my work all ready for me." And she sat down at the desk, adjusted the lamp, and picked up the sharpened pencil.

"Oh, Vi, I organized the papers for you. I hope you will be able to make sense out of this. I know you haven't seen the books in a while, and Edna and I work on them each month, but somehow, they don't come out even."

"I can see that. Part of the problem seems to be the amount of credit you are still giving. I know Pa did that too, but you just can't run a business without collecting at least some of the money owed. Let's start by figuring out which families owe the most, and if you can't collect some of the owed from them, you just can't extend them additional credit." Viola began to separate the piles of papers.

The two of them worked for about thirty minutes, and finally Edna came into the library.

"Is everything settled?" asked Violet looking up from the desk.

"Yes, they are all cleaned and tucked away. Viola, those boys of yours need some new pajamas. They are barely fitting into the ones they are in. I think we might have some laid away at the Emporium, and you and I can go there early tomorrow and find them. I am pretty sure they are in those boxes in the upstairs office. We ordered them last year, but they weren't big sellers."

"I know the boys are growing, and I was hoping those clothes would last for a while. I just can't spend any more money right now. John's business dealings are not doing as well as we had hoped, and money is tight. I guess it's still the same for everyone."

"Well now, Vi," said her big brother, "I think we can figure out something. After all, you are family, and those clothes aren't selling anyway. We will all get down to the Emporium early in the morning, right after breakfast, and just see what we can do for those twins of yours." Nathan gave a generous smile.

Viola looked at her brother, and then Edna, and then back at the pile of papers she was holding. She swallowed her comment and sighed and nodded her head in reluctant agreement.

"It's settled then. Right after breakfast. Let's get to work at this. We have a few hours of figuring ahead of us."

Viola moved over a bit as Edna moved a chair and sat down next to her. The three of them began what would turn out to be a long night of adding and subtracting and multiplying and dividing.

Upstairs in her small bed in the old back bedroom where she was forced to sleep while the twins took over her real bedroom, Edie thought through the plan for the morning. *Janet Lynn is right.* She grinned in the dark. *We can get to the Emporium right after breakfast before Ma decides to go, and I just know we can talk Pa into some of that candy. He will be happy to give it to us. I am sure of it!* And she turned over in her small bed and went to sleep with sweet candy dreams filling her head.

Returning

Poisoning is an imprecise act. The full force of this realization hit Viola when she saw John's car pull up to the side of Nathan's house. He came to collect his family and return them to their home after their visit, but she had hoped this would not occur. She had a plan, a partial-plan, in mind. She would pace for a while and suggest to Nathan and Edna that he must be detained for some reason. Perhaps he had to start the car several times to get it running. That often happened. She would look a bit worried and then very concerned. They would have the operator ring the telephone, and of course, there would be no answer. Eventually, Nathan would drive them home, and she planned to talk all the way home about where John could be, and that they might pass him on the road, and that she hoped he was not ill or had been called away. The actual finding of John's body and the ensuing sadness and shock would not be difficult to portray. So went the plan. And then John drove up. And got out of the car. Alive.

John Jasper looked ill. His skin was yellowish, and there were new wrinkles around his eyes which were bloodshot. He walked slumped and slowly, took one last long pull on the cigarette, and pushed his hat back before looking at the front stairs to determine how much strength would be needed to climb all six of them. He had been sick. He was angry, although he was not sure why, but he knew he would blame Viola. Whether she was the cause or not, it did not matter. It never mattered.

"Look, it's Uncle John," called out Edie unnecessarily since the entire group was pressed to the two front windows looking out.

John pulled himself up the front steps and reached for the door, but found it held open by Nathan. John entered and saw Viola standing there with the twins. They looked at each other. The boys said, "Hi, Pa," and ran to his side certain he would not push them away in front of their relatives. They were wrong.

"We were getting worried about you, John," said Nathan, "and I came home from the store because the women thought something had happened. Well, glad to see you are fine. Great to see you again. Don't be a stranger. I need to get back to the store. Safe driving home." And Nathan patted John on the back as he left to return to work.

They had never really liked each other, and Nathan did not want to give John a chance to ask about another order for the Emporium. Honestly, Nathan was pleased to see the boys go. It had been a long week.

Edna said, "John, come and have a cup of coffee before heading home. Tillie just baked a fresh blueberry pie, and that will be good with the coffee. Come into the kitchen and wait while Viola finishes packing a few more things," and she walked off expecting him to follow.

"Be right there," answered John, "Just coffee will do. My stomach has been upset lately." John looked at Viola. They had not greeted each other yet. He said a bit louder, "Must have been something I ate."

Viola pretended she had not heard the reference to what she assumed was the food she left for him. She turned, and as she walked upstairs, said "I'll finish in a minute and bring the bags down. Sorry to hear you have not felt well."

She yelled for the boys to quit their tussling and come upstairs with her to help carry things. They ignored her, but Edna left the kitchen to follow her up the stairs.

John went to the kitchen and flopped at the table. Tillie brought over the coffee and asked about a piece of pie, but he shook he head and sipped at the hot cup. Tillie glanced at the back of his head and wondered how deep a dent the frying pan would put in it. She knew better, of course, but she also had seen the bruises Viola had tried to cover up wearing a long-sleeved dress in the deep of summer. Tillie knew the kind of man John was. She knew it from the start of the relationship between John and Viola. She had wanted to say something to Viola's father before he gave his daughter away in this marriage, but the words would not come. She wasn't sure how to speak to him about it even though she had worked for the Mitchell family for years. There were lines that could not be crossed. So, she did nothing but wish John harm. She walked back to the box where she continued packing foodstuffs to send home with Viola. The blueberry pie did not get packed.

Viola came down the stairs carrying the suitcases. Edna came behind her carrying nothing but talking about how she and Edie would miss them. Of course, this was not true. Edna was looking forward to having her sister-in-law and those twin boys gone. putting the house back in order, and moving Edie back to her own room. That child had done nothing but complain about the boys being in her room all week. But Edna knew politeness and graciousness, and she also knew she was both polite and gracious even to this awful man her sister-in-law had married.

"John," called Edna, "Viola and the boys are ready. Are you sure you won't take some pie with you? Tillie could wrap it up."

John took up the box Tillie offered him, mumbled his goodbyes, and walked out to the car, past the boys who were slapping each other with great hilarity. John packed the bags and boxes in the car and yelled for the boys and Viola to get in. Viola hugged Edna once again and waved to her out of the car window as the Jasper family took off towards their home.

During the return trip, Viola kept up a constant monologue as John drove. She talked about the store and the difficulty of keeping it going, the old friends she was able to see, the adventures of the boys, and how good it was to see the family for an extended time. In the backseat, for the first time in a week, the boys were moderately quiet and cordial to each other. John did not speak. The ride to their house seemed to take longer than usual. Finally, Viola stopped speaking, and the only noises came from the murmuring of the twins in the back of the car and the tires clipping along the road.

The sky was bloodshot as they finally arrived in their driveway. The boys found their voices as they tumbled out of the car and ran to the shed to check on their pregnant cat. The adults carried in the bags and boxes and placed them on the table to be unpacked and put away by Viola. As she moved around the kitchen, she spied the hand-painted plate that was in pieces on the floor, but she said nothing and picked up the pieces and stored them on the counter. Later she would try to glue them back together.

John lowered himself into a chair and stared at Viola. "I been sick most of the week," he said in a petulant tone. "Don't know if those damn cookies or the food you left was the cause, but ..." and his voice trailed off.

"Did you eat them all?" asked Viola.

"What else was there to eat? I ended up at Mazie's for some meals. You did not leave enough and was gone for a week."

"Well, if you ate all the cookies, that could have been too much sweet for your system. I can make more tomorrow." Viola kept busy and did not look at him as she spoke. Some sweat, not due to the summer evening, formed on her brow and she patted it dry with her sleeve.

"No, I am done with them cookies. I thought you was becoming a somewhat good cook, but maybe not, and don't make more. Get me some water, will you? And put the coffee on."

John was not as angry as he could have been due to the lingering illness. There was even a sort of relief that his family was back, and now things would normalize. Viola brought him the water, and as she set the glass down, he grabbed her arm and pulled her towards him. His strong fingers tightened around her upper arm, and Viola knew from the pressure that there would be three new bruises there in the morning. He glared for a while at her face, and looked into her eyes, but found no answer there. He let her go, and she straightened out her dress and went to the stove to fix the coffee.

After putting the pot on, Viola went to the door and called for the boys to come in. When they finally did, she set them getting ready for bed. They asked to sleep in their tent that night, but Viola looked out, and saw the rain coming, and told them tonight would not be a tent night. They went to wash up and get ready for their own beds while Viola brought John a cup of coffee and placed it down before him. She poured herself a cup and sat down too.

"How about a piece of Tillie's blueberry pie?" John asked, looking at her expectantly.

Missing

"Just one more time, Mrs. Wells, when did you notice your little girl was missing?"

Emma Wells sat with Maddy on her lap while her twin brother, Jess, was asleep in the arms of Hattie who usually looked after him. Her oldest sons, Vernon and Leon stood leaning against the counter in the back, arms akimbo, trying to look fully grown and in charge, and the other four children spread around the cluttered, disordered kitchen, on the floor or laps of their siblings. The Wells family was known to be untidy and a bit contrary, but Sheriff Samms and his deputy, Ike Jackson, overlooked the disorder of the house and the reek of recently cooked cabbage as they continued with the questioning. After all, a missing child was a missing child.

"Sheriff, I told you three times. Rebecca has been gone for almost a week now. She did not come in to breakfast with the others six days ago, and we been looking for her ever since. I want to know who took my little girl and where she is. You been here for three times now and have not told me any news. Here, Esther, take Maddy outside. Go on out, the rest of you. Vernon and Leon, you stay here with me."

There was some shuffling and complaining and a few moans, but eventually the children scattered, slamming the screen door again and then again, and mumbling and talking was heard faintly as they distributed themselves throughout the yard.

"Yes, Mrs. Wells, I know we keep asking the same questions, but it is important to our investigation. We just have not had any information to go on in this matter. We have checked with your neighbors and questioned the Rivens, the Jaspers, and the Martins, but no one has seen Rebecca, and we have searched everywhere. We wish you had contacted us sooner. Why did you wait two days? We might have been able to catch some luck before this."

"I told you, we just figured Rebecca was out maybe looking for them cats she always wants, or maybe went for a long walk, or maybe was stayin' somewhere else. Sheriff, I got ten kids and it has been real hard with them all. My husband doesn't even know about this and there's no way to contact him, him being up near South Bend to look for work. He must've found something because he ain't back yet."

"We will keep looking, Mrs. Wells, and keep asking everyone we can. You say she was wearing a flowered sundress? What color again?"

"Blue. And she always has a ribbon she likes on her hair, and I don't think she had shoes on it being summer and all. Vernon, Leon, can you think of anything else to tell the Sheriff?"

Both Vernon and Leon stood thinking. Sheriff Samms looked at them, and they finally shook their heads. They weren't given to speaking much.

"Mrs. Wells, we will continue to look and question and will be back in a day or two. If your husband gets back before then, have him get in touch with us. In the meantime, anything else you or your children can think of, let us know. Boys," and the males all nodded at each other as the two older men departed and climbed into the Model A police car owned by the city of Everstille and kept in running order by Sheriff Edgar Samms.

They drove for a while without talking, and then Deputy Jackson took out a packet of Wrigley's gum and offered a piece to his partner. Sheriff Samms just shook his head, and Ike opened a piece and chewed for a time before saying anything.

"I don't know, Ed, a little girl disappearing in a small town like this. It just doesn't happen. Everyone knows everyone else, and people look after one another. I think we need to check on some of those hobos who wander around town. Could be one of them had something to do with it. They come and go, and we just don't know what they are all about. Don't know where else we can look, and, frankly, after all this time, that little girl is just gone."

"I know, Ike. But I couldn't say that to Mrs. Wells. She has her hands full of them children. Seems Bob Wells comes home about once a year and then we know how that turns out. He's not such a bad sort, just a poor sort, and we have plenty of them in this area. Can you think of anyplace we have not checked?"

"Nope. We interviewed all the neighbors. We checked as far back in those woods between the Jasper's and the Martin's places as we could see. We went out old Smokehouse Road to Jake and Lem's place and checked along there, and the creek and the hills over to the south… not sure who else we can ask or where else to check. Do you think we should call in someone else? Course, not sure we would get much help. Things are tough all over, and one little poor girl missing in a little town in one state in this big country won't get much notice."

"You are probably right, Ike, but we owe it to the Wells to keep looking and asking. Let's take a ride down to the south and look again. And let's have Dave Rivens go out with us to questions Jacob and Lem once again. I don't think they would do anything, being such quiet and dull creatures as they are, but no stone unturned…"

Sheriff Samms turned down Country Road 8 and headed back to the small hills and the creek and wooded area south of town. He did not have much hope that they would find anything, but he needed to look again anyway. He believed the oath he took and made every attempt to well and faithfully discharge the duties of his office.

***

Viola was getting the boys' clothes ready for school. Summer was nearing its end, and they would be entering second grade. They were outgrowing everything they had. She unpacked last year's items to check on what was still serviceable and which things could be of use at least for a month or so. There were some trousers whose hems could be taken down, and a few sweaters that were large for them last year, but should fit fine this year. Some of the socks were also useable but needed darning, and then there were the new things that she had received from Nathan and Edna. She had not wanted to take them because she could not pay for them, but they had insisted. She promised some payment just as soon as John came back from his trip, but there had not been much left over after bills had been settled. Hopefully the sales would be better this trip. John had recently left and would not be back for another week or so, and Viola hoped he would return with some profit.

Terrible things seemed to be happening all over. The world was a scary place to live, and horror had even touched their small town. Since the disappearance of Rebecca Wells, parents were keeping their children closer to them, and Viola was forever warning her boys about staying near home. The new rule was that they could no longer play in the wooded area behind their house and always had to stay within her sight. She was forever checking out her windows to observe them and to listen for their voices. Mike and Mitch were not happy about the restrictions on their adventures, but Viola had punished them twice and made them stay in the house when they had disobeyed. They then decided that playing in the yard and staying close to the house was not as bad as not being able to good outside at all, so they unenthusiastically kept their promises to remain within their designated boundaries.

Viola had been upset when Sheriff Samms had questioned the

boys and her about Rebecca. She had not seen the little girl since before she and the boys left for that week in town and was unsure exactly when she and her sister, Hattie, had last been around to play with the twins.

"Why, I believe it was a number weeks ago, Sheriff. In fact, I know it was. I don't remember those girls coming much after summer vacation started. I planted this year's garden earlier than last year, and I did see them around that time, but I don't remember seeing them before we visited my family in town. So, it has been a while since I have seen the girls here."

"Do you mind if I ask your boys about the girls? I would like to get as much information as possible. I promise not to upset them. And is your husband home? I doubt we can get too much information from him, being as he travels so much, but I need to interview all the neighbors."

"John is traveling and is not home now, but I will get the boys for you," and Viola called the boys in and sat while the sheriff asked them some simple questions.

That was well over a week ago, and nothing had been discovered. It was still the talk around town that one of those odd tramps might have been involved, but so far that was just talk. A few of the men in town even suggested that Jena Rivens' simple uncles who lived out in a shack by themselves were guilty. But that was merely talk too. And Rebecca was undeniably gone.

Viola thought over these things as she continued to sort through the clothes. Although it was not her usual wash day, she decided that because it was early and the sun was nice and bright that she would get a head start on her chores. She had a few things to launder, and John was sometimes careless about his clothing, so she would check the closet also.

She listened for the boys, and satisfied that they were close, she went around gathering up the wash. Sure enough, back in the closet there were some things that needed attending. Viola pulled out a sweater thinking it was ready for the rag bag, and there were some of John's pants that were muddy at the cuffs.

She took everything to the wash sink in the back room and thought that she had better let some of these things soak. Filling the wash tub with water was an arduous task, but it was necessary. It took time, and then she stirred in some soap flakes and then added a few more. Those boys had gotten into some mud somewhere, and she would just soak their clothes with those muddy trousers of John's. She was not sure any of them would be useful again, but she would try to save them.

She shook out the boys' things and stirred them into the tub. She held up her husband's muddy trousers and thought *I better check his pockets. Wouldn't it be fun if there was some money in them!* Viola reached into the right pocket, but it was empty. However, from the left pocket of John's muddy pants which she had found stuffed back in the closet on the floor, she pulled out a tattered red hair ribbon that had a small brown leaf dangling from a loose red string.

Weak One

Saturday

John rolled over in bed and covered his face with his arms to conceal it from the warm glare. Noises amplified in the crisp autumn air and echoed through the house causing him to become exasperated by the boys' laughing in the yard and the clanking of pots and pans in the kitchen. His head hurt despite the fact he had not had a drink in almost a week. He was attempting to improve his life, and clean up his act, and get back on track, and pull himself up by his bootstraps, and do all those things people swear to do when they look down to see how far they are from the bottom and realize they are standing on it. It had been a grueling week.

He sat up on the side of the bed and reached over to the bedside table for his cigarettes and then realized that he had forsaken them too. He took three deep breaths, then stood, and wandered out of the room into the bathroom, and spent some time attempting to make himself look as though he cared to live. He went to the kitchen for coffee. At least he still had that.

"Good morning, John. Coffee is ready, and I can make eggs or pancakes for you. Which would you like?" *Too perky*, thought John, *she is too cheerful, and that makes my head hurt worse.*

"Thanks, but just coffee and some toast will be fine for now."

He lowered himself into a chair wishing the sun would disappear.

"Do you think you could give me another driving lesson today? I would like to practice, and I believe I am getting better. Am I?"

Viola was excited that John seemed to want to be a better person. She was even more excited that he had agreed to teach her to drive.

"Sure, maybe this afternoon we can drive for a bit. The boys can sit in the back as long as they keep their mouths shut."

"I'll warn them about making so much noise this time, but they were just as thrilled as I was last time. The weather is just perfect, and maybe we can drive out as far as the Martin's farm today."

"Uh," spoke John into his coffee cup attempting to suck up the dregs of caffeine into his almost cleared up blood stream. "More coffee?"

Viola brought the pot over for a refill. She poured more milk in the chipped green milk glass creamer and held up the bread as a silent question. John shook his head and pushed the plate with the remains of the toast away. She leaned back against the sink and, with a smile, said,

"John, tomorrow is Sunday, and I know I can't drive to church, and I am hoping you will…," and John nodded, "and I am hoping you'll also attend church with us. The new minister, Pastor Richards, will be giving his first sermon, and there is a tea afterwards for the church members to meet him formally. Will you go?"

"Why? Is it Christmas so soon? No, Vi, I won't go with you. You know my feelings about that stuff. I will drop you and the boys off. Nathan can bring you home."

And that was that.

Sunday

"And this is my husband, John, Pastor Richards."

The minister leaned down and stuck his hand through the car window to shake John's hand. "Happy to meet you, John. You know you are welcome to come in and be with your family. Those twins of yours are really something."

"Thanks, but no thanks. I will probably see you at Christmas though." John narrowed his eyes and squeezed the minister's very pale hand extra firmly.

Pastor Richards was not quite sure what to say to this, so he simply smiled and retrieved his hand, trying not to massage it, and said, "Well, again, glad to meet you." He walked back into the church greeting other, real parishioners on his way in, shaking their hands in a normal, flaccid manner.

"We'll be home in a few hours, John," and Viola corralled the boys and went churchward.

John drove away. He did not feel quite as bad as yesterday although there was still a tinge of pain left. He decided to take a drive around town and journey down the country roads, and then go home and take a nap until his family came home, and Viola made Sunday dinner. Later, he might go over his travel plans for next week just to keep himself busy. He turned the car left and then left again and wound up on Main Street. He looked at the closed stores and shops and offices; there it was: The Emporium. The job and building that should have been his. His pulled the car over, stared at the building and sat for a while feeling his blood pressure rise and his anger elevate. Damn it. He was stuck in this damn salesman job when he knew he could have been much more successful than his goof of a brother-in-law and his nagging wife, Edna. His mood turned. John started the car, driving quickly forward, and narrowly missed hitting someone's runaway dog trotting across the empty street. He honked the car horn. He really needed a drink. At least a smoke. He decided to just go home. And go to bed.

Monday

John spent the day in bed.

Tuesday

John spent the day in bed.

Wednesday

John got up and drank a pot of coffee. Then he began to plan his next trip. He would leave next Monday. He was glad the boys were at school for at least part of the day, and Viola was busy with the laundry. He did not feel like talking to her. Or teaching her to drive. Or helping her do any of the tasks she needed him to do. He sat with his maps and sales books and spent some time planning. Then his head hurt again. Badly. He went to the bedroom closet and riffled through the pockets of his hanging clothes looking for a cigarette…just one…one damn smoke. Nothing. But he did find his flask. It was empty. He sat with it for a while and then put it in the bedside table drawer. Dinner was not good that night, and he went to bed fuming.

Thursday

His head really hurt. He was forced to get up and yell at the boys before they went to school. They were screaming. At least he thought it was screaming. Viola said it was not, but he knew screaming when he heard it. He yelled at Viola too. He slammed the bedroom door, and went to the bedside table, and took out the flask, and opened it just to recheck. Still empty. He stayed in bed the rest of the day holding the flask.

Friday

He had difficulty sleeping last night. The room was too warm. And then too cold. He could no longer stand the headache. He needed solace. He was up and dressed before the boys left. He told Viola he had many errands to run in preparation for his trip the following week. He needed to go out for the day. No, there would be no driving lesson today. He would be back late. Don't wait dinner for him. He tried to sound cordial. He sounded hostile.

Saturday Morning 2:35 A.M.

John staggered into the house leaving the front door wide open. He knocked over the small table in the parlor because it was in his way. He hit his knee against the bedroom door and swore loudly. He fell into the bed with his clothes on and snored almost immediately. He paid no attention to Viola who had her back to him but was wide awake as she wiped her eyes with a corner of the wedding quilt. She did not sleep that night.

Saturday, Noon

John's head still hurt but at least he knew why. He got out of bed and found a note on the kitchen table from Viola. She and the boys had walked over to the Rivens' farm to do some apple picking. Then they were going to make applesauce. They would be gone all day. Coffee was on the stove. John tore up the note. *I need some hair of the dog,* he thought. *No, I need to pack up and just get going. What difference does a day or two make?* His decision made, the suitcase came out, and the clothes went in. He gathered his sales books and maps and packed all the sample cases into the car. He cleaned himself up, dressed, and drank a cup of lukewarm coffee before he left his own note for Viola. It said: *Gone on trip.*

He stood for a while on the porch thinking about anything he might have forgotten, and then he went back to the bedroom where he opened the bedside table drawer and took out the flask which he deposited in the inside pocket of his tweed jacket, patting it protectively as he did so. He would fill it up once he left town. He closed the front door, walked to the car, and took a deep breath. There was a slight ache in his head, but he could stand it. John took out a cigarette and lit it taking an extra deep drag. It felt safe and right again…standing fully and solidly and securely on the bottom.

Sale!

There was too much stock at the Emporium. Boxes and boxes piled up in the back room, and under the stairs, and behind the desk and chair in the office area. Something had to be done with it, so a sale was scheduled. People were having difficulty paying bills, and money was tight, but who didn't like a bargain?

Nathan and Edna planned the big sale for a Friday and Saturday when John would be traveling, and Viola would be able to assist them. Even Tillie was going to be working at the Emporium on those days. Signs went up in front of the Emporium, and Edna talked about the wonderful bargains there would be at every church committee meeting she could attend. She designed and placed an advertisement in the Everstille newspaper which read:

Sale! Sale! Sale! Sale! Sale!

Mitchells Emporium and Dry Goods

Friday, November 3 !   Saturday, November 4 !

Many wonderful items! Women's blouses! New hats!

Munsing Underwear for all!   Household Goods!

Sewing notions! Toys for the Little Ones! Threads!

Many More Items! Something for Everyone! Come and Look!

Mitchells will not be honoring credit. Cash purchases only.

The exclamation points were important because, Edna explained, "They denote excitement, and people will know that something important and wonderful is happening. We can't list every item that is going to be on sale, but those listed are the boxed stock. Customers will specifically be looking for them. I am placing this in two issues of the paper that will come out before the sale."

There were two issues of the paper printed weekly. One came out on Monday and another on Thursday. Usually, unless there was something very unusual happening, the news was the same. Except for the dates, of course, and the Thursday edition contained the titles of the various church sermons for the following Sunday. Both issues of the paper contained the Emporium advertisement. But, the most important information the Emporium advertisement contained was in the small print at the bottom which proclaimed:

Mitchell's will not be honoring credit. Cash purchases only.

There were no exclamation points included in this part of the advertisement. Edna explained this sentence was very serious, and the periods let customers know that this was store policy. She was sure this was both proper and suitable and very businesslike. Nathan agreed.

Viola was excited to be part of this adventure, but she was careful not to mention it to the boys for fear they would say something to John. She had arranged for Jena Rivens to watch the boys after school on Friday, and on Saturday, she would have to take her chances and bring them with her to town. They would play with Edie, and Edna's parents would look after all three of them, and Tillie planned a big family lunch for Sunday after church. Nathan would drive Viola and the boys back late Sunday. Viola even found the pink smock she used to wear when she worked at the Emporium and washed and ironed it. Edna and Tillie sewed pink aprons, and the entire family was enthusiastic about the big sale. This would be the first time the Emporium would have such a sale, and hopes were high for selling old stock and maybe even some of the new.

Thursday evening before the Friday sale, Nathan and Edna stayed at the store once it closed for the day and opened boxes and organized and displayed the goods. They decided to move the candy displayed on the counter to the large glass divided case which allowed additional counter space for the children's caps they had found in a large box shoved behind the desk area. Neither Nathan nor Edna remembered ordering these caps. In fact, this box had never been opened. The caps were perfectly good. They were in fine shape and not even very dusty, although they were somewhat old fashioned, and Edna was afraid they would not sell. Then she had an idea.

"Nathan, what if we gave away a cap to every customer who has a child with them and purchases something? It will be a bonus. People love to get things for free. I only wish we had known about these caps earlier because I could have put that in the ad. Wait, no, then we would not have enough of them. Let's see how many we have and the kinds and sizes."

Edna pulled all the caps out and was pleased to find there were two dozen. There were all sizes: small, medium, and large, and while they were fashionable at least a decade ago, she was sure, in these still difficult times, that free items would be more than acceptable. She searched for and then found some large paper and writing tools and began to make two signs. One would go in the window to entice customers, and another placed right behind the counter, up high enough so that all could see it.

Free!

Child's Cap to Customers

Who Purchase Something !!

Good While Supplies Last!

One Per Customer!

Cash Purchases Only!

Edna was pleased with her signs. She wanted to ensure that customers who may not have seen the newspaper advertisement knew that no credit would be given during the next two days. She was particularly gratified with the exclamation points.

Signs up, stock displayed, candy moved, extra bags for the purchases placed on the counter, all made ready. Nathan and Edna, satisfied at last, and anxious to go home and rest, turned out the lights, locked the substantial entry door, and went home where Tillie had dinner made. She had finally talked her friend, Joseph, the butcher at the meat market at Clampet's Grocery, into a decent price, so they were having roast chicken. Edna's parents were staying overnight at the Michell house because it would be an early and busy morning for everyone. The roast chicken was delicious.

***

Nathan woke up early, dressed promptly, and left before breakfast to pick up Viola. Once the twins were off to school, they would head back to the Emporium in time for the opening of the sale. Nathan was apprehensive but eager as he drove in the early morning light. He was also surprised to see John's car parked in the driveway of the house.

He stopped his car behind John's and got out. Viola met him on the front porch. She had been crying, and her eyes were red rimmed. She closed the door quietly behind her and looked at Nathan. He could see she was attempting to maintain some composure.

"What?" he asked.

"I can't go. John came home last night late, and there is just no way I will be able to help. I am so sorry, Nathan. He is sleeping, and the twins just got up and are eating breakfast. I will have to stay here today and tomorrow." Viola wiped her eyes.

"I can talk to him, Vi. Has he been drinking? We need to do something about this."

"No, do not talk to him. He came home early from his trip. He could not finish doing his work, so he just drove home. There is something awfully wrong. Nathan, he is sick, and I mean physically sick, and not from the alcohol. Yes, he has been drinking, but this is different. I know he does not like Doctor Evans and has refused to see him in the past, but I am going to try and convince him to go today. Or at least as soon as he is able to walk."

"What is the matter? I think I should see him," but Viola kept her brother from entering the house. He was shocked at her strength when she held out her arms to stop him from entering the house.

"No, Nathan. I need to stay with him. Would you please do me a favor and stop at the Rivens' place on your way home and let Jena know I won't need her help today? That would be helpful. I can't telephone her from here. Honestly, I just feel so bad about this." Tears continued.

Nathan, not a person given to displays of affection, put his arms around his sister and hugged her. "O.K., Vi. Don't worry about the store. We'll be fine. I'm just sorry you will miss out. I know you were looking forward to being there again. I'll stop and speak to Jena. Please, use the telephone if you need me to come out here."

He walked back the stairs and into the car and backed up, driving towards the Rivens' place first and then back to the Emporium. They would just have to have Edna's parents in the store today. Things would work out. Edna would figure out what else they could do. She would have it all under control. He drove a little faster.

Viola watched him leave and then walked back into the house to check on her family. The boys were almost finished eating, and the bedroom was still quiet. She quickly finished up the cleaning and the dressing of the boys and got them off to wait for the school bus. She made a fresh pot of coffee and sat down at the kitchen table to wait until her husband woke up. Until she could figure out what the problem was. Until she could convince John to see the doctor. Until...

***

The sale was a success. Edna was annoyed at first that Viola would not be there to help, but then she got busy with the sale, and she forgot her annoyance. Her parents were happy to pitch in, and the two days of the sale went by swiftly. On Friday evening after the first day of the sale, before the Emporium closed, Edna had to remove the sign about the caps from both the front window and above the main counter. All twenty-four caps had been given away with cash purchases. She left up the sign about the *cash only* purchases and wished she could find more bonus gifts for the Saturday sale, but there was nothing else they could afford to give away.

***

At the next City Council business meeting, Nathan was honored for his innovative sales technique. He did not pay for either his dessert or drinks at Mazie's that evening. Edna, too, received praise. The church committee women admired both her creative give-away sales tactic and inventive use of exclamation marks in both the Everstille newspaper advertisements and the store signs. For weeks, townspeople stopped by the Emporium to inquire as to the date of the next sale. And for years, twenty-four children of the town, and then their younger siblings, could be seen running along the sidewalks, playing in the park, going to school or church, walking with their parents, or buying a Coca-Cola at Banter's Drug Store while wearing a somewhat old-fashioned, but still useful, and once free, bonus cap.

Business of the Day

John Joshua Jasper had certainly lost his looks. His face was lined and drawn, and he looked at least ten years older than his actual age. His tweed jacket hung loosely on him, and he had to use some old suspenders to hold up his trousers because he could not make any more belt notches without the belt end hanging down in an unattractive manner. He used to be vain about his clothes but not lately. He went out on sales calls, but the work was getting more taxing, and his trips were becoming shorter. No more two-week trips for him. Two days, and he was home again for a week. In bed or drinking. Or drinking while in bed. There were times he was in absolute agony. His headaches had increased and intensified. Whenever Viola suggested that John seek medical advice from Doctor Evans, he just laughed at her.

"That old fake! And what will he tell me? He don't know what the cause is, and then there's another bill to pay. If you ran a decent house and them boys weren't so ornery, then I would be fine."

John Jasper would continue the rant, sometimes punctuating it with fists, and Viola would grieve silently at her fate, and the boys would remain outside until the quiet in the house told them that it was safe for them to enter.

After an unusually lengthy and futile sales trip, John became so ill with one of his headaches, that Viola, daring to defy him, telephoned and asked Doctor Evans to examine him. The pain was so great that John did go into town to the office and allowed him to poke around. He asked the old fake for something to cure the pain.

"How long have you had this pain? Where is the pain the greatest? Can you point to it? Is the pain only in your head or are there other areas of discomfort? How much weight have you lost in the past three months? How much are you drinking, John?"

John sullenly answered and ungraciously took the white tablets offered him. When he left, Doctor Evans pulled out some of his old college textbooks. He looked up certain articles in recent medical journals. He read and studied. He thought. Then he called a colleague of his to discuss what he was sure was a cancer of the brain in the head of John Joshua Jasper. There was no cure. The headaches would become worse.

They did. It took a few months. John Jasper lost more weight; he became weaker and angrier, and neither the gin nor the white tablets, nor both taken together helped much. There were times that John was barely able to sit up or to deliver Viola's necessary marital corrections. Viola tried to keep peace and make meals for her family, but often, John threw his dinner against the wall or at her. Soon John was spending most of his time in the bedroom, too weak to leave the bed, alternately moaning and screaming. Viola was helpless and hopeless; her role reduced to bearing the brunt of John's anger and pain. The boys were gone outside or at the Rivens' farm most of the time. The late sun with its warmth and brilliance aggravated John, and whatever names he had not called Viola before in the years of their marriage, he managed to spit at her now.

Neighbors stopped by but were sent away. Viola met her few friends on the front porch and downplayed the ugliness within. She insisted Nathan and Edna and Tillie remain in town. Pastor Richards from the Methodist Episcopal Church came to comfort, but stopped making attempts after John told him, during one of his more lucid times, that he was looking forward to Hell and did not need the damn Pastor's help in getting there. Only Doctor Evans managed to get into the house and the invalid's bedroom where there was not much left to do anyway.

One day, when Doctor Evans came to visit, he brought with him a small bottle. He showed Viola how to deliver the drops to John and how much to give him.

"This is what we call *God's Own Medicine*," he said to Viola, "and while it will not cure your husband, it will ease the pain and make him tranquil for a while. I am sorry there is not much more to do for him. Eventually the pain will take over again, and he will need increasing doses of it. I can provide you with this, and it may make your job of caring for him somewhat easier."

Doctor Evans hoped to see relief in Viola's eyes. He did not.

"Thank you, Doctor. I appreciate what you have done and promise to pay you for your time and medicine when I can." Viola's sad acceptance was more difficult for Doctor Evans to face than the cancer eating away at John Jasper's brain.

"I will be back in a few days. And Viola...John's pain will get worse. Don't be afraid to use these drops. He won't last more than a week. I am sorry." And he was.

The drops worked for a while, but when John Jasper was awake, the fiercest part of him was his vile vocabulary. He relished using all the words he had learned on his many trips to remind Viola how awful she, the boys, and the marriage were. Viola tolerated the abuse and was thankful John was too weak to attack her physically except for the times she came too near his bed. The pain seemed constant now, and to protect her boys, she asked if they could stay with the Rivens. Jena was glad to help, and the boys were happy to go. As she watched Jena drive away with her sons, Doctor Evans drove up and parked in the driveway.

"Hello, Viola. I figured you were about out of the drops, and I brought more. Let's go in. Let me look at John."

Viola stood at the bedroom door as John moaned, and Doctor Evans did a cursory examination. He helped John to sip the water and drops. John's yellowish face turned towards the sunlight which did not seem to bother him much anymore. Doctor Evans motioned Viola out, and he shut the bedroom door quietly.

"John will not last much longer, Viola, and he will need more of these drops. Do not hesitate to give them to him as the pain will become almost unbearable. I am sorry to see you go through this alone. Let me get someone to assist. I know Tillie will be happy to stay and help you."

Viola answered without hesitation, "Thank you, Doctor, but John is my husband, and I know what he needs. I appreciate all you have done, but I can and need to do this by myself."

There was nothing more to say, and Doctor Evans picked up his bag and turned to leave.

"I'll return tomorrow afternoon. Telephone and let me know if you want me before then. Use as many of the drops as you need to. They will calm John and reduce his suffering. He can pass peacefully then." Doctor Evans rested his hand on Viola's shoulder. And then he left.

Viola stayed on the porch and watched as Doctor Evans drove away. She walked resolutely back into the bedroom where the late afternoon sun no longer warmed John's face. He lay silent, and a small bubble of spit came out of the corner of his mouth as he breathed heavily. A moan escaped, and he turned his head slowly from side to side. Viola stood and watched. She rubbed her upper arm where the latest greenish bruise was fading, and she tried to remember a happy time with him.

After a while, she moved the side table by the bed to the opposite wall. She unplugged the lamp, closed the window, and drew the flowered curtains across it. She went to the chair where John's clothes lay and put them in the closet. She made sure the wedding quilt covered John. She took the glass from the side table with her as she left the bedroom and closed the door.

Viola placed the glass in the kitchen sink, and then she moved the creaky rocking chair from the parlor, placing it in front of the closed bedroom door. She walked back to the kitchen table where the bottle of drops for John's ease had been placed by Doctor Evans, picked it up, and walking out to the back steps, poured the contents into a pile of chickweed that was growing wildly there. She closed the door behind her as she came into the house, placed the empty bottle back on the table, took off her apron, hung it up, and sat down in the creaky rocking chair to wait.

Other than the sounds from the bedroom behind her, Viola heard nothing that entire night except the creaking of the old rocking chair as she sat in it and slowly moved back and forth. Gradually the louder sounds gave way to tired moans and then to heavy breathing and then to total silence.

Viola waited until the gray ash of the sky became dark blue and then bright sunlight before she stopped rocking. She stood and walked over to the kitchen and threw into the trash a tattered red hair ribbon she had been clutching. She moved the chair back, put her apron on, made some coffee, and prepared for the business of the day.

Funeral

John Jasper was buried at North Cemetery during an early morning two days later. There was sparse attendance at Viola's request. She stood with her sons, and her brother and Edna, and Tillie, and Doctor Evans, and Jena Rivens, and they listened to supplications for John's soul fervently prayed by Pastor Richards. She glanced into the sky and thought that the day would turn out to be sunny and bright and the curtains in the bedroom needed washing. This afternoon might be a good day to hang them out to dry.

After the last prayer and before the lowering of the casket, Viola surprised the attendees and Pastor Richards by dropping the casket-bound flowers she held and walking away. Mitch called out "Ma…" but she ignored him. The mourners decided that sorrow had overwhelmed the new widow, and she simply needed to be alone. John's funeral concluded without her.

Viola walked the road towards her house and thought of nothing. She quickened her pace when she saw her home and entered the house through the back steps, glancing at the chickweed growing there. She went through the kitchen into the back room and knelt before her solid oak chest. Reaching over to a drawer, she felt around for the key to unlock it and pushed open the top. She stared at the embroidered napkins and table runners she had crafted when she was younger. A lifetime ago. She reached in and took out from the bottom the old apron which held three pieces of a pink floral formal china creamer and its matching sugar bowl. She thought of her mother and the table she would set for Sunday suppers. The pink flowered china had looked charming on the dining room table next to her mother's favorite vase holding the fetching dahlias from the backyard. She remembered family and friends gathered there, laughing, and talking. She recalled being truly happy.

Viola removed and carefully carried the pieces to her kitchen table. Using the only glue she could find, she meticulously bonded the pieces together, sat at the table, and cradled the creamer until she was sure it was secure. And then she held it a while longer. The creamer would never again hold liquid, but it would keep its shape. She placed the repaired set on the table next to the green milk glass sugar bowl and chipped creamer set her dead husband had given her. She wondered if she would miss him and decided she would not.

Viola pulled out a kitchen chair and dragged it underneath the very highest kitchen cabinet. Bringing the green milk glass set with her, she stepped cautiously onto the chair and lifted the set up. There were some Ball jars and an old mousetrap in the cabinet, and she moved them aside, and put the green milk glass set behind. Closing the cabinet, she stepped down to the floor and returned the chair to the table.

She stood still for a moment as though she did not know where she was. She took a deep breath and let out a settled sign; then, sat down on a chair at the kitchen table gazing at the flowered sugar and creamer, waiting for her sons to come home from their father's burial.

After

Mike and Mitch

Parents are not supposed to favor one child over another, but Viola knew she had broken that rule. She preferred one of her twin boys over the other and hoped it did not show. She kissed them both the same number of times before bed. She hugged them equally. When one of them fell and scratched his knee and needed it washed or needed a splinter pulled out, she did that, and then kissed both boys' knees or fingers. If one begged for an extra sugar cookie, and she relented, she made sure the other one received the same. She was fair and equal, but in her heart, there was more love for one of the boys.

Mike was the older one, being born five minutes before Mitch. He had a large brown splotch on his neck underneath his right ear. Other than that, the twins were identical. They grew at the same pace and parted their hair the same way. They wore each other's clothes because they were always the same size. Even when they lost their first set of teeth, they seemed to lose them at the same rate and in the same place. From the back, it was not possible to tell any difference between them. Only the brown on the neck of Mike indicated their identities. Physically they were a matched set.

In every other way they differed. Mike spoke loudly and played wildly. He took more chances and was not afraid of consequences. His grades were not good, and he was often in trouble at school. He tore his clothes at an exponential rate and bruised his knees and arms even faster. He was rude and messy and sometimes downright mean, even to his mother. He was the one who had received the most slaps from his father and probably earned some of them. Mike was robust and rowdy and rough.

Mitch was his opposite in every way. He spoke carefully and weighed his words as an adult would. He stayed to help his mother when Mike ran out to play in the wooded area back of their house. Mitch pleased his teachers with both his excellent grades and polite manners, and he was kind to others, noticing when someone needed his assistance and offering to help. He was the model of a considerate, generous, well-mannered child.

But it was the loud and messy and sometimes mean Mike who held Viola's heart. She was not sure why she felt this way, but she was certain about when she first admitted it to herself.

Modernity does not cease even in difficult times. The desire of the American public for contemporary objects, for state-of-the-art conveniences, for prevailing novel mechanisms is not quashed just because of a critical economy. And while Everstille was a small town in a rural area, power lines and telephone poles were installed practically as rapidly as the town itself was spreading outwards. Construction crews with linesmen, drivers, diggers, workers of all sorts were dotting the rural roads and town streets with lines and wires both underground and over trees. They hauled wagonloads of poles and heavy equipment alongside, into, and nearby, once dated settlements. Trifling towns transformed into major municipalities and, willing or not, were carted forward into the twentieth century.

All the digging and assembling and producing was a free show for the children of Everstille, especially in the summer months when there was not much to do, and the hot days precluded baseball games or hopscotch or hide-and-go-seek. They would gather around wherever the digging and assembling and producing was happening and sit and watch, and occasionally the workers yelled at them for being too close to the action. Then they would move back, and resettle, and very slowly creep up closer until an adult noticed, and they would have to move again. This became a game.

Mike and Mitch, living west of town, did not often get a chance to view close-up this modern-day effort, but when an opportunity presented itself, they joined the brood of youngsters and enjoyed the distraction. During those summery days when Viola was able to get to town to shop or visit family, the twins knew where the entertainment was. The summer between second and third grade was a pronounced traveling time for their father, and Viola was able to spend more time in town with her family and at the Emporium. The boys were always glad for these visits, especially when their amusement involved the scrutiny of construction.

The day Viola discovered which son she favored was one of those hot summer days. She and the twins were in town at the Emporium, and the twins were excited by the new building that was going up just three streets away. The building was not new; it was the old unused warehouse that was being turned into a new high school, and power lines and telephone poles were being installed, and all manner of unfamiliar equipment was around. The citizens of Everstille were not quite sure how this was all happening, but they did not question the City Council and its members who somehow organized this feat of progress. There was quite a crowd around the activity, and Mike and Mitch were anxious to be part of it.

"Ma, can we sit out with those kids and watch? They are digging really deep holes and we want to see it." Mike was always the one who asked, and perhaps for this reason, Viola always gave in.

"Fine, but you know the rules. Be careful and stay back. It's dangerous there. Edie, will you be there too?"

Edie was looking forlorn because Janet Lynn and her family had left for a visit to some relatives, and she was alone. Since there was nothing better to do, she agreed.

"Yes, Aunt Vi. I'll go there, but tell the boys that they have to listen to me and not run off like they do, especially Mike." Mike and Edie often quarreled, and Edie saw an opportunity to enforce her perceived authority.

"Thanks, Edie, and boys, do you hear? Edie will go with you and you are to listen to her. Do you understand? I will be right here in the store helping Uncle Nathan. Edie, please bring them back for lunch in about an hour."

Not willing to give up any more entertainment time, the three of them left with Mike and Mitch running ahead and Edie behind yelling, "You *have* to listen to me, you two! Your Ma said so. Stop and wait for me!"

The boys did not stop running until they reached the warehouse and joined the rest of the watchers. Edie ran after them to the site, but lost interest when she saw a schoolfriend and started a conversation with her. Not much was going on in the way of building, but the group of children were fascinated by the poles, and lines, and wagonful of wood and supplies. They watched as the diggers continued shoveling the dirt for some of the poles. They discussed the reconstruction of the warehouse. They commented to each other about how it would look and how excited their older brothers and sisters were to be in their own high school sometime later in the fall.

The actual workers were moving slowly in the heat, and only once did one of them yell at the group to back up. After another half hour, the crew leader told his men it was time for a lunchbreak and a rest. Then he came out to the children gathered there and spoke to them.

"Now, you kids gotta stay away from the stuff we been doing

here. There are dangers, and ain't gonna be no one here to watch you for a while, so go home for lunch or somethin'. Do you all hear me?"

Nods and *yeses* were answered, and some of the gathered children turned and began to walk home. It was hot, and they were hungry, and there was not much to watch. However, once the workers dispersed and no adult was in sight, Mike turned to Mitch and a few of the boys who stayed and asked, "Who wants to go with me and look in that hole they were digging? I bet it's not so deep, and we could see the bottom. Maybe there's something down there. Whoever wants to go can follow me," and being sure all of them would follow him, Mike marched off.

They all followed him. They gathered around the deepest hole and investigated it. There was only dirt, but Mike searched around, found a large stone, and threw it forcefully into the hole.

"I think this hole is small enough that I can jump over it," Mike claimed.

"No, Mike, you better not," Mitch was the cautious one.

"Sure I can. Does someone want to try it with me?" Mike was always up for a challenge.

"You go first," said one of the followers.

Mike moved backed and sized up the hole. He walked forward, promenaded around the circumference, and then returned to his starting point.

"Get far back so I have room," he directed the others, and they moved back.

"Wait, Mike, don't do it," Mitch knew it was probably useless to try and stop him, but he always made the attempt. "You could fall or something."

"I'll be fine," and Mike took a deep breath, ran quickly, and jumped the hole without a problem. He gave a shout and raised his arms like the winner he was. Then he challenged, "Who's next?"

No one wanted to take a chance, so Mitch said, "O.K., if you can do it, I guess I can too," and he sized the hole up just as Mike had done.

With Mitch back in the starting place, Mike again warned everyone to get out of his brother's way and said to him, "Come on, Mitch.

It's not that big. You can do it just fine."

It was at this point that Edie, who was walking over to gather her charges and take them back for lunch, saw what the boys were attempting to do. Mitch backed up, took a running stance, just as his brother had done, and was beginning his vault over the hole when he heard Edie yell insistently "Stop! What are you doing?"

Mitch turned his head to look at her, and his left foot caught the outer edge of the hole. His body revolved halfway midair, and he landed on the ground outside the hole on his right side. Hard. He gave a shriek and then was silent.

Edie and Mike and the other boys rushed to him as they yelled at him asking if he was hurt. Mitch did not answer. He was laying on his right side, his face scraped and his right arm, which he had thrown out to break his fall, was at a strange angle. Edie screamed at the boys to *stay with him* and *don't touch him,* and she ran at a speed she did not know she could attain, back to the Emporium yelling all the way.

"Aunt Vi! Aunt Vi! Hurry! One of the boys is hurt! Pa, you better come too!"

Viola heard her before she saw her and ran out of the store and without thinking, shouted at the racing Edie, "Which one is it?" and in her heart there was a slight break as she prayed, *Oh please don't let it be Mike! Please let Mike be safe!*

She tore down the street with Nathan after her, and as she came to the place where all the boys stood, some of them in tears, she saw her standing son, and as she came closer to the assemblage, the brown spot on his neck told her that it was Mitch who was lying silent on his right side with his face scratched and bleeding, and his right arm out at a strange angle. She could not help herself. She experienced something close to relief.

***

They all stayed with Nathan and Edna for the next few days until Doctor Evans could set Mitch's broken right arm and determine that except for a few bruises and scrapes, Mitch would be fine and ready for third grade when school started.

Nathan drove them home later in the week, and only after both the boys were tucked into bed with the new books, and the new metal toy trucks, and the new board game that their Uncle Nathan had bestowed on them, did Viola allowed herself to reflect.

She sat at the kitchen table with a cup of tea which she did not drink. What an awful mother she was! How terrible to have thought the way she did! Her first thought was for Mike and his safety. Why didn't she feel the same way about Mitch? She knew she loved them both, but she flushed with shame at her preference.

She determined that neither one would know about this and reviewed her past actions. She thought about the past years, about the hugs, and cookies, and gifts, and kisses. She concluded that she had been outwardly fair with both of her sons. She had been judicious in her observable dealings with them. She would continue her unbiased and impartial mothering, and no one would even know, would ever suspect that Mike, despite his bad choices, and poor grades, his sometimes cruel attitude and callous actions, held a greater and deeper place in her heart than his brother did.

Purge

Raising her two boys without John was easier than raising them with John. In fact, after the shock of his death, and the distress of the funeral, and the difficulty of the burial, life seemed settled and reasonable in a way it never had before. Mike and Mitch and Viola emerged from the chaotic existence of living with John and entered a serene maintenance of life without him. Gratefully, without him. It was not a sudden lifting of grief and fear, but a gradual, gentle shifting of reality; a soft entrance into the ordinary; a neutral sort of life. And as she had done throughout her time with the Mitchells, Tillie helped.

After the funeral, Tillie came for a temporary stay with Viola and the boys. It lasted the rest of her life. Tillie and Edna, with some input from Nathan, made some changes. A year before John's death, Edna's father had died, and her mother was living alone in the big house across the street and three doors down from the Mitchells. Edna's mother, Millie, was lonely and sad, and Edna worried about her even though she was nearby; so, having Tillie stay with Viola and the boys seemed a natural exchange. Tillie for Millie.

Tillie always planned to go back to her life at the Mitchells. She offered to stay with Viola and the boys just to see them through the transition from four to three, and Viola agreed. On a late Sunday afternoon, two weeks after the funeral, Nathan drove Tillie, her suitcase, some large bags, a blueberry pie, and her favorite cast-iron pans out to the Jasper house and helped her to move in. She would stay in the back room where there was a daybed and some furniture and a small closet. Viola had cleaned and readied the room for her, and after Nathan left, she helped Tillie get settled.

When she arrived, the boys ran in from outside and hugged her before asking for a piece of pie. In the kitchen, the boys gobbled their treat, then ran back outside where they were creating something of great importance with cardboard and sticks. Tillie made Viola some tea and told her to say seated while she cleaned things up.

"Viola, just sit and talk to me. Let's do some planning and talk about some of the things you'd like to do in this house now that I'm here to help. Before the weather turns too cold, we can take down those curtains in the bedroom and wash them. I know you meant to get around to it, but we can both work at it and give this house a good cleaning. Out with the bad and in with the good."

"That would be helpful. There are a few other things I would like to clear up. I am grateful you are here, Tillie. This entire time has been awful."

"I know," and Tillie came over and hugged Viola. "You don't need to tell me anything I don't already know or at least suspect. Let's just concentrate on making this house a safe, happy place for you and your boys."

And that is what they did. The next day Tillie was awake early and started the coffee and breakfast. She peeked into Viola's bedroom since the door was open and saw the bed was made, and Viola was not there. She was not in the bathroom or outside, but when Tillie went to the parlor, she saw her curled up sleeping on the sofa. Nothing was said, and Tillie went back to the kitchen to finish the morning meal. Soon Viola got up and woke up the twins. They rushed around getting ready for school; they ate breakfast and ran out to the road to wait for the school bus. Once they left, Tillie, came right to the point.

"Viola, how long have you been sleeping on that sofa?"

She thought for a second and then answered, "Honestly, Tillie, on and off through the last almost seven years. I started sleeping there all the time when John got sick so as not to disturb him, and so I could get some sleep too. So, I suppose most of the last six months."

"And why aren't you sleeping in the bed now? Is it because John died there?"

"Partly. But also, because...well, there are just some bad memories there. And that is all I am going to say about it."

"I think you need a new bed."

"That's my plan, but I do have something I need to do. If you will help me tomorrow, I would appreciate it," and Viola explained what she wanted to do. What she needed to do.

Tuesday morning turned out to be one of those muggy autumn days that force a reassessment of which season it is. The boys complained about the heat in school and suggested they stay home to get just one more day of summer under their belts. But they were marched out to the school bus and unhappily took their seats along with the other hot and unfortunate children. Once gone, Tillie and Viola prepared the purge.

They moved the bedroom furniture out of the way and propped the back door open. They cleared the back steps and shifted toys and brooms and rakes and shovels to the side to create a clear path. Viola and Tillie went back into the house and into the bedroom, lifted the mattress off the bed, and dragged it through the kitchen, and out the back, and down the steps. They dragged it into an area far back from the shed, and in front of the woods, a cleared area used for burning garbage. They pushed and piled the mattress onto the center of old ashes.

Tillie brushed her hands together and wiped them on her apron, and they walked back to the steps to grab a rake.

"Are you ready?"

"Not yet. I need to get a few more things." Viola went back to the house and returned with an armload of men's clothing...John's clothes. They went back to the mound.

"Maybe you should check the pockets," suggested Tillie, "it would be a shame to burn any money he left."

"Already found two dollars and some change," said Viola smiling ruefully.

She walked to the mattress and placed the clothes pile on the top.

"Now stand back while I start this fire."

Viola had some matches and lit one side of the mattress and then moved over and lit the other side and then threw a burning match on top of the clothes. And then she lit and threw one more.

She and Tillie stood back and watched the effects blaze and burn. Now and then, Tillie would take her rake and push some of the scorching ashes back to the heap, and Viola, thinking the inferno was waning, would lite and throw another match. Neither spoke. They watched the conflagration, making sure everything burned, and the flame consumed what it needed to. The fire was dying, and the energy was disappearing, and the two women wiped the sweat from their faces as the sun continued to beat down, on, and around them, and the Hell-like atmosphere that was this project slowly faded.

Tillie dragged her rake along the ground and stood next to Viola. She stared at Viola until finally, Viola looked up and back at her and immediately collapsed into a sobbing heap. Tillie let the rake drop and held her, and their tears combined.

After some time, they wiped their eyes and made sure the fire was exhausted before walking back to the house. Inside, they washed and changed their smoky clothes, and Tillie poured some iced tea. They sat and drank the tea in silent companionship.

Tea finished, they washed and cleaned the bedroom. They laundered the floral curtains and hung them out to dry. The closet was reorganized and straightened and, with only Viola's clothing in there, looked uncluttered and wholesome. Then they rearranged the furniture in the room. Finally, Viola used her telephone to call her brother Nathan and place an order through the Emporium for a new mattress to be delivered in a month. She would sleep on the sofa until then. One more month made little difference.

They met in the kitchen and worked together making supper, and the boys came home from school. Schoolwork and chores done, the four of them ate, and afterwards, the twins threw a ball back and forth while Tillie and Viola sat on the front porch watching. Once the boys cleaned up and were settled in their beds, Viola spent some time reading a new book to them. The evening turned cool, and the sleeping that night was going to be comfortable. Tillie and Viola made plans for cleaning the parlor the following day, and before going to her bed on the sofa, Viola hugged Tillie and whispered, "Thank you."

Viola spread out the sheets and placed her pillow on the sofa. She had a blanket next to her in case she needed it during the night. She lay down and stretched out to the extent she was able, closed her eyes, and listened to the sounds of the night which surrounded her. All was quiet, and she was almost asleep when her eyes flew open. Noiselessly, she sat up, placed her feet on the floor, and stood up. She traveled over to her upright piano and reached to the top to remove the iridescent carnival glass vase that John had given her years ago.

Noiselessly she walked through the kitchen, opened the back door, and moved carefully down to the bottom step. Holding the vase in her right hand, she pulled her arm back like a quarterback going for the long pass, and hurled the vase against the shed where it shattered. Walking back up the steps and entering the house, she went to her sofa/bed and arranged herself one more time. Tomorrow she would clean up the pieces.

Drama in One Act

CHARACTERS

NATHAN MITCHELL   Owner of Mitchell's Emporium and Dry Goods
EDNA MITCHEL   Wife of Nathan Mitchell
MR. GRAYSON and
MR. MELWORTH   Prospective buyers of the Emporium
MR. WICKS   Partner in the law firm of Granger and Wicks

TIME

Tuesday morning at 10:00 A.M.

PLACE

A large room in the offices of Granger and Wicks. Characters sit at a round table with coffee cups and water glasses in front of each. Men are in business suits and ties. Edna is wearing a navy suit with a small yet tasteful red hat containing two red feathers tilted to the right. It is raining outside, and wet umbrellas are in the corners of the room leaning against the wall upon which hang the law diplomas of Mr. Granger and Mr. Wicks. A portrait of FDR hangs on the wall.

MR. WICKS

(An older man of medium height with no unusual features and a forgettable face. He wears glasses.)

Now that we have settled that, are there any other items for discussion?

(Looks from person to person and smiles inquisitively.)

MR. GRAYSON

(A tall man with a thin moustache.)

Well, now, I would like Mr. Mitchell to clarify just once more where all the unsold stock is located. Did you say it was behind what you call the

Men's Corner or in the office area?

NATHAN

(No description necessary. Speaks after clearing throat.)

Actually, the stock can be located both places.
The newer boxes are on top of the older ones, and there are some additional boxes stored in the large closet in the back hallway.

MR. MELWORTH

(A short man with a thin moustache.)

What exactly do you have as far as additional stock goes?
What do the boxes contain?   Is there a list of the extra stock?
We have not seen a list in the papers, have we Arthur?

> *(Turns to his partner who is shuffling through papers and who slowly shakes his head. Both men look expectantly at the Mitchells.)*

NATHAN

(Turns to Edna who shrugs and frowns.)

I am not exactly sure.
A few years ago, we had a big sale and did sell quite a lot of the extra,
but since then, we have accumulated additional stock
I am not even sure we know exactly what the new stock is.
Do you remember, Edna?

> *(Edna shakes her head and the two red feathers jiggle merrily.)*

MR. WICKS

I am sure that the Mitchells can get a list of additional available stock to you. Isn't that possible, Nathan? Edna?

(He turns to the Mitchells and raises his eyebrows.)

NATHAN

(Clears throat once again.)

Absolutely. We will begin working on that today.
How does having a list to you by the end of the week sound?

MR. MELWORTH

That will be acceptable.

(He looks at his partner, Mr. Grayson and it is possible to see both men thinking the same unkind things about the Mitchells and deciding that they were basically bumbling country clods and how their family stayed in business for three generations is beyond comprehension.)

MR. GRAYSON

Fine.

MR. WICKS

Well then, I guess that all that is needed are a few *John Hancocks* on these papers, and we have a transfer of the business.
Nathan, if you would sign these, and Mr. Grayson and Mr. Melworth, if you would do the honors on these,
and then we can exchange and sign again, and we will be through. If there are any additional questions, please do not hesitate to get in tough with this office.

(There is a general shuffling and moving and signing of papers among the three men while Enda simply sits and watches

because, being a woman, she had no say-so in these important
business matters. Besides, the business is solely her husband's.
Her red feathers are still.)

MR. WICKS

There. I will make sure copies are delivered to all parties, and at the end
of this month, the transfer will be complete.
Thank you, gentlemen.
I believe our business is concluded.

(Everyone stands and there is handshaking all around. All the
men, that is. Edna stands back and watches. And as they leave,
Mr. Grayson and Mr. Melworth tip their hats to Edna who bows
her head in acknowledgement.)

(Once the door is closed, Mr. Wicks looks at both Nathan and
Edna and motions for them to be seated. They all sit down at
the table, and Nathan reaches over and takes Edna's hand. They
are all silent for a few seconds.)

Well, Nathan, I guess that is that.
How are you feeling?
Have you and Edna decided what you will do?

(He looks inquisitively at Nathan and Edna as he sips the water
in front of him.)

EDNA

(Pats Nathan's hand and looks at Mr. Wicks.)

Nathan and I will be fine.
He has asked Viola to help us figure out some things…

(Looks side-eyes at Nathan. She was not particularly happy
with this.)

…and she has been great.

Nathan will be starting work at Jim's store after the Emporium is officially sold. Jim said Nathan's year at Purdue will be helpful, and he can be
assistant to him. He won't be able to do anything with the actual medicine, but Jim will need him for everything else.

(*She smiles at Nathan*)

NATHAN

We will be fine.
It's just a bit hard letting go of the family business.
We have had it for so long and there are so many memories there.
I mean, that was my father's life.
And, you know, he died there too.
Actually, I feel a big relief that it's sold.
I am looking forward to working at Banter's.
Jim is a good man and a better friend.

(*He smiles. There is relief on his face. He has never really liked
working at the Emporium.*)

MR. WICKS

I am glad things will work out for you.
By the way, is Tillie still out at Viola's place?

EDNA

(*Nods her head. The red feathers shake.*)

Yes, she is.
    My mother is living with us and doing much of the cooking.
Once Nathan begins to work at Banter's, I will be staying at home.
There is talk of Tillie making a permanent home with Viola and the boys.
We are not completely sure what will happen yet.

NATHAN

(Sighing.)

No, we are not.

MR. WICKS

I am sure things will work out.
For now, can I ask you to get the list of stock together for these
gentlemen? The sooner, the better.

NATHAN

(Nods his head.)

We can begin that tomorrow morning.
We'll get Viola and Tillie to help during the day while the boys are in
school. Viola can drive in tomorrow with Tillie and begin to look at what
needs to be done.

MR. WICKS

(Looks surprised.)

Well! Viola is driving?

EDNA

(Looking just a bit annoyed because she does not drive.)

Yes, she is.
There have been a few changes after John's death.
Viola said that John had started to teach her how to drive and that it just
didn't seem that difficult. She had been practicing, and Tillie said she is
doing a good job. No sense in wasting that car.

MR. WICKS

(Smiling and standing up, indicating that the Mitchell's time with him, in the office of Granger and Wicks, is done. To further clarify this, he takes out his pocket watch and looks at it with interest.)

Alright then, Nathan and Edna,
I am glad to help you and if there is anything else you need, let me know.
As soon as you can get that stock list to me, do so.
Thank you both, and have a pleasant day.

(He shakes Nathan's hand and then, because he has known Edna since she was young, shakes hers also.)

NATHAN

Thank you, Mr. Wicks.
We'll get the list to you as soon as possible.

(Nathan and Edna walk out of the office door. They travel down the steps of the building and cross Main Street. The rain has ceased but the wind blows Edna's red feathers and they slowly move. At the Emporium's substantial entry door, they open it using their key and go inside. They close the door.)

END SCENE

Clouds are Gone/Sun is Out

John Jasper always kept a nice automobile. He liked Buicks because they were affordable and large enough to fit all his sample cases and a suitcase, and still, when necessary or expedient, roomy enough to spend the night in, sleeping it off. He knew cars and took care of his, and if there was one bill that was always paid first, it was anything having to do with his car. The last car he bought and owned was the 1934 Buick Series 40 4-door sedan in, of course, black, with the three-speed manual transmission and the side mount spare tire. He was looking forward to one of the new Buick models, perhaps even some sports model although that might not be large enough for his needs, but then, he died. Viola inherited the Buick.

She had four driving lessons in the car her husband had kept in tip-top shape, and after just two, could drive, but John insisted she could not drive the car alone without him and his explicit instructions. A week after John's death, after the boys left for school, Viola got in the car and drove to the town's gas station, filled it up with gas, and had Mackie, the owner, check it out to make sure it was running well. There were one or two minor adjustments Mackie had to make, and the car was, as he put it, "It's A-OK. It's all jake!" Viola drove the car home, parked it in the driveway, and continued to drive it for years. She always meant to obtain a driver's license, but did not because she never really drove very far.

And then Nathan and Edna sold the Emporium. For most of a week, after the boys left in the morning, Viola and Tillie would get into the Buick and travel to town where they would help inventory stock and manage the Emporium while it was still Mitchell-owned. At first, Edna was disconcerted that Nathan had asked his sister and Tillie for help, but they were so handy, and Viola was so organized, that she got over it quickly. Despite the rainy week, customers were still coming in, mostly to commiserate with the Mitchells about the sale of the Emporium and wonder about their credit options from the new owners. Some of them did pay part of the money they owed, but most were not in financial shape to do so. It was a long, sad week.

Among the boxes of stock found stored all over the building, were some small boxes of clothing, serviceable but old-fashioned, that for at least a decade had not been unpacked. When Viola saw the variety of clothing that would fit both boys and girls, she spoke to Nathan.

"Nate, there are those boxes of unsold clothes there. I am not so sure they will be saleable. I would like to take them and a few more things with me. I know someone who could really use them. What do you think?"

"Sure, Vi. I have no problem with that. Maybe you or Tillie could quietly get them in your car without Edna seeing. Not that she would mind, but…"

"Thanks, Nathan. I can do that," and she did.

All of them worked throughout the week, organizing the stock and store, and creating the necessary lists for the new owners. On the last day, with everything finally systematized, Viola and Tillie finished the final tasks by noon. The rain had stopped, and although it was not sunny, the clouds were dissipating

"Thank you both for helping. This was a much bigger job than I thought it would be," Edna spoke earnestly and gratefully to them. "Would you like to stay for lunch? My mother is making a casserole, and she would be glad to see you both."

"Thanks, Edna, but Tillie and I have some work of our own to do. We were glad to help you out. After church on Sunday, why don't Nathan and you bring Edie and your mother out to our place and have Sunday dinner with us. Would that be OK?"

"That would be great. Thanks," and Edna hugged both the women as they left the Emporium.

Once seated in the Buick, Viola turned to Tillie and said, "We need to stop at Clampet's for some things. I know I did not ask you about cooking for Sunday, but I can help."

"Oh," replied Tillie, "that is fine. You know I enjoy cooking for a crowd. Yes, we can stand to pick up a few things, and I will say hello to Joseph."

Viola drove to the lot at Clampet's Grocery Store and parked. They went in, and while Tillie went to the back to see Joseph and check on the meat prices, Viola began to gather items. Rice, beans, flour, sugar, some dried fruit, oatmeal, and canned goods, were piled on the front counter. When Tillie came to the front with her goods, she looked at the load that Viola had gathered and turned to her.

"Are we out of all this? I didn't notice the pantry was so low.

Or will there be a much larger group for Sunday dinner than I know about?"

"No, Tillie, this is not for us. Would you help me to get this in the car? And before we go back home, there is a short trip I need to make."

They piled everything into the Buick. Viola drove out of the main town and west towards their house, but she did not make the turn to their lane. Instead, she continued driving straight down the road. Tillie turned to her.

"You are headed to the Wells, aren't you?"

"Yes. I am going to drop off some clothes and a few groceries to them. We won't stay long and will be back before the boys are home from school."

Tillie just nodded. She sat and stared at the road ahead and said nothing. They soon turned and drove into a path next to the large cabin that was the home of the Wells and their nine children. There used to be ten.

"Hello, Emma! I wanted to stop by and drop off some things for you," Viola spoke cheerfully. She wanted her tone to carry over to Tillie and let her know this was to be a friendly neighborly visit, and not a mission of mercy. Which, it was.

"Oh, Viola, it is so good to see you again. My oldest boys are not here, but I can help bring those in," although that was doubtful since she had hoisted one child to her hip and another held her hand.

"That's fine. You have a handful already. Tillie and I can bring these boxes in."

They delivered the groceries. Viola went back to the car to get the box filled with clothing she had taken from the Emporium. She carried it in and placed it on the table next to the other boxes.

"I am not sure of the sizes of your children, but I suspect some of these will fit. I hope they do anyway. And who are you, little one?' and Viola bent down to see a two-year old face looking up at her.

"That's Maddy, and this is Jess. They just turned two. The rest of them are at school and the oldest boys are out in the back woods huntin' for rabbit or squirrel. Viola, I do thank you for this bounty. Your kindness is appreciated. It has been hard. Bob was back for a while but then left again on a work search. I think he got a job at a car plant near South Bend. Anyway, I thank you for this. Maddy, leave the lady be. Are you thirsty? I can offer you some cold water."

"Thank you, but we need to get back. My boys will be home soon too. By the way, have you met our family friend? This is Tillie Smith."

Tillie smiled and nodded, and Emma Wells said, "Glad to know you."

As Tillie and Viola turned to leave, Viola went to the box containing the clothing and pulled out a bunch of colored ribbons. She handed them to Emma and smiled as she said, "I know girls like something pretty in their hair, so these are for your girls."

"So thoughtful of you," Emma said, and a sadness clouded her face. "My Rebecca loved her red ribbons. Thank you. The girls will enjoy these," and she gathered the ribbons and looked at all the colors in her hand.

As Viola drove off and down the road towards home, she waved to Emma Wells standing with Maddy and Jess. They all waved back.

Once they were out of sight, Tillie turned to Viola and asked, "So, how many times have you been there dropping off groceries?"

Viola just smiled and shrugged. "There is always someone who is worse off, Tillie, you know that. I do what I can. I have only been out there a few other times. They are in need. You can see that."

"Well, you are a good woman, Viola. Your Ma and Pa would approve," and Tillie reached over and squeezed her shoulder and Viola did not cringe because there were no longer any bruises.

Viola drove carefully and surely. She lowered the car window and brought in an easy breeze.

"Look, Tillie, the clouds are gone and the sun is out. I think when we get home, I'll gather the last of those zinnias to decorate the table for dinner. They remind me of Mother."

And driving home in her Buick with Tillie in the passenger seat, and anticipating seeing her boys come home from school, and watching the sun, and knowing it was drying up the rain-soaked zinnias in her garden was exactly where Viola wanted to be.

Moving Day

During the following months, there were many changes:

1. Joseph proposed to Tillie again and suggested they move to one of the new houses being built. She turned him down again, although, as Tillie qualified, maybe sometime in the future it would happen.

2. Tillie gave up her room at the Mitchell's and sold most of her furniture and household goods.

3. The Martins sold their farm and moved to South Bend.

4. Millie Johnson, Edna's mother, held an estate sale and sold most of her belongings because she moved in permanently with her daughter and son-in-law, Nathan, and granddaughter, Edie.

5. Viola sold her house and property, and she and the boys and Tillie moved into Edna's childhood home across the street and over three houses from her childhood home.

6. Both Tillie and Viola began to work: Tillie, once again baking pies for the town's expanded Peterson's Bakery, and Viola working as part-time bookkeeper at that bakery, Banter's Drugs and Pharmacy, and to everyone's surprise, the no longer owned by but continued to be called *Mitchell's Emporium.*

7. Everstille grew and expanded with more families coming to live in the bustling and popular town.

These changes did not happen in the numbered order. Some were simultaneous, others were months in the making, others happened quickly. All were inaugurated, in one way or another, by the Goodwin Construction and Building Company buying the land which included Viola's house and property, the wooded area behind it, the Martin farm and all land west up to but not including the Wells' place. Too bad for the Wells, although Bob Wells was now at home because he was working clearing land for the Goodwin Company.

The land was to be divided and sold to families who wanted clean living and a fresh start, having purchased one of the many Sears Modern Home kits available. Now they needed some land for their houses. Prosperity loomed on the horizon after a long and difficult Depression, and the country saw hope again.

Moving day for Viola, Tillie, Mike, and Mitch had come. They had cleaned, organized, and moved many of their belongings through numerous trips taken in the Buick. But on this day, Nathan had borrowed Jim Banter's truck and had taken part of the day off to help move the last of the larger furniture, and the boxes from the kitchen, and the closets into what would be their new residence. The Johnson house was Viola's to live in as long as she maintained it. She had received enough monetary compensation from the Goodwin Company to pay off her mortgage, most of her bills, and to enable her to buy new beds for the twins who were growing and elongating and looking forward to high school in another year.

"Mike and Mitch, grab that large box and put it in the truck first. Then put these smaller boxes on top and next to it."

Nathan was ordering and instructing. The boys were following their Uncle Nathan's directions and were happy to be doing such man's work. They accepted the move because they had no choice, but they would miss the freedom they had grown up with: the woods, the large, spacious yard, the shed cats who had mostly disappeared. There were advantages to the move: no bus ride because they could walk to the grammar school and to the high school next year, proximity to the town and to their town friends, and the excitement of a larger house in which they each had their own bedroom. Small rooms, but they could decorate them any way they liked, and the new beds were set up and in place for the night's use.

Tillie and Viola were piling clothes into the Buick and trying to determine if there would be two or three more trips into town and back.

"Nate, please be careful with that oak chest!" and Viola stopped to watch as Nathan and the boys hoisted the oak chest containing her wedding staples onto the truck. "Here, cover it up with this blanket so there are no scratches."

Through yells and shouts and questions, both the truck and the Buick were loaded, and the first caravan to the new house set off. Once they were unloaded, there was a final delivery, and then the unpacking and organizing began. Because the empty Johnson house was cleaned and part of the furniture had been moved in, there was not as much to do as if the move had been a one-day event.

It was a pleasant autumn Saturday, and Viola opened the house windows allowing in the warm breeze. The boys were in their second-floor bedrooms, placing their possessions in the proper order, and Tillie was busy getting the kitchen and dining room arranged. Across the street, Millie Johnson was making her specialty, a Kitchen Sink Casserole with bacon and beans, for a family dinner later. She was doubling the recipe so there would be leftovers for both families. Once Viola heard what dinner would be, she warned the boys and cautioned them about complaining. No one particularly liked the dish. Nathan drove Jim's truck back and went to work for the afternoon, and Edna was working in her garden while Edie and Janet Lynn were plotting something in the upstairs bedroom. Everyone was busy, and Viola had something to do.

"Tillie, I need to fill up the Buick with gasoline and make one more trip to the house just to check and make sure nothing was left. Is there anything else you need? No? OK, I'll be back in a while," and she went out to the car. She drove to Mackie's for gasoline and then took the long way out to the house.

There was no real reason for the trip. She drove slowly and deliberately down the road, and when she came to the edge of her former property, she saw trucks and digging implements left idle until the next work day. She parked and walked the short distance to her house. The Goodwin Company's house now. She still had the keys, and she walked up the front steps and went in, closing and locking the front door behind her.

Viola went to the parlor and looked around at the emptiness. Then to the kitchen and the back room. She checked all the closets and the pantry. Empty. The bathroom still contained a forgotten towel, so she claimed that and went to the boys' room. It seemed larger without their books and toys and beds. Her bedroom was next, and she stood in the middle and turned around slowly. She peeked into the closet, and in the corner, saw one of John's ties that she had missed at the burning. She left it there. The light floral curtains were still up, but she did not remove them. Instead, she pulled them closed so the room darkened. As she went out the back door, she held on to the wooden railing thinking: *This is loose. I would need to fix it if we were still here.* The large pile of chickweed close to the steps had been pulled out last summer.

As she walked around the side of the house, she saw one of the shed cats and bent down to pet it, but it scooted out of the way of her hand. Over the years they had slowly disappeared, and the ones left had turned wild. She wondered what would happen when the new families built the homes and moved here. Would there be cats around? Walking to the side garden plot which she had not planted this year, she saw it overgrown with weeds and the spreading Lily-of-the-Valley and Hemlock. A few stray vegetables had insisted upon producing, but they had rotted on the ground or animals had gnawed at them. Viola moved back a few steps, took one last look around, then returned to her Buick, threw the towel on the passenger seat, backed up, and drove away without scrutinizing the property in the rearview mirror.

That evening, after the family had gathered and eaten the casserole (and no one said anything negative about it) and the pie Tillie had made the previous day, the boys and Edie left to get Janet Lynn, and the four of them walked to town and to Banter's Drug Store where the newly installed soda fountain was becoming the meeting place for the town's young. Nathan retired to his library while the women packed up the leftovers and did the dishes. Viola and Tillie said good-night, crossed the street, and walked down three houses to their new residence.

"I'll put this casserole away in the icebox," said Tillie, "although I doubt it will get eaten. Then I think I'll get to bed early if you don't mind. I am beat. This has been quite a day and I am looking forward to trying out the new bedroom."

"That's fine, Tillie. I'm going to sit on the porch swing for a bit and wait until the boys get home. Oh, I see them now."

Viola went out to the porch and sat down on the swing. She watched as her boys ran across the street to their new house and chattered to her about the soda fountain and the friends they saw there. Viola listened to them, seeing the happiness in their faces. She sent them to clean up and go to bed and told them she would be up to check on them in a while. For once, Mike and Mitch did not complain about having to go to bed but went into the house and ran up the stairs. They were as eager to settle in their new bedrooms as Tillie had been to settle in hers.

Viola sat down on the porch swing and looked around the neighborhood she used to know so well. There was her childhood house, the first floor dark, but lights shining in the upstairs windows. Down Main Street was the Emporium, once owned by her family and now her place of work. Peterson's Bakery was next to it, and Banter's Drugs and Pharmacy was on the corner. She was in walking distance to them all and looked forward to going to work on Monday. Her Buick was in the driveway, and stillness surrounded her. Nights in the town were less

noisy than nights in the country, and she would need to become reac-
quainted with the quiet. She sat on the porch swing and pushed it using
her toes and swung back and forth, back and forth, back and forth.

Smooth Roads

Predictability and repetitiveness are not necessarily unpleasant. Rising in the morning, readying for the day, completing required tasks, preparing for bed, and repeating the motions bring a sense of steadiness and stability to life. It is the smooth road and not the bumps and hills that humanity desires. At least Viola found this to be the case.

Because of her past work experience and excellent organizational skills bolstered by the business courses she took in high school, Viola was offered a part-time job keeping the books at Banter's Drug Store. When her expertise and quickness with numbers was noted, she was asked to work at Peterson's Bakery, and then, Mitchell's new owners needed someone to help with their expanding business. Her schedule became organized around the three businesses. She spent Mondays at Mitchell's Emporium, Wednesdays at Peterson's Bakery, and Fridays at Banter's Drug and Pharmacy. On Tuesdays and Thursdays, she completed paperwork from the businesses. If there was nothing to complete, she stayed home and helped Tillie with her baking.

Tillie delivered pies on Wednesday and Saturday and did the baking on the other days. Sometimes, if Viola had spare time and there was space to work in the kitchen, she would make a few dozen of her special sugar cookies for the bakery. They always sold quickly, and the bakery would place a handprinted sign on their front window stating:

Special Today: Sugar Cookies while they last!

The money they earned paid for the pie ingredients, the upkeep of the house, the monthly bills and needs, and there was even a bit for each of them to store away. The family's needs were slight; everyone was used to making do with little, and Viola's discount at the Emporium was useful. All in all, life in town was easier than life used to be in the small house west of town.

Mike and Mitch enjoyed living in town. Being closer to school meant they did not have to rise early to catch the school bus. They appreciated having their own bedrooms on the second floor of the former Johnson house, and they relished periodic jaunts to the soda fountain at Banter's Drug Store. School was, well, school. Mitch's grades were exemplary as was his behavior. Mike's were not, and Viola made numerous trips to the school office to discuss his grades. Or his behavior. Often on Friday nights, due to some trouble at school (although it was never, according to Mike, his fault), Mike stayed at home with his mother and

Tillie while Mitch visited Banter's and indulged in an ice cream treat. However, it was not unusual, on those evenings, for some sugar cookies to find its way into Mike's hands. Or a half-melted ice cream cone was hustled into his bedroom.

Across the street and three houses down, Nathan and Edna were busy with their lives. Nathan discovered that he enjoyed working at Banter's Drugs with his friend, Jim Banter. The regular hours and pay-check made life easier, and Nathan found that working for someone who was not his father overseeing and censuring his every move, made a job pleasurable, and he was fast becoming a favorite with Banter's customers. While he worked, Edna was at home with Edie, and once Edie did not need or want her constant attention, Edna found church and civic activities that were in want of those attentions. Edna's mother, Millie, was happy having a family to cook for again and enjoyed creating new versions of her Kitchen Sink Casserole recipe to her family's unspoken aversion.

Edie was in high school and saw herself an undisputed star. She had an unobjectionable voice, and sang in the school chorus and the church choir and badgered her parents into getting her a piano. She studied voice and piano with Mrs. Wilson, the church choir director, and was sure stardom was in her future. Her parents were not as certain, but they indulged her and thought her aspirations harmless. They were grateful that Viola was willing to have her childhood upright piano moved back across the street and three houses down so that Edie could practice singing and playing. And, as the neighbors could all attest, she enjoyed practicing singing and playing.

Mitchell's Emporium, newly reorganized and renovated, emerged as a flourishing, thriving business. Store changes reflected cultural changes and specialization was the new by-word. There were monthly sales, and the first one involved all the tools and equipment from the *Men's Corner* which was dissolved to make space for the expanded ready-to-wear men's and women's clothing section.

The owners, Mr. Grayson, and Mr. Melworth, decided Jensen's Hardware and Agricultural Needs could provide necessary tools and equipment to the town, and Mr. Jenson was pleased with this decision. The following month, the sale included the sewing, quilting, and needle-work stock. That section was not totally discontinued, but condensed and modified. A new department which sold different and newer electric items: six-tube radios, toasters, irons, clocks of all sorts, was popular. There were items which could be special-ordered from the

Emporium's updated catalog: a Westinghouse cleaner with attachments kit, a Tappan gas range, a wringer washing machine, all expensive, but with the Emporium's new Layaway Credit Line, available for the ever growing and desirous population in Everstille to, eventually, acquire. Personal credit of the type Nathan Mitchell and his father and before him, his grandfather extended to the citizens of the town, was no longer obtainable.

Mackie's Gasoline and Service Station was consistently busy due to the increased number of cars and trucks the expanding population of the town owned. In fact, Ian MacKenzie, owner of Mackie's, decided to expand and build an additional service station just outside of the town limits. He was discussing the legalities of it with Mr. Wick's son, Jason Wicks, who was the new junior lawyer at the Granger and Wicks Law Office.

Clampet's Grocery Store needed to expand and enlarge, and build out onto the lot used for parking. Mr. Clampet was anxious to purchase the empty lot one street over for a new parking area, and Joseph the butcher, was training an apprentice to help at the butcher shop in the new back section of Clampet's.

Mazie's restaurant recently renovated, added new counter space, and was waiting for updated tables and chairs to arrive from Chicago. Mazie could no longer wait on all the customers herself, so she hired two waitresses who wore frilly white aprons over their black uniform dresses which had the tag line: **Mazie's Best Food** embroidered across the top left breast pocket. And a new, expanded library was the topic for discussion at the next City Council meeting.

Everstille's population continued to rise in the morning, get ready for the day, complete required tasks, prepare for bed, and repeat the motions, all of which brought a sense of steadiness and stability to their lives. Travel was smooth; bumps arose, but were surmounted, and life was repetitive but satisfying. It was when the unpredictable happened that unpleasantness occurred.

A Secret

Spring brought soft soil and pliable ground, and the Goodwin Construction and Building Company was working diligently at clearing and parceling out the land they had purchased. The workers hired were usually on time and completed the difficult physical tasks of chopping and removing the trees and prying out the area's enormous rocks. Martin's farmhouse and barn had been razed. Viola's house and shed were gone. The woods in the back and to the west of her property were the most difficult because the trees, while not wide, were tall and closely grown, and the men removing them were genuinely earning their fair wages of forty-eight cents an hour paid to them by the Goodwin Company.

The deeper into the wooded area they moved, the more difficult it was, and two men, Joe and Pete, were sent to scout the area and figure out how to proceed when it was not possible to drive trucks or large equipment into the thickets. Joe and Pete walked to a darkened place, a remote area where there was such scant light that the green was insignificant, and the gloom was encompassing, and they came across a small stream. They walked across it and went further into the dark area, and in a little while, they turned and sprinted back to their foreman, Don, who gave the crew leader the key to his truck and sent him into the town of Everstille to speak with Sheriff Samms.

Sheriff Samms and his deputy, Ike Jackson, drove out to the woods where the workers had been given an early and lengthy lunch break. They went to the spot that Joe and Pete had found, and after discussing the situation with Don, decided that work for that day would stop. The workers were sent home with the promise of a full day's pay, and while they did not know exactly why this had happened, they did not mind.

Sheriff Samms and Deputy Ike drove back to town to complete some necessary paperwork and make several important calls.

"Now, Ike, we need to keep this quiet. Eventually the news will get out, but we do not need anyone to know for as long as we can keep it secret. Got it?"

"Absolutely, Boss," and Ike finished his paperwork, and they both took a brief lunch break. Ike went home where his wife, Betty, had lunch waiting.

Betty asked about how his morning went, and Ike, in the manner of married men who share everything with their spouse, told her the news and swore her to silence, and Betty, who knew how important it was to not tell anyone, agreed. When Ike left, the telephone rang, and Betty answered it, speaking briefly to her sister, Joanie, about the birthday party they were planning for their father that evening. During the conversation, Betty may have mentioned the news, but extracted a promise from her sister to not say anything to anyone. Joanie agreed.

Joanie's husband, Charlie, happened to walk into the house because he forgot a tool that he needed for his job at Mackie's Gasoline and Service Station where he worked as a mechanic. He said *hello* to Joanie and grabbed one of the cookies she was making for the birthday party that evening and asked about her day. Joanie mentioned the news from Betty, but told Charlie he absolutely could not say a thing, and he concurred.

Charlie went back to work at Mackie's where he was finishing up a minor repair on the automobile of Peter Hopewell. As he and Mackie were working on the car, it is possible that Charlie let slip the news his wife had told him, but knowing its importance, he made sure Mackie knew that nothing should be mentioned about it. Mackie, never one to gossip, assured Charlie that he would say nothing, and then was interrupted by Peter Hopewell who had come to pick up his car. Mackie let Peter Hopewell know that it would just be about ten minutes more, and Charlie would be finished. They had a brief conversation while waiting for the work to be completed, talking about nothing, really, but it is possible that Mackie let slip the intelligence he learned from Charlie. Peter Hopewell paid for the mechanical work and left, going back to the town to pick up the items his wife needed from Clampet's Grocery.

Peter Hopewell parked next to Clampet's and entered the store to purchase the required items. He was waited on by Mr. Clampet himself because it was a slow day, and Mr. Clampet's usual clerk, Tom, had called in sick. There was something going around, as Mr. Clampet explained to Peter Hopewell, and they spent a minute or two discussing their health issues, and in the discussion, Peter Hopewell may have let slip the gossip told to him in confidence by Mackie. Of course, he obtained a promise from Mr. Clampet that he would say nothing, then paid for his groceries and left to deliver them to his wife.

Mr. Clampet watched Peter Hopewell leave his store, and then, because it was the slow time of one-thirty in the afternoon, he walked back to see how Joseph, his butcher and friend, was doing. Joseph just finished instructing his apprentice in the intricacies of grinding fresh hamburger meat and was washing his hands as Mr. Clampet came back to shoot the breeze. They talked a while and, by mistake, Mr. Clampet mentioned the news he had heard from Peter Hopewell. Then the door's bell jingled, and he left to see who had come in.

Tillie Smith walked through the door of Clampet's in search of some freshly ground hamburger meat to make the potato and hamburger meat casserole that was Viola's favorite. She greeted Mr. Clampet and proceeded back to the meat counter to get what she needed from Joseph. Joseph was glad to see her, and as he weighed out the freshly ground meat and made plans to see the new movie at the Bijou Saturday night, Joseph, who knew he could trust Tillie with any kind of secret, let her know about the one he had just heard. Tillie paid for her purchases and left Clampet's to walk home.

Tillie entered the house and greeted Viola who had come home from a short day of work. She had been at Peterson's Bakery working on their books and receipts and was busy making some coffee. Tillie placed the freshly ground hamburger meat in the icebox and gathered the potatoes and onions for the casserole that evening. While she worked at thinly slicing the vegetables, Viola sat at the kitchen table, the old one they had moved from the house west of town and which was still shiny and bright, and they chatted.

Tillie knew that Viola could be trusted, and so she told her the secret that had been imparted to her by Joseph just a few minutes ago at Clampet's where Mr. Clampet had been told, in friendship, by Peter Hopewell who had learned of the occurrence from Mackie who knew of the news from Charlie whose wife, Joanie, had been told about it by her sister Betty, whose husband, Deputy Ike, had told her but sworn her to silence. It was in this way that Viola, at two-fifteen in the afternoon, learned that just a few hours before, the workers for the Goodwin Company who were scouting the wooded area behind the house she and her boys and her dead husband, John, used to live in, had discovered the remains of a young child buried far into a darkened place, a remote area where there was such scant light that the green was insignificant and the gloom was encompassing.

Special Wednesday Edition

THE EVERSTILLE NEWS

Martin Chessworth, Editor

Building Company Finds Child's Remains
Possible Missing Child: Rebecca Wells
Story by: Martin Chessworth

Two workmen from the Goodwin Construction and Building Company found the remains of a child as they searched in the wooded area west of Everstille in preparation for portioning the land for additional buildings planned in conjunction with the City Council Planning Committee of which the editor of this newspaper is a member. Upon finding the remains which had been buried in a shallow grave, Sherriff Edgar Samms and Ike Jackson were alerted and immediately went to the site to check on the discovery. Additional help from the South Bend Police and Detective Departments was sought. Officers came down and prepared to help in the investigation.

Rebecca Wells, age 7, young daughter of Emma and Bob Wells went missing about four years ago. A thorough search was made by the Everstille Police Department at that time. Additionally, a search party of helpful citizens, including the editor of this newspaper, spend many hours and days looking for the child. While there were no clues, and Mrs. Wells, herself, thought that the little girl had just wandered off, at the time, there were a number of tramps who had been noticed in the area, and it was thought that one of them could have perpetrated the foul deed. However, nothing came of that investigation. Meanwhile, the police who were involved in

(cont. on page 3)

In Other News...

Act of Contrition

Rebecca Wells was buried in a small casket at North Cemetery. The casket and cemetery plot were donated by the citizens of Everstille. Bob and Emma Wells had no extra money to spend on the amenity and were both grateful and embarrassed by the charity of the town. A joint service of the Baptist and the Methodist Episcopal Churches was held in the sanctuary of the Methodist Episcopal Church because it was larger, and it was expected that there would be quite a crowd in attendance. There was.

The Wells family were ushered to the front pew, and Bob Wells kept his arm around his wife, in part, to keep her from falling to the ground. The older boys, Vernon and Leon, had recently joined the United States Army, so they were absent, but the rest of Rebecca's siblings: Bernice, Clyde, Hazel, Ester, Hattie, and the twins, Maddy and Jess, who would begin first grade in the fall, sat straight and silent. Hattie who was closest to Rebecca probably remembered her best, and wore in her braid that fell over her shoulder, a red ribbon, a tribute to her sister. A small bouquet of flowers bedecked the casket which remained closed. Only Rebecca's father had beheld what was bundled inside, in a shroud of white satin printed with angel wings and donated by Mr. Jamison, the undertaker and owner of Jamison's Livery Stable and Funeral Home Services. Bob Wells was ill for weeks afterwards.

The service was brief as befitting Rebecca's ephemerality. Mr. Jamison directed the pallbearers to lift the casket onto the wagon-hearse pulled by two of Jamison's kindest and oldest black horses although the weight of the casket was such that only one horse was really needed. The wagon-hearse led over a dozen cars and trucks, filled with the townspeople who were acquainted with the Wells, out to the cemetery in a gentle, deliberate procession. The Wells family crowded into the first car driven by Mr. Jamison himself. All the children sat on each other's laps and were as excited to be in a real car as they allowed themselves to be when burying their sister. The last car in the queue was a Buick containing seven people squeezed together, and driven by a tearful woman.

The graveside service was succinct. A short appropriate poem, a Bible reading, and a prayer. There was to be no repast luncheon, at the request of Emma Wells who could not tolerate additional kindness. After the brief ceremony, Mr. Jamison drove the Wells family home while the cars and trucks containing neighbors and townspeople maneuvered out of the narrow cemetery lanes and returned the passengers to their familiar lives and ordinary tasks.

Viola had taken the twins out of school for the morning but returned them for the afternoon classes. She then drove the Buick back to her house and parked it in the driveway. When Tillie heard the car drive up, she came to the front door, leaned out and called to her, "Come on in, Vi, I have coffee going and am making some sandwiches."

Viola closed the car door and replied, "Thanks, Tillie, but I can't eat anything right now. I'm going to take a short walk to town. I'll be back before the boys come home from school."

Tillie shook her head and went back to complete her lunch, and Viola began to walk down the street towards town.

The official conclusion of the Rebecca Wells case was *homicide by person or persons unknown,* and most of the townspeople thought the blame fell on the tramps who roamed the region and were often found making camps in various wooded areas. Now that the Goodwin Company was clearing the trees and selling the vacant lots, the hobo camps were abolished. There continued to be strange men around, but their numbers had lessened.

Unofficially, Sheriff Samms and the South Bend police and detectives he had worked with were not so sure a tramp was to blame. Years had passed, and nature had taken her toll with any evidence that might have helped. Inquiries, interviews, and pages and pages of reports, were completed, but nothing specific was determined, and the lawmen chalked this case up as unsolved.

Sheriff Samms and Deputy Jackson had been part of the funeral procession, but upon returning to their office, Deputy Jackson drove out to see to a minor accident near Mackie's Service Station. Sherriff Samms sat down to work at paperwork which always crowded his desk and sipped the cup of coffee he had picked up at Mazie's. He was feeling hungry and thought that when Ike returned, he would wander home and see what his wife had for lunch. When he heard the office door open, he expected to see Ike, but was surprised by Viola Jasper.

"Hello, Viola. How are you? Is there a problem? Something I can help with?"

Viola's lips barely moved in a contortion meant to be a smile as she spoke, "Hello, Edgar. No, there is nothing wrong. I thought I might be able to talk to you about something. Do you have a minute?"

The Deputy moved away from his desk and nodded to a close table and chairs. "Yes, let's sit here. Would you like something to drink? I can telephone Mazie's for some coffee or tea."

"No, thank you. I don't want to take up too much of your time. Is Ike here?" Viola was hoping to speak to the sheriff alone.

"No, Ike is not here. There was a minor accident, and he went out to check on it. We're here alone, and you and I can speak freely."

Sheriff Samms pulled up a chair next to Viola. Something told him this was a very personal issue, and he should not take an official position behind his desk. He sat back and let Viola speak.

"I saw you and Ike at the service today, Edgar, and there is something I need to say. I know you've spent a great deal of time working on poor Rebecca's case, and I need to tell you something."

"Well, the case is officially closed. We interviewed many around town including you and the boys and even John. Is there something else you remember?"

"Edgar, this is difficult for me to say, but I think John may have had something to do with poor Rebecca's disappearance." Viola could not say the word *death*.

Edgar Samms sat perfectly still. He waited for Viola's next statement. He thought that if he moved, she would hurry out the door and disappear herself.

Viola took a deep breath and stared at her hands which clutched each other desperately. She took another breath and said, "Once I found a red hair ribbon in some trousers of John's. I think it might have belonged to Rebecca. I don't know. I never asked John about it, but it has worried me ever since."

"Do you still have the ribbon, Viola?"

"No. I threw it out when John died."

"Do you have any other proof that John would have had anything to do with the disappearance?" Sheriff Samms, too, avoided the word *death*.

"No, no proof, but John was not a ... kind man. And it seems that the disappearance happened around the time John was home, but then I tried to remember, and he was gone so much, and those were diffi-cult times, and…" Viola's voice faded. She was unsure exactly why she even came in to talk to Edgar.

"Well, then, let's examine this. You found a red hair ribbon in John's trousers but don't have it now. You never talked to John about it and are not sure about exactly when he was home or when he was gone, but think it could be around Rebecca's disappearance. Viola," and here Sheriff Samms knew he had to tread gently, "Viola, there were rumors about John and his visits to, well, to places where red ribbons might have made their way into his pockets. I don't know exactly what you know about John's activities when he traveled, but small-town police depart-ments share some information." He was not sure how to proceed or exactly what to say.

"Yes, Edgar. I am aware of John's actions, at least some of them. I guess I never thought about the fact that a red ribbon could have come from elsewhere. I just have worried about this for years and wondered if I should have said something to you sooner. Not that it would have helped that poor child, but I felt guilty. I still do."

"John was awfully sick, wasn't he?"

"Yes."

"Well, since there is not any real evidence, I think you might ease your mind about John. Whatever he might have done, I suspect he suffered for. He suffered mightily at the end, didn't he?"

Viola studied the floor and then looked directly into Sheriff Samms' eyes. She sat up straighter and said, "Yes. Yes, he suffered."

They were quiet for a few seconds, and then the sheriff spoke. "Viola, this is a conversation between two neighbors, two friends. I see no reason to make any official notes about it. Thank you for coming in and letting me know your thoughts. I suspect we will not ever know what really happened to Rebecca. Let's hope she rests in peace."

"That poor child. That poor family. Thank you, Edgar. I should be getting back home now. I appreciate you listening to me."

Viola got up and walked to the door and Edgar, her friend, opened it for her and saw her out. She thanked the sheriff again and turned to walk towards home. Sheriff Samms watched Viola walk down the sidewalk and across to the next street. He let out a sigh, quietly closed the door, and went back into the office.

He sat at his desk where he leaned back in the chair and laced his fingers at the back of his head. He looked up at the ceiling light and thought for some time. Then he sat forward, picked up the cold coffee from Mazie's, and drained the cup. His hunger pains had disappeared, replaced by a knot of queasiness. The papers on his desk called for his attention, and he began to distractedly move them around.

***

Viola walked down Main Street, and crossed to the corner where Banter's Drug Store was located. On the front window a sign read:

Get a Bottle of Coca-Cola Here for Only a Nickle!

Delicious smells still came out of Peterson's Bakery which was closing for the day. The Emporium next door had placed in its front window some of the new clocks it was selling. The last couple of letters at the end of the word *Goods* had peeled off, and the sign that had been so carefully painted on the window years ago now proclaimed:

Mitchells Emporium and Dry Goo

Viola noticed it all as she walked pensively to her home. Tillie was inside, waiting with fresh coffee, and her sons would be running energetically through the door in a short time. Viola crossed the street to the house and stopped at the bottom step. She did not yet want to talk to another person. She sat down on the steps and watched as a truck slowly make its way down Main Street. It stopped at the town's only stoplight and turned right, disappearing around the corner. Viola glanced up and noted the sky was clouding over, and a nippy gust of air blew into her face. She took a couple of deep breaths, trying to calm down, and wondered why the enormous pressure that had been lifted from her shoulders had settled solidly and profoundly in her heart.

Mea Cupla.

July Fourth Weekend Celebration, 1941

Patriotism was at an all-time high in every city, town, and village, and Everstille was no exception. The Fourth of July parade had been a complete success. The fireworks display produced by the City Council Committee for the Fourth of July, chaired by editor of *The Everstille News,* Mason Chessworth, was the best ever seen, and the weather was perfect for the celebration. Because July Fourth was a Friday, there were celebrations throughout the weekend. Saturday picnics and neighborhood parties abounded. The conclusion of the weekend festivities on Sunday, July 6, would be at the city's park where both churches in town, Everstille's Methodist Episcopal and the First Baptist would combine their congregations. A joint sermon by Pastor Richards and Minister Evan Edwards was entitled "God and Patriotism: Both Needed Now More Than Ever!" Afterwards, a strawberry festival, with the Rachel Circle presiding would be held. Flags flew on everyone's porch and there were enough baked goods to put Peterson's Bakery out of business. Citizens celebrated and rejoiced, and Kate Smith's rendition of "God Bless America" played again and again and again. Five months later, patriotism would be indisputably required.

Viola and Tillie made their sugar cookies and blueberry and sour cherry pies for the Saturday neighborhood picnic which was in the spacious Mitchell yard. Friends and neighbors attended, and a pot-luck lunch would be served at one o'clock with dessert available the rest of the afternoon. Homemade ice cream was being churned, and children of all ages took turns turning the handle, at least until their small arms gave out. Tables and lawn games were set up, and chairs were dragged out for those adults who just could not get up and down from the blankets spread out under the trees and through the lawn. The partying continued until fireworks faded. Cleaning up, gathering the leftovers, moving chairs and blankets and corralling the children, were completed and the second day of celebration was over.

The following day was one of those impossibly hot, humid summer days, and by the end of the joint Sunday morning service, after the strawberry shortcake was enjoyed, everyone went back to their homes with only one desire, and that was to remain cool. Mike and Mitch would be spending the day with their Uncle Nathan who had promised to take them to the old pond where he and Edna used to fish. Tillie had packed a large basket filled with leftovers from the previous day's picnic for them to take along, and the boys planned to cool off in the pond.

Edna and her mother, Millie, would finish cleaning up from the previous day's party and then take a nap. Edie and Janet Lynn were laying on a blanket in the yard planning their summer activities. Viola and Tillie would be visiting North Cemetery.

***

Each year, at the start of summer and, again at the end of autumn, Viola and Tillie took a trip out to the cemetery to tidy up the family graves. They dressed in old clothes and piled the paraphernalia needed into the Buick's back seat. Tillie knew they would be out there for a while, and they would need nourishment, so she packed some cookies, fruit, and a large jar of cold water. They lowered the car windows to allow a breeze to cool off their sweaty faces.

Viola drove slowly through the town, looking at the few children who were leisurely walking around the closed stores and traveling to the park. They drove past the Emporium, and Peterson's Bakery, and Granger and Wicks Law Office. Sheriff Samms was on a chair which leaned against the building, and he saw Viola and waved to her. Viola smiled and waved back. The high school that Mike and Mitch would attend in the fall was closed and silent, and Jensen's Hardware and Agricultural Store could be seen down the side street.

As they traveled the road towards the cemetery, they could see the new Sears Modern Houses scattered around the area. Some were completed, and families could be seen on the porches and in the yards. Others were in various stages of being built. Martin's farm was gone, and Viola's house had been replaced by two partially constructed Sears homes. Viola glanced back where the woods used to be. Only a few trees dotted the now flattened land. They drove on without talking and came to the entrance of North Cemetery. They turned into the third narrow lane and drove up to the top.

After sitting for a few minutes, Tillie, wiping her forehead, turned to Viola, and said, "It is so warm today, we could put this off for a week or so."

"No, we are here and should just do this."

Viola opened the car's back door, and they pulled their equipment out. They walked to the right where the graves of Tillie's mother-in-law, husband and young son were located. Tillie knelt to pull out the weeds that had grown around the headstones while Viola swept the loose dirt with the whisk broom. They took a brush and scrubbed off the caked mud from the stones and stood back to view their work.

"Tillie, do you ever miss being married?"

Tillie smiled dolefully and replied, "Really, I was married for such a brief time, I barely remember it. Herman was a good man, and our son was so young and small when he died, it's as though that was another life. And here," Tillie pointed with her foot to the space to the right of her son's grave, "here is where I will be. Perhaps, one day I will get familiarized with them again."

"Did you ever love anyone after Herman? What about Joseph? He would marry you in a minute. I know that for sure."

Tillie thought for a while, but then decided not to divulge the secret in her heart.

"No, there was only Herman. Joseph is a kind and good man, and I am very fond of him, but marriage at my age would be a real hard thing. And what about yourself, Missy? You are still young, and there are a few men in the town who would be happy to call you their *Missus*."

Viola smiled and shook her head. "No, Tillie, I don't think so. Come on, let's finish up the rest."

They walked to the right again, across another lane to the graves of Michael and Mary Mitchell and cleared the weeds and cleaned them. Viola kissed her fingertips and laid them on the headstones, and there was only one left to do. John's grave was across from the Mitchell's spot. They cleaned and weeded. Viola's fingertips did not stroke the stone. Tillie reached over to the basket she had packed and pulled out the jar of water.

"Here," she gave it to Viola, "take a sip. It's too hot to be standing here. How about some fruit? The watermelon is sweet."

Viola took the jar and drank from it and handed it back. She wiped her face with an embroidered handkerchief from her pocket and said, "No thanks. No fruit."

"Well, I packed some cookies if you would like one."

Viola thought and then said, "Yes, I'll take a cookie."

Tillie reached into the small basket and took two of the sugar cookies Viola had baked a couple of days before and handed one to her. She took a bite of the other one and chewed slowly. Viola took the cookie but did not eat it. She walked to the far corner of the cemetery, back where there were plenty of spaces, back where there were few head-stones, back where a small grave, newly dug had only a small makeshift cross as a marker. She bent down and put the sugar cookie on the grave. Then she stood and whispered something to the ground.

Tillie watched her walk back. When she got closer, she said, "You know, some animal is going to get that."

"I know," said Viola, "I know."

***

On the drive back, Tillie looked up through the windshield at the sky and predicted there would be a thunderstorm. Viola nodded in agreement, and they continued in silence. Viola drove slowly through the town again and pulled into the driveway where, once parked, they emptied the back seat, went inside to clean up, and change their clothes. Tillie pulled out some of the picnic leftovers, and they ate a cold supper at the shiny kitchen table. They cleared the dishes and went out to the front porch to await the fishermen.

Within fifteen minutes, Nathan drove up with Mike and Mitch who yelled out at them and waved. They came back carrying their poles, and an empty food basket, and no fish, although Mitch had caught a small one, but then he threw it back. The twins were hungry, so Tillie took them into the house to feed them. She declared her weariness and intention to go to bed.

It was just starting to get dark, and a coolness was underway. Far in the distance a flash of lightening was observed. Fireflies flickered, and there was a moist breeze that would sometime in the early morn-ing turn into a drizzle and then a downpour. Viola reminded herself to get out the umbrella for her walk to work the next morning. The boys came out to hug her goodnight, and she told them she would be up later to check on them. Exhausted with patriotism and picnics and pleasures from the long celebratory weekend, her sons went into the house, up the stairs, and to their bedrooms.

Viola was alone on the porch. She sat on the swing and pushed herself back and forth with her toes. She allowed her mind to wander and refused to settle on any one thought. Preferences and guilts, passions and griefs, propitiations and gratitudes intertwined in her mind. She honored them with her acceptance and lingered in the dark becoming acquainted with the quiet.

War and Peace

A Late August Morning

"…and you know what Ma has told us, Mike. Why are you bringing this up again?"

Mitch threw the basketball across the yard hitting the last row of dry corn stalks standing. The Victory Garden was mostly late summer vegetables, and the ripened tomatoes needed gathering. Mitch walked over to the corner, picked up the ball, and tossed it towards his brother who sat on the tree stump.

"I know, Mitch, but we are seventeen, and you know how many of the guys have joined. No one cares about age, and if we wait another year, the war might be over. I don't want to miss this opportunity. Ma will be fine with it once she gets over the shock. I'm going with the others, and if you don't want to, well, then that's that." Mike held the ball and spoke quietly; then, Mitch sighed.

"Let me think about it. O.K.? I just don't want Ma to be here alone and both of us gone. Who knows how long it all will last?"

"Well, Tillie will be here, and Uncle Nathan and Aunt Edna are just across the street, and there are all the neighbors. Ma won't be alone. Think of all the others who have joined up. All I am going to say is that I've decided. I'm not going to wait months until we are eighteen and then the war will be over. Frankly, I have had all the schooling I need. You are a better student, and I guess if you want to stay home with Ma and finish high school, that is your choice. Tom and Buck and I are going on Friday to South Bend and sign up. There is room in Buck's car if you want to go along. You still have a couple of days to decide."

Mike put the ball down and walked out of the backyard gate toward the stores along Main Street. He thrust his hands deep in his pockets and kicked the stones in his way.

Mitch watched his brother walk out of the gate and down the street. He walked to the tree stump and sat down. This was not the first time for this discussion. The brothers had talked about joining the army since the war began. Of course, they were much too young, but now that they were seventeen and closing in on eighteen and the war continued to be the number one topic for everyone, the possibility of becoming a soldier had gotten closer to a reality. Foregoing his senior year in high school was not much of a sacrifice to Mike. Mitch was a better student and planning to attend college, so he was not as anxious as his brother. But the twins were close, and it would be difficult for them to separate.

There was no way to talk Mike out of this plan. Mitch had tried all summer. Mike was absolutely determined, and now Mitch had to make a decision. It was not that he was frightened about joining the army, but he was certain this would devastate their mother. Viola had kept Mike in school simply by the strength of her will. He would have ended his education a year ago had not been for Viola's insistence that they complete high school. Her hope was that by that time, the war would be over. Now Mitch had to make a decision in a couple days.

He got up from the wooden stump and walked over to the back porch where he picked up Tillie's gathering basket, walked over to the garden, and began to collect the ripe tomatoes Tillie had asked the boys to gather for her. She would be home soon from the civilian volunteer group meeting at the church, and wanted to begin her canning. Mitch collected everything he could and then went into the house and placed the basket on the kitchen counter next to the waiting tomatoes. He sat on the front steps and waited for Tillie or his mother to come home and find out if there was anything they needed done. Meanwhile, he would consider what to do.

Mike was right. Most of the eighteen-year-old boys at Everstille High School had joined a branch of the armed services already. Some of their friends were gone, and even their cousin Edie's fiancé, Ned, was somewhere in the Pacific with the United States Navy. Patriotism was the key word in all American small towns and large cities. Volunteer groups met weekly at churches and homes and gathered materials and scraps for the war effort. Letters of encouragement to service men were written, and a general bolstering up each other's spirits was encouraged. Most houses and businesses flew the flag, and church services either started or ended with the Pledge of Allegiance. War bonds were purchased even if they could not be afforded. The elementary school's play yard transformed into an enormous Victory Garden, and the school children took turns caring and weeding it. The garden helped to feed those who were living in apartments or whose own yards were not sufficiently spacious enough for growing needed vegetables. Everyone was involved in at least one war-time civilian activity, and many spend much of their free time in completing volunteer work. Mike was determined to do his part.

Mitch wasn't so sure. It was true that a few Everstille's boys, aged seventeen and even one sixteen-year-old they knew, had been accepted into the services. If a boy was tall enough, his voice deep enough, and he swore that he was eighteen, most recruiters would accept their word, stamp their papers, and fill their quotas. And Mike and Mitch, at six feet tall, with baritone voices, and steely looks, especially Mike, would not have much trouble looking older. Mike had explained this to Mitch again and again, and Mitch thought he was most likely right. Especially since every other seventeen-year-old they knew had come back from the South Bend Army Recruiting Station, packed a few things, hugged their sobbing mother, shook hands with a proud but nervous father, patted their younger siblings on their heads, and headed off to fight.

Mitch looked up from his seat on the steps and saw his mother walking home. She was carrying a bag and her purse, and Mitch rose and ran over to take the bag from her. He gave her a willing smile as Viola smiled up at him.

"Where is Mike? Is he at home?"

Mitch shook his head as they crossed the street. "No, he went off for a walk. But the tomatoes Tillie wanted are in the kitchen, and I can help you do whatever you need me to."

Viola smiled again. "Thanks, Mitch. I am just a bit tired and think I will lay down for a while until Tillie gets home. She should be here within the hour, and I will help her then. Tillie and I appreciate the help you boys give us."

Mike never let either Tillie or his mother know that he was the one who generally did what both boys were asked to do. A brotherly bond and loyalty kept him from claiming the credit for himself. He did not want Mike to get in any more trouble than he was likely to get into.

That night, after supper and dishes were done, Tillie and Viola sat down in the front room to listen to their radio program while Mike and Mitch went out to the back yard to talk.

"O.K., it's all planned. Buck has the car ready, and we are going to take off for South Bend early Friday about seven-thirty. It will only take an hour or so, and we plan on being at the Recruiting Station before it opens at nine. The other guys wanted to know if you were going to come with us, and I just told them *maybe.* It'll be fine, Mitch, if you don't go. No one will think less of you, and Ma will be satisfied if you stay here. But I want you to know there is a seat for you if you decide to go. Have you made up your mind yet?"

Mitch looked at his brother. In the semi-darkness he could see the partial beard along his brother's jawline and cheek. Mike had gotten a short haircut just a week ago, and Mitch could see him in a uniform: tall, and proud, and loyal. Mike was soldier material. Mitch brushed his longish hair away from his face and stared at his shoes for a bit.

"I don't know, Mike. I'm still thinking."

Mike nodded and looked at Mitch. "That's fine. Whatever you decide will be O.K. with me. But, remember, don't tell Ma. I don't want to argue with her, and once it's done, I know she'll accept it. Listen, I'm going to take a walk over to Buck's house. Want to go along?"

"No, not tonight. I'll see you later." Mitch watched his twin brother walk out of the back yard. Then, just like he had done earlier that day, he went over to the tree stump and sat down to think.

***

Friday morning at seven A.M., before Tillie and his mother were awake, Mike dressed quietly and carefully, tying the freshly shined shoes, brushing back his hair, putting his suitcoat on over a freshly ironed shirt. He glanced in the mirror, gave his image a nod, left his room, closed the door, and walked quickly towards the stairs. Before he started down, he looked over to the closed door of his brother's room but decided not to knock. He had told Mitch that whatever he decided was fine, and he meant it.

He walked down the stairs, glancing once more up at Mitch's closed door and went to the front hall. He opened the front door and closed it silently, moving out into the gray dusk of a late August morning. A movement attracted his attention, and Mike looked to his left. Mitch was sitting on the front porch swing. He was also wearing his suit coat over a freshly ironed shirt.

Mitch grinned at Mike and said in a whisper, "Come on. Where you been? I hear they get us up really early in the army."

Mike stood up, and the brothers walked down the front steps of their house. Buck's car came around the corner and stopped to allow the twins to crawl into the back seat. The car headed down Main Street, through the still sleeping town of Everstille, and towards the city of South Bend.

Movie Night

The Bijou Theater in Everstille was directly across the street from Clampet's Grocery Store and Meat Market where Joseph worked as a butcher. He always knew which new movie would be shown on Saturday night because James Smithy, the theater's owner, came in each Thursday with a list of his wife's grocery needs and told him. Joseph and James had struck up a friendship over the years, and every month Joseph received movie passes from him.

Joseph and Tillie had a standing Saturday night movie date. This week's movie was *A Tree Grows in Brooklyn*, and while Joseph was not particularly eager to see it, he knew Tillie was. While she wasn't much of a reader, she had borrowed the novel from the library on the recommendation of Ruth Evans, the head librarian, and was looking forward to seeing it played out on the big screen.

"I just think it can't be as good as that book was, but I'm anxious to see it. I'm looking forward to Saturday! But I have a favor to ask you, Joseph."

Joseph was weighing out the hamburger meat Tillie ordered, but he stopped and looked at her. "You know that whatever it is, I'll be glad to do. What do you need?"

"Would you mind if I asked Viola to come with us this week? She has been so gloomy since the boys left, and I would just like to get her out of the house. I'll be glad to pay for her ticket."

"Why, that's not much of a favor, Tillie. Sure; ask her to come along. I would be delighted to escort the two best looking women in this town on Saturday night! And I have plenty of passes from Jim, so don't even think about money. It will be good for Viola to get out and have some fun. What do you hear from the boys?"

"Well, if you are calling this old woman *best-looking*, then you do need those glasses, but thanks, and I will try to get Vi out of the house." Tillie took the wrapped meat and placed it in her basket and her smiled faded.

"The boys are good at taking turns writing, but those V-mail letters get lots of censorship. We're not even sure where the boys are stationed right now. As far as we can tell, they're somewhere in France or maybe Italy. Viola lives for the mail, and when there is nothing, she just sits and stares. She keeps busy, working extra hours at the Emporium filling in on the floor, and she volunteers at church many nights, but she needs a break. I'll try to get her to go with us. Thanks, Joseph. See you Saturday at the usual time."

Tillie paid for the groceries with both cash and ration stamps. She wrapped her winter scarf tightly around her and pulled on her gloves before she picked up her grocery bag and headed out the door. There was old snow on the ground, but none was currently coming down, and despite the cold, she enjoyed the short walk home. She got to the corner and decided to stop in at Banter's Drugs to say *hello* to Nathan.

The warm air hit her in the face as she walked into the drugstore, and it felt good. She unwrapped the scarf and saw Nathan standing at the back stocking some of the shelves. She walked over to him and smiled as he turned to her, remembering how she had held and rocked this tall, grown man when he was a baby.

"Tillie, how are you?" Nathan put down the box he held and hugged her. "Been to Clampet's, I see. Is there something you need? You aren't getting a winter cold, are you?"

"No, I am fine, Nate, but I wanted to ask you if you would do something."

"Absolutely. What do you want?"

"Joseph and I are going to the movies Saturday night, and I'm going to try to get Vi to go with us. Honestly, I don't think my chances are very good, but I can't stand to have her sitting alone and worrying about the boys for another night. Not sure what you and Edna are busy with this Saturday, but if I can't get her out, and if I let you know, do you think someone can go over just to keep her company for a while?"

"We can do that. I have soda jerk duties that night, but either Edna or Millie can get over there for a time. Stop by before you and Joseph leave, and if you do not come by, we will assume she did go along. It would be good for Vi to get out. The war has had us all in knots for years waiting and worrying. I am glad you stopped to ask. I'll say something to the women tonight."

They spoke for a bit about Edie's future wedding plans, and her sailor fiancé, Ned, and neighborhood gossip, and then, Tillie wrapped her scarf again and walked the short distance around one street and down another to the warmth of the home she and Viola share.

***

Tillie was right. As much as she tried, Viola would not join them for the movie. She said there was a musical program she wanted to listen to on the radio, that she was going to embroider some additional placemats for Edie's wedding, that her closet really needed cleaning, and that she might begin the vegetables for Sunday dinner. The fact was, she planned on getting out all the letters she had received from her boys and rereading them and then writing an additional letter to them. Tillie gave Viola a look and left with Joseph. But before getting into Joseph's car, she walked across the street and over three doors and let Edna know that Viola would be by herself.

Thirty minutes later, a figure, carrying a sewing basket, came out of the Mitchell house and walked across the street. Edna knocked on the front door, and when Viola opened it, she smiled and said, "Evening, Vi, I thought I might keep you company tonight. Nate is at work at the soda fountain, and Mother is busy cooking for tomorrow and said she did not need my help."

"Well, come in out of the cold, Edna."

Viola held open the door as her sister-in-law came in, placed her basket down and removed her coat and boots. The two women moved into the kitchen where Viola heated water for tea and got out a plate of oatmeal cookies Tillie had baked earlier. Edna reached into her basket and pulled out some socks, put her glasses on, and began to darn.

Viola moved her embroidery into the kitchen and adjusted her hoop over the area of the placemat she was working on, but after a stitch or two, put the hoop down and looked at Edna. "Tillie asked you to come over tonight, didn't she?"

Edna looked back at her and contorted her face in that certain way she had when forced into telling the truth. "Yes, she did. She's worried about you and did not want you to sit alone tonight. She's the closest thing you have had to a mother since Mary died, but, Vi, I needed some company too. Sometimes Mother just gets on my nerves, so this is a break for me. Do you mind so much?"

"No, I am glad to see you and spend time with you. It's just that Tillie harps about me worrying and wondering about the boys, and while I know she is as concerned as I am, she does not have both her sons thousands of miles away fighting in a foreign country. I get a feeling, sometimes, Edna, and it's a sickness in my heart that I can't explain. The boys and I had quite an argument when they joined the army, but I knew I would lose both if I didn't just give in, so I did. We made up, but if I don't hear from them a couple times every week, I about go crazy. I did get a letter earlier in the week, but the V-mail is so censored that sometimes I am just not sure what is really going on."

"Vi, why don't you get the letter and read it to me? I'd like to hear it."

Viola got up to turn the boiling water off and poured it into the teapot to seep. She went to her bedroom and took the latest letter from the top of the bureau and came back to the kitchen. She poured two cups of tea and put them on the kitchen table alongside the teapot with its cozy on top. Then she sat down and cleared her throat. She read:

Dear Ma and Tillie,

It's my turn (Mitch) to write, so that's who this is.

So glad to get your letters and the two of us fight

over who will read them first. Mike usually wins.

Ha Ha. We are both doing good, and are safe,

so there is no need to worry although we know

you will anyway. We are in █████████████

We are not always sure just where we go

because the army sometimes tells us one thing and

then changes at the last minute. Anyway, we always

need to move at the quickest time just like when we

████████████████████████████

No, to answer your question, the food is not good

here, at least not like home with your cooking and

Tillie's cooking. Well there's the bell for breakfast,

and we want to get this letter out as soon as we can.

Mike will write next and we both love you. Say

hello to the rest of the family and all the

neighbors and keep us filled in the any news from

home. We miss it all.   Love Mitch (and Mike)

Viola folded the thin paper and placed it on the table. She took a sip of her tea and stared at the letter. Edna took her glasses off and laid the sock on top of her basket as she reached over and took Viola's hand and squeezed it.

"Vi, I worry too, and you can just imagine how upset Edie is all the time about Ned. We are planning this wedding, but the truth is we have no idea when or even if it will take place. War is hard on everyone and maybe hardest on those of us who just sit at home and wait and worry. I wish I could comfort you. I just don't know how to or what to say."

Viola looked up and wiped the wet from her face. She breathed deeply and tried to smile. She returned Edna's squeeze, and they sat soundlessly for a few moments while the tea in their cups cooled. Then Viola took up her hoop and continued her stitches, and Edna picked up the sock again, moving her needle through the split in it.

For a long while, the two women sat working their needles, sipping their cold tea, maintaining an affable silence, and thinking of those who, in remote places, were thinking of them. Outside, the early March weather changed, and a soft snow began to fall. It instantly covered the sidewalks and the streets and, through the light from the streetlamps, looked like silent projectiles plummeting to the earth.

Friday the 13th of April, 1945

Dear Ma, Tillie, and all the ships at sea!

It's me, Mike, and I am sure you can tell that! My turn to write and I wish
I could let you know what is going on, but I am sure there would be a
whole lot of blackouts on this letter. Anyway, we are Okay and neither
of us wants either of you to worry. Mitch looks after me and I look after
Mitch. Brothers to the last! It is Friday the 13th, and that is supposed to
be unlucky although I don't believe it. There's a whole bunch of guys here
who think that but I just laugh at them. You make your own luck. Or not.

███

███████████████████ One of my pals here overheard a couple of the big
wigs talking and there will be ████████████████████████████████████
██ I don't
think what I wrote will get though the censors, but at least I gave them
something to do! But listen, don't worry. We will be fine. Ma, something
had been bothering me. I know you and I had words before we left, about
our joining up, and, you are right, I am sure I sort of talked Mitch into it. I
am sorry. You are right about so many things, and when the war is over, I
am going to do what you want and finish high school. So that is a promise.
Love to you both. Tillie, we really miss your great meals and can't wait until
we get home to eat them. Kisses and hugs and Mitch wants the last space.

Love, Mike

Ma, Mike is right, we do watch after each other. Love, Mitch

April 22, 1945, Northern Italy

Somehow, they ended up in Italy in the Po Valley as additional support to the 85th Infantry Division which had been stationed there for almost two years. Somehow, they had ended up living and moving, and fighting alongside Italian and Polish and British soldiers. But strangest of all, somehow, somehow, in this mess of a war and crazy movement around Europe and blind following of orders, somehow, Mike and Mitch ended up stationed together. This was surely an army mistake. Perhaps being twins, and their names being so similar, and everything about them being identical except for that brown splotch on Mike's neck underneath his right ear, had something to do with the mix-up. They did not attempt to straighten it out. They were glad to be with each other.

Their basic training was at Camp Atterbury in Indiana, but their friends, Tom and Buck, had been sent to Fort Sheridan, Illinois even though they all joined up the same day. The Jasper boys tried to stay in touch with them, but it was difficult to do, and then, they were given a series of orders, and moved from one place to another, and ended up waiting in New Jersey to be shipped over as support. They just followed the orders. That was what they were trained to do. That was what they had signed up for: to fight for their country, these seventeen-year-olds.

It was code named *Operation Grapeshot* and was the Allied offensive in Italy meant to destroy the German Army positioned there. The *Grapeshot* appellation must have tickled whoever thought of it, Italy being known for its wine, but to the average soldier, to Mike and Mitch, it was just a war, cold and wet or humid and hot, but all the time, miserable. They had trained for being shot at, and had trained to shoot, but there was a frightening difference between the training and the reality.

According to all the authorized reports, April 21 ended the Battle of Bologna. The Allies had triumphed. The Poles had entered the city, stopping the German forces who were there fighting half-heartedly, already sure they had failed. The city greeted the Allied soldiers with elation, and everyone assumed that war would soon be over everywhere.

Sunday morning after the official end to the Battle of Bologna, Mike and Mitch and some soldiers they had struck up a conversation with, decided to walk the roads through and around the city, listening to a few church bells left standing, ring and chime, expressing delight in ending. The day was cloudy, and the smoke and powder from the weeks of war had not settled. They all felt grimy and dirty and discussed how satisfying it would be to finally take a long shower, and rejoice in lathering sweet-smelling soaps, and have plenty of hot water, and put on clean clothes...really clean clothes. Such simple things. Such foolish soldiers to wander out into the countryside, into the unknown, thinking that they were safe, that this Sunday would be quiet; assuming, just as the Italian city had assumed, that it was over, that they would soon be home enjoying those long hot showers and lathering with the sweet-smelling soap.

The city of Bologna rests next to the Apennine Mountains where small hills and rocky areas lead up to them. This territory coupled with the day's dusty, sooty, humid air allowed the sizable band of rogue German soldiers who had resisted capture and maintained a reasonably significant stash of weapons, to take aim at the strolling soldiers, their enemies, their nemeses. Hearing remote instructions of *Feuer auf mein Kommando* and then *Feuer Frei,* Mike and Mitch, and the other soldiers whose names they would never know, were suddenly at war again. They all broke into a run.

As the bullets zoomed over their heads, the two brothers ran side by side with their helmets pulled low over their faces, their rifles in their hands, running quickly, down low, down near the mud and muck and patches of torn grass. Explosions were so thunderous, they made their ears sting, and the dirt from their rushing boots flew up and smacked their eyes and filled their mouths. A light above in the sky held for just one long second, and Mike glanced up to get a better view of the incandescence. He grabbed Mitch's arm and pulled him down under him just as the single light split into a million smaller ones and filled the space around them with sharpen rays. Mitch fell to the mud with Mike covering his body, and they held on to each other just as they had when they were newborn. Mike flung his rifle to the side as he clutched his brother, pushing him into the mud, throwing his arms around him, encompassing him, gripping him, holding on while shards of fury covered them.

They lay there for a time, holding each other, enfolding each other possessively, listening to the gently falling slivers. Dust and fog arose, and the sounds of soldiers shouting surrounded them. Muffled yells, and rifle shots, and foreign screams informed them that there would soon be peace again. Mike's arms fell limp, and he rolled to the side. Mitch lifted himself up, wiped his eyes so that he could see, and when he saw Mike's mouth moving silently, he yelled, "Hold on, Mike, the medics are coming!" into his brother's ear, and then he soothingly brushed the spiky pieces away from Mike's face.

Mike turned his eyes to Mitch and quietly, so quietly that Mitch almost missed it, murmured, "Did you remember that today is our birthday? We are eighteen."

Mike breathed a yearning sigh, and Mitch watched his brother shudder, saw his eyes glaze over, and noted that a dribble of blood, as red as a small girl's hair ribbon, crawled out of the side of his mouth, down his chin, curving and coiling, arriving and settling at the brown splotch on his neck just under his right ear.

Sunday, April 22, 1945, Everstille, Indiana

Viola woke up suddenly from a disturbing sleep and sat up on the side of her bed. She put her hands over her face and tried to remember the dream but could not. She took a deep breath and realized the date…April 22…her twin boys were eighteen years old today. She sat for a minute and allowed the uneasy sadness she felt to rush over her and then stood up and shook it off. She washed up, taking care to comb her hair, pulling it back into a Victory roll, leaving it flatter on the top so her Sunday hat would fit there. She went to her closet and reached for her best white blouse and then took her two-piece gray Victory suit out. As she finished dressing and leaned down to put on her Sunday pumps, she thought *Victory everything…suits, gardens, hair styles, bicycles, cakes, mail…when will there be a real victory? War and propaganda…I'm tired of it.* She spent a bit of time at the mirror and then walked into the kitchen where Tillie, still in her housecoat, was making coffee and stirring the oatmeal.

"I don't have much of an appetite today, Tillie, just some coffee for me."

Tillie looked at her and grimaced and said, "You are getting too thin, Vi. I know you are worried. We all are, and I also know what today is. You need to keep up your strength. Try just a little bit." And Tillie placed much more than a little bit in the bowl she placed before Viola who readied the oats and pretended to take a few bites to appease Tillie.

"I thought I would make something special for dinner today and ask Nate and Edna and Millie over later, so I won't be going to church this morning. Is that fine with you?"

Tillie asked as a matter of respect although Viola generally agreed with whatever she decided. Today was different. Viola took a sip of her hot coffee and then set the cup down. She looked at Tillie and shook her head.

"I know what you're doing, Tillie, and not today. I cannot celebrate the boys' birthday without them here where they should be. I am not in the mood for it. Just make something simple. Maybe we can have company later in the week. But, not today."

Tillie stood still for a moment and then filled her own cup of coffee and took some oatmeal in a bowl and sat down at the shiny kitchen table.

"Fine, Vi. I just thought it would be nice to have a distraction. Everyone is anxious. And you have every reason to be so, but it is not healthy to work as hard as you do and then volunteer most nights and not enjoy a dinner with family."

"I will enjoy things again when the boys are home. I received only one letter last week which was so censored, I am not even sure exactly where they are. I'll feel better when another letter comes. Tillie, I know you are worried too, and I appreciate your concern for me. Do you want me to wait while you dress for church?"

"No. I think I will just praise the Lord in my heart today. And maybe bake some bread."

Viola moved her coffee cup and uneaten oatmeal to the sink, bent down to kiss Tillie's head and said, "Be back in a little while. Today I feel the need to be in a church, and I think I'll walk there. The weather isn't bad, and I want some air."

She moved to the front closet, opened the door, and reached back for her light spring coat. Placing her hat on her head, she glanced in the hall mirror to ascertain its levelness. Viola removed her purse and gloves from the side table, and reached over to the stand, pulling out a black umbrella, just in case, walked out the front door and down the steps.

The day was chilly but not cold, and Viola breathed deeply as she pulled on her gloves and turned to walk the few streets to the Methodist Episcopal Church. Tillie stood up from the table and went to the kitchen window to watch until Viola turned the corner on the next street, and she could no longer see her. Then she washed the breakfast dishes, got out the flour, measuring implements, and her biggest mixing bowl. She began to bake.

Thursday, April 26, 1945
9:00 A.M.

Tillie was up early again and working in the kitchen. She had left Viola sleep and was busy baking pies. She had to forego the pleasure during the war because sugar and flour and other necessary ingredients had been rationed. But recently, supplies were getting easier to obtain, and she thought a couple of pies might perk up Viola's dwindling appetite.

She had not heard from the boys since the letter last week and was upset. So was Tillie. Viola went to work at one of the stores, and then to volunteer, and after picking at the dinner Tillie made, would sit and stare into space until late into the evening. She spoke rarely and answered perfunctorily, and seemed to find no pleasure in the radio shows Tillie turned on at night, or her embroidery which she had taken up again, or in meeting and talking with any family or friends, and Tillie could not get her to perk up in spite of her attempts. She had just put the pies into the oven when Viola came into the kitchen to get some coffee.

"Why did you let me sleep so late? It is almost nine o'clock and I told you I would help with the baking today. I was even thinking about making some sugar cookies if butter and sugar are available. I haven't done that in a while, and they sound good." Viola poured and fixed her coffee and sat down at the table to drink it.

Tillie smiled, glad Viola had the energy and inclination to bake. "Well, I knew you were not working today, and I though you could use the sleep. There is the whole rest of the day to bake."

Tillie finished washing the bowls and placed them to dry on the towel she had spread on the counter. She turned to say something to Viola when out of the kitchen window, she saw a green army Jeep drive up and park in front of the house. She let out such a gasp that Viola, coffee cup in hand, got up to see what was there. They watched as two soldiers looked at a piece of paper one of them was holding and then up at the numbers on the front of the house. The day was cool, and soft drizzle trickled from the clouds to the ground, leaving tear marks on the khaki green the soldiers wore.

Viola set her coffee cup down and walked to the front door. She opened it and stepped out onto her porch, still in her bathrobe and slippers, ignoring the wet. She stood there as Tillie, positioned on the other side of the screen door, watched. The soldiers, wearing their brisk, clean, and now damp uniforms, slowly walked up to the front steps, assumed a military stance, saluted the two women, and delivered the message that Viola feared but fully and completely expected.

Coming Home

The United States Army was kind. They allowed the brothers to come home together. Mitch sat quietly on a side bench in the back of the army truck where he had insisted on being. He could tell by the lack of city sounds that they were traveling home, to Everstille, and they were on the country roads. The ride was not smooth, but the two soldiers in the front were trying to steer the truck and be as gentle as possible. Hearing was difficult over the noise, but Mitch did not let that stop him. He talked loudly all the way home, explaining to Mike where they were and reliving some of their memories.

"Do you remember the time you brought that big bug into Edie's bedroom and threw it at her? Boy, did you get in trouble for that! I wonder how her Ned is doing and if he is home yet? I guess we'll find out soon. Ned is quite a guy, and I am guessing that this war will be nothing compared to his marriage to Edie." Mitch grinned at the thought. Edie never stopped demanding to be the center of attention. He would be glad to see her.

The soldier in the front riding shotgun glanced back into the truck through the small plastic window flap that separated the front and back and yelled, "How's it going back there? Everything O.K.?"

"Fine," said Mitch, "we are fine. How much longer do you think?"

"Maybe half an hour."

Mitch gave a thumbs up to him and the soldier turned around and faced the front. Mitch glanced down to check his watch and then remembered that it had been lost somewhere in the mud in Italy.

"Well, I'll have to get a new one," he said to Mike, "I wonder what the Emporium will have on sale? Ma wrote last time that there was quite a bit of new stock, and you could get stuff for cheap because no one could afford it. Guess I will have to wait and find out."

Mitch unbuttoned the top shirt button and loosened his tie. He was in his dress uniform, and the bumpy ride was making the wearing of it uncomfortable. He sat back and tried to figure out exactly where they were. The truck was slowing down and periodically making full stops.

"Must be near home. These roads are new. Lots of changes

since we've been away," and Mitch buttoned up again and straightened the tie and ran his hand through his fresh army haircut. He wanted to look good when he came home.

The truck was making slower turns and was not as noisy as before.

Mitch yelled into the flap, "Are we here?"

The soldier turned and looked at him and said, "Yep, we're coming to the place now. We should be stopping in a minute or two."

Mitch stood up although it was difficult to stand in the slowly moving truck. He glanced at Mike and said, "Almost there. We are coming home now, Mike. Coming home."

The truck began to drive slower and slower, and then came to a complete stop. Mitch put his hat on, placing it at the correct angle, and stood to attention as he heard the soldiers get out of the front and speak to someone. He could not quite hear what was being said, but he could guess. The soldiers came around to the back of the truck and opened the door to let the brothers out.

Mitch blinked a few times at the sunny sky, and climbed down the steps from the truck. He watched as the two soldiers and two other men in long black coats walked up into the back of the truck and released the latches that were holding the flag-draped casket in place. With a practiced air, they moved, and then lowered the casket containing Mike onto a gurney-like contraption, repositioning it slowly and carefully.

Through all this, Mitch stood at attention, saluting his brother, the only movement being his quivering chin. He did not release the salute until the casket settled in the back of the long black hearse which had across its side in small, unobtrusive gold lettering the name: *Jameson's Funeral Home*. The two soldiers saluted Mike, and then in military precision, turned towards Mitch and saluted.

It was only after the two soldiers and the two men in the long black coats had all come over to him and shook his hand that Mitch turned to the small crowd that was standing on the sidewalk. He saw his mother and Tillie, his Aunt Edna and Uncle Nathan, and cousin Edie, along with a few neighbors, quietly standing, wearing black mourning, men with hats off, and women holding handkerchiefs to their eyes.

Mitch waited until the hearse pulled out, traveling down the street slowly, conveying Mike to Jameson's, and then he walked over to the crowd. He bent down and enfolded his mother in his arms in much the same way Mike had enfolded him in their last embrace. He kissed her cheek.

Viola looked up at him, her face red from weeping. She clutched the black-bordered handkerchief she had just finished embroidering, working throughout the night, her sleep stolen from her by sorrow. It was saturated with her tears. She was not able to speak.

Mitch looked at her, and kissed her once again, and uttered softly enough so that only she could hear, "Hi, Ma. We're home."

Adjustments

Mitch

It was Tillie who discovered that Mitch was sleeping, on those nights he did sleep, in Mike's bedroom. She asked Mitch to bring down the bed linens for washing, but after two weeks, when he still had not, she walked upstairs to find that his bed had not been disturbed. She peeked into Mike's room and saw the sheets and cover and quilt tumbled and rumpled and thrown to the floor. Mitch was not there, and as Tillie glanced out of the window in Mike's bedroom, she saw him, still in his pajamas and slippers, sitting on the tree stump in the backyard, twirling and playing with the basketball the brothers used to share. Tillie gathered the sheets into her arms and made her way down the stairs.

For Mitch, sleeping was feast or famine. There were some nights that he never slept more than an hour or two. He would go to bed, and toss, and twist, and pull himself to the edge, and shake his head. He would travel downstairs thinking he was hungry, and make a sandwich which Tillie would find the next morning with only a bite or two taken. On hot summer nights, he poured a large glass of ice water and sat outside on the tree stump, sipping at it, and periodically taking out an ice cube to rub around his sweaty neck. Some nights he would dress and quietly walk down Main Street looking at all the closed stores and offices, and travel to the high school, and the Victory Garden planted at the grammar school. He would go to the park where he and Mike spent so much time, sit on the swings, and move back and forth until the light gray in the sky told him that Tillie would soon be up making coffee and breakfast.

Then there were the evenings, the early evenings, sometimes just after dinner, when he told Viola and Tillie that he was going to bed, and he did. He would drag himself up the stairs, brush his teeth, wash up, and put on pajamas. He would go into his own bedroom and sit on the bed, and after ten minutes or so would move to Mike's room where he would lay on the bed and stare at the ceiling until his eyes fell shut. He turned on his side with his arm under Mike's pillow and slept, barely moving all night. And the next day at noon or one o'clock or two o'clock in the afternoon, he would wake up and dress and come downstairs and eat the breakfast Tillie had left. Viola and Tillie never told him that they would take turns quietly climbing the stairs, sliding open the door to Mike's room and peeking in at him just to ensure themselves that he was still asleep; still alive.

Summer lingered while the war concluded. V-E Day was celebrated, and the Japanese mourned their burned and dead. *Victory* was declared, and still Mitch was edgy. Some of his friends came home, and he was glad to see Tom and Buck. They would spend hours with each other in dialogue and distress, and on those nights after returning home, Mitch did not sleep. Despite Tillie's culinary efforts, he did not regain he weight he had lost eating the army's flavorless fodder. His face was drawn and angular, and he appeared taller than the six-foot height specified on the driver's license he had obtained. His light hair had darkened, and it grew around his ears giving him a somewhat disreputable aspect. He remained ever polite and courteous and even loving to Tillie and his mother, but there was a creeping sadness that played around his mouth and raided the luminosity that used to flourish in his eyes. His previously willing smile, given as greeting, was extinct.

Tillie

From the time Tillie first held Viola's twin boys, she considered them her grandchildren, and she lavished a grandmother's love on them. She took pride in their accomplishments and pleasure in their achievements. She was the assuager, the softener, the mollifier as Viola sometimes struggled with the raising of the two boys. Tillie consoled the boys after a punishment from Viola, and then consoled Viola who felt guilty for enacting it. She was the stalwart pillar and the common-sense post. Mike's death shook her and made her quake with a pain she had long forgotten, and by its fact, intensified her love for Mitch.

On those nights Mitch did not sleep, Tillie lay awake listening to him wander the house and the yard. Her bedroom was next to the kitchen, and she listened to him opening the cabinets and the icebox and making the sandwich he would never eat and knew she would throw the bread out to the birds in the morning. At first, she considered getting out of bed and keeping him company, but her good judgement won out. She knew that the demons Mitch was fighting were his to defeat, and she remained in her bed, whispering a prayer or two for him, and slowly fell back to sleep.

There was the one time she heard Mitch quietly leave the house, and she was worried. She got up in the dark and threw on her clothes, and not wanting to wake or worry Viola, slipped out the back door in the murky blackness and scrutinized the night for Mitch. She saw him walk up one street and turn down another, and in her supremely sneakiest manner, she followed him. Skulking along the storefronts and slinking between the doorways, Tillie watched Mitch noiselessly travel from place to place until he wound up at the park. So that there would be no chance of being seen by him, she pressed her body close to a parked car and strained her eyes to see what he would do. She did not really have a plan in mind should Mitch be determined to somehow harm himself, but she thought that running towards him at the top rate that an almost six-ty-year old woman could attain, and screaming *Don't* might be enough to stop him. So, she waited with that plan in mind, and was relieved when Mitch sat on a swing and simply moved back and forth causing an incon-sequential breeze to flow around him and through the peppery summer night.

After watching him sit and swing for a long while, Tillie decided that he was going to be safe, and she retraced her steps soundlessly and cautiously back to the house where she let herself in through the back door, went to her bedroom, and fell into a partial sleep. Sometime later, through the fog that was her slumber, she heard Mitch come back to the house and return to the upstairs room and settle down for what remained of the hours before the dimness cleared.

Viola

The guilt that pressed into Viola's soul was so intense, there were some times she thought the only relief would be death. She was positive that no one knew of her preference for Mike over Mitch, but then Mike died, and she spent disconcerted darks and desolate days attempting to sort it out. Was this what was known as *Karma*? Was she being pun-ished for loving one son more? How much fiercer would the guilt have been, had Mitch died instead of Mike? How could she even consider that? She berated herself constantly for her preference, and felt shamed by every thought she had. She loved Mitch, and admitted to herself that he was now doubly precious because he was the only son left. Her self-reproach could not have been any more profound, and her unsettled nights did double duty: she lay awake racked with guilt over her pref-erence and love for Mike and, at the same time, beset with worry about Mitch.

She ached with the lingering love she felt for Mike knowing he would never again receive it. Her hands shook as she folded and ironed clothes that would be worn only by Mitch. Her stomach wanted to reject the food expertly cooked by Tillie, knowing that Mike would never again be there to grin at sneaking an extra piece of her blueberry pie. How was it possible to feel the amounts of both relief and guilt she felt and still survive?

Viola echoed Mitch's sleep pattern. On the evenings he went to bed early, Viola did not stay up much later. Mitch's sleep meant she could rest. He would remain slumbering until noon or later, and Viola needed to get up for work, but knowing he was safe in his bed would allow her to close her eyes until the alarm clock woke her in the morning. On those nights, she heard his agitated movements, his wandering from room to room, to kitchen to backyard, and she would lay still and listen, not sure what she was expecting to hear but fearful of going to sleep and missing it.

She knew Mitch would periodically leave the house. The first time he did this, she was unsure what to do. She sat up on the side of her bed, reached over to move the curtains aside, and peered out the window which faced the front street. She thought she might dress and follow him, but as she was deciding, she perceived another figure at the front of the house. She frowned out the window and saw Tillie move slow-ly behind Mitch. Viola watched until she could no longer see either of them, and then she pulled a chair to the window and studied the gloom, unsure what she was going to witness. After a long while, Viola saw the figure of Tillie move towards the house and heard her walk along the side and come in the back door. She waited for Tillie to come in and give her some horrid news, but all she heard was Tillie opening her bedroom door next to the kitchen, and then close it again. Viola remained alert, and in a while, she heard another sound, and Mitch came in, and mounted the stairs, and the house became tranquil. She let out a breath she had been holding for what seemed like hours and laid back on her bed. What remained of the night was undisturbed

.***

Slowly, incredibly slowly, Viola and Tillie and Mitch settled into a pattern. Changes gradually materialized. The three of them became attuned to living together again, and their sleep habits eventually became regulated. Mitch almost stopped cringing at loud sounds, and Tillie nev-er complained about needing to clean both upstairs bedrooms. Viola first acknowledged and then bore her faults. They all adjusted to a reconciled world, a peaceful country, and a tranquil town; but it was a lengthy pro-cess and a difficult one, and it left a legacy of shrouded heartaches and blanketed wounds.

Summer's End

Certain dates carry importance. August 6, 1945 was one of those dates because:

1. Edie received a letter from her sailor fiancé, Ned, in which he wrote that he was going to be home for good in two weeks.

2. Edie and her mother, Edna, and Ned's mother, Jennifer set the date for their wedding: September 23, 1945, only seven weeks away.

3. Edna put in a rush order for the invitations which needed to be mailed in a week. They would be ready by Friday, August 10.

4. Janet Lynn, Edie's best friend, was the Maid of Honor, and Janet's mother arranged for the baby-blue bridesmaid dress to be made by the same dressmaker who was making Edie's wedding dress. They even paid the extra rush order fee.

5. Edna arranged for Edie's final wedding dress alteration for Thursday, August 9.

6. The United States dropped the atomic bomb on Hiroshima on August 6, and another on Nagasaki on August 9, the day Edie was having the hem on her wedding dress adjusted. An extra layer of lace was added to it. To the wedding dress.

And on Saturday, September 2, 1945, the day when Japan signed an unconditional surrender, Edna and Nathan hosted an Open House from three o'clock P.M. until seven o'clock P.M. at their home to welcome back Lieutenant Commander Theodore "Ned" Patterson, and to officially celebrate the engagement of their daughter Edie to him. It was an eventful and exhilarating end to the summer of 1945.

> **You are invited to an**
> **Open House**
> to welcome home
> Lieutenant Commander Theodore "Ned" Patterson
> United States Navy
>
> and celebrate the engagement of
> Miss Edith Mary Mitchell
> and
> Lieutenant Patterson
>
> On
> Saturday, September 2, 1945
> at the home of
> Mr. and Mrs. Nathan Mitchell
>
> From 3:00 P.M. until 7:00 P.M.
> Cocktails and Hors d'oeuvres served

Edna pressed friends and family into creating the Hors d'oeuvres to be served at the Open House, and two books, *Entertaining is Fun! How to be a popular hostess* by Dorothy Draper and *The Settlement Cook Book* by Mrs. Simon Kander became the women's bibles for the event. Both cold and hot appetizers were chosen from the suggestions and recipes in the books, and while certain substitutions were still necessitated by the war (crabmeat was just impossible to get!), the foods placed on the best platters borrowed from the neighbors, looked lovely.

A pre-party tasting was arranged. Viola and Tillie, Janet Lynn and her mother Jennifer, and Millie, Edie, and Edna all gathered at the Mitchell home, bringing with them the samples of their assigned foods to scrutinize, to taste, to evaluate, and to alter, if Edna deemed that necessary. The women sipped the special gin cocktails that would be served and enjoyed their time together. Tillie, however, was somewhat put out about the changes recommended by Edna to her celery bites stuffed with cream cheese and chives.

"Tillie, these are good, but I believe the chives are a bit overwhelming. Perhaps fewer chives and additional sour cream would help. What does everyone think?"

There was a pregnant silence as the women examined their

cocktails, and pondered their answers, and contemplated the wisdom of choosing one side over the other.

Viola, always the conciliator, declared, "We could try that, Edna, as long as sour cream is available. I do like the taste of the chives, and they are still growing quite well in our garden. Tillie is just a wonder with the fresh herbs," and she smiled at Tillie and gave her a slight wink.

"Humph," muttered Tillie, and she repeated her alternate suggestion for the menu, "I still don't see why all this special fuss. Won't people be expecting more than just these bits and pieces of *horses orders*? Really, I think some good stew and some of my home-made bread would do nicely."

Edna relocated her lips into a straight line, gave Tillie a long look, and then, with a sigh, said, "Tillie, we have talked about this before. This is not a dinner, and the guests will be wandering around talking and eating the canapes and coming in and out of rooms. It is an *Open House*."

"Yes," replied Tillie, "I *know* that, but these small bits of food just don't seem like enough. And I do think the celery bites are just fine. Perhaps they could even use more of the chives," and Tillie finished her gin cocktail with one large swallow.

Edna sighed again, and then produced a smile of sorts. "Well, do what you can. Let's discuss the possibility of deviled eggs. I know eggs are still difficult to get, and how many do you think we could come up with, or does someone have an idea for a substitute?"

The conversations, and tastings, and suggestions continued through the afternoon. Eventually the menu, which, all agreed, would include smaller versions of Viola's large sugar cookies as part of the desserts, was decided upon. The women cleaned up the table, washed the dishes, and covered up the leftovers. Before everyone left, Edna spoke a few heartfelt sentences about family and love and togetherness, all those things people talk about when important events like weddings occur. Edna stood by the front door and gave everyone a hug as they left, and Tillie received an extended one. Tillie hugged her back, and they gave each other a genuine smile. After all there was no sense in starting a war.

Continuing Education

After Europe celebrated V-E Day in early May, it was assumed that World War II would presently be coming to a close, and those young men from Everstille who had survived the fighting would be returning home soon. Some of them had already. In fact, the Everstille City Council honored those returned men by making them march in the July Fourth Parade which traversed the entire half-mile down Main Street and ended at the city park where the veterans were further honored by being seated on the large dais in the hot July sun and remained there to listen to each of the members of the City Council speak in turn about the bravery and patriotism which the day esteemed. Mason Chessworth, *The Everstille News* editor read his latest poem entitled "Ever Brave; Still Patriotic", a title whose play on words he explained at length to those remaining audience members.

The Everstille School Board convened the following week also determined to do something for those men who had left high school to fight for their country and had not received their diplomas. Special School Board meetings were held throughout July and early August, and the board devised a plan by which returning vets could receive their diplomas, if they so desired, and do so with a minimum of effort.

The high school principal, Tobias Pickerton, chaired the sub-committee of the School Board which organized schedules and classes for those who wanted to obtain the diplomas as members of the Class of 1946. Their plan was judicious and generous. Returning veterans would need to make up minimum required classes. All the classes would be scheduled for the morning so that if the students were lucky enough to have a job, they could work in the afternoons or the evenings. This became one of the first School/Work Programs in the Midwest, and Principal Pickerton was quite proud of himself. And the subcommittee.

The Senior Classes of 1942 and 1943 counted eight students who quit school to join up, and of them, three survived to return. None of those three were interested in reentering high school. Being in a schoolroom with much younger students and completing actual assignments seemed laughable when compared with the carnage they had both witnessed and participated in. Count them out. Besides, one of the returning soldiers arrived home missing his right writing hand and had not yet learned to complete the required five-page essays with his left.

The Class of 1944 contained ten veterans... half the males in the class. Four of them had returned and two were interested, but only one signed up. Unfortunately, he had not been that conscientious of a student, and did not make it past the deadline for the first five-page essay, even though he had come through the war with both of his hands intact. Five members of the seven in the Class of 1945 returned, and four of them took advantage of the program. Three of them completed it and earned their diplomas.

Clyde Wells was the oldest of the Class of '45 returning vets. He and his large family lived in the cabin west of the town, and Clyde, like his older brothers Vernon and Leon, had joined the army. Vernon was MIA in France, and Leon stayed in England after the war. Clyde, despite being a decent student, was determined to be a farmer. While no one in town knew exactly what had happened to his parents, Bob and Emma Wells, the gossip was that they had come into an inheritance, and Clyde, with his father's help, bought a farm in the next county. A high school diploma was not much use to him, so he politely declined the School Board's offer

Ben Clampet was the nephew of Mr. Clampet, the owner of the now larger and expanded Clampet's Grocery Store and Meat Market. Ben, always a quiet and studious young man, regretted joining the army and not finishing high school, so he was anxious to go back and receive his diploma. He only needed to complete two required classes, which he did, and as soon as he was able, he took advantage of the G.I. Bill and entered Purdue University where he began his study of medicine.

Buck Travis was never a good student, but his mother insisted he take advantage of the offer, so he began again. He had been scheduled for four classes (partly because he had failed a couple before joining the army) and had every intention of completing them, but he could not get interested in getting up and going back to classes. Or completing those essays. He was, however, quite clever with his hands, and since the newly built Mackie's Gasoline and Service Station just outside of town, needed another mechanic, Buck found his calling.

Tom Everett was a better student than his friend, Buck, and had only two classes to complete. While he did not have any desire to continue his education beyond high school, Tom wanted to please his parents, especially his mother who sobbed when he joined the service because her son would have been the first person in their family to obtain a high school diploma. Tom went back to school for his mother, and the party that the Everett family gave upon his receiving the diploma lasted through the entire weekend.

Mitchell Jasper had always been an excellent student. He enjoyed studying and planned to go to college and become a teacher. All that changed when he and Mike joined the army. He needed to complete two classes for the diploma and was happy to do so. Mitch believed he was fulfilling the promise Mike had made their mother: to go back to school and graduate. On the day Mitch received his diploma, he gave it to his mother and said to her, "This is for you, and while it has my name on it, it is actually Mike's." Viola hugged her son, and they stood quietly for a while allowing some of the shrouded heartaches and blanketed wounds to fade.

The School Board met at the end of the 1946 school year to review the Pinkerton subcommittee's plan. From the beginning of the war to the end, there had been twenty-five students from the high school who had joined the service. Of those, twelve had returned. Of those, three earned their diplomas. The outcome was not what the School Board had originally hoped for, but the plan had been judicious and generous, and in the difficult days of settling again into a normal life, that was the best that could be expected.

As further tribute to the soldiers, sailors, or marines who did not return, the School Board had individual plaques created and inscribed with their names. These plaques hung in the Everstille High School first floor corridor, next to the Main Office, where passing students could see them and know that their bravery and patriotism was remembered.

Cousins

It was the Monday afternoon after the Mitchell's Open House, and Edie was returning the borrowed platters. She filled them with leftover desserts as a thank-you to the neighbors who had lent them. The party was a great success with everyone enjoying the gin cocktails, the hors d'oeuvres, the conversations, and while the party was scheduled to end at seven o'clock, it continued into the early morning hours. The church pews at Sunday morning services were rather empty.

The last platters she returned were to her Aunt Viola and Tillie. She was hoping to see Mitch. He came to the Open House and welcomed Ned home, and hugged Edie and congratulated them, but did not stay long, and Edie did not have a chance to talk to him. Except for seeing Tom and Buck periodically, Mitch stayed alone most of the time. That was understandable, but Edie, who was very much like her mother, thought she could get him out and into society again. She knew the next few weeks before the wedding would be busy with all sorts of tasks and requirements, and this might be one of the last times she would be able to talk to him for a while. Edie and Mitch had always gotten along better than Edie and Mike.

Edie knocked at the front door and yelled into the screen, "Hello, it's Edie. Mitch, are you there?"

From the kitchen she heard Millie answer, "Come on into the kitchen, Edie. I'm making dinner."

Edie let herself into the house and walked into the kitchen with the platters.

"Thanks, Tillie for the wonderful hors d'oeuvres and the use of your platters. Mother sent some of the sugar cookies back and a few of the petit fours for your dessert tonight. I hope you and Aunt Vi had a good time. Is she home yet?"

"Not yet, but soon. Thanks for these. I didn't have any sweets for dessert. Yes, we did have a wonderful time, and I understand the party went on with you young folks for quite a while. You aren't working today?"

"No, I took today and tomorrow off to help Mother clean up. Yes, the party was fun, and I hope our music didn't disturb you here. Some of Ned's Navy friends stopped by later after you and Aunt Vi left.

I was hoping Mitch would have stayed longer. He would have enjoyed trading stories with them. Is he here?"

Tillie pushed the vegetables to the side and washed her hands. As she dried them, she turned to talk to Edie.

"Yes, he is in the back yard. I know he did not stay long Saturday, but he's not been himself since coming home. I'm glad he got over to the party for a time because I was afraid he wouldn't show up at all. Maybe you can get him out of the dumps he is in. He hasn't talked much about the army, and truthfully, me and Viola haven't pushed him to. We figured he still needs some time to sort it out. Anyway, go on out to the back and see him, but steer away from army talk. O.K.?"

Edie nodded assent and headed out the back door. She walked down the three steps and saw Mitch sitting on the tree stump in the back, twirling a basketball and bouncing it between his feet. She walked towards him and called out, "Hey, cousin, how are you?"

Mitch caught the ball and looked up at her and said, "Hi, Edie. Thought you would be busy with wedding stuff."

"I am. But I was returning platters and wanted to see you. I am glad you came by last Saturday, but we didn't talk much. You would've had a good time if you had stayed. Some of Ned's friends came later, and we talked and danced until late. When Aunt Vi left, I asked her to send you back over."

Mitch moved the ball back and forth between his hands. He waited a few seconds and then said, "Yeah, well, Ma did come upstairs, but by that time, I was in bed. My sleep habits have been weird lately, so I get sleep when I can. Glad you had a good time. It was a nice party. Sorry I couldn't come back over."

Edie spread her skirt, and sat on the grass in front of him.

"That's fine, Mitch. Some of the kids from the neighborhood were there too. Janet Lynn was looking for you. She wanted to know how you are. She is excited about the rehearsal dinner and the wedding. Her dress is just lovely, baby-blue and her gloves match exactly. I guess you aren't interested in this stuff."

Mitch shrugged and looked at her. "I know this is a happy time for you and Ned, and I really am pleased for both of you. It's just that coming back has been difficult. I can't really talk about what happened, and don't want to. Trying to be normal again is something I'm struggling with. Just so you know, Ned might have some problems too, so give him a break if he does."

"Alright, Mitch. I will. I hope things ease up for you. I heard the School Board is going to give you vets a chance to make up classes and get your diplomas. Aunt Vi told me that you were going to do that. I think it's a fine idea and might make things seem normal again. School begins Thursday, doesn't it?"

"Yep. I only have a couple classes to finish, and will start this week. I guess Buck and Tom and Ben Clampet are going to start too, but I am not sure we'll be in the same classes. I'm taking Senior English and the second part of U.S. History, and then I have that part-time job delivering for Banter's Drugs. I started working last week. Your dad helped me get it, and Ma is letting me use the Buick for the deliveries. You're right...doing normal stuff might make things normal for me again. The last few months have been rough."

Edie nodded and they were quiet for a while. Then Edie cleared her throat and looked at her cousin.

"Hey, Mitch, I have a suggestion for you. I know you have been pretty much by yourself, but maybe you might want to think about dating again. I know lots of girls, and I can fix you up with someone. What do you think?"

Mitch looked her and then back to the ground. "I don't know, Edie. Not so sure I'm ready for that. Maybe I just need to work for a while and go to school and wait."

"I do have someone in mind for you, Mitch."

Mitch just looked at her.

"Well, to be honest, Janet Lynn was looking forward seeing you and talking to you last Saturday. I know she's a couple of years older than you, but really, what difference does that make? I probably shouldn't tell you this, but she thinks you are a great guy and would love to see you socially. Just think about it, and let me know. If you want to come to dinner some time, that would be fine, although maybe after the wedding. Ned and I have rented one of those apartments over on Summer Street, and once we're settled in, we could do that. What do you think?"

"I know you mean well, Edie, but let's hold off. Janet Lynn is nice enough, but I just don't think I am ready for any dating. Appreciate your thoughts though."

Edie got up and Mitch stood up too.

"Sure, Mitch. The offer stands. Janet Lynn is a great friend, and I think you two would hit it off. Anyway, good luck with school and work. You were always such a good student that it should be easy for you. How's the old Buick running.?"

"Good. Buck looked it over and made a few adjustments, and it's fine. Ma doesn't drive much because we live so close to her jobs, and she said it will be a good thing to keep it going. Thanks, Edie for coming over. And thanks for thinking of me."

Edie wanted to hug Mitch, but she hesitated. He looked at her and reached over to pull her in. She hugged him and stayed close to him and said to him tearfully, "Mitch, I miss Mike too. We all do."

"I know," replied Mitch, "I know."

School Days

Wednesday afternoon, Banter's Drug Store and Pharmacy

"…and when you drop this one off to Mrs. Jeffers at 235 Cherry Lane, the other goes to Mrs. Barrows on the corner at 245. Her daughter has bronchitis and a bad cough…so this will help. And when you return, would you mind sweeping out the back and straightening those boxes? We just have not had a chance to do it." Nathan looked at Mitch with raised eyebrows.

"Sure, when I get back, I can do that. Anything else? Did you remember that I start classes tomorrow? I won't be in until later. Is that O.K.?"

"I think that will be it for today, Mitch. Both Jim and I know about the classes, so why don't you come in after lunchtime tomorrow? That way you could get some homework done if you need to. And, Mitch, we appreciate you helping around here with the odds and ends we ask you to do. Especially since you were hired just to deliver. How is the Buick running?"

"Fine, Uncle Nate. The Buick's running just fine. My friend, Buck, looked it over…he's handy with mechanical stuff. Ma is glad for it to be driven since she doesn't have much of a reason to drive. And I don't mind helping here. Keeps me busy and I like that. I better get going. See you later," and Mitch picked up the box filled with the deliveries and went out the door to the parked Buick.

He stored the box in the passenger seat and arranged the bags in the order to be delivered. Mitch liked doing this. It was easy work. It was mindless work, but it kept him busy, and he was grateful that Uncle Nate had arranged for the job. That was why he did not object to doing the sweeping or stacking or general cleaning and organizing he was asked to do. The work helped thrust memories away and made him feel normal. Or almost normal. Once classes started, he would be even busier, and he was looking forward to that. Looking forward to busy. To normal.

Thursday Morning, Everstille High School

Tillie pushed the bowl of oatmeal towards Mitch. He just looked at it and then got up to pour himself a second cup of coffee. It had been a sleepless night. They did not happen as often anymore, but they still came and kept Mitch and Tillie and Viola awake as they listened to each other's movements and worried about each other's sleeplessness.

"You need to eat something and not just drink that coffee."

Tillie watched Mitch. He was still too thin, and now that he was working and starting school again, he needed to get some food in him. He needed to put on a few pounds, and Tillie was cooking and baking everything she could think of to encourage this. It was not very successful.

Mitch sipped his second cup and pulled the bowl towards him. He took a few bites and then put the spoon down. "Thanks, Tillie, but I'm not hungry. I promise that I'll eat lunch today after classes and before I go to work. I shouldn't feel nervous, but I do. Not sure why."

"Oh, you'll be fine. Your Ma wanted to walk with you, but she needed to get the Emporium early. She had to fill in and open the store this morning. I think Mr. Grayson takes advantage of your mother's good nature with all he asks her to do, but she just does it. Anyway, she is as anxious as you are, so I have two *nervous Nellies* to deal with today. She didn't eat much either. Got your supplies and books?"

Mitch looked at Tillie and said, "Yes, Ma'am...I do remember what school was like."

Tillie shrugged. "I know I'm fussing. Just forgive this old woman for it."

Mitch nodded, "Forgiven, old woman!" He perched his head sideways and leaned forward so Tillie's gentle slap would not hit his arm. "I need to get going. See you later."

Mitch got up and placed his bowl and cup in the sink. He grabbed his jacket although he did not really need it, and took the notebooks and books from the table. A pencil and a pen were slipped into his back pocket, and he went out the back door just as he and Mike had done for years. This time, he walked alone.

Mitch was early, but Mr. Pinkerton had asked him and Tom, and Buck, and Ben to stop and see him before they went to their classes. He said he wanted to welcome them back. There were a few students waiting around the front of the high school when Mitch walked in. He did not recognize any of them and thought for a minute that this just might be a mistake. He walked down the first-floor corridor to the Main Office and entered. The school clerk, Mrs. Green, was moving some papers back and forth and finishing up a conversation with a teacher. After the teacher left, she turned to Mitch and recognized him. She smiled and said, "Welcome back, Mitchell. Mr. Pinkerton said to bring you in when you got here, so come on."

The half door that separated the outer space from the Principal's Office swung open and Mitch walked through and thanked Mrs. Green. As he entered the office, Tobias Pinkerton got up from his desk and came around to shake Mitch's hand.

"Welcome. Glad you are back, Mitchell. You were always a stellar student, and we are glad to offer you this opportunity to complete your course of study and get your diploma. I know you had plans to continue your education, and I hope that is still what you intend to do."

Mitch took his hand and shook it and said, "Thank you. Principal Pinkerton. I appreciate this, and yes, I still do plan to go to college. I always thought I might be a teacher, so I am glad for the opportunity to finish up here,"

The principal nodded his approval.

"Well, I will say the same thing to all you boys, actually, men, who are entering this program. And that is, we welcome you back, and thank you for your fine service. The past years have been hard on all, especially those of you who were away fighting. If there is anything we can help you with, please let us know. And Mitchell, on a personal note, please accept my condolences to you and your family on the loss of your brother, Michael. We lost some brave and honorable young men, and your brother was certainly one of them."

Mitch swallowed hard. Condolences, he knew, were meant to comfort. They did not.

"Thank you, Sir."

"Well, the entrance bell will be ringing in a few minutes. I suspect you will be able to find your classroom. Glad you are back, Mitchell, and I meant what I said."

Mitch nodded his thanks, and as he walked out of the office, he saw Tom and Ben waiting their turn for the official welcome back. Buck was not there yet, to no one's surprise. Mitch greeted them and then walked out of the office and turned right to find the Senior English classroom.

When he got to Room 125, he pulled open the door and walked into the empty room which seemed smaller than he remembered. There were a few minutes before class and the seniors were waiting until the last minute to take seats, so he had his choice of them. He looked at the back of the room, then walked to the last row, the last seat, and sat down. He hoped he would be less conspicuous here. The bell rang, and the noise in the hallway began.

He took out his notebook and pencil and put them on his desk and watched as some of the students slowly came into the classroom laughing and talking to each other. He recognized a few of them as the younger siblings of his friends, and he thought, for the second time, that perhaps this would not work. But he was here and had this chance, and would just make it through these two classes. He straightened up at his desk and observed a young woman walk into the room and move to the back, to the seat next to his. He knew her, but was not sure how, so when she looked at him, he was quiet, waiting for her to speak.

"Hello, Mitch. I heard you were going to be in this class. I'm glad you will be able to finish your diploma work. Everyone said you were one of the best students here. I am so sorry about your brother. He was always so much fun. Oh…do you remember me? It has been years, and I don't suppose you do."

Mitch looked at her. She was tall with long auburn hair that curled around milky skin, and brown eyes that contained hazel flecks, and dimples in both cheeks. "I know that I know you, but, sorry, your name is just not coming to me. Did I go to school with one of your brothers or sisters?"

The young woman smiled showing her dimples. "We used to play with you and Mike years ago when you lived out at the house west of town. My sister and sometimes Clyde would be there, but mostly it was Rebecca and me. I am Hattie Wells." Hattie held out her hand for him to shake. "Welcome home, Soldier!"

Mitch took note of her dimples and her hazel-flecked eyes as he took her hand and shook it. He observed the auburn curls around her forehead and said, "Thanks, Hattie."

For the first time in over half a year, Mitch smiled.

Winter and Wells

The Winter Family

In 1861, Leon and Greta Winter moved out of eastern Tennessee and traveled to the established city of Vincennes, Indiana to live and farm. They were newly married and youthfully rebellious and heartily disagreed with the state of Tennessee seceding from the union to join the Confederacy. Neighbors, particularly those who owned slaves, mocked the beliefs of the Winters, and whispered that because they could not afford to keep slaves and were dreadful at farming, they were forced to move. They were not completely wrong. One quiet Monday morning, after having sold the farm to a neighbor at a great loss, the Winters packed their wagon with belongings and began the lengthy, arduous journey to the North, to Vincennes where they purchased a small farm close to the Wabash River and set up housekeeping.

The Winters were not very adept at farming but made every attempt at it. When Greta found herself pregnant in 1862, Leon decided his plan to join an Indiana regiment and fight in the Civil War was not a wise one, and so he stayed on the farm. Early the next year, Greta bore the first of their three sons: George Washington Winter. Five years later, Thomas Jefferson Winter was born, and five years after that, Benjamin Franklin Winter showed up. It was in a spurt of Northern patriotism and an attempt to honor past rebellions, that their father named them.

The boys grew up in the farmlands around Vincennes, and when George was sixteen, he told his parents that he intended to take his chances elsewhere and set off for the northern part of the state. George traveled from Vincennes to Bloomington where he worked at the limestone quarries and spent some time helping to build the growing university there. But he was not one to settle down, and after some time, Indianapolis and the natural gas boom that was taking place there called to him. Eventually George traveled further north to South Bend and found work at the Studebaker factory. He was prudent and careful with his earnings, and because he never found a woman who wanted to marry him, there was no need to spend money on niceties and fripperies such as a woman would want.

In the early part of the twentieth century when George was in his fourth decade, he traveled to a small but emerging town just south of South Bend and decided to purchase some land, refurbish a cabin that was on it, and live back in the wooded area west of the town. He kept in touch with Thomas via biannual letters which he painfully wrote out with a small pencil sharpened with a large hunting knife. In this way, he learned of recent family news, including the birth of Thomas' daughters.

While their brother, George, traveled and worked and seized chances, Thomas and Benjamin stayed and worked on the family farm. Thomas, at nineteen, married a neighbor's daughter, Beatrice, and brought his bride to the farm where they both toiled, and struggled, and cared for Leon and Greta who had grown old quickly and died during one grueling, hostile winter. Their youngest son, Benjamin Franklin Winter joined his parents the next spring, and Thomas and Beatrice inherited the farm and the struggle.

Thomas was not any better a farmer than was his father, so he sold the farm, visited the graves of his family one last time, and moved with his wife to Bloomington. He had received a letter from George which told of the opportunities available there because of the expansion and growth of the university, so Thomas and Beatrice followed George to the bustling town. The three of them even lived together for a while until George, hearing a clear call of opportunity, left for other places.

After George left, Beatrice gave birth to Kate Anne, and not too long afterwards, a second daughter, Emily Jean. Beatrice and Thomas moved into a small house just south and west of the main Indiana University campus, close enough for Thomas to walk to work every day. Kate Anne and Emily Jean grew up loved and given the best six years of education available to the children of the Bloomington workers. Because their parents were barely literate, education was not venerated in the same way as were housekeeping competences. They grew up knowing essential elementary reading, writing, and arithmetic, but once formal schooling was over, both began to work as apprentice housekeepers in the same house as their mother.

Kate Anne was a pretty girl, taking after her mother with her dark eyes and hair. But Emily Jean was a beauty. She looked like her father, Thomas, with her thick auburn hair that curled around her face, kissing the pale smooth cheeks containing dimples and enhancing her brown eyes with their flecks of hazel. While Kate Anne was just five feet tall with ample curves, Emily Jean was five inches taller than her sister, and her form was straight but shapely. When the sisters walked down the street, they gathered looks and smiles at their combined comeliness, but Emily Jean was begrudgingly noted by other females and appreciatively studied by males.

The sisters were close. They were friends, and when Kate Anne met and married a man who had traveled to Bloomington to obtain temporary work, Emily Jean was delighted for her and her new brother-in-law, Ronald. However, when the newly married couple decided to move back to Illinois, to Ronald's hometown, Emily was distraught and cried nightly until her mother took her by the shoulders and demanded she stop, and that this was life, and this was the way things happened. A few years later, after Emily Jean met and married and moved, Beatrice became distraught and spent night after night crying until Thomas told her to stop, and accept that this was life, and this was the way things happened.

After Kate Anne and Ronald moved, Beatrice and Emily Jean were obliged to find new jobs since the family they had worked for sold their house and left the state. Beatrice found work with another family, but there was no need for an additional housekeeper, so Emily Jean continued to search for work. Luckily, Thomas had heard that there was an opening at one of the best households in Bloomington, and his daughter applied, interviewed, and was hired as an assistant housekeeper at the house of the late esteemed lawyer Grayson Robert Wells. The house was owned by his son, the widowed Classics Professor, Alexander Wells who lived there with his son, Robert Alexander Lucius Wells.

Emily Jean was interviewed by the Head Housekeeper and Manager, Mrs. Pendant who thought her new assistant's name too countrified, so *Emily Jean* became *Emma*. Emma enjoyed her work in the fashionable, elite Wells household and was pleased to think that her excellent wages were helping her parents who were growing old and tired. She bloomed under the tutelage of Mrs. Pendant, and what she lacked in formal education, she gained in common sense knowledge.

Robert Wells, the son of Professor Alexander, was not in the house when Emma began her work there. He was at Camp Sherman, Ohio waiting for a discharge from the United States Army. However, once he was home, and after a proper rest, the paths of the beautiful, auburn-haired assistant housekeeper and the tall, former Doughboy would often cross.

Cabin in the Woods

George Washington Winter was one of the few men working at the Studebaker plant in South Bend who actually owned a Studebaker Light Four Touring car. George lived carefully and frugally, spending very little for anything other than the absolute rudimentary essentials. He owned a work shirt and pants worn daily, and then while they dried from the weekly cursory wash he gave them each Sunday, wore his dress outfit or, if he was not leaving his rented room, remained naked and wrapped himself in a thin, worn blanket. His dress outfit was almost twenty years old, and it was due to his careful eating of simple meals twice a day that he could still fit into it. Once part of his work outfit wore out and he could no longer wear the patched and ragged shirt or pants, he would bargain at the second-hand store and purchase a replacement. One pair of shoes and two of socks got the same treatment. A raggedy coat to wear only when the weather absolutely demanded it was also his. Long underwear was worn year-round. George kept long hair and a beard, and trimmed them himself, thus saving himself barber costs, and if there was anything he splurged on, it was a beautifully milled soft soap to wash himself daily. He could stand the dirt on his outer clothing but not on himself.

He read when he could find a used newspaper or book, and in that way, improved his proficiency. He had no friends, and because his life was rather nomadic, even those acquaintances he possessed were temporary. This never bothered George because he lived for himself and his thoughts. Years earlier, he had purchased a dozen Ticonderoga pencils and a ledger, and he kept track of his purchases and wrote down important dates and items and stray thoughts, and twice a year, tore out a page to write a letter to his brother, Thomas Jefferson Winter. By the time he was in his mid-forties, he had filled almost a dozen ledgers. Those and his Studebaker were his treasured possessions.

When the opportunity to purchase a used automobile came up, George bargained with the man who was desperate to sell it so that he could afford the wedding trip his fiancé wanted. George examined the car, overlooking scratches on the driver's side and realizing that he could most likely maintain the car himself, bartered with its current owner and then, paying with the bag of coins and some paper money he brought with him, drove away in his own car. He drove for a while and then settled on a place to park it. He moved the car every other day to a new place so no one would think it abandoned, and in this way, the car remained in decent driving shape for his Sunday drives.

On most Sundays, George would arise early and complete his few chores including the washing of his work clothes. He would hang them up around his room, opening the window slightly when weather permitted, fill a large jar with water, pack a bologna sandwich and fruit if he could find some, and go out to his parked Studebaker. He spent time examining the car, making sure everything was in working order, and at the time when most people were trekking to church for the early service, George would start the car and take off exploring. His food was on the passenger seat, his dress hat on his head, and his eyes were on the road before him. It was the best time in his week.

He would travel the roads and find the small villages and towns dotting the countryside. Driving down unpaved roads was sometimes a challenge, and he had learned to bring enough tools with him to repair whatever needed to be whether it was a tire or a mechanical part. *Lucky,* he thought, *lucky I work at that plant,* and he smiled, and if any of his fellow workers were to see him, they would not recognize the smiling man whose beard was freshly trimmed and whose blue eyes could be seen sparkling under the visor of his almost twenty-year old dress hat.

George traveled some of the roads again and again because there were certain small towns to which he took a liking. As he became more familiar with the places, he would, periodically on a late Saturday afternoon after working the early shift, travel the roads and stop for a meal and a drink in a town restaurant as a special treat to himself. His birthday (which was in February but he celebrated in May so the weather would cooperate) was one of these days. His brothers' birthdays were celebrated in this fashion as were the birthdays of his two nieces whom he had never seen. Holidays were ignored.

There was one town south and a bit east of South Bend that he could travel to in just about an hour, and George found himself often visiting it. It had a pleasant main street containing various business-es, a lovely park, and a mixture of old and new houses that he liked to examine. One Sunday, George took a slow drive through the town and continued to travel west. He passed some farms and a few houses and came to an obscure road which lead into a wooded area, so he turned his car to the left and slowly drove into a clearing where he saw a cabin. He stopped the car and got out to explore.

"Hello," he called and again, "Hello, is there anyone here?"

There was no answer, and upon looking into the cabin which was empty, he opened the door and went in. The cabin had two small rooms with a fireplace at the end of the larger one. The smaller one was meant to be a kitchen with a sink area and a door which lead out to the back to an outhouse. The yard was overgrown, but George could see that there had at one time been a rather large garden   Towards the back was a well and some small trees which had been cut into planks. It looked as though someone had started to divide the wood in preparation for additional building. George closely examined the back of the cabin and decided it would not be difficult to continue to expand and build additional rooms. He spent the afternoon looking around the cabin and land, and when he realized it was abandoned, he thought of a plan.

When he returned to his room that evening, he took out his latest ledger and opened it up to the page he had written in just a few days ago. He examined the entries.

Money Found		February birthday dinner will be on May 10
April 3	1 cent	
April 5	2 cents	
April 10	a nickel (good day)	New socks needed
April 18	1 cent	
April 28	1 cent	
May 5	3 cents (2)	
	(one was a button)	

George thought that he would need to make some changes. He would eliminate the birthday celebration this year and forgo the purchase of the new socks. He had a rather generous amount of money in his secret hiding place, but more was necessary. He thought and considered. Taking out one of the Ticonderoga pencils and sharpening it with the large knife, he made some changes:

Money Found		February birthday dinner will be on May 10
April 3	1 cent	
April 5	2 cents	
April 10	a nickel (good day)	New socks needed
April 18	1 cent	Save money by:
April 28	1 cent	No birthday celebration No new socks
May 5	3 cents (2)	Continue to look for coins Drive only every other week
	(one was a button)	Work additional shifts

For the first time in years, George planned for his future.

***

Some months later, George surprised his supervisor at the plant by explaining that he would need a day off to attend to some important family business. Supervisor Miller was so astonished by this request that he granted it, and the following Thursday, George was not at his usual position at the Studebaker plant. Instead, he put on his dress clothes after making sure he had thoroughly washed himself with his beautifully milled soft soap, carefully packed some papers and a great deal of his secreted money, and took off in his Studebaker for the small town about an hour south and a bit east of South Bend. He drove into the town, having forgotten it was a week day, and the array of people going about their daily tasks surprised him. He found the Sheriff's Office, parked the car, and knocked firmly before opening the door.

"Excuse me," he said to the young man who was holding some papers and walking towards a desk. "My name is George Winter and I thought to inquire about a cabin I saw empty a couple miles or so west of town. I am looking into buying it and was wondering if you knew the owner or a person I could talk to about it?"

Deputy Samms looked at George and nodded. "You must mean the old Harvey place. Yes, it's been empty for a few years now. Not sure exactly why Mr. Harvey left, but I am sure you could find out some information from Mr. Granger, the town's lawyer. I believe the land and cabin were left in his care, and as far as I know, no one has bought it. His office is just down the street on the west side across from the Emporium."

"Thank you, Sir. I'll go and inquire now."

He held out his hand which Deputy Samms shook.

George walked out of the building and down the street to the office of Mr. Granger. Upon entering, a woman informed him that the lawyer was out but would return in an hour, and suggested George wait out the hour at the town's diner, a place called *Mazie's*. George said he would return and decided to walk around the town to look at the shops and businesses. He did not enter any of the places because he decided that it would be unfair to give any of the shopkeepers false hope that he would purchase something. His money was already spent.

An hour later, he appeared back at the law office where he took a seat to wait for Lawyer Granger to appear, and fifteen minutes later he did. Mr. Granger and George Winter went into the back office and talked and discussed the property for the better part of two hours, and when George left and walked back to his Studebaker, he had arranged to purchase the cabin and land he had visited and, as a legal precaution, to create a will since now he was a property owner. The move from South Bend to his new home would not happen for some time, but George was excited and delighted. He would be a nomad no longer.

***

That is how about a year later, when Thomas Jefferson Winter received a large official envelope, he was shocked and surprised. Should something happen to his older brother, George, he would be the heir and legal owner of a cabin built on some land located a bit south and east of South Bend, in a small but growing town called Everstille.

Fathers and Sons

During the 1840's when divorce was a dirty word, Indiana became acknowledged for its cordiality to the edict. As unhappy couples took up residence in the state to take advantage of the increasingly tolerant divorce laws, there became a need for additional lawyers to guide them through the tangle of confusing and ever-changing regulations. Grayson Robert Wells, recent graduate from the Indiana University School of Law, took note of the lawyer shortage and set up an office in Bloomington where he gained so many clients that his practice expanded as swiftly as his bank account.

Grayson Wells was one of the most eligible men in the area, and for a wife, he had his choice of Bloomington innocents. His law practice did not dissuade him from possible matrimonial mis-steps, so he chose a lovely woman whose local cabinetmaker father and brothers were equal in wealth to him. After a fashionable wedding and a proper honeymoon, Grayson built a large, beautiful home for his new wife, Sarah, and they set up housekeeping and became part of the social elite in the bourgeoning town of Bloomington, Indiana.

A year into their marriage, a son, Alexander, was born. He was schooled, and tutored, and trained, and given the most and the best of everything. He remained the only Wells child because Sarah's constitution did not allow her to produce siblings for him although she tried. In fact, when Alexander was ten, Sarah, in a final attempt to produce just one more offspring, succumbed to the effort and died.

After a long period of mourning, and with the assistance of various housekeepers and nannies and tutors, Grayson and Alexander settled down to live together companionably. Although courted by many eligible Bloomington ingenues and youngish widows, Grayson Wells never remarried. He spent his time counseling clients, educating his son, and functioning as a member of many, many committees for Indiana University. Grayson Wells became an extraordinarily important member of the University family and instilled in his son, Alexander, a love of the institution. When it came time for Alexander to enter the school, he did so with an intensity approved of by his father.

Alexander Wells excelled in the studies of Greek and Latin. Upon completing the course in the ancient classics and receiving his Bachelor's Degree, he, with just a smidgen of help from his father, became the youngest member of Indiana University's Classics Department and began to lecture and teach.

The University began promoting a series of lectures given by various professors to stimulate interest in the school as well as to inform and educate the public. The talks were particularly popular with Bloomington's elite, and the youthful and handsome Professor Alexander Wells always addressed a full audience. And in the audience, and always in the front row was Marcella Edmonds, who, with her mother, Mrs. Alfred Edmonds, attended each lecture.

The Edmonds family was in the hotel business which had proven quite lucrative. They owned the South Bend Grand Oakerton Hotel, the Indianapolis Twin Oaks Hotel, and were in the process of opening the almost completely remodeled hotel to be known as the Bloomington Oaks. (Mr. Edmonds admired the sturdy and strong oak tree.) They had temporarily relocated to Bloomington from South Bend where the newest hotel would be managed by Marcella's father, Alfred Edmonds until his son, Peter, graduated from Indiana University and took over the family business. Meanwhile, the Edmonds were on the lookout for a proper husband for Marcella. They found one in Alexander Wells.

The wedding reception breakfast took place in the Bloomington Oaks Grand Ballroom, and no expense was spared. Fresh flowers and ribbons wreathed all the tables and encircled the enormous, light, and airy *bride's cake* which Marcella and Alexander cut together according to the newest custom. The breakfast meal itself was created by the South Bend Grand Oakerton's Chef de Cuisine who had been imported especially for the affair. Marcella's wedding dress and trousseau had kept Bloomington's dressmakers busy for months. All in all, the wedding was the highlight of the season.

After the wedding, with their daughter and son-in-law properly settled in the beautiful Wells house, and their newly graduated son firmly in control of the family business, the Edmonds left for a trip abroad followed by a return to South Bend. The newly married Alexander and Marcella took a brief tour of the east coast, visiting Boston and New York. They had a wonderful time, and when they returned to Bloomington, Marcella was thrilled to write to her mother announcing the arrival of an addition to their family. Within months of this letter, Marcella wrote another, sadder one, informing of death of her father-in-law, the esteemed lawyer, Grayson Wells.

History repeats. Marcella and Alexander were delighted to usher into the world their only child, Robert Alexander Lucius Wells. The birth was a difficult one, and it left Marcella weak and unable to produce another child. But Robert, called "Bobby", was adored, and loved, and unfairly, when he was only five, his mother was ushered into the next world. And again, the Wells household became strictly male although several female nannies, and housekeepers, and servants were there to help raise young Bobby as his father continued to lecture and teach at the University.

Bobby, or as he grew older, Bob, grew up wishing he had some brothers or even sisters around him. He pretended that some of the younger maids were his sisters and enjoyed playing with them as their housework allowed.

"When I grow up," he would tell them, "I will have a really big family. Me and my wife will have lots and lots of children. Won't that be fun?"

And the maids would nod their heads, thinking about the housework they needed to do, and considering their own sizable assemblages of siblings, pitied little Bobby's future wife.

As he grew older, Bob Wells received the best education a string of tutors could give him. There were no private or boarding schools close enough or proper enough for him to attend, and there was never a thought about sending him to any of the public schools with common children. So, the finest and brightest tutors from the University, were hired by Alexander to prepare Bob for his eventual entrance into Indiana University which coincided with his eighteenth birthday.

As a youth, Bob was educated in both the Latin and Greek languages, mythologies, and histories, so there was never any doubt that his first formal degree would be in the Ancient Classics, and he would follow in Professor Alexander's footsteps. From age eighteen to age twenty, Bob studied at the University, excelling in his classes, and distinguishing himself so that upperclassmen, struggling with Greek declensions and Latin conjugations, sought to hire him as a tutor.

Once declensions and conjugations were clarified, the tutoring sessions often ended with a lively discussion of current politics. The older students would regale Bob with their stances on the country's entrance into World War I. Almost to a man, they were in favor of it, and most of them willingly exchanged their Homer and Virgil for olive drab and boots. Encouraged by their commitment and influenced by their patriotism, in 1918, after the late spring semester ended, Bob went to the army recruiting station with the last two of his tutees and joined up.

Professor Alexander was not pleased. He was of the mind that neutrality was a wiser choice, and upon the entrance into the war, he wrote two blistering letters. One was sent to the *Bloomington Evening News Newspaper*, and the other was sent to Indiana's Senator, Harry Stewart New. However, once Professor Alexander saw his son wearing his khaki-colored army tunic and hat, and managing to carry, without dropping, his newly issued Springfield rifle, the Professor's eyes welled up and a burst of patriotism, fully formed and rising as the legendary Phoenix from his brightly blazing heart, filled his body. He then rewrote the letters, explaining at exorbitant length, why he had this change of heart and sent the letters off to the newspaper and Senator New at the earliest possible post.

Even though the army required additional soldiers to fight the Great War, the massive paperwork that accompanied each recruit slowed things down. Eventually, Bob was assigned to Camp Sherman, Ohio to begin his training in early August. The object was to send qualified, competent soldiers to fight in France by December.

The camp was nothing like Bob's home. Intensive training was held at an artillery range, a rifle range, and the maneuver grounds. Soldier Bob learned to dig and work in trenches, to do his own laundry, to cook his own food, to sleep in uncomfortable positions and places, and to wake and jump up ready for a fight in a few seconds. He surprised himself by, if not exactly enjoying it all, at least surviving it. And the skills he acquired were to bear fruit in future years.

But the war ended on November 11, 1918, and Bob's deployment to the trenches of France was cancelled, and by Christmas of that year, he was back in Bloomington with his father, Professor Alexander. He was glorified, and honored, and pampered just as though he had fought in France. While he was encouraged to rest at the lovely and spacious Wells home, it was his father's ardent intention to reinstate him at the University just as soon as possible.

But no one, especially Bob, had planned on his friendship with the young and beautiful assistant housekeeper, Emma Winter, to turn into a romance, and then a marriage, and that eventually the two of them would produce the large family that little Bobby had once told the young maids who he pretended were his sisters, he would one day have. The late Grayson Wells, the eminent lawyer, would not have approved. Alexander Wells, the renowned Classics professor, definitely did not.

Christmas Bonus

Professor Alexander had not envisaged that Bob would resign from the university after two and a half years, join the army, train to fight in World War I, return an unused Doughboy, meet and marry an uneducated woman who not only was unable to read or understand Latin or Greek, but also regularly used such poor grammar that the Professor shuddered upon hearing her speak. But, indeed, Bob did.

Bob returned home after finishing his training at Camp Sherman, Ohio in time to partake of the Christmas celebrations. He had gained muscle, but lost the childish weight his lanky six-foot-two-inch body contained, and his father instructed the cook, Mrs. Pat, to make rich, nourishing foods to build up Bob's slender frame. Delicious desserts: walnut butter bread, caramel custard, ice box cakes, and the newly popular Jell-O pudding, were always available. Baked Virginia ham, roasted chicken, and all the appropriate side dishes were served regularly. While Prohibition was the new law of the land, alcohol was still available if the money was available, and money in the Wells household was available. A complete wine cellar was in the house, and the doctors hired by Professor Alexander to tend his son encouraged medicinal alcohol in the form of whiskey, and brandy, and hot toddies. The Christmas season provided plenty of opportunities to serve the foods and drinks, and to rejoice that Bob was home and safe.

While Bob had a somewhat spoiled youth, manners and civility had been drilled into him by his father and reinforced by the army. He may have been an overindulged young man when he left, but months of rugged training completed his education and changed his world view. He returned a muscular, angular man who was slightly despondent about the fact he was never able to use his training overseas. But he was grateful to be home.

A traditional Christmas celebration was planned for the entire staff who came dressed in their best and partook of the elaborate dinner where, after a brief speech by Professor Alexander, they would receive their generous bonuses. Mrs. Pendant, head housekeeper and manager, had worked diligently to create a proper menu of foods and drink, and with the head cook, Mrs. Pat, created a feast for the employees which included the second-best of everything. The chauffeur/mechanic, Harold; the gardener/ handy-man, Wilson; the sometimes maid Jane; the kitchen assistant, Mary; and Mrs. Pendant's new assistant, Emma, were invited into the formal dining room to sit, to eat, to imbibe, and to enjoy the evening with Professor Alexander and his son, Bob, as they were served by the specially hired and highly compensated temporary kitchen/wait staff.

These celebrations were instituted by Grayson Wells and his wife Sarah, continued after the marriage of Alexander and Marcella, and persisted as Alexander and his son, Bob, took their places at either ends of the finely hand-crafted, long and lovely oak dining room table, designed and wedding-gifted to Grayson and Sarah from her cabinet-maker father and brother. These holiday dinners were a chance for the staff and family to meet as equals, and enjoy each other's company in the sparkling, tastefully decorated formal dining room of the Wells house. Dinner was delicious and plentiful with the leftovers being split among the staff. Professor Alexander visited the wine cellar to gather half a dozen bottles of wine, and the traditional individual mince-tarts that Mrs. Pat made only during the Christmas season, and whose secret recipe she never divulged, completed the fine meal. Afterwards, Professor Alexander would stand and thank each member individually for their fine service as his son approached each person to shake hands and present them an envelope containing a cash bonus commensurate with their length of service.

On that dry, cold December evening, with seasonal good will in plenteous supply, and the remains of the mince tarts coagulating on the second-best china plates, Professor Alexander stood to make his usual speech filled with appreciations and good wishes for the assembled. Everyone settled comfortably to listen, and while all except Emma, had heard the speech before, they attended with anticipatory smiles on their faces.

"Welcome, and holiday greetings, and thank you all for your years of service. I am grateful and happy that we can share another year of accomplishments and joy. I am most gratified that my son, Robert, is safely at home with us and that the world is once again at peace. Allow me to honor the past year and welcome the new year. Please let us all raise our glasses to what the ancient Romans would claim: "Always towards the better" …*Semper ad Meliora!"* and the Professor led the entire congregation in the toast for the year. Each year's carefully chosen phrase would take the Professor a day or two of thought, and he prided himself on never repeating one.

As the glasses were lowered and the seats taken, Professor Alexander remained standing, placed his wine glass on the table, and cleared his throat. He began with Mrs. Pendant who had been hired originally by his father and mother and started as assistant housekeeper and eventually became the director of the staff and had continued to keep the household running smoothly, or as the Romans would say: *Quae est nonumy*. Then Mrs. Pat, whose cooking he enjoyed as a young man, who knew all the ways of his stomach, and whose delectable efforts were enjoyed by all. Wilson, the gardener, and general handy-man, kept the grounds and the house in tip-top shape, and grew the lovely winter camellias which he brought in from the greenhouse and which decorated the dining table. The chauffeur/mechanic, Harold, was ever ready with both automobiles which worked remarkably well even in the coldest of Indiana winters. And Mary, Mrs. Pat's assistant, and Jane, the serving maid, had both always been at the ready whenever their services were required. Bob was familiar with all these people and they knew him, and the warmest of handshakes were exchanged, with Mrs. Pendant and Mrs. Pat claiming their familiar seasonal hugs. The only staff member Bob did not know and had not formally met was Emma.

When Professor Alexander said, "And finally to our newest staff member, Miss Emma Winter, who has been with us over four months and has admiringly completed her tasks: Merry Christmas!" Emma pushed back her chair and stood up, her auburn hair curling along the sides of her dimpled face. Bob walked towards her carrying her bonus envelope, holding out his hand to shake hers, ready to verbalize "Merry Christmas" in the same way he had done for the previous six people.

But as the Latin phrase goes: *Amore tussisque non celantur* (*Love and a cough cannot be hidden*), and at the moment the two of them met, there was such a spark of obvious electricity connecting them, that it lit up the room, causing sparks to fly down upon the heads of all there, setting their hairs on fire and producing a reaction in each of them.

Mrs. Pendant pursed her lips, looking across the table at Mrs. Pat who slowly shook her head as the corners of her lips drew downward, while Harold looked sideways at Wilson as his left eyebrow hiked up to his forehead, and Wilson glanced sideways at Harold as his right eyebrow did the same, while Mary glanced at her folded hands in her lap, trying not to smile, and Jane's right hand came up to her face to hide her silent gasp, while Alexander Wells, Classics Professor, felt the heat from the flush that began at his forehead and worked its way down his face to his mouth where it created a scowl. The thunderous hush created resounded throughout the house, the neighborhood, the city, and far, far into the sky.

Neither Bob Wells nor Emma Winter noticed any of this. The moment Emma's hazel-flecked eyes engaged Bob's gray-blue ones, and Bob's hand enfolded Emma's in his, those few seconds expanded and stretched, reaching eons back into the past and lightyears ahead into the future, and surrounded them in such a cloud of wonder that for what seemed like decades and decades, they stood there, engulfed in the essence of unexpectedness, and the only humans, the only people, the only souls anywhere on the planet, were each other.

Wednesdays the Library Gets Tidied Up

The newest appliances and latest up-to-date technology helped streamline the tasks required of the employees in the Wells house who worked collectively, having bonded over the years. The staff, both full-time and part-time members, fulfilled their tasks professionally, and were moderately content with their renumerations. When the previous assistant housekeeper left to marry and move away, and Emma was hired, she knew that jealousy and resentfulness often polluted a staff. But she met with politeness and cordiality and was relieved to find herself accepted without too much animosity.

Emma was grateful for the camaraderie shown and enjoyed her work. She was busy from the time she arrived at 7:00 A.M. until she left around 6:00 P.M. She had Sunday and most Saturday afternoons off unless she was needed for service during dinner parties which occurred twice monthly. On those evenings when she helped Jane serve, and it became too late to walk home, she and Jane shared the bedroom next to the large room where Mrs. Pendant resided. For her work, Emma received the fair wage of $14.50 per week. She arose at 5:45 A.M., left her parent's house by 6:15, and walked to the Wells' house, arriving before her required time at seven in the morning.

Emma had specific duties. During her first two weeks, she referred constantly to the hand-written schedule Mrs. Pendant had provided for her. After those two weeks, she was familiar enough with the tasks to arrive daily, and once changed into her required uniform, begin her day. Her scheduled tasks included daily chores such as cleaning, dusting, and sweeping, and weekly tasks like washing, ironing, and mending, and a weekly deep cleaning of the Library. Monthly, Emma polished and washed the silver, china, and glassware, then deep cleaned the upholstery and rugs. And occasionally, as needed, she helped Jane serve at the Professor's dinners, assisted Mrs. Pat in the kitchen with food preparation, and did, as Mrs. Pendant said, "Anything and everything else that we need you to complete." The new assistant housekeeper was perpetually occupied.

Emma's favorite day was Wednesday. Professor Alexander began his teaching and lecturing early, and there were always meetings and usually dinners for him to attend, so he would generally not return home until late at night, and therefore, not use the Library. She completed her daily tasks in the morning, then took her time tidying, and cleaning, and dusting, and browsing in the extensive second floor room whose bookcases ran from the floor to the ceiling. She was not much of a reader and had little time to improve her sixth-grade skills in that area, but she loved the room with its elegant light, and gratifying aura, and assurance of knowledge.

For the almost five months Emma had worked at the Wells' house, she cherished her time alone in the Library. On Wednesdays, daily duties done, and lunch eaten, she would climb the sweeping staircase, lugging her cleaning supplies in a special basket, and pause at the balustrade to look down at the glittering entryway. She continued to the center door on the second floor, and opening it slowly, would stand and smile and take a deep breath knowing that the next few hours she could hold the books, many of them written in strange languages, and pretend to be able to understand and appreciate them.

It was the week between Christmas and New Year's Day, normally a time Professor Alexander would have no classes or meetings due to the University's winter break, but he had been invited to a colleague's home for a special meeting and dinner, and would not be working in his Library. Emma brushed back her curls, took her basket filled with supplies and said to Mrs. Pendant, "I am going to the Library now. Is there anything you need me to do before I begin?"

Mrs. Pendant shook her head at Emma who then walked up the stairway, stopping and looking down at the entryway, and then opened the Library door.

She looked around and saw that there was quite a bit of tidying to do since the Professor had spent most of the last few days working in this space. Emma began working by emptying the trash basket which overflowed with rejected ideas, and cleaning up the various teacups whose liquids apparently had sustained the Professor during his efforts. She piled the trash and cups close to the door where she would bring them downstairs with her after she concluded the cleaning. She began to wipe the tall casement window behind the desk. The weather outside was cold, but not snowy, so she cranked open the window to allow some fresh air to enter. The desktop was covered with papers and books, and if they were still on the desk, she knew not to disturb them, but pick them up, clean underneath, and place them back exactly where they had been.

Books needing replacement in the large bookcases were always on the small table to the left of the ornate desk. This Wednesday, there was a large pile since the Professor was currently creating a lecture about the Latin Love Elegy with a concentration on the poems of Ovid.

She picked up two of the books, searched out the empty spaces where they needed to be replaced, and moved the library ladder to the correct spot. She climbed the ladder, found the space for the first book, and slid it into position. As she held on to the ladder with her left hand, and the second book with her right, she heard a noise which so startled her that she dropped the book and grabbed onto the ladder with both hands. She turned her head and looked towards the sound. Standing inside the library door was Bob Wells who, upon entering, had kicked the trash and cups, causing the clatter. For a fragment of a second, the eons past and lightyears future visited the Library. Then Bob regained his ability to speak and apologized for startling Emma.

"I am sorry. I did not realize anyone was in here. I just came in to get a book."

Bob carried off the lie beautifully. He was aware that Emma was in the Library, and aware that his father was not, and aware that the rest of the household was busy with their chores, and aware that for the past week he had trouble getting the memory of those hazel flecks in Emma's eyes out of his mind. He walked over to the dropped book, picked it up, and read the title.

"Ah, Ovid's *Ars Amatoria*. This is quite some reading you are doing." Bob smiled as he handed it to Emma. "What do you think of it?"

Emma took the book and placed it in the correct space before she turned and looked directly at him. "I think we both of us know I ain't the reader here. I just put 'em back. Don't have any idea what they're about." And she carefully climbed down the ladder and stood and looked at Bob.

"Well," he said looking for the hazel flecks in her eyes, "that book gives advice to men."

"What about?"

"Women. And love. Perhaps my father is looking for another wife," and Bob hesitated think he might have gone too far with his teasing.

Emma looked at him for a longer time than he was comfortable with, and then, unexpectedly, she laughed so that the dimples in her cheeks jumped. Bob laughed with her.

"Sorry," said Emma stopping, "I don't mean to poke fun at your father; you just made me laugh. Is that truly what that book is about?"

"Actually, it is. And there are parts of it that are thought by some to be not quite decent. In fact, some people think that book is what got the author thrown out of his homeland by the Emperor. I am sure my father is just using it for reference. I know he is working on a lecture for next month. What other books are you putting back? Can I help you with them?"

"I can do this. It's my job. You have things to do, I'm sure," and Emma walked over to the pile of books still on the small table. She picked up two more and looked at the empty places in the book shelves.

"How do you know where these go? I mean, I know my father wants these placed in a specific order. Here, let me get those and hand them to you." Bob took the remaining books from the table and turned to face Emma.

"Well, when I first started workin' here, Mrs. Pendant would help me. She showed me how the different spines went along together and to look at the books before and after the spaces, and then I figured it out. Not so hard. Really, I can do this."

But Bob had taken the books and moved to the ladder, and Emma climbed up to the next spot, and the two of them worked together placing the books back, and talking about them, and about the weather, and about the new year, and about nothing, and everything. And when the task was completed, they stood for a while in silence and complete comfort. Their breathes echoed each other's, and the stillness in the Library was not unpleasant.

Finally, Bob asked, "What else do you need to do? I am here and don't mind at all helping you."

Emma glanced at the clock on the table and noted that her day was almost done.

"That's all I need to do here. Thanks. You didn't need to help. I just have to get the cleaning and trash and things downstairs. You gonna get that book you came in for?"

Bob looked puzzled for a minute until he remembered what he had told her.

"I can get it later. Let me help you with carrying everything. You can't get it all down the stairs by yourself. Come on, and tell me what you need to do."

Emma walked over to the opened window, and as she closed it, noticed that the street lamps were on, and there was a gentle snow beginning. She walked to the door and picked up her basket and said, "These things need to be taken to the kitchen, but I don't feel right about you doin' it. I can get it all."

Bob grinned, "No, you would drop some of those cups and then what would Mrs. Pendant say? I can get those and the trash."

He picked up the cups and trash and stowed them in the crook of his arm while he opened the door for Emma to go out before him, just as a gentleman would. As she passed, he caught a whiff of a sweet lemon smell. Perhaps it was the cleaning solution she had been using, but it would keep him up that night. That and the hazel flecks and the dimples.

Emma and Bob walked down the staircase carrying their items and continued talking about nothing much. They walked through the hallway into the back part of the house where Mrs. Pat and Mrs. Pendant were putting away some dishes. Both women stopped their chatting and looked first at Bob as he deposited the cups on the counter and the trash near the bin. Then they stared at Emma.

"Mr. Robert," said Mrs. Pendant," Is there something wrong? Why are you doing Emma's job?"

Bob looked at her and grinned. "Just helping out. She had a load to carry, and I was in the Library to get a book, so I helped. Don't fuss, Mrs. Pendant. I can carry a few things downstairs."

He turned to Emma and said, "Good-night. It was great talking to you." Then he left.

Emma nodded and said, "Good night," and then placed her basket of cleaning supplies in the closet. She turned to Mrs. Pendant and reported, "The Library is done. Is there anything else I should do?"

Mrs. Pendant glanced at Mrs. Pat who had stood by and said nothing, but the corners of her mouth were turned downward and her head was slowly moving back and forth.

"That's all, Emma. It is late and beginning to snow, so you need to start home. However, tomorrow I'd like to talk to you. Good night."

Emma was unsure if she had done something wrong but thought that since it was getting dark and snowy out, she would leave and face whatever the problem was tomorrow. She changed her uniform, and gathered her things. She put on her coat and boots, and wrapped her winter scarf around her head, and said her good-nights to the two women. Emma closed the door behind her, and as she walked home in the lightly falling snow, she felt a pleasing warmth despite the snow, and a glad smile played around her lips although she was unaware of it.

Once Emma left, Mrs. Pendant looked at Mrs. Pat and pursed her lips in the same fashion she had done on the night of the Christmas dinner when the electricity had lit up the room and a thunderous hush had resounded throughout the universe.

March 15, 1919

Dear Mr. Thomas J. Winter:

I am saddened to inform you of the death of your brother, Mr. George W. Winter. The Everstille Sheriff's Office surmised Mr. Winter went to the woods to hunt and met with an accident in the harshness of the snowy season. His body was discovered, and according to his wishes which were filed with this office, he is buried at North Cemetery in Everstille, Indiana.

Mr. George Winter filed a Last Will and Testament with this office and left you his sole heir. The cabin is on Smokehouse Road about a mile west of the main town of Everstille, located on two acres of land which he also owned. Over the years, Mr. Winter paid off the mortgage on the property, so the cabin, the property, and his automobile belong to you.

On a personal note, Mr. George Winter, while a quiet man, was friendly and when he came to town was kind and considerate to all. Deputy Edgar Samms and I recently went out to the cabin to check on it and to lock it up safely. We found that the cabin had been expanded. George had built on additional rooms and was in the process of adding an indoor bath- room. The cabin and the Studebaker which he owned are in good shape. We brought locks with us to ensure that the cabin and its contents remain safe. By separate post, you will receive keys to the cabin, the locks, and the Studebaker. I have a second set of all the keys in my office.

Additionally, George had a savings account which contained $127.88, and a check for that amount is enclosed. Cost of the locks were taken from this account. The receipts are enclosed.

If there is anything I can do for you, please let me know.

Sincerely,

Richard J. Granger

Sent by separate post: Keys to cabin and Studebaker

Copy of Will

Letter from Geo. Winter (sealed)

Ars Amatoria or *The Art of Love*

Book One (To Men): How to Find a Woman

"…and then there is Annette Jennings, a perfectly suitable young woman. Or the Crandalls have a daughter, Catherine, I believe her name is. Honestly, Robert, the MAID? She is lovely, but hardly suitable and not of our class, and I am insisting you *not* have anything more to do with her. Otherwise, I will instruct Mrs. Pendant to let her go. That may be the best thing to happen anyway since this is like something from an appalling Victorian romance novel!"

At this point, Professor Alexander took a seat in his fine leather chair and a sip of his fine French brandy from the fine crystal snifter recently washed and polished by Emma. The maid.

"Father, the class nonsense is just that. This is not the nineteenth century, and we are not ruled by Queen Victoria. Emma is not just lovely, she is fun to be around and interesting to talk with, and much more alive than Annette Jennings or Catherine or any of the other snobbish, pretentious daughters your friends have been trying to foist on me over the years. Just get to know her. I am certain you will agree with me. Anyway, we are just friends."

"Do you think I am unaware of what goes on in this house? Friends? I understand the two of you went out to a movie the other week. A MOVIE at a PICTURE PALACE. Can you be any more plebeian?"

Bob looked at his father and sat down in the other fine leather chair. This was the third discussion concerning Emma, and the language was escalating. He would not tell the Professor that he had to use all his focused skills to convince Emma to meet him at the picture palace, and that it would be acceptable for them to do something together just as friends, although he did not want to be just friends. But he was apprehensive about scaring Emma away, and it had taken quite a few Wednesday library discussions to persuade her. Bob reminded himself to return all the books he had pretended to need.

"Father, even if Emma and I were to …marry…we…"

"MARRY!" Professor Alexander exploded. "Now you have gone too far. That would never be allowed, or I would have to expel you from this house. There would be no help or assistance from me. I cannot believe you would do such a despicable thing. This is enough. She will be dismissed, and you are forbidden to see her! Do you understand?"

He could not help sounding as though he were quoting from a bad melodrama. His son had changed. Since his return home from the army, the two of them had continually argued. Robert did not want to continue his education at the University, would not attend dinners they were invited to, ignored the parties hosted by his father, and had adopted some strange political ideas. Professor Alexander was beginning to wonder if Robert's army time had corrupted him.

Bob rose from the chair, and stood over his father, and looked down at him. He was not angry, but sad. Bob knew something had changed in him, and he knew Emma was a part of that. He had never meant to mention the word *marry*. He had not realized he was thinking of it. But here it was.

"I am sure, Father, that you do not mean what you say. You are only upset, and there is not any reason for it. However, I have some savings, and will be twenty-one in a few months. Then I will have access to the money Mother left me. I do not want to upset you further, so this conversation is ended." He left the room.

But the Professor was not finished and yelled after him, "And how long do you expect that money to last? You need to come to your senses, Robert. This is ridiculous!"

He sat back in his fine leather chair and let out an oath…language he never used. He picked up the fine crystal glass and drained the brandy as he listened to his son's fading footsteps. The Professor placed the empty glass down on the side table and took some deep breaths and thought. He sat for a while feeling his heart thumping rapidly. Then he rang the bell for Mrs. Pendant.

Book Two (To Men): How to Keep a Woman

On Tuesday, when Mrs. Pendant dismissed Emma, she was not only kind, but generous. Emma left with a munificent letter of recommendation, the full week's pay, and a lead on another job at the Owens house on 16th Street. Emma was unsure of the reason for the dismissal because Mrs. Pendant assured her that her work was satisfactory, even excellent. The reason for it was something about a return of the previous assistant housekeeper, or the possible return of a woman who had been known to the Wells family, or something which Mrs. Pendant mumbled about, but Emma was sure it had to do with her friendship with Bob. The day after Bob had helped her carry things, she had been gently but sternly chastised by Mrs. Pendant. And then Mrs. Pat had a say-so about her actions. And Emma understood. But Bob seemed to find her wherever she was working, and he was so easy to talk to, and Emma enjoyed being with someone her age who was so friendly and handsome. And so obviously attracted to her.

Emma thanked Mrs. Pendant and walked around to find the other workers she had labored with for the past ten months to tell them good-bye, and wish them luck. She then walked over to the Owens household to discuss a job and meet with the head housekeeper. She would start the following day doing the same sort of work but for a dollar less. She went home for the remainder of the day, laid on her bed, and cried. When her parents, Thomas and Beatrice, came home from their jobs, she had dinner ready for them, and explained about her new job, and what had happened at the Wells, leaving out any mention of Bob and their friendship. She went to bed an hour earlier than usual wanting to be alert for her new job in the morning. She cried some more.

***

Bob waited until he was sure lunch was over, and Emma was at work in the Library, and then he pushed open the door to the second-floor room. The smile disappeared from his face when he saw that the books were being placed into their spots by Mrs. Pendant.

"Oh, hello Mrs. Pendant. I just wanted to get a book."

Once again Bob thought he needed to return the dozen books piled up in the corner of his room. He walked to one of the shelves and pulled out the first book. Mrs. Pendant finished wiping the casement window and left it open so that the spring air refreshed the room. She turned to him and spoke.

"Good afternoon, Mr. Robert. Isn't it a lovely day today? By the way, I believe Mrs. Pat is making your favorite sour cherry crumble today."

"Sounds great," and Bob began to walk to the door. He stopped and turned to the housekeeper and spoke, using what he hoped was a spur-of-the-moment, disinterested intonation.

"So, where is Emma today? I thought the Library cleaning was hers to do on Wednesdays. Is she doing something else?"

Both Mrs. Pendant and Bob knew what he was asking. In fact, Mrs. Pendant, who was fully aware of Bob's Wednesday visits with Emma, had decided that she would clean the room herself and not send either Jane or Mary to do it. She fully expected that Bob would visit and knew what she would be asked, so she had prepared her answer.

"No, Mr. Robert, Emma is not working elsewhere in the house. She is not working for your father anymore. Yesterday was her last day. I believe she has found work elsewhere," and she continued dusting the desk.

Mrs. Pendant had decided that a complete, succinct, specific, and truthful answer was the best one. She stopped dusting and looked over at Bob. She expected he would be surprised and ask several follow-up questions. But when she appraised Bob's face, it was blank, and his lips were in a perfectly straight line, and in a quieter voice than she expected, he said,

"So, he did it. Thank you, Mrs. Pendant. Please tell Mrs. Pat that I won't be home for dinner tonight," and Bob left the room closing the door quietly.

***

Emma had worked at the Owens' house for a week now. She tolerated it. The work was not difficult, but the head housekeeper and the other maids, and the cook, and the gardener, were not as friendly as the ones at the Wells' house. And today was Wednesday. The Owens' house did not have a Library. She missed the Wells' Library. She missed looking over the balustrade at the top of the staircase. She missed cleaning and opening the Library's casement window. She missed climbing the Library ladder and replacing the books. She missed the books and their soft leather bindings. She missed wondering what the strange language of the books said. She missed looking at the ornate desk and dusting the top of it. She missed Bob. She could not get in touch with him and was not sure she would have even if she could. He had not attempted to find her, so she supposed their friendship was over. She thought that it might have been more than a friendship, but it no longer mattered.

The days were getting longer and the sky was still light. Emma was finished working for the day. She was walking slowly home and was almost to her street. She crossed at the corner, and as she came closer, she noticed an automobile in front of her small house. She did not recognize it, and no one on their street could afford such a thing, so she thought it must belong to a neighbor's visitor.

As she came to her door, her mother opened it and said, "We have been waiting for you," and looked at her with wide eyes and an unusual contour to her lips.

"What is wrong? Is Papa sick? Should I go and try to find the doctor?'

"No, your Papa is fine. But there is company here for you."

As her mother moved aside so that Emma could enter, she nodded her head to the small kitchen area where, at the table with the teapot and cups in front of them, sat her father and Bob Wells.

When he saw her, Bob Wells stood up and come close to her. Examining the curls in her hair, and her eyes which held a look of astonishment, and the sweet lemon scent that he was sure was cleaning solution but would forever be connected with her, he took her hand and held it. Bob turned to Mr. and Mrs. Winter and said to them,

"Thank you for the tea and your time, and if you don't mind, your daughter and I will go for a brief walk," and turning to Emma, he said, "Please, we need to talk."

Emma placed her bag down on the closest chair and regarded her parents. They studied her. Bob held the door open for Emma, and the two of them went out and walked down the street. Bob had not let go of Emma's hand. She had not let go of his either.

"It took me a while to do what I needed to, and then I had to find where you live. I think I surprised your parents by showing up as I did, but they are understanding and kind, and your father and I talked. You never said anything about me to them, did you?"

"No. There was no reason to. What did you need to discuss with Papa?"

"I told him that I intended to ask you to marry me and asked his permission."

Emma stopped and turned to him. She stood so still for such a lengthy time that Bob began to worry. Then she smiled and nodded her head.

"And did he give it?"

"Well, he wanted to know about finances and living spaces and all the things fathers generally want to know about. Then he said that no matter what he said, you would have the final say-so, and I needed to get your answer. I guess I need to ask you the same question. I know we have only known each other for a few months, but I feel that I have known you forever. Will you marry me?"

They stood on the street, engulfed in the essence of unexpectedness, and the only humans, the only people, the only souls anywhere on the planet, were each other.

"Yes. Yes, I will," and Emma's dimples jumped.

Book Three (To Women): How to Please and Keep a Man

Bob had spent the week moving into a small furnished apartment he rented with the savings he had accrued. He bought a used car and moved his personal effects into the apartment, then looked for and found Emma's address. It took another day to get up the courage to visit her home and talk to her father. It also took courage to tell his own father what he intended to do. That went about the way he expected it to go which was badly. His savings would support them for a time while he searched for a job and waited until his twenty-first birthday at which time, he would come into a small monthly inheritance left him by his mother.

The wedding was simple. Bob and Emma were married by the Baptist minister at the church she and her parents attended. This was the first shock for Bob who grew up attending the Episcopal Church. The second shock occurred six months later.

Emma continued her job at the Owens house, not telling anyone there that she had married since married housekeepers were frowned upon and usually dismissed. But when she became so ill, she could not retain her morning tea and bread, she knew her working days were limited. She was delighted but scared. Living costs were more than either she or Bob had expected, and they were barely making it even though Bob had found a part-time tutoring job, and she was still working. Once Bob turned twenty-one which would be in about another month, there would be some additional money coming in, but then Emma would not be working much longer.

The evening she was positive that another seven months would bring a grandchild for her parents, she prepared a special dinner for her husband. When Bob came home from his long day, he saw that the table was set with special care and smelled a stew that very obviously had some meat in it.

"Oh, oh, have I forgotten a birthday? I thought yours was in January, and we have been married less than a year, so unless we are celebrating my birthday early, what is the occasion?"

Emma went over to him and reached up to hug him. She was unsure how he would take the news.

"Let's sit down and have some tea. I got something to tell you."

They went to the tiny table and two chairs they had found in a second-hand shop. (Perhaps *this* was the second surprise for Bob...he had not realized such places existed.) Emma brought over the teapot and cups her parents had given them for a wedding gift and poured tea for them. She sat down and looked at her husband. Over the past months, she realized that this man she had married was exactly the right one. She was happy in a way she had not known she could be, and was worried that introducing a new person into this relationship would be a problem.

"Well, soon you will get a new name."

"New name? Are we changing ours? What will I be called?" and Bob took a sip of the tea which was hot and sweet.

"How's about the name *Father* or do you prefer *Pa* or *Papa?*" and Emma looked into his eyes. She was not prepared for his reaction.

Bob sat stunned for a minute, and then he threw his head back and yelled. He got up from his chair, and pulled Emma up and into his arms, and twirled her around. He hugged her and kissed both cheeks where the dimples were.

"I guess you're happy?" Emma was relieved.

"Delighted more than you know. I have always wanted children, and I can't wait. This is wonderful news. I love you so much. I always wanted a *large* family. Are you up for that?"

"Well, maybe a few. Let's start with one," and Emma grinned.

"I hope it's a boy. I have the perfect name for him. How do you like *Lucius Ovid Wells* for a son? But a girl would be wonderful! We could call her *Valentina Celesta Wells*. Latinized names would be perfect!"

"We'll see," and Emma smiled.

Problem and Solution

Their first son was named *Vernon*, and when Emma named their second son *Leon*, Bob gave up his plan to give all his children Latinized names. He loved his sons. They rolled around like puppies, and he rolled with them whenever he had time. When Emma became pregnant for the third time, and her other children were only one and two years old, she cried. Money was limited even with Bob working two jobs and the monthly inheritance from his mother coming in regularly. Emma tried doing some piece work at home, but with the two babies and the cooking and cleaning and playing, she did not get much accomplished. She was worried.

"It will be fine," Bob reassured her, "I will look for additional students to tutor and maybe I can get up an hour earlier for the K-U job." Bob worked early in the morning as a *knocker-upper*. He knocked on people's windows to get them up in time to get to their jobs, usually at the factories. "I should be able to take on another ten streets or so. I'll check on it tomorrow."

"Bob, you don't get much sleep now. You'll end up gettin' sick, and when winter comes, it's more likely in the cold. I guess I can ask Mama and Papa for some help. Maybe I should. We are so cramped now, and with another baby, there's not even room for another small bed."

"No. Don't bother your parents. They have been too generous already, and they can't afford it any way. Just wait. I'll see if there is a bigger place for us. I'll look around in the next few days. What's for dinner? Potato soup again? You make the best soup, Em," and Bob kissed his wife and pushed her curls behind her ears.

Saturdays were Bob's busiest tutoring days, so Emma decided to visit her parents. She organized her babies, and all their paraphernalia, and on an early fall Saturday, she walked the eight streets to her parents. Her father was home, and her mother would be soon. After she put the boys down to play in the small parlor, she told her father to sit, and she would get the tea ready.

"How are things?" asked Thomas.

"Papa, they could be better, I guess. Bob is great with the boys and works hard, but we are so crowded in that small apartment, it just ain't easy."

Emma placed the teapot and some of her mother's freshly baked bread down on the table for them. She sat down to her tea when she heard her mother taking to the boys in the parlor.

"Well, look who came to visit! Come here, Lovies; give me a hug!"

The two babies toddled and crawled over to her, and she picked them up and sat them on her lap as she sat on the chair in the parlor. Beatrice smiled at her daughter, but her smile faded as she saw the circles under Emma's eyes and noticed the drawn look on her face.

"There now, the two of you play here while I check out your Ma," and the boys were put back on the floor as she went to the kitchen to join her husband and daughter. "Glad to see you. You looked a bit peaked, Emma; how is this one doing?" and she nodded to Emma's middle.

Emma stood to hug her mother and then, unexpectedly, burst into tears.

"Sorry Mama, I am just tired and worried."

Beatrice patted Emma's back and moved her back into the kitchen chair. She brushed her curls back much in the same way Bob had done a few nights ago and nodded knowingly.

"It's always hard in the beginning. The tears are at the ready," and she pulled out her handkerchief and gave it to Emma to wipe her eyes.

Emma sat back dabbing her face and looking at her children who were busy with some wooden blocks she had brought along. She sat back in the chair, took a sip of the tea, and sighed.

"Oh, this new baby is fine, and I'm not feelin' bad now, but I can't think where we will put him when he gets here. We are stuffed in that apartment and just can't get another because the cost is so high. Bob said he's looking for one, but the money ain't there. No gettin' blood from this turnip."

The three adults sat and sipped their tea, and Thomas reached for a piece of the cut bread. There was not much to say because they all knew it was true… money was tight, there were few places to move into with a growing family, and times were tough. Beatrice looked at her husband and raised her eyebrows in a silent language known only to them. The difficulties of Emma and Bob had been something they had discussed, and they were just waiting for the right time to make a suggestion to their daughter and son-in-law.

"Well," started Beatrice, "maybe we can do something about that."

"No, Mama, we are not askin' and will not be takin' money from you. You need to put aside what you can for your old age. I just came with the boys to get out of the house and spend some time with you because this is Bob's late night to work. We will get by."

"No, it's not money we would offer. Your Papa and me been talking about something that happened a few years ago. We just hung onto it partly because we didn't know what to do, and partly because we thought it might come in handy. Seems like it might."

Emma had picked up her cup to take a swallow, but she put it down and looked at her parents.

"What are you talkin' about?"

Thomas cleared his throat and said, "Now you know I had two brothers. Benjamin died long ago and is buried in Tennessee. And my older brother, George died a few years ago."

Emma nodded. "I never met him, but remember you talkin' about him. You never told me he died."

"It seems that George did good for himself. He never married and lived a ways in a cabin in a small-town north of here. Never been there, but a lawyer sends me a regular accounting of the place and the land. Guess the cabin has about four rooms and can have more added on. There's a garden space and some land, and there is a whole bunch of furniture and tools that he left. And a car there, I think. Your Mama and I just let it as it is because we're too old to move, but if you and Bob are willing to, we could help you out."

Emma leaned forward to her parents. Placing her elbows on the table, the three of them talked about the property, and the possible move, what would Bob say, what money would be needed, and how could Bob earn more. The group discussed and talked until the two boys playing in the parlor began to cry with their needs to be cleaned and fed. When Emma walked home late that afternoon, she felt better than she had in weeks.

She put Vernon and Leon to bed that night and waited for Bob. When he came in, tired and hungry, she greeted him at the door with a kiss and hugged him so long that he pushed her away, and looked at her and saw the hazel flecks in her eyes and the dimples dancing and was glad. He had missed them.

"Well, Miss Emma, you are in a great mood! What is the news you have? "

They walked into the small kitchen where Bob washed his hands at the sink and threw some water on his face. Emma dipped out the leftover potato soup she kept heated on the stove, and placed it in in front of him with some of the homemade bread her mother had sent with her. As Bob ate his dinner, she smiled at him. Then she tilted her head to one side and asked with a deep grin that showed off the dimples again:

"Have you ever heard of a town called *Everstille?*"

***

That is how the following spring, as Emma awaited the birth of their third child, she and Bob and their sons, Vernon and Leon, moved into the cabin in the woods that George Washington Winter had bought and developed with the money he had saved for years because he had been prudent and careful with his earnings, and had never found a woman who wanted to marry him, so there was no need to spend money on niceties and fripperies such as a woman would want.

Home Sweet Home

Thomas Winter, father, and Richard Granger, lawyer, kept up a lengthy correspondence until, finally, it was settled. The Everstille cabin and property was deeded over to both Emma and Robert Wells with the stipulation (written in the legal document fashioned by Mr. Granger who did not agree with it) that Emma be listed as co-owner of the property. Bob had no objection.

Emma and Bob worked and scrimped through the rest of that year and the winter. They schemed and saved, stored, and salvaged, and readied for the move in the spring which was more difficult than they had anticipated. They sold whatever they could, planned the journey, and when the day for their move came, they packed the car, leaving late one night in spring after the threat of constant snow was gone. They thought it would be easier for the boys to sleep as Bob drove because the trip would take about eight hours with stops for gasoline and oil and water for the car and the humans inside it. They planned to arrive in Everstille at Lawyer Granger's office very early in the morning. From there they would complete some paperwork, travel to the cabin, and clean one room where they would spend their first night.

But the boys woke up while being settled in the back seat, snuggled in with all the quilts and pillows and blankets, and did not go back to sleep. Eventually, Bob needed to pull over, and Emma got out of the front seat to reorganize items. Bob's Latin and Greek books and the packed foods and canned goods Beatrice had sent with them, were rearranged in the front while Emma moved to the back. Leon began to cry, and Vernon eventually joined him, and Emma did her best to comfort and persuade them that this uncomfortable ride would soon be over, and they were going to their new home, but she did so with tears in her eyes.

As the grayness of the morning came, the boys, exhausted from hours of weeping, fell asleep. Emma watched out the back and surveyed the passing towns and farms, and occasionally she would ask Bob a question just to keep him awake and alert. There was one time they thought the car was on fire, but Bob was able to correct the problem with some water a helpful farmer offered them, and they continued. They stopped at gas stations along the way to tend to the car and to allow themselves to stretch while the boys continued to sleep. After a few more hours, Emma, who was continually adjusting her bulging middle, was so uncomfortable that they stopped once again and moved the books and foods back to their original space, and Emma took her place in the front seat.

The entire trip took almost eleven hours.

They pulled into Everstille, located Mr. Granger's office which was across the street from a building whose large window boasted that it was the *Mitchell Emporium and Dry Goods,* and parked at the curb. Bob and Emma sat still, just breathing, too tired to talk. After a couple of minutes, Bob reached over and took Emma's hand and held it. She looked over at his gray-blue eyes and her dimples appeared. Bob took her hand and pressed it to his lips. "We're here, Em; we're home."

They got out of the car and stood and stretched, and the boys woke up in the back and whimpered until Bob reached in and pulled Vernon out to stand next to his mother and held Leon in his arms. As they turned to find the door to the Granger Law Office, Mr. Granger came out to greet them.

"Well," and Mr. Granger shook Bob's free hand, "I was wondering when you would arrive. Guess the trip took longer than you expected. How is everyone?"

"Thank you for meeting us. Yes, it was a long trip, and frankly, we are all hungry and tired. I know we have business to complete, but I think we could all use a few minutes to wash and clean up and get something to eat. Is there a place we could do that?" and Bob shifted Leon who stared at the strange man, then hid his head on his father's shoulder.

Richard Granger sized up the situation with his keen lawyer eyes. Standing before him was a woman who looked five or six months pregnant, and her husband who looked as though he had not slept in days, and two small children who were just on the verge of tearful collapse, and a car which was piled high and filled with their belongings, and was dirty and dusty, and the front tire looked almost flat. He deduced that they needed some rest. And probably food.

"Actually, my wife and I would like you to stay with us for a few days. I think the cabin will need some work before you can all settle down, and we have the room and would enjoy the company."

"Mr. Granger," replied Bob, saying words he did not mean, "that is terribly kind of you, but there is no way we could impose upon you and your family. We just need a bit of time to rest, and then we should get to the cabin," and at this time, Leon who had been close to crying, began to do so. Then Vernon joined in and pulled on Emma's hand to remind her that he was still there. Emma stood looking stunned, thinking that her swollen feet were now numb.

"Nonsense. My house is just a few streets from here and you can follow me in your car. Just give me a couple of minutes to get my keys and lock up, and we can go. Go on now, and get settled in your car. I'll be right out."

Mr. Granger smiled at Emma, and patted the crying Vernon's head, and hurried into his office to call his wife and tell her to expect company in about ten minutes and start rendering the back-guest room ready. And there would be an extra four people for lunch.

Emma and Martha Granger connected immediately. The Grangers had four grown children and a big batch of grandchildren and, as it happened, were well prepared to host the Wells for a few days. The few days turned into ten because the cabin needed a great amount of cleaning and fixing after the years of emptiness.

Mr. Granger introduced Bob and Emma to their closest neighbors, Ethel and Samuel Pinkerton were delighted that there would be someone living close to them. Samuel Pinkerton was newly retired and anxious to have something to do, and while Bob knew a few things about being a handy-man, he learned more from Samuel. In the week they worked together, they fashioned a mostly clean and livable cabin. A bit at a time, Bob unpacked his car and brought their belongings into the cabin. It would be at least another six months until things were sorted, and structured, and shaped.

Martha Granger took Emma and the boys for daily walks into town and introduced them to the various stores and the necessary people. One of the first things Martha did was to visit Emmanuel Evans, the town's doctor who was to become an important adjunct to the Wells family in future years. Doctor Evans, upon examining Emma, pronounced that she was in fine shape although obviously tired, and that he would be ready to assist at the birth of the third Wells child in three months or so.

Ten days later, with most of the cabin's dirt swept out, and the furniture cleaned, and water and electricity in working order, Emma and Bob and the boys thanked the Grangers and climbed into their car, and drove to the cabin west of Everstille where they would live, and over the years, entertain sorrows and joys and revelations.

Ten Hearts and Counting

During the depth of the Depression when Emma was 31, she had her eighth child, Rebecca, and Doctor Evans had a serious discussion with her. And then one with Bob. They both understood and agreed. Four years later, in early December, when Emma was 35, she found herself at Doctor Evans' office, tearfully hearing the pronouncement and asking the good doctor some pertinent questions. Doctor Evans closed the door to his office and spoke quietly.

"I do not generally practice the procedure, but there have been times I have agreed to do so. This is not generally known, so I am depending on your discretion, and on Bob's, should you both want this done. It is early enough that the procedure should be safe enough, and you will be back doing whatever you need to do quickly. However, you and Bob must discuss this, and both of you must agree, and Bob will need to bring you in, and take you home, and be prepared to watch after you for a while. If this is to be done, you must come in by no later than next week. The sooner, the better. Do you understand?"

Emma wiped her eyes and nodded her head. Even with the addition of two large rooms that Bob, with Samuel Pinkerton's help and guidance, had added on to the cabin, the family was pressed into the space, and another child would be problematical. The country was slowly recovering from the Depression, but families, many like the Wells, were barely making it. Even with Bob's periodic jobs, the monthly inheritance they had from his mother, and the large garden which produced much of their food, life was a challenge. Emma thanked Doctor Evans and went into the outer waiting room where the two youngest girls were sitting. She gathered them up, seated them in the old Studebaker she had learned to drive in case of emergencies, and headed back to the cabin.

Emma drove through the town, turning onto old Smokehouse Road which would lead home. She passed the large and sprawling Rivens' farm. Next was the Pinkerton's house, which now belonged to the Jaspers. Lights were shining, but no car was there, so John Jasper must be gone, traveling for his job. Emma missed the Pinkertons and thought of all the help Samuel and Ethel had given them when they first moved. Now, Samuel was resting at North Cemetery, and Ethel had moved with her son, Tobias, to Chicago to live with her daughters. From the back seat, Hattie complained that she was hungry, and Emma answered that they would be home shortly, and then they would all start dinner.

The six older children were at school, but the school bus would be dropping them off in another hour. Bob was due home in another day, and then they would sit down and talk. She honestly did not know what she wanted. Bob loved the children, and she did too, but with him gone much of the time working at part-time and temporary jobs whenever and wherever he could find them, she was left with the children, and the cooking, and cleaning, and organizing, and she was simply tired. They had been so careful the past four years, thinking she might be too old to have more babies, but apparently not as careful as they should have been. Emma maneuvered the car into the narrow lane that led to the cabin and was surprised to see that her husband's car was there. He was home early.

Hattie and Rebecca saw their father waving to them from the front porch and began to climb out of the car barely allowing Emma a chance to stop it.

"Daddy! Daddy's home!"

The two girls scrambled up the steps and into the arms of Bob who hugged, and kissed their small faces, and took them inside to the warmth where they tugged at him to see something of great importance in the girls' bedroom.

"Wait, wait, I want to see Mama first," and as Emma came in and closed the door to the December cold, Bob enfolded her in his arms while Hattie and Rebecca pulled on his trousers.

"Em, it is wonderful to be home again. A month away and you have no idea how I missed you and the children. Is everything O.K.? I came home and worried when I saw the car gone. Is someone hurt? Is there something wrong?"

"No, Bob. I just had a need to run into town for a bit, and we can talk about it later. I'm so glad you are home. We missed you. How was the job? You feel thin! You been skipping meals again to save money, right? You need to stop that and eat!"

Bob was thin. He did skip meals, and when the weather allowed it, he slept in his car to avoid spending money. It was difficult to find jobs, and he worked intensely and honestly when he did because he had a large family to support. The last night of each job, before he came home, Bob would splurge at the cheapest boarding house for one night so that he could use the bathing facilities. He did not want to be dirty and unkempt when he greeted his family, but Emma was not fooled. She loved him even more for his self-sacrifice and worried about him constantly.

Hattie and Rebecca were relentless in their tugging, so with an additional kiss for Emma and a laugh, Bob went with his girls. Emma went to the kitchen area to begin preparing supper, wishing she had some meat to add to the dinner to celebrate Bob's homecoming. She pulled out the vegetables and two of her largest pots to begin preparing the Kitchen Sink Casseroles which would contain everything she could think of. Luckily, she had baked some of the last of the season's apples that morning, and she readied a few more while the vegetables and beans were cooking. She was just finishing up when she heard the shouts and laughter of the rest of the children coming home from school.

"Mama, is Daddy here? His car is here!" and flinging off their coats and throwing down their books and papers, they began a search of the house.

Bob was coming from the back of the cabin holding Rebecca, and his children swarmed around him waiting for their individual hugs. Emma stood back and smiled. There was no doubt that her husband was happiest when surrounded by the family. His thinness disappeared into the fullness of his arms, and for the first time in weeks, her dimples showed.

After supper, the dishes were washed and put away. All ten hearts slowed to normal, and Emma and Bob and the children crowded into the front room where the fireplace was throwing out heat. Bob sat in the old, overstuffed, ratty chair holding Hattie and Rebecca on his lap. The rest of them gathered around him in their usual groups. Vernon, Leon, and Clyde lay close to the fireplace, looking at the flames and talking softly. Hazel and Beatrice were playing checkers while Ester looked on, and Emma sat, darning the hefty pile of holey socks.

"Daddy, tell us one of your stories. We didn't hear one in forever, and Mama says she don't know them like you do. Please?" Clyde looked up from his place, and they all looked expectantly at Bob. Bob read books and told stories to his brood most nights when he was home. *Aesop's Fables*, myths, legends, and histories of the Greeks and Romans entertained them. It appeared that Bob's classical education was not totally wasted.

"Have I told you about a king who thought he wanted gold more than he wanted anything else in the world? No? Alright, this is the story of King Midas and his daughter…" and he launched into the tale, and even the older boys who were beginning to think they were much too advanced for stories, stopped and listened, and were content that their entire family was together.

Emma worked at her darning and listened and watched and thought. There was no doubt that Bob loved being home. He was attentive, and patient, and kind to the children. He listened to their complaints and settled their arguments judiciously. He taught them whatever he knew about keeping a house repaired, and assisted in their schoolwork. *He is a better parent than me*, thought Emma, *but, of course, he is not with all of them every day.* She smiled ruefully.

Later, when they were all in bed for the night and the coverlets and quilts and blankets were protecting bodies from the December night, Bob and Emma hugged in their bed, and talked about the news from the town, and Bob's job, the possibility of him getting additional work after the holidays, and all the things they needed to catch up with after a month apart. Bob kissed the side of Emma's curling auburn hair, now with a few slivers of silver showing and asked, "Why did you go to town today?"

Emma hesitated and then sighed as she spoke. "I was at Doctor Evans. I'm pregnant."

She waited for Bob's reaction, waited to tell him the rest of the conversation, waited for a clue as to what they would decide. In the dark, lying against her husband's side, her arm thrown around his chest which she realized was thinner than the last time she had touched it, Emma felt her husband smile. His arms tightened around Emma, and she knew he was glad. She waited for his comment.

"I know you, Em, and you have already been thinking of names. So, tell me, what would you name this baby?"

Over the years, Bob had told enough stories about the ancients to both her and the children so that she understood and could name this moment. The Rubicon had been crossed.

"I thought that *Madeline* for a girl and *Jesse* for a boy would be nice. But, Bob, since this is absolutely the very last baby," and Emma emphasized the word *last*, "I thought that maybe this time, you should name him. Or her. Maybe one of them fancy Latin names you always wanted to give the others. I guess that after eight, it's your turn."

Bob hugged her and kissed the top of her head. He could not see her eyes in the dark, but knew the hazel flecks were there, and her weight in his arms was that of a mother and a child. He smiled again and conspiratorially whispered to her:

"Actually, I think that either *Madeline* or *Jesse* will do. They are fine names, Em, perfect names. Perfect."

Nine Pairs of Feet

Sheriff Samms and Deputy Jackson stood at the entrance of the Wells' kitchen with their hats in their hands as Emma Wells sat with Maddy on her lap while her twin brother, Jess, was asleep in the arms of Hattie. Vernon and Leon stood leaning against the counter in the back, arms crossed, and Clyde, Beatrice, Ester, and Hazel sat around the crowded kitchen. The Wells family was known to be somewhat untidy and sometimes contrary, but the Sheriff and the deputy overlooked the disorder of the house and continued with the questioning. Emma told Beatrice to turn off the cabbage soup which was cooking and which filled the air with a pungent aroma. Rebecca was missing.

"Mrs. Wells, please tell us once again about when you noticed that Rebecca was missing,"

"Sheriff, you have been here three times, and I told you three times. Rebecca has been gone for almost a week now. Six days ago, she was not at breakfast, and we been looking for her ever since. We didn't think much about it at first because she was at the Rivens' place once before and spent the night sleeping in the barn with them cats. We looked all over for her and thought she might be hiding and upset because I told her that she could not sneak anymore kittens into this house. I want to know who took my little girl and where she is. Esther, take Maddy outside. Go on out, the rest of you. Vernon, Leon, you stay here."

There was some shuffling and complaining and a few moans, but eventually the children scattered, slamming the screen door again, and then again. Faint mumbling and talking was heard as they distributed themselves throughout the yard.

"Yes, Mrs. Wells, I know we keep asking the same questions, but it is important to our investigation. There's been no information in this matter, and we have checked with your neighbors and questioned the Rivens, the Jaspers, and the Martins, but no one has seen Rebecca, and we have searched everywhere. The Riven's barn was searched thoroughly, and all the out buildings were too. We wish you had contacted us sooner than two days after she was missing. We might have been able to catch some luck before this."

"We just figured Rebecca was out maybe looking for them cats she always wants or maybe went for a long walk or was stayin' at somewhere else. Sheriff, I got ten kids and it's been real hard with them all.

Bob don't even know about this, and there's no way to contact him. He's near South Bend and must've found work because he ain't back yet, but should be in a few days. He's been gone almost three weeks."

"We will keep looking, Mrs. Wells, and keep asking everyone we can. You say she was wearing a flowered sundress? What color again?"

"Rebecca had on her blue-flowered dress and probably a red ribbon in her hair. I don't think she had shoes on it being summer and all. Vernon, Leon, can you think of anything else to tell the sheriff?"

Sheriff turned to look at the two lanky boys who appeared to be thinking, and they finally shook their heads. They weren't given to speaking much around strangers.

"Alright, Mrs. Wells, we will continue to look around and question everyone again. We should be back in a day or two, but if your husband gets back before then, have him get in touch with us. Also, let us know if you or your children remember anything else."

Sheriff Samms turned to Vernon and Leon and nodded to them. "Boys…" and Everstille's Police Department went out the front door and down the stairs to their Model A car which had *Everstille Police Department* painted on the side of the doors.

Emma sat for a couple of minutes and then looked at Vernon and Leon.

"Boys, I want you to go on out again and look around for Rebecca. You know her hiding places, and I just need you to look again. Don't argue. I know how many times you done this, but do it again. Just be safe and quiet, and be home for supper. Send the rest in to me."

Vernon and Leon had spent most of the last week searching for their sister. Everstille's citizenry had helped, but there were no clues and no luck. Vernon and Leon went out the back door and told their sisters and brothers to go on into the house where Emma kept them busy and under her control by giving them chores to complete and ignoring their complaints of repression.

The summer was ending early for many of the children in the town. Parents were unsure what had happened to Rebecca, but were not taking chances. The groups of children usually allowed to wander freely, and explore, and play until hunger or darkness drove them home, were stymied. They became tethered to their own back yards by the strident voices of their parents; they were allowed no summer leeway; they even entertained the thought that when schooldays came, there would be some form of independence. Terrible things seemed to be happening all over. The world was a scary place to live and horror had touched their small town.

***

Emma did not know what to do about the sorrow and misery she felt, but she knew less about how to deal with the anguish and pain Bob endured. He returned home, expecting a joyous homecoming. He had found a very lucrative although temporary job in South Bend and returned with more money than expected. Enough to live on for a while, pay off some of the bills owed to Clampet's Grocery Store and Banter's Drug Store and Pharmacy, and purchase new school shoes for those feet that had grown the most. He came home to only nine pairs of feet.

For months Bob searched everywhere. He walked through the town and the countryside. He drove over to the next county and stopped to talk to strangers. He parked his car by the side of the country roads and wandered through the meadows yelling Rebecca's name and frightening the cows. He harassed tramps and stray people he ran across, yelling at them, and accusing them until they feared him and left the town. He visited the neighbors and townspeople again and again, asking, inquiring, demanding anything they might know about Rebecca's disappearance. No one knew anything, although they understood the pain and anguish and sympathized with him.

Eventually, Sheriff Samms found the need to call on, and speak to Bob, and mandate that he end his inquiries. The Police Department would continue to look and search and question. They would not give up and had called on the Police Detectives in South Bend to look over their reports and papers, and if anything could be found, they would find it. Bob listened to the Sheriff and then broke down and sobbed as Emma shooed the nine pairs of feet off and tried to comfort him.

The months passed and the money Bob had brought back with him was almost gone. He needed to find work again. He took low paying jobs around Everstille, sometimes working for the Martins or the Rivens at their farms in exchange for foods and goods he could no longer afford to buy. He swallowed whatever pride remained and accepted the government's aid. He would not, could not be far from his family anymore. He counted his children's heads nightly and kissed them each time he saw them. He thought that if he had any gold, he would, like King Midas, give all of it up just to see his daughter once more. Just to tie the ribbon she wore onto the ends of her messy, lovely, childish, missing braids.

Rebecca

No old tramp man never killed me. No one found out who really did. I should feel mad about it because Mama and Daddy and my brothers and sisters carried on awful when I went missing. But I can't seem to feel much anymore. I just think about what it was like, and what happened, and what my family was like. Sometimes I think I could see them again for real if I knew where they were.

I can't remember it all. Sometimes I think real hard but can't. I think I don't want to.

Those Jasper boys was always teasing me 'cause I was almost their age. But they had a real nice cat that had kittens, and they said I could pick one, and I picked the small one that was black and white and its nose was white. But when I took it home, Mama said I couldn't keep it because there were too many living creatures in our house, so I kept it in the back building. I made it a nice bed, and it was fine for a few nights. Then one morning it was gone. I called and called for it, but I could only call *Kitty* because I hadn't named it yet. It just disappeared.

When I went back to the Jasper house and told those boys about the kitten, they said I could have another from their other cat. But it didn't have them yet, and I should just keep coming back to check. Maybe if I hadn't, I could still see my family. I could still play with Hattie. I could still hear Daddy's good stories.

I have four brothers and five sisters and me. That makes ten. One for each finger. I was number eight, and then Maddy and Jess came along and made nine and ten. And also Mama. And Daddy who was out earning a living and trying to raise money, so Hattie said. Hattie and me are real close. We share a bed and Hattie tells me some of Daddy's stories when she can remember them. She helps me put ribbons in my hair and shares cookies when we get some. Mama is nice, sometimes. She would hold me before Maddy and Jess came, but she said she was too tired to do that, and then I had to care for Maddy, and Hattie took Jess.

Those Jasper boys were Michael and Mitchell, but I never could tell who was who. They were twins like Maddy and Jess, but Maddy was a girl, and Jess was a boy. So, they was easy to tell apart. When I went to the Jasper place to play in their yard, Mrs. Jasper was nice to me and gave me sugar cookies. I was glad to get those because Mama never made any because sugar was too dear and vegetables from our garden was better for us, but they didn't taste as good.

Sometimes Hattie and me played with the Jasper boys. We would run into the back woods and hide in the short trees and the ditches. Once we found some bones, and we would hide them and play with them. We found a dead squirrel, and I was going to take it to Mama because she sometimes had squirrel meat in the vegetables, but the boys said it was spoiled so we just poked at it and left it. Later, me and Hattie went back to find it but it wasn't there. Funny how stuff just disappears.

That day I went to see if that cat had kittens yet, but the only one there was Mr. Jasper. He said *Hi, little girl, are you looking for my boys?* I said *Yes* and he said *My wife and them went to town to visit some family.* And I turned to go back, but he said *I been watching you play. You like to play in those back woods, don't you?* The boys' Pa seemed nice, and he said he might have some of them good sugar cookies, so I talked to him about the trees and the ditches and the squirrel. He seemed nice and smiled and then said *Do you want me to play with you since the boys ain't here? I know where there's some good stuff in the woods to play with.* And I thought it would be like playing with the boys only he could lift me up into the high trees, so I said *Sure.* I wanted to ask about those cookies, but then thought I should wait until we were finished playing.

So, we walked into the woods where the boys and me had never been. It was dark, and the trees were really high, and I was scared a little, but then being with a grown man, it seemed safer. Now and then, he would stop and pick up something to show me, and I would be polite and say something like *That sure is nice*, even though it wasn't much to see. I was polite because of the cookies. We walked to where the trees grew real close, and it was darker than before. Once he patted my head and said *You are a nice little thing,* and I smiled at him, but I don't think he could see me because it was so dark.

We came to a small stream, and he said *Don't try to jump it, I can pick you up and take you across,* so he did. But when we got across the stream, he didn't put me down. I said *Thanks but I can walk.* Then I am not sure what happened. I remember trying to get down, but I felt his hands pick me up again and he laughed. I thought, *I won't get the cookies*, and when I could remember, I was here, and I knew I was dead.

There is a sad feeling where I am, and I do not know where that is. If my kitten is dead maybe I could see it and have it with me. If I had named it, I could call it, but I only called it *Kitty.* It is bad that Mr. Jasper killed me. If I had that kitten and maybe some cookies it would be good.

If Hattie is looking for me, she can't see me. I don't know if I could see her anyway. She might have Jess with her. I wonder who is caring for Maddy now? Mama and Daddy might get another baby because now when I count on my fingers there are only nine used up, but maybe nine is enough for Mama.

What Was Lost, Now is Found

It was an early spring. Crocus and hyacinth peeked out over the bits of snow that had not yet melted, and children balked at wearing coats and hats. It was Saturday, and Mitchell's Emporium was having their monthly sale. Bob and Emma left the older children at home with assigned chores, climbed into Bob's car with the twins, Maddy and Jess, and drove into town to see if it was possible to find some reasonably-priced shoes for them. This would be their first pair of shoes that were not hand-me-downs, and the twins were excited.

Bob Wells had met with some luck lately. The Goodwin Construction and Building Company was clearing the land they had purchased, readying it for the Sears Model Homes bought and built by newcomers to the neighborhood. Bob was hired to work at chopping and removing the trees, and prying out the enormous rocks from the ground. The men working at this back-breaking task were genuinely earning their forty-eight cents an hour. Because the Goodwin Company was operating at the area close to the Wells' cabin, Bob could walk to work and eat lunch he brought from home and earn, at least for a while, an actual salary. Thus, he was able to purchase new shoes.

Almost four years had passed since Rebecca's disappearance. The Wells family, while settled into the present, still mourned the past. The hollowness that was fashioned in the family unit had not been plugged, and evening story-time was never the same, especially for the storyteller. Other changes added to the emptiness. At age eighteen, Vernon had joined the United States Army and, just recently, Leon had done the same. In the fall, the twins would begin school, and for the first time in many years there would not be a child or two or five running around the cabin. Beatrice, Clyde, Hazel and Ester were all in high school, and Hattie, having skipped a year because of her academic astuteness, would be there in the fall. Joshua Rivens was courting Beatrice, and there was talk of a wedding in the approaching future. But Rebecca's specter was always present, and the rip in Emma's and Bob's hearts had never mended.

The shopping trip was a success, and Maddy and Jess admired their new shoes all the way home. Jess wanted to wear his, and he kicked his legs back and forth to admire one and then the another. Maddy did not want hers on. She held them in her hands rubbing their softness, and bringing them to her nose to smell the novel newness. The story that evening was about the gods' messenger, Hermes, and his winged sandals, and Jess wanted to know if it were possible to return the new shoes for some winged sandals, but Maddy was thrilled with her new pair and wore them to bed that night.

The weekend was a quiet one. The twins wore their new shoes to Everstille's First Baptist Church's Sunday morning service, and the supper that night included some ground meat in the casserole. Everyone went to bed feeling content, and when Monday morning arrived, there was the usual rush to get ready and out the door to the school bus and, for Bob, to work.

***

Spring brought soft soil and pliable ground, and the men working for the Goodwin Company were glad because the large rocks that would be easier to pry out and move. The Goodwin Company workers were proceeding deeper into the wooded area where the trees grew tall and thin and thick, and canopied overhead, blocking out most of the light. It was not always possible to drive trucks or large equipment into the thickets, so two of the men were sent back into a remote region where they walked into the scant light and across a small stream, and entered a darker spot where they poked around and examined, and then, stopped. In a short while, they turned and sprinted back to the foreman, Don, and spoke quietly but animatedly to him. Then Don called the crew leader over, gave him the keys to his truck, and sent him to town to get the sheriff.

Sheriff Samms and his deputy, Ike Jackson, drove out to the woods to investigate. The Goodwin Company had stopped all the clearing, and the workers got an early and lengthy lunch break. Sheriff Samms and Deputy Jackson walked with the foreman to the remote region in question, and after discussing the situation, decided that work for that day would stop. Don announced to the gathered workers that they should go home, but he promised they would receive a full day's pay. No reason was given for this and the workers did not question it. A day off with pay was an extraordinary occurrence, and they welcomed it. Bob left the wooded area and walked home to the cabin where Emma was in the back hanging up washed clothes in the spring sun.

"You're home! Why? What's wrong?" Emma was astonished to see Bob.

"Not sure, Em. There is something going on, and the company shut down work for today, but with full pay, so all of us left. There was some talk about something found, and a few of the men joked it was buried treasure. Not likely. Anyway, I have the rest of the day off and can be here with you and the twins. Where are they? Let's go for a walk."

"Let me just finish this up and we will go. They're in the back bedroom. Go on in, and I'll be there in a bit."

She finished hanging the clothes, and Bob went in to find Maddy and Jess. Once they were ready, the four of them walked down their narrow path and out to the country road where they strolled, and talked, and laughed, and looked at the spring flowers poking up and the bugs crawling around. They went back to the cabin, and Emma made some cookies for an after-dinner treat while Bob pulled the twins onto his lap and told them the story of Persephone and the seasons.

Much, much later that night, after the shocking news, and after Sheriff Samms returned Bob to his home, he and Emma wondered to each other how such a joyful day could have ended so tragically.

After dinner and chores were completed, and the Wells children were finishing up schoolwork and getting ready for bed, there was a loud knock on the front door of the cabin. Beatrice was the closest to the door and opened it. Sheriff Samms was standing there.

"Good evening. Sorry to knock so late, but is your Daddy home? I need to see him."

Beatrice backed up, and asked him to come in, and went to find Bob. When he came to the front room, he looked at the man standing at the doorway and turned and told Beatrice to go and help her mother get the young ones ready for bed. He examined the Sheriff's expression.

"What's the problem?"

"Mr. Wells, I need you to come with me. There is something you might be able to help with, and I'll drive you home later. I know you have questions, but I would rather not talk about this in your home. We can talk in the car on the way to town. Please let your wife know that you will return in a couple of hours."

Bob stood silent for a few seconds, and then he went to Emma who came back with him to the door. She looked at the Sheriff, and then back at her husband, and nodded her head. Bob touched her cheek and then grabbed his hat as the men went out the door.

The two men got into the car and closed the doors. Sheriff Samms started Everstille's only police car, backed out of the narrow lane, and began the journey into town. As he drove the country road, he disclosed to Bob what it was which had been discovered in the tightly wooded area in the back woods where the Goodwin Company was clearing the land for the Sears Model Homes bought and built by newcomers to the neighborhood.

Hattie

That Friday morning, I put my hair in one long braid and pulled it over my shoulder to tie on the red ribbon I had found in Mama's sewing basket. Rebecca loved red, and she loved to have a ribbon in her hair even though they often fell out because her hair was so fly-away. I miss my sister more than the others do, I think, although we all cried for weeks after she could not be found, and we cried for days after she was. During that week, Mama was sick in bed, and Beatrice, Clyde, and Hazel acted really grown up and took over the chores of cooking, and cleaning, and laundry. Ester and I cared for Maddy and Jess who just wanted to be with Mama, but she said she couldn't see them. Of course, the twins didn't remember Rebecca. They were too young. Daddy said we could stay home from school that week, but would go back to trying to live a normal life after the Friday funeral. He was so sad.

We weren't told what happened except that Rebecca's body was found, and she would be buried in the North Cemetery after a church funeral. None of us ever went to a funeral. Even when Mama's daddy died a while ago, only Mama went to the town in southern Indiana where he was buried. That was a sad time too, although we never really knew our grandparents and never visited them. I guess they had come here to our cabin once a long time ago, but I wasn't born yet, so of course, I don't remember. And now that Mama's mother is living near Chicago with Aunt Kate (we never met her), I don't guess we will see her either. We know that Daddy's mother died when he was little, and his father is around, but when we ask him about his daddy, he just says, *That's ancient history, not worth telling*, so we don't know anything about him. I guess it's good that we have so many brothers and sisters because we sure don't have any other relatives.

***

The service was at the Everstille Methodist Episcopal Church and not our own First Baptist Church because our church is so much smaller, and Daddy said there would be so many *gawkers* there. I had to look up that word and it means: *someone who stares at something but tries to hide the fact*. When I asked Daddy why he said *gawkers*, he just said that perhaps he should not have, and that most people were kind, and he told me not to repeat it. I won't.

That church was really pretty, and there were quite a few people there, and they would not have all fit into the Baptist church, so I guess it was a good thing to have the funeral where it was. Rebecca was in the casket in the front, and there were some real pretty flowers on the top. The men that Daddy worked with bought them for her. Too bad she could not see them. Too bad we could not see Rebecca.

After we knew Rebecca had been found, Ester asked Mama and Daddy if we could see her and tell her good-bye. Mama just put her hand to her mouth and ran into the bedroom and closed the door, and Daddy had a sick look on his face. He said, it would be best just to remember her as she was: laughing, and funny, and loving all those cats. Then he went into the room with Mama. Beatrice and Clyde and Hazel just looked at each other, and then Beatrice said, we should get our chores done. I didn't even argue, and we all just did what she said.

Mr. Jamison came out to the cabin on that Friday to pick us up in a big car, and we went to the funeral. Our whole family fit in his car. Mama sat next to Mr. Jamison, and then Daddy, and Maddy and Jess were on their laps. The rest of us got in the back seat, and we were scrunched together, and I had to sit partly on Beatrice's lap, but the ride was slow, and I liked being in the car. We don't get in a car often except when we all go the church on Sunday, and Daddy's car can't fit us all, so when he can get Mama's old one started, we take turns going to church in both of them.

After the church funeral, Rebecca was put on a wagon that two black horses pulled. The ride out to the cemetery was slow, and there were a bunch of cars following us. I saw the Jasper boys and their mother, and she was crying, and there were a few others I knew from our church, and some from the town. But there were some people I did not recognize, and they still all came out to the service with us. The *grave-side burial service* (that's what it was called) was short. There was a poem that I think Daddy asked our minister, Reverend Edwards to read and it was:

> I fall asleep in the full and certain hope
> That my slumber shall not be broken;
> And that though I be all-forgetting,
> Yet shall I not be forgotten,
> But continue that life in the thoughts and deeds
> of those I loved.

Afterwards, I asked Daddy what that poem was and he showed me the book it was in written by someone called Samuel Butler. Then there were some Bible verses, and the one I know is Mama's favorite,

Psalm 23, was said, and then Reverend Edwards said a really long prayer. That was all. What took the longest was when all the people came to say *I'm sorry* and *You have my condolences* to Mama and Daddy, even the people I did not know…those were the gawkers, I guess. Maybe I shouldn't call them that.

Mr. Jamison took us home afterwards. Daddy told us to go into the cabin, and let Mama rest, and we should get a lunch started. He and Mr. Jamison talked a while on the front porch, and when Mr. Jamison left, Daddy stayed out on the porch for a long time. Once when Clyde went out to ask him if he wanted lunch, he came back and said Daddy was just sitting there and crying, but not loud, and just the tears were coming down his face. This made us all feel bad, and then we did not want to eat except Maddy and Jess did. In the afternoon, we just sat and read or played some checkers. When it was almost time for supper, Mama came out, and she seemed like herself again. She said to get out one of the casseroles that neighbors had dropped off, and we would have that for supper. Then she went out to see Daddy.

No one talked much that night, and we didn't ask Daddy for any story. We all went to bed early, and then the next day Mama said we all needed to become a living family again, and Daddy told us that Rebecca would be with us forever in our hearts and our thoughts and our deeds. No one went to church that Sunday, and Monday we all went back to school, and Daddy went to work.

Since then we have become almost like we used to be, and Daddy is telling us stories again but not very often. He helps with our schoolwork if we need him to. I heard him tell Mama that the Goodwin Company gave him some partial pay for the days he didn't work, and that they were a noble and virtuous company. He was not sent to work in the wooded area, but was doing things someplace else, and he said he was grateful for that kindness. I am not sure what he meant, but I am pretty sure if Daddy said the Goodwin Company was *noble and virtuous*, he would not name them *gawkers*, so I won't either.

Saturday Night

"Mama, we can't find the checkers set. Know where it is?"

Hattie and Ester were prepared to continue their week-long championship games with the loser making the winner's bed for the following week. They were tied, and tonight would decide the winner.

"Clyde and Hazel were playing with the set this afternoon, so ask them, but I don't want to hear any fighting about this."

Emma finished drying Maddy's hair and then began to comb through it, and cautioned her, yet again, to stay still while she worked at the tangles. This job was usually Beatrice's who had begged off because Joshua Rivens picked her up in his family's old truck, and they were going to get an ice cream soda at Banter's Drug and Pharmacy. Beatrice was gentler than Emma, and the tangles came out easier. At least that is what Maddy complained to her mother about.

It was Saturday night. Weekly chores done, the family was ready to sit in the front room of the cabin by the fire that Bob was busy starting, and play games, and read, and perhaps, listen to a story. Emma would bring in apples if available, or sometimes corn would be popped, and she would darn the socks, and pants, and shirts that were always waiting in her sewing pile.

In summer, they would go out to the front porch and try to stay cool, and talk, and play until the darkness and mosquitos drove them in. These were times Bob treasured, and he yearned for all the children to be together again. Vernon and Leon were in Europe with the army. Beatrice was out with her beau. Rebecca was in North Cemetery.

Emma finished combing and braiding Maddy's hair and then went to check on Clyde who was making sure Jess was bathed. He was, although he was no more patient with that process than his sister had been with hers. It was late spring, and the weather was still cool enough to have a fire, but since there were no more apples available, Emma got out the bowls and makings for the popcorn. She called for some help to carry in the necessary equipment, and Hazel and Ester came to the kitchen. Once everyone settled and the fire was going, she asked Clyde to pop the corn while Maddy and Jess waited nearby with the bowls.

"Be careful, you two," Emma warned the twins, "back up some and let Clyde handle that pot. You're too close to him." The twins backed up one step.

Hattie and Ester were placing the checkers on the board, and Hazel was watching. As soon as they finished determining the winner, Clyde and Hazel were going to play a set of three games with the loser having to help Jess bathe the following week. The stakes were high.

Emma darned, and Bob had before him volume three of Gibbons' history of the Roman Empire. He had been working his way through the six-volume set which he brought from Bloomington years ago. He never had much time to read, and it was a slow, laborious task because he spent much of the time answering questions and holding Maddy and Jess in his lap as they shared their popcorn with him. They were more entertaining than Rome's fall anyway.

Bob watched the group eat, and play, and talk. Tonight, they engaged in a favorite wishing game called: *If I had money, I would get...*, and the object of the game was self-explanatory in its title.

"Well," began Clyde, double jumping Hazel's checkers, and placing her in the precarious position of losing the second game, "I would get a farm. I know I'd be good at it."

He would be. Clyde had a proclivity for growing things. In the past few years, he had taken charge of organizing, planting, and harvesting the crops grown in their back-lot truck patch, and found delight in the work. He had started with the usual vegetables harvested in the summer and fall, and then worked on growing some winter crops like cabbage and kale, and then added a few flowers for the prettiness. He tried some strawberry plants and was thinking about blueberries this year. The strawberry plants did not do well, but Clyde had made a trip over to the Martin farm to talk to Richard Martin about what he had done and how to correct it. He was certain the plants would grow this coming summer, and he was anxious to try.

"You always say the same thing, Clyde," Ester alleged, "Why don't you change it?"

"I don't want to," and Clyde decided to stop talking because Hazel's kings were closing in on what he thought was a certain win.

"I still want a horse," declared Hazel.

She took the game that Clyde thought he had won, and he sighed. They were tied. At this point, Jesse climbed down from his father's lap and walked over to the board which was being set up for the deciding game. He was interested in the outcome. Hazel had assisted in his bath before, and she was serious about getting the job done in record time. If she won, there would be little splashing allowed, and he knew his ears would take the rough scrubbing that Clyde just didn't care about. The stakes were indeed high.

"If Clyde got his farm, then you could have a horse there, and you could live on the farm with him," pronounced Jess as he wondered if this could possibly happen before his next bath.

"That would work out," and Hazel smiled at Clyde as she took another of his checkers, and Jess, sitting himself down next to the board, anxiously hoped she would win.

"I would like to have a radio," and now Ester spoke, "and I would share it on Saturday nights and let everyone listen to it."

Emma smiled at her as she finished up a sock, "That would be a kind thing to do, Ester."

Ester nodded, "But the rest of the time, it would be only mine."

So much for benevolence.

The family laughed, and Hazel called her sister *selfish* and then got back to her game which now looked like it would belong to Clyde. Jess swallowed hard.

"Mama, what would you want?"

Hattie, having lost to Ester and facing a week of making two beds, was sitting quietly munching popcorn. She looked at her mother.

Emma sighed. *So much*, she thought to herself. Out loud she said, "I know we can only name one thing, and I can't decide. That old stove is about to give out, and a washing machine would sure be helpful, but a real nice thing to have, especially since them lines are out here, would be a telephone. And I guess that would be my choice."

Maddy clapped her hands and said, "I will give you my wish, Mama. And then you could get the telephone and maybe the stove too."

Her father kissed the side of her head and said, "That's sweet, Maddy, but you get a turn too. What would you like?"

"Another pair of shoes that I would only wear on Sundays. They would be pink or maybe purple." Her favorite colors.

"Pink shoes! Or purple! That is weird. I bet they don't even make them like that!"

Jess spoke as he looked up from his surveillance and added, "Well, I would like a new bicycle. One of my very own. One that no one ever owned but me. And it would work all the time." He went back to watching his future play out on the board in front of him.

"I think pink or purple shoes would be beautiful, Maddy, and I am sure you could find some in a big city at a big store," Hattie smiled at her sister. "What I want is to be a nurse, but I don't think money will buy that, could it, Daddy?"

Bob looked at Hattie. "That's a great thought, Hattie. I guess if there was some money for education at a nursing school, that's how money would help. But there would be quite a bit of work on your part."

"I could do that, and I didn't know about the education part. So, Daddy, everyone has answered except you. What would you want?"

At this point, the checker game finally done, Clyde gave a groan, Hazel a yelp of joy, and Jess stood up and yelled, "Yeah! Hazel won!" and rubbed his ears which would have a week's reprieve.

Then he echoed Hattie, "Yeah, Daddy, what would you want?"

Bob looked around at his family. He wanted to give Emma her stove and washing machine and telephone. He wanted Vernon and Leon home and safe. He wanted to give Beatrice the beautiful wedding dress they could not afford. He wanted to grant all the wishes of his children and get a pair of pink shoes for Maddy. He wanted Rebecca back with the family, and the least he wanted was a lovely headstone to place at her grave. One that said:

Rebecca Wells

Beloved Daughter and Sister

Securus Dormies

Bob looked around at the group and over at his wife, busy darning. He took a deep breath, swallowed the lump in his throat, and smiled.

"Well, I'm not so sure we need money for it, but I think I could use a bit more popcorn, and maybe a story?"

The six children who were there agreed that this was a wish that could be granted.

JACOB L. HILLSTOCK

423 Pennsylvania Street   Bloomington, Indiana

September 15, 1945

Dear Mr. Robert Wells:

I am the lawyer for the estate of the late Mr. (Professor) Alexander G. Wells who died February 30, 1945. The late Mr. Wells had directed me to contact his only son six months after his death.

The purpose of this letter is to inform you of the Last Will and Testament of your father and to advise you of your inheritance.

Mr. Wells wanted his assets liquidated and sold, and the resulting money, less debts, taxes, and my fees, divided into three equal parts. One third is to go to Indiana University Classical Department, another third to be divided amongst the servants and staff who were with him through the years, and the final third to his son.

The amount of your inheritance is $18,086.19

It would behoove you to retain the services of a lawyer who should get in touch with my office at the above address, and we can work out the transfer of the money into your bank account.

Please accept my condolences on the loss of your father. We were rather close during the past decade, and he wanted me to assure you that whatever the issues that divided you, he never lost his affection for you. He also wanted me to tell you that while he never answered the yearly letters you sent, he kept them all. They are included in the packet that accompanies this letter. He also wanted the enclosed book sent to you.

I look forward to hearing from your attorney in the very near future.

Sincerely,

Jacob L. Hillstock

Enclosures: Death Certificate for Alexander Grayson Wells

                     Packet of letters

                     Book: Ovid's *Ars Amatoria or The Art of Love*

Trips

Trip to Town #1

"...and then sign here and initial there."

Jason Wicks pointed to the places Bob Wells needed to sign and initial. Bob did so and sat back while Jason Wicks, son of George Wicks, partner of the Granger and Wicks Law Firm, examined and reread some of the documents in his hands. Jason Wicks had taken over most of the work from his father who was semi-retired and all the work from Richard Granger, founder of the firm, who was fully retired. The young Mr. Wicks was the up-and-coming, full-time lawyer in the town of Everstille. He was the only full-time lawyer in the town of Everstille.

"Well, Mr. Wells, congratulations. You are now officially a rich man. Do you have plans for your inheritance? I could advise you in some things if you want me to, so think about it, and let me know. Do you have a bank account set up for the money transfer?"

"No, up until now, there was no money to place into a bank," and Bob smiled ruefully at the lawyer. "I'll go to the bank after we are finished here and open one."

"Let me call Howard Jones, the bank's manager. I'll explain the situation, and he can get the process started. Excuse me for a minute," and Mr. Wicks got up from his desk and went into the outer office to telephone from there.

Bob got up, stretched, walked over to the window, and looked out onto Main Street. Across the street was Mitchell's Emporium and next to it was Peterson's Bakery. He wondered what their bakery goods tasted like. The few sweets he and the family had eaten had come from their own kitchen. *Next trip*, he thought, *I am going to stop and get some treats for the family. Won't they be surprised?*

Bob turned as Jason Wicks came back to his office and motioned him to have a seat.

"I spoke with Howard Jones and explained the situation. He said to tell you that he will get the paperwork started, and when you get there, the process will only take about half an hour or so. When you finish, he can call me and give me the account information. That way I can immediately contact Jacob Hillstock's office and get the transfer under way.

Will that be acceptable?"

Bob said, "Yes. That will be fine. When will this be done and the money be available? Honestly, there are some debts I would like to take care of."

"I believe it will only take five days or so. Why don't you stop back in a week from today? We can tie up any loose ends. Perhaps you would like to bring Mrs. Wells with you also. You mentioned that you want her to know about the legal side of all this. We can clear up any questions you think of between now and then."

"That's fine, Mr. Wicks. Thank you for all your help. I can't pay you right now, but I hope you know that I will have the money soon."

Jason Wicks looked directly at Bob Wells to see if he was serious. When he saw the playful smile, he also grinned. "As the newly richest man in this town, Mr. Wells, I am sure you will be able to pay my fees."

Bob Wells held out his hand to shake his lawyer's. "Thank you for your assistance. I'll go to the bank and see Mr. Jones. And, Mr. Wicks...I am asking that this news be kept between us, for reasons I am sure you understand."

"Of course. Lawyer and client privilege and all...and Mr. Wells, please accept my condolences on the death of your father."

Bob nodded, stood, picked up his well-worn hat, and walked down the stairs to the outside of the building. He looked up at the sky and then down to the corner where, at the Everstille Bank, Howard Jones was waiting for him. Before he walked there, he glanced over at the Emporium and made a decision. He walked across the street and into the building, and in a little while, came out holding a large wrapped package. He placed it in the back seat of his parked car and went to the bank where he was greeted by Mr. Jones and ushered into his office to complete the process of being the town's richest man.

Thirty minutes later, Bob was driving down the country road towards his home. He turned into his lane and parked the car. Reaching into the back seat, he took out the package and walked through the front door. The children were at work or school, and he placed the package down on the kitchen table and went to find Emma. She was finishing hanging up some wash, and as she walked into the house holding the clothes basket, she was surprised to see her husband.

"Bob, you are not at work? Is the job finished? Are you sick? Why are you home in the middle of the day?"

Bob took the basket from her and placed it on the floor. He led her to the kitchen where he nodded towards the package on the table.

"What is that?"

"Open it up, Em."

Emma tore off the wrapping and gasped as she looked at the brand-new wooden Philco table radio.

"Bob, have you lost your mind? We can't afford this!"

Emma put her hands on her hips and shook her head. When Bob laughed and leaned over to kiss her cheek, she was further shocked.

"Sit down, Em. I have something to tell you."

Trip to Town #2…One Week Later

"…so, because the twins are sick, Emma was not able to come today. I will bring her in just as soon as we can and have you explain it all to her. I hope you won't mind repeating what you just told me."

"That will work, Bob. Are there additional questions?"

"I think that is all. Again, thank you for your time, Jason. As I said, there are some debts I need to take care of. I intend to go to the telephone company and get a telephone installed as soon as they can manage it, so when I have a telephone number, I'll call your office and let you know what it is."

"That's great, Bob. Are you and the family looking for a newer place to live? My sister could help with that."

"No, we are happy where we are and will stay in the cabin. There are going to be some changes and updates, but the place is solid, and sound, and large enough for our use."

"Alright, Bob. Call with your new telephone number when you get it, and again, anything else I can help you with, let me know."

The men stood and shook hands and Bob walked down the stairs and out of the building. He looked across the street at the bakery and reminded himself to stop in after his tasks were complete. Walking across Main Street and down to the corner, he pushed open the door of Banter's Drug Store and Pharmacy. He walked to the back where he saw Jim Banter and walked up to him.

"Good morning, Jim."

Jim turned around and when he saw Bob said, "Bob, good morning. How are you? What can I do to help? Are one of the kids sick? Is there something Emma needs?"

"No, Jim, the twins have a cold, but that is all it is. I came in for another purpose. I want to thank you for all the credit you have extended to me over the years. I am in a position to pay off my account and, if you would look up and check what I owe you, I could do that now."

Jim was stunned. This had never happened before. Most of the townspeople owned him money, and he just figured that he would collect a bit at a time but probably never get it all. He stood still for a moment and then said, "Sure, let me get the books in the back. I'll return in a bit."

Bob nodded and walked around looking at the odds and ends on the shelves. When Jim returned, he walked back to the counter and looked expectantly at him. Jim cleared his throat.

"Well, Bob, there is quite a bit on your account. Are you sure you can pay it all now? You could give me part of it and maybe more later. Things are still rough, and we are all feeling the war's effects yet."

Bob nodded and said, "What do I owe you, Jim? I can pay it now."

Jim handed him a list of the medicines, and drugs, and tablets, and paraphernalia that the Wells family had needed over the years. The bill came to $18.75. Bob reached into his pocket and pulled out two ten-dollar bills. Jim's eyes got wide, but he did not say anything and just made change for Bob and gave it to him. He marked the bill *Paid in Full* and gave a copy to Bob.

"Thank you, Bob. I appreciate your business, and I hope the twins get well soon."

"I am sure they will, Jim. I need to get going, but again, thank you too," and Bob turned to walk out of the store.

Jim watched him go. He shook his head and murmured, "Well, yessirreebob, yessirreebob!"

Bob turned to his left and walked to end of the street. He crossed over and entered Clampet's Grocery and Meat Market and replayed the same scene with Mr. Clampet. This bill was a little higher. It came to $20.35, and when he left, thanking Mr. Clampet in the same way he had thanked Jim Banter, Mr. Clampet stood shaking his head and said, "Well, I'll be…"

As he walked back towards Peterson's Bakery, Bob felt a weight-lessness in his body and grinned at the sensation. A delicious smell greeted him as he neared the door and watched the clerk put up a sign in the window that read:

Special Today: Sugar Cookies while they last!

Bob smiled at the sign, and went into the bakery, and bought all the sugar cookies that were available. He left and crossed the street to his parked car as the clerk took down the sign.

He placed the box of sugared treats on the front seat, got into the car and sat quietly for a few minutes. He had one more mission. Bob drove down two streets, turned right, and went down to the end of the second street. He sat in the car for five minutes allowing the aroma from the cookies to fill the nostrils and waiting for his heart to beat normally. Then he got out of the car, walked to the front door of Jamison's Livery Stable and Funeral Home Services and went in.

Trip to Town #3…still another week later

"Come on, Em, we have things to do today."

Bob walked his wife to the old car and opened her door. He turned and leaned over and kissed her cheek. Then he walked around to his side, got in and started the car.

"Bob, you have sure been happy lately. I know we are better off than we were, but there is still something you ain't told me, like where we are going today."

"To town, Em, to town. I told you that Jason Wicks needs to talk to you about the legal things involved with the inheritance. So, that will be our first stop."

"The first one? So, there are more? We could use some groceries from Clampet's, so if there is time, could we stop there?"

"Absolutely, Em. But that will be the last stop."

"So where are we going between the lawyer's and Clampet's? Come on, Bob. You been as tight-mouthed as a clam."

Bob continued driving down Smokehouse Road into town as he spoke, "Think back to a while ago, Em. Remember when we last played the *I Wish* game with the kids? Do you remember what you wished for?"

Emma sat and stared into the distance. She had wished for several things that night, but had she said them out loud? After thinking quietly for a bit, she answered.

"I wanted a telephone for one. Then that stove is about on its last legs, and it still is, and a washing machine would be great." She sat for another minute and then turned to Bob.

"Are you telling me that we are going to get one of those things?"

Bob grinned. "No, Em. Not one…all of them."

Emma looked at him with disbelief on her face. "Bob, how much money did you get? What ain't you sayin'? What don't I know?"

"Em, when we get there, Jason Wicks is going to review it all with us. Once he's done, we will go to the telephone company to place an order for a telephone. Then we'll go to Mitchell's and look at their catalogue. I want you to order the exact stove and washing machine you want," and here, Bob glanced into the rearview mirror at his head. "I think I am going to get a new hat."

"Bob, can we afford all that?"

Bob turned the corner onto Main Street and looked for a parking place near the lawyer's office. He carefully pulled into the space and then backed up and pulled forward until he was directly in front of the door. Bob turned to his wife and replied with a grin:

"Yes, Em. Yes, we can."

Sorrows and Joys and Revelations

At eighteen, Vernon Wells left home to join the military. Less than two years later, his brother, Leon, did the same. Clyde wished to follow his brothers before his senior year in high school started, and when he told his father, it led to the only real argument Bob had ever had with his children. He wanted Clyde to complete high school and then reconsider joining up. Neither of his brothers had graduated, and while Bob understood the reasons his older sons had for becoming soldiers, he believed his family had donated enough manpower to the war.

The argument lasted for a week, and Clyde brought up Bob's own patriotism in leaving school and enlisting during World War I. Bob answered that he left college and not high school. Clyde replied that since he was privately tutored, it could not be considered a true high school. Bob demanded that he finish the last year and said that he would not sign papers for Clyde since he was only seventeen, but Clyde turned eighteen that fall, and he went anyway. They made up at the train station as Clyde left for the army, and they both cried upon saying farewell. On their drive home, Emma joined her husband in tears.

Between the discovery of Rebecca and the inheritance, there were additional sorrows. Vernon was declared *Missing in Action* in France. Eventually, his name was listed with other MIA's at the Brittany American Memorial in France, but that did not happen for many years. Bob was determined to have a proper headstone for his first-born at Everstille's North Cemetery. One day, he did.

Leon was injured fighting in England, but recovered, and after the war wrote to his family that he would be staying in England for a while. Eventually, he, too, returned home. Clyde did return, and he and his father were glad to see each other. Past arguments forgotten.

It wasn't just the inheritance which eased living for Bob. It wasn't just the end of the war and the return of Clyde. It was the autonomy he felt. He continued to work his usual part-time jobs for a time after he received the estate money until finally, after one particularly difficult work day, Emma spoke to him,

"Bob, there is no need for you to continue looking for them jobs. I could use your help here, and really, you been away from me and the kids for such long times in the past, I think you might want to be around." And he did want that.

He was able to return to his Latin and Greek texts and started on the fourth volume of Gibbons. He began to jot notes down for a possible book. He was able to assist with schoolwork. The older children did not need much help, but the twins did. Especially Jess. Maddy was quite the scholar.

One evening Bob came to the front room to find Maddy holding Caesar's *Bellum Gallicum* and the Cassell's Latin dictionary Bob used in his youth. She was attempting to translate the first sentence: *Gallia est omnis divisa in partes tres.* When Bob saw his daughter trying to work out the Latin sentence, he was more pleased than he thought he should be, and the two of them spent many evenings working at the text and learning Latin words and beginning Latin conjugations.

Late one evening, as they lay in bed talking about their family, Bob said to Emma, "I think we may have a classics scholar on our hands, Em. Maddy has quite a knack for the language."

He laughed when Emma answered, "Great. Now, if she can only learn to comb the tangles out of her hair..."

Beatrice graduated from Everstille High School and was the first Wells child to do so. Her parents were unquestionably pleased. The following fall, a small wedding was held for Beatrice and Joshua Rivens. Beatrice was able to have a lovely wedding dress after all, and Maddy was thrilled with her pink shoes found at Robertson's Department Store in South Bend where Bob and Emma took the family to shop for new clothes. That had never happened, and it was a toss-up as to whether the wedding or the shopping trip was more exciting.

Bob and Emma had long discussions about their good fortune and decided to invest in their children. They would make some repairs and update the cabin. They would add some new appliances and eventually, new furniture. They were determined to stay where they had lived through the burdens and blisses of family life. A new and larger car was purchased, and the old, dilapidated Studebaker that had belonged to Uncle George Washington Wells, was sold to Mackie at the service station in town. He wanted it, although Bob was never sure what he would or could do with it until he saw Mackie's mechanic, Charlie, driving around town in the car which appeared rehabilitated.

There were some rumors among the townspeople about the sudden luck of the Wells, but Jason Wicks kept his promise and said nothing despite continual questions. Bob and Emma had been seen visiting his office a few times, and a small town thrives on gossip and tales. It was also observed that new furniture and appliances were delivered to the cabin. A new telephone number appeared in the Everstille Directory, and when Bob Wells, his new hat set at a jaunty angle, drove his newer and larger car into the town, heads swirled. But Bob and Emma kept their finances, and their windfall, to themselves.

The Wells children only knew that some money had come to their father. They were not informed of the amount and were not spoiled by it. They continued to work their after-school jobs and do their chores, and when deemed appropriate, given financial help, via the inheritance, to achieve adult goals.

The newlyweds, Beatrice and Joshua, were living on the Rivens' farm while Joshua and his brothers built a new house for them. It was not far from either the Rivens or the Wells, and a monetary wedding gift from the inheritance was helping to create it. Clyde had come back from the war and seemed at loose ends until he and Bob had a serious discussion about his future. In the next county, a small farm had come up for sale, and after several trips to examine it and many consultations with the retiring farmer, the farm was purchased with a down payment from the inheritance. Hazel had completed high school and was unhappily working at Clampet's Grocery Store. When her brother asked if she wanted to live and work with him at the farm, she quickly agreed. There was not a horse there for her yet, but the inheritance purchased chickens and two goats named Hi and Lo. In the meanwhile, they were acceptable substitutes.

Ester completed her high school business courses and supplemented that education with a course at secretarial school, paid for by the inheritance. She found a job at the Everstille Bank and was pleased with her career decision. Only Hattie, Jess, and Maddy were still in school, with Hattie in her senior year of high school. She aspired to be a nurse, and Bob encouraged her in this quest. Now that the inheritance was available, he told her, it would only take the hard work on her part.

Then Leon sent a letter from England. He had stayed there after the war because he had met and married Elizabeth who had been a volunteer at the hospital where he was recovering from his injuries. They were saving their money, and as soon as they could afford it, he wrote, he and his bride would be coming back to the States, to Everstille, to the cabin. Money for the trip was wired to him as soon as Bob could get to town. The Wells cabin was filled with contentment. Thanks to the inheritance.

Late fall had arrived, and most of the leaves were off the trees and covering the ground and the porch. The Wells were anxiously awaiting the arrival of Leon and Elizabeth in another week. New furniture was due any day, and the house was being given a thorough cleaning by Emma. It was late afternoon, and the twins were home from school and completing schoolwork. The fireplace was lit, and the smell of baking apples filled the cabin. Bob was sitting in the front room by the large window, working his way through volume five of the Gibbons work when the telephone rang. He listened as Emma spoke into it and waited to hear who had called. Emma came into the room holding a dishtowel and stopped to speak to the twins.

"When the two of you are finished, Jess, the trash bin needs emptying, and Maddy, set the table for supper. And put an extra plate on. We're having company." She looked at Bob. He looked at her.

"Who?" asked Bob.

"Hattie just called and said she did not take the school bus but stayed to finish a report. She also asked if she could bring a friend home for supper."

"Oh, is it Rita or Jane?" Bob was used to these friends coming over to spend time with Hattie.

"Neither. I don't know who it is, but Hattie said *he* would drive her home, and they would be here in about twenty minutes."

"*He*? Well…," and Bob watched as Emma and the twins went back to the kitchen to complete their tasks.

He put down the Gibbons, marking his place with a slip of paper, and sat at the window looking out. In just about twenty minutes, as the sky was becoming that orangey-red hue often seen in late autumn, he heard a noise and watched as an old Buick pulled into the lane next to the cabin. A young man jumped out of the driver's side and dashed around to the passenger side to open the door. The late afternoon sun grew brilliantly bright as Hattie, looking up at the man, took his hand and stepped out into the glow. They stood for a moment and considered each other. Bob watched as his daughter's auburn hair, so like Emma's when she was young, fluttered in the fall and flew into her face, and as he rearranged the curls behind Hattie's ear, Mitch smiled.

Endings and Beginnings

Hattie and Mitch

Mitch steered the car around the cow in the middle of the road as he and Hattie laughed. She turned around and watched as the animal ambled over to the pasture and into the grass and began to munch.

"There she is again, old Gertie, the wandering cow, loose from the Rivens' farm."

"Is that her name?" asked Mitch, "I didn't know that."

"That's what Daddy called her. A few times she wandered over to our cabin all the way from the Rivens, and Daddy would send whichever of us were around to walk her back. We just called her that. I know she wanders, and David and Jena can't seem to keep her contained unless they tie her up. And Gertie doesn't like that."

It was a late Saturday afternoon, and Hattie and Mitch were both in a cheerful mood as they returned from a trip to South Bend. Mitch had been saving money to buy a new suit, and had asked Hattie to take the trip with him. They both took a day off and traveled to Robertson's Brothers Department Store in South Bend to find just the right suit. It had not taken too long, and then they had lunch in the Tea Room on the sixth floor. Hattie had the chicken fricassee and Mitch the grilled boneless ham dinner, and afterwards, they spent an hour walking around the Potawatomi Zoo. Neither of them had been to a zoo before, and they stared with wonder at the polar bear and the monkeys, and walked through the Cat House, and watched the lions. The peacocks on the grounds were not particularly friendly, but Hattie loved their colors and Mitch told her that her eyes belonged in their tails. It was an incredible day.

They talked all the way there and back about the future. Hattie, having graduated high school in May, was working at the library shelving books and cleaning up, saving up her money. She was accepted to the Main County Hospital Nurses Training Program in Chicago and would begin the three-year stint in the fall. Mitch was still working at Banter's Drugs and now also Clampet's Grocery Store, making deliveries, sweeping, cleaning, and saving his money for college. He was hoping to attend Indiana University's recently opened branch in South Bend where he would study to be a teacher. He had not yet heard from the school nor from the Veterans' Affairs Office where he had filled out the papers for a G.I. loan but was sure he would soon.

The summer day was warm but not sticky, and with the windows rolled down on the old Buick, they enjoyed the breeze that fanned through the car, pressing Hattie's long auburn curls into her face so that she had to hold them back with her hand. As they traveled eastward down Smokehouse Road towards Hattie's home, Mitch slowed the car down, not yet wanting the day to be over. Hattie glanced over to her left and pointed and asked, "Mitch, would you pull in here for a minute, please?"

Mitch glanced sideways at her and then slowed down even more, finding the narrow path leading into Evervstille's North Cemetery. He stopped the car for a minute and turned to Hattie.

"This is where you want to go? Which lane should I take?"

"Just drive to the top. I want to find Rebecca's gave. I hope you don't mind."

Mitch nodded and pulled up to the top of the lane where he parked. They got out of the car and stretched. Hattie held her hand over her eyes to look for the correct area and pointed. They walked across some grassy patches and Mitch stopped in front of some graves.

"These are my grandparents. I never knew them because they died before we were born."

Hattie did not ask who *we* were. She knew. She looked at Mitch and waited for him to speak again.

"Over there is where my father and Mike are," and the two of them traveled over to the next section. Mitch placed his hand on Mike's stone and was silent.

"You never talk about him," said Hattie, "I know he died in the war. Were you together then?"

Mitch was silent for such a long time that Hattie was afraid she had made a mistake asking about Mike. She stood nervously waiting, unsure what to do or say.

Mitch looked at her and said, "It's O.K. I miss him. Yes, we were together when he was killed in Italy. One day I'll tell you about it. But not today. Alright?"

"That's fine, Mitch. Whenever you want to talk, I'll listen," and Hattie smiled. "Over there is where Rebecca is." She began to walk across the grass and the stones.

Mitch followed. When they got to the spot, he was surprised to see two headstones side by side. One had a stone engraving of a kitten on it and declared:

Rebecca Wells

Beloved Daughter and Sister

Securus Dormies

The stone next to it was engraved with the words:

Vernon Alexander Wells

MIA France, World War II

Fili, Frater, Maria

Mitch read both out loud, stumbling a bit over the Latin phrases. They were both quiet and then Mitch asked, "I took Latin, but don't remember much. What do they mean?"

"Rebecca's means *Rest in Safety* and Vernon's means *Son, Brother, Soldier.*"

"They both fit," said Mitch, "Why aren't there any dates on them? I think there usually are. At least the rest of them seem to have them."

"Daddy said that their lives were both so brief that he didn't want to be reminded of it, so he didn't have them engraved. I know what it is to lose someone, Mitch. I really do."

They stood still and Mitch reached over and took Hattie's left hand. She was wiping her eyes with her right one. After a time, they turned and walked back to the car. They were quiet as they got in, and Mitch did not start the engine immediately. He sat there and then turned to Hattie.

"Hattie, I hope we stay in touch when you leave for school. I haven't heard yet about the University, but I really think I will get in, and

Ma and I talked about me finding a place to stay in South Bend so I can stay near the school. I will get a part-time job there, and really, Chicago is not so far away. We can visit each other or see each other when we come hone for holidays. I know your studies are year-round, but I want to keep in touch. We can write too."

Hattie turned to him. "I was thinking the same thing, Mitch. And a few years is not such a long time."

They stared at each other. Reflections of the future unspoken. Then Mitch started the car. He backed out of the narrow lane carefully and pulled forward, inching the car slowly to the cabin in the woods, neither of them particularly willing to end their day. The sun was collapsing into the horizon, pulling its light into itself, making way for the evening and the stars and the moon.

Viola and Tillie

"Mrs. Jasper. Where should I put these new hats?" Eva was holding a large box, and she had placed a soft gray fedora on her head.

Viola looked up from the papers she was examining and laughed. "Put them in the back for now. We need to decide which of the old stock will go on sale next week. Then we'll replace it with the new stock. And, Eva, you look quite attractive in that!"

Eva and Janie, the part-time clerk, both laughed. Their jobs had become more enjoyable since Viola Jasper had taken over the management of the Emporium two years ago. Mr. Grayson and Mr. Melworth, the owners, were decent enough bosses, but they had no sense of humor or appreciation of any, and when they were at the Emporium, the mood was one of dull business. The entire staff of the Emporium began to look forward to coming to work, and staff turn-over ceased once Viola took charge. In fact, many townspeople applied for jobs at the Emporium because Viola was known to be fair, reasonable, evenhanded, and the homemade sugar cookies she brought in weekly for breaks were an extra enticement.

Mr. Grayson and Mr. Melworth had been alternating weeks of managing the store, but once they instituted the necessary changes, they began to look elsewhere to invest in additional businesses. This entrepreneurship created both a hectic schedule for them and the need for a trustworthy manager. Since Viola was so conscientious about her bookkeeping and accounting and had saved them overhead costs with her suggestions, they asked her to take over managerial duties as well. After all, who better to run their now flourishing business than the daughter of the original owner who knew the business? Viola quit her part-time jobs at Peterson's Bakery and Banter's Drug Store and was satisfied to be back at the Emporium where she resumed the activities of ordering, receiving, stocking, organizing, cleaning, and selling.

The new owners had expanded business hours on Wednesdays and Fridays, when the Emporium remained open until eight o'clock P.M. Viola was at the store one of those evenings each week, and because she lived so close to the store, she often filled in the other evening when the younger clerks who worked there had an important date or party to attend. Her consideration was appreciated. That is the reason that no one minded working for Viola when she shortened her schedule and stopped working late evenings to spend additional time with Tillie who was not well.

***

Tillie had stopped baking pies for Peterson's Bakery because the task had become too tiring for her. She was often out of breath and her heart pounded. She began having headaches, something she had rarely had before, and she needed to rest after even the slightest effort. Doctor Evans had retired and moved down south to be with his sister and her family, and Tillie had put off going to the town's new doctor until Viola forced her to with constant nagging and arguing, an unpleasant experience for both women. Doctor Luke Grenville was a newly graduated M.D. who had bought the practice from Doctor Evans, but his youth and baby-faced appearance kept many of Doctor Evans' older patients from trusting him. What could he possibly know that the older, seasoned doctor did not?

"Mrs. Smith, You have hypertension, and I am going to do a couple things. First, you need to change your diet. Stay away from sugar, and restrict your sodium."

"Sodium? I don't even think I take that," Tillie was pretty sure this baby-faced doctor knew nothing.

"Salt, Mrs. Smith. Do not put any salt on your food. Also eat healthier vegetables such as cabbage and turnips. Cauliflower if you can get it."

"Do you mean I am supposed to eat those kinds of foods without salt? Doctor, they need some seasoning, and if there is not salt, they are tasteless. Why, I have cooked all my life with salt. Everyone in the town does, and I am not sure what you expect me to eat!" Tillie was thunderstruck at this obviously terrible advice.

"Mrs. Smith, salt will only increase your high blood pressure and lead to other problems. I will have the nurse give you a sheet that will help you make some changes in your diet. The second thing is I am going to prescribe a low-dose of a drug called *Reserpine*. It has been out for a year or two, and some patients are having great success with it."

"Some patients? So not all patients?"

"We will try this one, but if you find you suffer from insomnia or feel depressed, you should let me know. Also do not over-do. Are you still working?"

"I have stopped baking for Peterson's, but still keep house for Viola. Really, there is not much to do, and we have pretty much left the back-yard garden go, so I am not raking and hoeing and such."

"That's good. Walking is good exercise. When you feel up to it, you can walk to town in the good weather. Just don't do heavy work like gardening, or shoveling, or lifting. I want you to rest, but not have a completely sedentary life style. That is not good either."

"And what kind of life style is that *send-in-tery*?"

"Doing nothing, just sitting all day."

Tillie thought this doctor was being a smart-aleck. First telling her how to eat and then to walk and then to rest. Maybe he couldn't decide what she should do because he didn't know. She thought about just leaving the office, but Viola had badgered her so much, she did not want to face that again. She crossed her arms and stared at this youngster.

"Now, here is the prescription, and Banter's can fill it for you. Let me know if you are feeling any ill effects from the pills, and I want to keep a check on your blood pressure. I'm going to ask you to stop in every week for a while so my nurse can check your pressure. Then, if you are tolerating things well, we can make monthly appointments for you. Are there any questions?"

Tillie had a few, but since they were about his general upbringing and behavior, she kept them to herself. He left the room, allowing her to redress, then go to the nurse who made her next appointment and handed Tillie papers instructing her about the diet. Viola was waiting for her and speaking to the doctor. He ended the conversation, wished both women a good day, and left to practice medicine on his next patient. *Practice. He needs to do that*, thought Tillie.

Viola and Tillie went out to the Buick. Although the office was only a few streets from their house, Viola insisted on driving since Mitch did not need the car. She started the Buick and drove over the couple of streets to Banter's Drug Store.

"Give me that prescription, Tillie, and I'll run in and have it filled. Mitch can bring it home with him tonight."

"Oh, now I'm sick? I can't even get out of this car and get my own medicine? Just what did that baby-doctor tell you? And did you know I am not supposed to even salt my food? I swear…"

Viola sighed. "Tillie, if you want to go in, go on. I just thought I would save you a few steps and then I would say *hello* to Nate. I also want to go to Clampet's and tell Mitch to pick up the prescription before he comes home tonight. Doctor Grenville is young, but he knows what he is doing. You need to give him a chance and follow his directions. Come on then, we'll both go in."

They got out of the car and entered the Drug Store. Nathan greeted them, and they talked for a bit while Tillie went to Jim Banter with her prescription. There was no need to tell Mitch to pick up the medicine because Jim Banter said it would only take a little while to get it together. While they waited, Tillie complained about the new doctor and Nathan listened. Viola just stood back and only once did she sigh. And then they left for home.

Tillie had already made supper for that night, and she, following the doctor's orders, did not add any extra salt to her meal. There had been plenty added during the cooking of the stew. They had the sour cherry pie she had made for their dessert although she only had one piece. One small piece. *Maybe this won't be so difficult after all,* she thought as she decided to add just a small scoop of ice cream to her tiny piece of pie.

Salt-Less Cabbage Soup

Ingredients

1 head shredded cabbage	1 or 2 medium onions
Some minced garlic	2 green peppers
8 stalks celery	About 4 or 5 crushed tomatoes
8 cups broth	2 tablespoons olive oil
1 bay leaf	black pepper to taste

Instructions

1. Heat olive oil over medium heat in a large stock pot. Add onion, garlic, pepper, and sauté until onions cook down.

2. Add remaining vegetables to pot (except for cabbage) with tomatoes, broth, and bay leaf.

3. Bring soup to a boil, lower to a simmer, and cook covered for 15 minutes. Add cabbage. Cook, covered an additional 15 minutes.

4. Season with more pepper to taste.

"Needs salt," said Tillie.

Tillie's Last Thoughts

On the Sidewalk Just Outside of Clampet's Grocery Store

10:35:15 A.M.

What is the matter with me? I feel light-headed and my heart is beating quickly. Is that Joseph? Why is he running and why are people staring? Where is the list I had? I am not sure where my purse is. I remember Viola handing it to me as I left. She said she would drive me but the weather is nice, and I said I would walk. That doctor said I should walk. The high school is right on the next street, and Mitch said he would walk me, and we parted, and I came down here to Clampet's. Mitch is doing so well, and I think he likes that Wells girl although I just can't remember her name at this time. Mike is gone. Wait. Is he? Yes, he died in France or maybe it was Italy. When was that? My mind is not working today. The house west of town is where I live. No, that is not right. We moved into town and live...where do we live? We live. Who is *we*? Wait, I think I remember. Something seems wrong, but I am not sure what that is. We live ...no, I live with Viola and Mitch and Mike. Wait, Mike is dead. We used to live west of town. I remember the house when John was there. I never liked him. He is gone. Yes, John died. He was not a good person, and I never liked him. I should tell Mr. Mitchell that. I will tell him when I get home. No, he is dead too. So is Mary. Now I re-member. Mary died and then years later Michael died, and I found him. I found him on the floor of the store...what is the store's name? Well, I found him, and I never told anyone I loved him. I only barely admitted it to myself. And those two children, Viola and the boy. The boy's name was Mitch. No, that is not right. The boy was Nathan. Yes, Nathan and Viola, and I worked for the Mitchell's. I will need to make a blueberry pie when I get home. That is Mr. Mitchell's favorite. And I need to get the best china out and clean it. That Sunday supper is this week. I think. I will check with Mrs. Mitchell when I get home. Where is it again? West of the town, I think. No, that is not right. I lived there with the girl, with Viola. And the boys. Mitch and Mike. Mike is a stinker, but he is still a love. Mitch is so sweet and helpful. And they both love to play outside. They should stay away from the fire. No, they were not there when Viola and I burned the bed and the clothes. Why did we do that? Oh, I remember. John. He just comes too often to dinner at the Mitch-ell's, and I like Ted. That is who Viola should marry. I think so, and I always have. But those flowers in the garden. Mrs. Mitchell wanted me to get some for the table. Is that John coming? No, wait, she never knew him, did she? She died. Mary died many years ago. After Herman and our boy did. We lived west of town too. I think we did. I lived in a house with…with…Viola and the boys. Who is Edna? I lived with her; I think. Edna and Edie. Edna and the boy. Ted? No. Nathan. Yes, Nathan and Edna. Their wedding was lovely. That woman that I helped. She is about my age. And her name is Tillie. No, that is my name. Millie. And her husband, but what was his name? Joseph? No, that is the man I have known for years. We got married. No, he wanted to marry me, but I married Herman. I can't remember what Herman looked like. He was tall and had a beard. I think. We had a child. What was his name? Herman and, I think Little Herman. But they died. That was a terrible time. We lived in an old house. It was falling apart and then that old woman died. That was…Herman's mother. Mrs. Schmidt. Was that me? Yes, I remember. I married and we lived…no first we were with my mother and my brothers. What were their names? I think we stayed there in the back room. I remember the room was blue. Or was it green? I am not sure. I should know. I lived there with my husband. Herman. Herman Schmidt. And then we moved. But why did we? Oh, his mother. I was pregnant. I didn't tell him until we had moved. We were so happy. I wanted a little girl, but then we had a little boy. A boy. Where is he? I know. He is dead. He is buried at a place…the cemetery. We go there yearly. Who goes with me? That woman I live with. She is…? I can't remember. Maybe I need to go to the doctor. Something must be wrong with me. Old Doc Evans. He could help me, but I think he is gone. I know this…there is a new doctor in town. In the town where I live. And that is where we moved after someone got sick, and we moved and Mother was not happy. She said I needed to quit school and work. I didn't want to, but I had to because there was no money, and I had three brothers. Three. And they lived with Mother and with me, and I have to tell Mother that I still want to go to school. I don't want to have to work. But we need the money because someone else is gone. Father. Where did he go? I don't know. He was gone one day. Mother would not talk about it. I need to get to school now. I like to do the work. Reading is my favorite subject. My dress is too short because I grew, and the other girls laughed at me. I need to tell Mother. I need to work. Where are the books? Where am I? There is some yelling and I can't tell who it is. It is getting cold, and I need to get the sweater. Where is it? I need to get the sweater and go to school, and I need to tell Mama I need a new dress, but there is no money, and I have to work and Jimmie is crying and I am getting colder, and I want to go, and I want to go, and I want to look outside, and the sun is gone, and the…the sun…and it…it is…

On the Sidewalk Just Outside of Clampet's Grocery Store

10:36:50 A.M.

Getting Familiarized

Everyone had gone. Just the three of them: Joseph, Viola, and Mitch, were there. They stood together looking at Tillie and thinking their separate thoughts. Viola rested her hand on Joseph's arm and waited for him to look at her. Once he could look at her without tears, he gave her a despondent smile and sighed.

"I loved her you know. For years I wanted to marry her, but she wouldn't. She said we were just fine as we were, and she didn't think she could be married again."

"We know, Joseph. She loved you too. I once asked her why she didn't remarry and she said that it would just be too hard, at her age. She was happy with you, and I know she enjoyed being with you and going to the movies every week. I don't know what we'll do without her. She was my friend and my mother," and at this point, Viola let out a sob.

Mitch put his arm around her. He hugged her. They stood together and Mitch spoke.

"Tillie was a grandmother to Mike and me. We are all going to miss her," and he looked up into the sky, "I think it might rain, so we should probably go."

Viola wiped her eyes and turned to Joseph.

"Why don't you come over to the house for a while? We could sit and talk and I can offer you some coffee and a piece of pie…Tillie's pie."

Joseph smiled at Viola and Mitch and nodded his head.

"Thanks, I think I might. Mitch is right. We should leave. I feel some rain."

The trio walked rapidly to their cars. Viola opened the passenger door to the Buick and sat down, and Mitch got into the driver's side and started the car. Joseph started his Ford truck and followed the Buick out of North Cemetery and down Smokehouse Road onto Main Street and through the town. They turned, and as the Jaspers pulled into their driveway, and Joseph parked in front of the house, there was a loud clap of thunder. They hurried onto the porch where Viola opened the front door and they entered, just missing getting drenched.

"Come on into the kitchen, Joseph. I'll put on the coffee. Mitch, would you please close the window in the front room? And are there any open upstairs?"

"I'll get the windows, Ma. And I'll check upstairs, but I think they're all closed."

They went their separate ways, and as Viola and Joseph entered the kitchen, she flipped on the overhead light and motioned for Joseph to sit down at the kitchen table.

"That's a good boy you got there, Viola. You had two great kids. I enjoyed the stories Tillie would tell about them. I felt so bad that Mike met such an end. He was a great kid, and Tillie was heartbroken over it."

Viola had her back turned to Joseph as she listened to him. She took some deep breaths and then busied herself gathering the cups, and spoons, and forks, and plates, and bringing the pie over to the table. She nodded as he spoke. They were both quiet, thinking about their anguishes, past and present. Viola went to the icebox, took out the milk, and brought it to the table. Then she brought the readied coffee and poured three cups. She sat down on a chair and looked at her guest.

"We have all had our sorrows, Joseph. And, I guess, our joys too. That's what life is, I suppose."

They added milk and sugar to their coffee, and Viola cut a piece of pie for Joseph and set it before him. She cut another piece for Mitch and a smaller piece for herself. Mitch came into the kitchen and sat with them at the table. He looked at the pie and nodded. He took a large bite and chewed and then said:

"I will miss many things about Tillie, but possibly her pies most of all."

He took another forkful and held it up as if he were making a toast.

"To Tillie," he said, and as Joseph and Viola took a forkful of their pie, they repeated:

"To Tillie."

They all ate their bites and then smiled at the attempt to interrupt sadness with some silliness.

There was a comfortable silence as they ate the rest of Tillie's last pie and drank their coffee. Joseph leaned back, wiping his mouth with a napkin, and smiled. Viola gathered the empty plates and placed them into the sink. She brought over the coffee pot and poured another round of hot coffee. Then she sat down.

"Joseph, we have known you for all these years, but don't know your last name. What is it?"

"Joseph."

Viola tilted her head and looked quizzically at him and clarified, "I meant your *last* name."

Joseph smiled. "My last name is *Joseph*. My first name is Francis. I was called *Frank* when I was young. Years ago, when I started at Clampet's, people called me Mr. Joseph, and, over time, the *Mr.* got dropped. I suppose most folks just thought that was my name, and I never bothered correcting anyone. Been called that so many years, I almost forgot about my first name."

Mitch laughed. "That's some story. Did Tillie know that?"

"Honestly, I don't know. I think it came up once, but neither of us thought it important. She called me the same as everyone else, and that was fine with me."

"So, *Frank*, what will you do now?" Viola sipped her coffee as she talked. "A few months ago, Tillie said you were thinking of retiring. Are you still considering that? Will you stay here? Were you originally from here?"

"I grew up in Wisconsin, in a small town called *Appleton*, although I guess it's larger now. My family was a big one, and I had five brothers and three sisters, although a few of them are passed on now. We had a large farm just outside of town, and most of the family, even the younger ones, are still around there. In fact, my youngest brother and his sons are still farming on part of the family land. I married young, but my wife and daughter both died in childbirth. I guess that is one of the things Tillie and I had in common…youthful sorrows. When that happened, it was a bad time for me, and I just took off. I wandered around the country, and after tramping around a few years and working at a bunch of jobs, I ended up here."

Mitch finished his coffee and placed it down. His wrapped his hands around the cup, holding on to its receding warmth. He looked at Joseph and slowly nodded.

"I guess there are histories, stories, about everyone. Sometimes you get to know them. Most of the time you don't. I think that is what history is...stories, known and shared. I think that is one of the reasons I want to teach history eventually. We know some of the stories and can pass them on to others."

"Why, Mitch," said Viola, "I believe that is the first time you ever said what you wanted to teach. I think that's a wonderful idea. Have you heard from the Veterans' Affairs Office yet?" She turned to Joseph and explained, "Mitch is going to South Bend to the Indiana University, and is just waiting to hear about the finances. I wish I could help, but I'm not able to."

Mitch answered, "Not yet. I am sure I will get some money though, and I will get a job there to help with my expenses. I think I will be able to start in the fall. I hope so, anyway. So, Joseph, are you retiring?"

"I am. I was hoping to talk Tillie into marriage, and then I was going to steal her away and go back to Appleton to be with my family. Guess not now. I'll still go. It's time. My youngest brother and I are in touch, and he wants me to live there with him and his family. They are good people and I miss them. I did let Mr. Clampet know that I would be leaving soon. The apprentice I've been training is ready to take over now. He's a good kid...new to the town, and brought his young wife with him. I will miss Everstille and all the folks here. I'll miss both of you."

Viola patted his hand. "You will be missed Frank. You need to stay in touch with us."

Joseph nodded and then glanced out of the kitchen window. The storm had stopped, and the late afternoon sun was drying up the puddles. He moved his chair back and stood up as did Mitch and Viola.

"Thanks for pie and coffee and the talking. I feel a bit better now, but need to get going. I have some things to do. Mitch, you are a fine young man. I hope you know how much Tillie loved you and thought of you and Mike as her grandchildren. And, Viola, you could not have had a better mother than Tillie. The rest of my life, I'll miss her."

Viola put her arms around Joseph and hugged him, and Mitch

shook his hand. They walked him to the front door and said their fare-wells. As he walked out the door, Joseph stopped and turned to Mitch.

"Mitch, I am asking you to do something. Next Monday, after you finish work, will you come and see me? You know where I live, right? Great, I will see you then. And again, thanks."

He walked to his truck and waved once again before taking off. Mitch and Viola waved and stood there until he was out of sight. They closed the front door and walked back to the kitchen where Mitch helped his mother clean up the remains of the coffee.

"I wonder what he wants you for next week? He might need some help if he is planning on moving soon. We should have asked when he was leaving and have him over to dinner before then. When you see him next, would you ask him, Mitch?"

"Sure, Ma, I will," and they finished the cleaning in companionable silence.

A Surprise

After work the following Monday, Mitch drove over to Mrs. Beckett's house. Joseph had rented her two back rooms and lived there for years. He parked in front of her house and walked up to the door. He knocked loudly because Mrs. Beckett was deaf in her left ear. He knocked again. Louder this time. Finally, Mrs. Beckett came to the door.

"Why, hello Mitch. So good to see you. Come on in," and she pushed open the door.

Mitch walked into her front parlor which had a strange mothball smell, but he was too polite to wrinkle his nose. He stood next to the horsehair sofa, very much like the one that was in his childhood house, and waited for Mrs. Beckett to close the door and walk over. He smiled at her and spoke loudly:

"Hello, Mrs. Beckett. I have come to see Mr. Joseph. Is he here?"

"Could I offer you some tea? I know young people like that Coca Cola, but I do not have any. I do have some milk, and I think there are some shortbread cookies left. How is your mother doing? So sad about Tillie. I so enjoyed sitting next to her at church. Did you say *tea?*"

"Thank you, but I don't want anything. I'm just here to see Joseph. Is he in his room?"

"Oh, you are here for Joseph! But he is gone."

"What? Where is he?"

"He left early this morning. He packed his truck yesterday and left for his family in, where is that now…I think maybe somewhere south, no maybe north…"

"Do you mean Wisconsin?"

"Yes! That's it. I will so miss him. Such a nice man. Are you sure you won't take some tea?"

"No, thank you, Mrs. Beckett. Joseph asked me to come here today. I don't understand."

Mitch was not sure what to think. He had not seen Joseph in

Clampet's for a few days, but he knew they had arranged to see each other tonight. He turned to leave when Mrs. Beckett spoke to him.

"Well, I am sorry you missed him, but he left this for you." She walked slowly over to the ornate side table and picked up a box somewhat larger than a shoebox with an envelope taped on the top.

Mrs. Beckett gave to box to Mitch who took it. It did not weigh much. He wondered what it was, but would wait until he got home to find out.

"Thank you, Mrs. Beckett. I'm sorry to have missed him. I'll go now."

"Are you sure you won't stay for some tea? No? Well, tell your mother I send my best, and I hope to see her in church. Watch out for that last porch step. Good night, now."

Mitch walked out of the house, down the steps, expecting to trip on the last one, but there did not appear to be anything wrong with it. He went to the car and placed the box on the passenger seat and drove home.

He walked in with the box under his arm and yelled, "Ma?" but there was no answer.

In the kitchen was a note which informed him that Viola was at the church for a committee meeting, and she would be home later. Dinner was warming in the oven. He placed the box on the table and sipping a glass of water, sat down. He took the envelope off, set it to the side, and opened the box.

Once, when Mitch and Mike were young, their father had come home from a long trip and was in a particularly vibrant mood. His trip had been successful...very much so. He had collected the money on most of the contracts he had sold, had signed a number more, and for other reasons his sons never knew about, had thoroughly enjoyed his sales trip. He had enough cash in his pockets to pay all the bills due, to purchase new tires for his car, to give his wife some extra household cash, and to give each of his sons a five-dollar bill. A new, fresh, uncreased piece of paper, and they were excited, and pleased, and more than anything...surprised.

That was how Mitch felt as he poured out the contents of the box on the table; as he emptied the wrinkled, creased, and sometimes torn

ones, fives, tens, and twenties, onto the shiny kitchen table. Mitch counted the money and then recounted it. There was one thousand dollars in
all. One thousand dollars. He straightened all the bills, placing them
in piles. He looked at the money before him and finally reached over,
opened, and read the letter.

Dear Mitch,

I don't like good-byes. Had enough of them lately. Sorry for just leaving.

I keep thinking that if Tillie and me had gotten married, and since she
thought of you as a grandson, you would have been mine too. I been
watching you as you worked at Clampet's, and you are a good worker. A
hard worker. Life's not been very easy for you, losing your brother, and the
war and all, and sometimes a person needs a hand up.

Don't you worry about the amount. I never believed in banks and always
kept my pay close. I never bought much and just kept stacking cash away,
so there is more than this left for me to live out my life. My needs aren't
much.

I want you to go and be that teacher. Go and tell them history stories to
others. And let this cash help make things easier for you. Maybe get yourself a newer car. Or maybe a ring for that girl you are with. I notice things.

I am going back to Wisconsin to live with my youngest brother and his
family. I only hope his boys turn out as good as you. If you are ever near
Appleton, come and find me.

Tell your Ma she is lucky Tillie was in her life.

So was I.

Yours,

Francis (Frank) Joseph

Journey

Viola opened the passenger side door and sat down while Mitch got into the driver's seat and started his new car. Well, new to him. Mackie from Mackie's Gas Station helped Mitch get the year-old car which was *gently used*, according to Mackie. The car, a 1946 Chevrolet Stylemaster in a dark blue, was purchased with Joseph's bounty, then checked out and tweaked by Mackie. When all the bills were paid, Mitch still had a few hundred of the creased and torn dollars from the box Mrs. Beckett had handed to him.

Mitch checked his mirrors, pulled out from the front of his house, and took off, driving down Main Street, and then turned and traveled around the high school, around a few more streets, past the Methodist Episcopal Church, and then over to the highway past Mackie's new gas station. As he passed it, he noticed Mackie checking the tires of a car, and honked his new car's horn, and waved. Mackie looked up and waved back and shouted, "Lookin' good, Mitch!"

Driving carefully and moving smoothly down his home street, Mitch turned left and drove around the block, turned right, and pulled up in front of the Mitchell house where Nathan and Edie were standing on the curb waiting for him. He grinned as he stopped the car, and as Viola stepped out, his Uncle Nathan got in.

"So," said Nathan looking around the car and placing his elbow on the lowered side window, "this is your new car. How does she ride?"

"Great!" answered Mitch. "Want to go somewhere?"

"Maybe after we eat. I think Millie and Edna just about have dinner ready. I think Edie wants a ride later too," and Nathan looked out of the lowered window at his daughter.

Edie was standing there admiring the car. She held her back as she bent forward to look into the opened window and smiled at Mitch. Her back hurt constantly now due to her growing pregnancy.

"This is some car, Mitch. I love the color. After dinner could we go for a drive?"

"Absolutely, Edie. How are you feeling?"

"Not bad today. My back hurts, but that is apparently normal according to Doctor Grenville."

She stood up, straightened out, and gave a small moan. Only a couple of months now, and the baby would be here. Edie and Ned were looking forward to becoming parents. They were also dreading becoming parents. As Edie walked towards the house, Edna came out of the front door and called them in. Sunday dinner was ready.

The family gathered around the dining table and passed around the platters and bowls of food Millie and Edna carried in. They filled their plates and began cutting, biting, chewing, and swallowing. After a few minutes of semi-silence, Nathan looked up from his plate.

"So, Mitch, are you all packed and ready for your South Bend trip?" Nathan motioned to Ned to pass the butter for his rolls.

"Pretty much, Uncle Nate. But it's not just a trip. I'll be living there while taking classes, so it's a move. I'm leaving Tuesday morning although my classes won't start until next week. Figure that will give me some time to settle and look for a job. Already have a few ideas and saw some *Help wanted* signs near campus, so I'm not too worried about finding one."

Edie pushed her plate to the side and sipped at her water. Lately she just could not eat much before she started to feel bloated. "I heard there aren't many places for all the new students to live. You won't be in a dormitory, will you?"

"No, there are none right now. So many returned soldiers are taking advantage of the G.I. Bill and college opportunities that living places are tough to find. I rented a space above the garage of a nice couple, the Bensons, so I'm lucky. I already took most of my stuff there, and when I leave Tuesday, I'll fill the car with the rest."

"Above the garage?" Millie looked shock. "Is there a bathroom? What about a kitchen? That doesn't sound very comfortable. Are you sure you should do this?"

Mitch smiled. "It's more of an apartment, and yes, Grandma Millie, there are all the necessary parts. It's perfectly fine. Ma was there and she saw it, right, Ma?"

Viola looked up from her plate. She had taken just a few bites and was pushing her food around. She did not have much of an appetite. She assumed that Tillie's death and Mitch leaving for South Bend accounted for her appetite loss and stomach problems. While she was pleased that Mitch was going to do what he wanted, she knew she faced a great loneliness. She looked up at Ned and then around the table.

"The apartment is fine, Millie. Mitch is lucky to have found a place close to campus with a space to park his car. It isn't home, but I do feel better knowing he will be somewhere safe. The Bensons are good people. Mitch introduced us last week. I have heard that some of the college boys are renting attic or basement rooms, and they aren't as nice as Mitch's place."

Edna looked around and asked, "Who would like more potatoes? Here Ned, you enjoy these, and Mitch, you should eat some more while you are here. I doubt you will get home cooking like this for a while."

Ned nodded as he took another helping of the potatoes. "These are the best, Mitch. You know, you will be missed around here, especially by your mom."

"I will miss Mitch," and Viola reached over to her son and squeezed his hand, "but I know this is what he wants to do, and I'm happy for him."

Mitch put his fork down and looked around the table. Here was his family. Tillie was no longer here, ensuring everyone had enough to eat, guarding Viola, giving him the largest piece of pie. His brother was gone for years now, no longer available to cajole him into new experiences, advise him about life choices, shield him from dangerous events. Hattie was away in Chicago, having left a week ago, and would be at Nursing School for the next three years. He missed all of them. He would miss those sitting around the table. Mitch was not sure how to express all these thoughts, so he didn't. He raised his glass of water and declared:

"Thanks. I'll miss all of you and count on your letters to let me know what's happening in Everstille. I'll be anxious to hear about my new little cousin too."

He grinned at Edie and Ned, drank the water, and placed the empty glass on the table. He sighed and looked around. Then he asked, "So, who wants to go for a ride in my new car?"

***

Tuesday morning was unclouded and clear. Mitch was up just as the sun was brightening the sky. He maneuvered the box he was carrying down the stairs, trying to be quiet as he placed the last of his belongings into the car, but Viola heard him. She was awake and dressed and came out of her bedroom to help him.

"Sorry, Ma, I didn't mean to wake you."

Viola shook her head as she replied, "I have been up. Have had a difficult time sleeping lately, and I wanted to get up early anyway. What can I help you do?"

"Almost finished. I'll put this box in the back-seat, and then I'll be ready for coffee."

Viola smiled and held the front door open as Mitch carried out the last box. She went to the kitchen to make coffee and start a breakfast. This was a new task for her since Tillie had done most of the cooking over the past years, but she remembered how to scramble eggs. She set the table and was just pouring the coffee when Mitch came in. He pulled out the milk from the icebox, put it on the table next to the sugar bowl, and then sat down.

"Ma, just some toast for me, please. Don't fuss. I'm not hungry and want to get going in the next hour. I kept out some clean clothes, and after a shower, will get on the road. I hope you don't mind. This afternoon I have an appointment at a drug store for a job, and I want to get settled in the apartment before then."

Viola nodded and put the bread in the toaster. She put the butter dish and the last of the strawberry jam Tillie had made on the table. As she waited for the bread, she leaned against the counter and looked at Mitch.

"I didn't know you had an interview today."

"Actually, Jim Banter set it up for me. It's with a friend of his from pharmacy school. He called last night and told me about it, so I just found out too. I told him I really appreciated his help, and he said it would be clerking and doing some of the same stocking and cleaning up jobs I did at his place. Anyway, that's why I want to leave earlier than I had planned."

Mitch buttered his toast and spread the jam. He took a few bites and thought about Tillie.

"Ma, I know there are some big changes in your life, and I am worried about you. Will you be OK?"

Viola sipped at her coffee and looked at Mitch over the cup's rim. She placed it down and was silent for a few moments. There were so many things to say, countless emotions to express, a lifetime of sentiments, and thoughts, and cautions. She said none of them.

"Mitch, I will be fine. Write me and let me know how everything is going. When you get a chance, telephone, and reverse the charges. Keep in touch so I don't worry about you. Now, finish up and get into that shower. I need to get to the Emporium today. We have a big delivery coming."

They both stood up from the table, and Mitch came over and put his arms around his mother. They hugged each other and stayed still for a moment while the remainder of the shrouded heartaches and blanketed wounds they bore vaulted from their hearts, drifted out the front door, and dissolved into the Tuesday morning expanse. Mitch kissed the top of Viola's head and bounded up the stairs, two at a time, and readied himself for his journey.

Telephone Calls

Sunday Evening...Mitch calls Viola

"Hi, Ma. I am glad to finally find you at home. I called Friday night and again last night, but the operator said there was no answer. I was starting to get worried. Is everything fine?"

"Oh, Mitch, sorry I missed you. Yes, all is fine. Edie had her baby early this morning, and I was either at the hospital waiting with Ned and Edna and Nate, or staying with Millie. She has a terrible cold, and I was nursing her. But the baby is here, and Millie seems to be better, and the new grandparents are at home. Everyone is trying to get some rest. In fact, once we finish talking, I am taking a hot bath and going to bed too."

"Is this early for the baby? And what is it?"

"Yes, little Mary Edna came a few days early, but she is fine and Edie and Ned are just thrilled. Looks like she might have hair like Ned's too. Tell me about you and the job and your classes. From where are you making this call?"

"I am calling from the Benson's. They said that if it is a collect call to you, they don't mind me using their telephone. The last two nights I was at work and called from the telephone booth there. Work is good, and the job is like what I was doing at Banter's. I'm not making many deliveries, but if the guy making them is not here, I can use the store's truck, so I don't need to use my gas which is still hard to get."

"And classes? Did you get the money issue straightened out yet? I worry about that, and I can find something to send you if you need it."

"Thanks, Ma. I'm fine. The money should be straightened out this week. Anyway, I am working, and remember, I paid my rent through the end of the year. I still have a bit of the cash from Joseph, so that helped the first few weeks."

"How are your classes?"

"They are good. I am really enjoying the philosophy class, and the math class is easier than I thought it would be. Since it's been a while for the high school math, I thought I would forget, but..."

"This is the operator. Your five minutes are up."

"O.K. Ma. Tell Edie and Ned I can't wait to see little Mary. I will write this week and try to call in another week or so. Love you, Ma."

"Bye, Mitch. Love you too, and be safe. I'm putting some cookies in the mail this week, so watch out for them."

Thursday Afternoon…Janet Lynn calls Edna

"…and are you sure I can't bring over a casserole for Edie and Ned? I know she will be tired when she gets home."

"Janet Lynn, that is kind of you. There is enough for them to eat now, but why don't you bring them something in a few weeks? That seems to be when they will settle into a schedule with the baby, and Edie will appreciate it them."

"I'll do that. I am so excited to see little Mary. That was Edie's grandmother's name, right?"

"Yes, Nathan's mother was *Mary*, and even though Edie was too young to remember her, she liked the name and Nathan is delighted she decided to name her that. And Edie's middle name is also *Mary*. Of course, the baby's middle name is mine. I am delighted too."

"Well, I'll call once they are home and see if Edie is ready for me to visit this next weekend."

"Janet Lynn, how is married life? I see Tom is now working at the bank, and he seems happy. I did tell him to say *hello* to you."

"Tom did, Mrs. Mitchell. We are fine. I think that we might look into buying one of those houses west of town soon. There are a couple of them for sale, and we are going to view them this next week."

"That will be exciting! I'm happy for you."

"Thanks, Mrs. Mitchell. It was good to talk to you."

"Good-bye, Janet Lynn. Perhaps I'll see you this weekend. I think I'll probably be spending plenty of time helping Edie."

The Following Saturday Afternoon…Hattie calls her Parents

"And the weather? Do you have enough warm clothes?"

"Mama, stop worrying about me. Yes, I have plenty of warm clothes. The winter nursing cloak and the coat are both wool and warm, but I don't need them yet. I also have those cardigans. How are Leon and Elizabeth settling in? And are they going to stay in Everstille? How are the twins? I write to everyone when I can, but just Daddy seems to be good about answering."

"Leon and Elizabeth are fine. They're happy, but I think Elizabeth finds the United States strange. Not so sure they will stay in Everstille, but for now they are living in a cute little rented house in town, and Leon is doing well. He has a job with the telephone company here, and everyone else is good. The twins are fine. Maddy is doing well in school, and Jess is getting along. He is more interested in playing basketball and baseball, but then he is good at both. Wait, Maddy just came in and wants to say *Hi*."

"Hi, Hattie! I miss you. Did you get the letter Daddy sent yet? I put a short note in it for you."

"Not yet, Maddy, but the mail's not here until later, and I'll check then."

"Well, I listed my grades in that letter, and they are all good. Daddy said I might be able to go to Indiana University after high school and study Latin and Greek there. He is helping me learn some of the stuff I will need, and I am getting good at it. I like it too."

"That's exciting, Maddy! I am so glad you are doing well. Looking forward to reading the letter. Love you, and keep up the good work. Is Daddy there?"

"No, Daddy took the car to Mackie's for something, and Jess went with him. Mama wants to talk to you now. Bye, Hattie."

"Hattie, how are the classes going? I know your Daddy will want to hear about them when he returns."

"They are good but hard, and I have a lot of work to do for them. But I will be O.K. The beginning anatomy class is hard. Tell Daddy I must learn all those Latin names…he will get a kick out of that. Also, I'll let you know when the Capping Ceremony will be. I am pretty sure

Mitch will be there too."

"Yes, as soon as you know the date, write. It will be good to see Mitch. Do you think you will be home for Thanksgiving?"

"Mama, I don't think so. A bunch of us are invited to different doctors' houses for dinner, so don't worry about me. Apparently, all the doctors take turns inviting the student nurses for holidays. I will miss all of you though. Tell everyone I said *Hi*. I'll call again next week, and tell Daddy to stay home then so I can talk to him."

"I will, Hattie. Take care and be safe. That Chicago is such a big city, and I worry about you there. There are so many things that can happen."

"Don't worry, Mama. None of us have much time to travel around, and anyway, we never go out alone. We have had lots of lectures about that too. I know time is up, so, bye Mama."

"Good-bye, Hattie. Take care of yourself."

The Next Week, Sunday Afternoon…Mitch calls Hattie

"I am sorry, sir, there is no answer."

"Thanks, operator, I'll try later."

The Following Week, Wednesday Evening…Mitch calls Hattie

"I am sorry, sir, there seems to be no answer."

"O.K., thanks."

The Week After that, Friday Evening…Mitch calls Hattie

"There is no answer, sir."

"Well, thanks. Guess I'll try another time."

Bravery

Viola never thought herself particularly brave. But on three occasions she was.

The first incident happened when John was still alive. It was late summer when the boys were nine years old. They were playing outside near the shed back of the house, and John was sitting on the front porch. He had almost finished his bottle of gin and was considering driving into town for more when there was a horrendous sound from the backyard. He got up to check on it and found that Mike and Mitch had somehow pulled down part of the shed and were standing there trying to figure out what to do. The shed was old and dilapidated, and the boys did not have to do much to get it to collapse, but John, for some reason, took this as a personal affront and began to shout and shriek at the boys. He cornered Mitch against the shed, having removed his leather belt, was screaming that he would *beat the tarnation out of this brat.* John often threatened the boys with beatings, and a few times he had slapped whichever one was closest to him for whatever offence had been committed, but a full out and complete beating had yet to take place.

Mike ran into the house to find Viola, but she had just come out of the backdoor. She came down the stairs and grabbed the spade leaning against the back of the house. She hurried over, placing herself between John and Mitch and held the spade over her head.

"Don't you dare hit him with that belt!" Viola shouted at John.

Without turning, she ordered Mitch to get into the house. Mitch ran from behind her and scooted past his father just as the belt came down and caught him on the back of his leg, not hard enough to break the skin, but enough to cause a scarlet mark. John pulled back his belt to lower it again on the fleeing boy, but the upheld spade smacked the belt. Had she better aim, Viola would have wacked John's hand too, but he pulled back as she whipped the belt out of his grasp and into the ground.

The boys ran into the house, and John turned with surprise and fury towards Viola. She held the spade upright and spoke menacingly.

"I'm warning you, John. You may beat me, but if you ever touch those boys, I won't stop. Do it now; only one of us will be left."

John halted and swayed a bit. Viola had never fought back against him, and her actions stunned him. He was not certain what to do, but he obviously believed her and the spade she was still holding. He screamed as many foul words at her as he could think of, staggered to the car, and drove off wildly. He was gone for the better part of a week.

The second incident happened at the Emporium. Viola was working a late Wednesday evening with Eva. It was a slow night, and they were cleaning, straightening, and refilling items. Viola was near the candy counter when she heard the tinkling of the bell above the door. She looked up and stared at the strange man who had entered and was slowly walking towards the front counter. When she realized who it was, she took a deep breath and felt her heart begin to pound.

Last Saturday, Sheriff Samms had visited all the businesses and spoken with the owners, managers, and clerks. A warning message had come from South Bend Detectives. A man had robbed several small-town stores, but had not been apprehended. A description and sketch of him was available, and Sheriff Samms brought a copy to all the Everstille stores. The sketch was on Viola's desk in the upstairs office, and she had just looked at it again before coming down to assist Eva, so she was positive that the man who had just entered the Emporium was the same.

She did not look straight at the man, but spoke cordially to him and said, "Good evening. I'll be with you in a minute. I just need to complete this task."

She picked up a large stack of aprons from the counter and walked over to Eva saying loudly, "I need you to take this pile to the back, please," and as she placed them into her arms, whispered that she should quietly leave out the back and get Sheriff Samms.

Eva took the pile and walked rapidly to the back of the store. Viola came towards the man who was standing and watching at the front candy counter. As she came closer, she spoke.

"Would you like something? Let me get you a sample of our delicious, fresh bridge mix. Our distributor just brought this in early today and wants customers to try it. Let me know how you like it. The nougat is fresh, and the licorice is wonderfully soft."

She continued to chatter as she took a small white bag and filled it with candy. The man watched as she came around and held it out to him. She was smiling as she appeared to stumble on the wooden floor, then hurled the very full bag of bridge mix into the man's face, turned to the front door, pulled it, and ran out quickly. She almost bumped into Sheriff Samms who, gun drawn, darted through the door only to see

Deputy Jackson, who had come through the back, on the floor handcuffing the thief. The man's gun was over to the side, laying in a pile of fresh nougat and wonderfully soft licorice.

The third incident was when Doctor Grenville told Viola that due to the lung cancer, she had between six and twelve months to live.

**

Viola suffered with an aggravating cough for a year or so, but it would seem to clear up and then come back, and she thought she was keeping it at bay with her homemade remedies and teas. For months, through the dampish fall, the cough got worse, and she would find it difficult to catch her breath. She blamed it on the change of seasons and the cold weather, but it continued. She waited through the end-of-the-year holidays, until the next year when spring was on its way, and then decided to see the doctor.

Doctor Grenville took her vitals and examined her thoroughly. He asked her many questions and wrote furiously in her chart. He told her to get on the scale, and when she got off, he looked at her chart, and then asked her to reweigh.

"Mrs. Jasper, are you trying to lose weight?"

"No, Doctor. I don't have much of an appetite, but I need to eat and keep up my strength. I know I have lost some weight because my clothes are looser, but I'm not trying to. Why?"

"Since I saw you last year, you have lost about eleven pounds. Tell me about how you are feeling in general."

Viola explained that she could not rid herself of her cough, she was sometimes short of breath, was very tired, and lately, she had a pain in her chest and rib area. As she spoke, she had to clear her throat, and the doctor noticed her voice seemed hoarse.

"Alright, why don't you redress. We can speak in my office."

Viola dressed, picked up her coat, hat, and purse, and went with the nurse to the office. She sat in the chair in front of the doctor's new desk, and he checked some of his notes. She coughed forcefully again and tried to clear her throat, and the doctor called for the nurse to bring her a glass of water. Viola sipped at the water and waited for the doctor to finish looking at his notes.

"Mrs. Jasper, I would like to send you for some tests at Elkhart General Hospital. They will do some blood workups and an X-Ray there. I can have my nurse call and make an appointment for you, and if you can get there this week, that would be good."

"Doctor Grenville, is it tuberculosis? "

"I can't say. An X-Ray is the only way to tell, and we need to have certain tests done to make a determination. Will it be possible for someone to drive you to Elkhart? It's closer than South Bend and not quite as busy."

Viola thought for a minute. She had never driven that far in the Buick, and was unsure she wanted to do this by herself. She missed Tillie more than ever, and if Joseph were still here, she knew she could count on him. Even if Mitch were home and not completing his last college year, she wasn't sure she would burden him with this. But there was no other choice, and she knew who she would need to ask.

"Yes, I can get someone to take me," and at this point, Viola had another coughing fit and had a difficult time catching her breath.

Doctor Grenville helped her sip some water when she was able to and called in the nurse. He told Viola to stay seated; the nurse would stay with her, and he would go and make the arrangements. When he returned, he gave her a sheet with directions on it and told her that the appointment was in two days. He should have some information for her a week after that, and the nurse made another office appointment for her.

Viola left the office. It was early spring but deep cold, and she had driven the Buick, not sure she would be able to walk the few streets to the doctor's office. She started the car and drove to the corner where she turned it around, drove back down the street, and parked in front of Banter's Drug Store. She went in to talk to her brother, Nathan.

***

The results took more than a week, and Doctor Grenville sent Viola back to the hospital for some additional tests and to see a specialist there. She was exhausted, and Nathan was worried. He could not say anything to any of their family or friends because Viola had sworn him to secrecy until she found out what the diagnosis was and decided what she would do. Finally, Doctor Grenville called Viola, and she went into his office for the results.

There was no easy way for Doctor Grenville to break the news. Viola was resigned and even stoic hearing the diagnosis. She sat back for a minute and stared down into her hands which were cold and trembled. She looked up at the doctor, thinking that he was not much older than her sons. Her son.

"The only treatment is surgery and radiation?"

"That is the current practice."

"And the best cure rate I would have after that is about thirty percent?"

"Yes, Mrs. Jasper. Those are the figures. You need to know everyone responds differently, and there's no guarantee for thirty percent. On the other hand, there are cases where patients have a higher rate of success. Yours is an unusual case. Lung cancer of this kind is rare in women. I am sorry you are one of those women. I can suggest some excellent doctors and specialists for you, but I would recommend that you not wait too long to do this because the cancer is advanced."

Viola then asked what the effects of radiation would be. Doctor Grenville did not hesitate to explain them to her. She sat quietly and listened. She asked additional questions and heard the terrifying answers. She asked about pain.

"There is pain, but again, it is relative. Usually women have a higher pain tolerance than men, but it depends on the individual. There is *Codeine* which can help control coughing and pain, and then *Morphine* for more severe pain. Both drugs are tolerated well, but you need to be careful with their use. Are you in pain currently?"

"Not particularly. I just want as much information as I can get to help me make some decisions."

"Are there other concerns or questions you have? No? Well, I am here should you need further information or help. And, once you have decided what you want to do, I will help with that."

Viola thanked the doctor and left the office. Spring was early, there was little visible snow, but the weather was still harsh. However, the sun and blue sky gave the promise of a different season. Viola walked to the Buick and got in. There were two things she needed to do.

***

She drove slowly to North Cemetery. Snow could still cover the graves, but she knew where she was going. She turned and drove into the cemetery thinking that she should have gone home first to get her winter boots. At the top of the lane, Viola stopped the car and stepped out. *Be careful; don't fall and kill yourself,* and she giggled at the irony. She walked to the place where her parents rested and looked it over. She looked around the cemetery noting the space that was available. Then she went to the graves of her husband and son. She wiped off the bit of snow which was on top of Mike's stone and ran her fingers over the chiseled name: *Michael John Jasper.* Viola stood for some time, then bent and kissed the top of Mike's stone. She walked carefully to the car, backed out of the narrow lane, and headed into town.

Once on Main Street, she drove to Jamison's Livery and Funeral Home to speak with Mr. Jamison who was surprised to see her. They sat down in his office on the overly heavy leather furniture, and Viola spoke, explaining what she required. Mr. Jamison did an excellent job of not looking startled or shocked, and assured Viola that her wishes would be carried out. There was a discussion about finances and payments. Once all was settled, Viola stood and held her hand out to Mr. Jamison who cradled it for a while before letting go.

As Viola left the building, she felt inexplicably satisfied. She drove home and did not cough even once. As she parked the car, Edna leaned out of her house and waved *hello* to her and Viola waved back. She entered the house, hung up her coat, and put away her hat. Walking into the kitchen, she turned the kitchen light on, put the teapot to boil, and began to bravely live her remaining six to twelve months.

Letters and Calls and Visits

It was not that Hattie and Mitch did not want to see each other, but they were both so busy with school and jobs, that time and distance took their toll. At first, letters came a couple times a week, but as the years passed, one might appear every six weeks or so. Telephone calls were not always successful since Hattie was not able to call Mitch; he did not have ready access to a phone and needed to rely on the phone booth at work. While there was a telephone in her dorm room, Hattie was not always there to receive the calls. The student nurses had devised a method of placing a small sheet of paper on the phone when they were gone. The ringing of the telephone would shake the instrument, knocking off the paper, and that would be the signal that a call had come in. Of course, there was no way to tell who the call was from…a beau or the cleaners wanting to know when you were going to pick up your cleaned nurse's cloak.

Visits were rare. Hattie grew used to living in Chicago. She seldom came home and her family visited her infrequently. Her parents and Mitch came to her Capping Ceremony during her first year, and during one summer, her sister, Maddy, visited for a week. The brief winter breaks were the only times she came home because during the summers, she took additional courses and worked in the hospital. At graduation, her parents, a couple of her siblings, and Mitch came to watch as she received her Registered Nurse Diploma, and they celebrated with a dinner in a Downtown Chicago restaurant. Then Hattie and a friend rented and shared a small apartment while they both continued to work at the Main County Hospital.

The G.I Bill provided Mitch with an education. It paid for his tuition and gave him a small stipend for his rent, but there were other necessities and the upkeep on the car, so Mitch was grateful to have the job he did. He worked as much as he could and that included weekends. About every five or six weeks, he would drive home and spend a weekend with his mother and the rest of his family. On his drive back to school, he acquired the habit of stopping at the Wells' cabin to say *hello* and often spent an hour or two talking with Bob Wells. They enjoyed discussing historical events, especially ancient ones, and shared that interest. Mitch was as fascinated with the stories Bob told as were the Well's children. A friendship was forged.

Hattie and Mitch would see each other once or twice during their winter breaks. They would go for a dinner at Mazie's and sometimes meet up with friends and catch up with the news of their lives. They had decided years before that there would be no exchange of gifts or serious talk of a permanent bond, although there was an unspoken understanding between them. Both were content to let their friendship take its course. Whatever that might be.

Hattie's fourth year in Chicago was Mitch's last year in college. She was busy working and finding her way as an adult, and Mitch was preparing to finish up his degree and complete a round of student teaching. The new year's undertakings were demanding, and they found themselves writing fewer letters, and Mitch attempted fewer phone calls. They did not forget about each other, but assumed that this was friendship's path.

***

In the late spring of that year, on a weekend Mitch was home, Viola sat down with him and spoke seriously about the fact that her future would not be a long one. The conversation was painful and tearful for both. Mitch tried to talk his mother into at least attempting the surgery and radiation Doctor Grenville had suggested, but Viola would not be swayed.

"Mitch, you are almost finished with your education, and I am determined to go to your graduation in a few months. I'm as proud of you as I can be. But I know what is best for me. I won't undergo a surgery and that awful radiation when the chances of it helping are so low. I intend to be able to stand and applaud for you as you walk across that stage, and there is no guarantee that will happen if I have the surgery."

"Then I am moving home as soon as I graduate to be with you."

This was not his plan. Mitch had been offered a temporary position at the South Bend high school where he was doing his student teaching. He would teach a summer course, and then be a substitute teacher in the fall with the hope of obtaining a full-time position in a year. He planned to continue renting the apartment from the Benson's and keep his job at the drug store on week-ends and nights. Viola knew what the plans were, and she would not let him change them.

"No, Mitch. This is your life and you need to get on with it. However, there are some things I want you to know and to do for me."

There was a serious discussion, some questions, and instructions. Mitch listened sorrowfully and answered reverently. The day was getting late, and although he wanted to stay longer, Viola told him he needed to get back for his classes, and teaching, and jobs. She would not let her son interrupt his life for her.

"I am fine. I'm still working at the Emporium although putting in fewer hours, and Eve is a great help. So far, I have been able to handle the little pain I have. Doctor Grenville has been wonderful with his help, and Edna and Nathan check on me daily. In fact, it's getting somewhat annoying! Edna calls me each morning just to wish me well, although between you and me, she is checking to see if I'm still alive!"

Mitch was shocked at his mother's cavalier attitude, but Viola just laughed and hugged him.

"Mitch, I know it's difficult for you to understand, but I am at peace with my decisions, and I want you to be too. Now, let's pack up some food for you to take back. Those sugar cookies are going, and I can make some sandwiches for your next few lunches. Make sure you let me know how the classes are proceeding, and when you find out the date for your graduation, tell me so I can make sure Edna and Nathan and I can all get there. Also, think about a place you would like to eat after the ceremony. You know better than we would where a good place would be."

Viola got up and went to the kitchen to organize the food, and Mitch went upstairs to finish packing. Once she was alone, Viola opened the kitchen cabinet where she kept a small bottle and shook out two more tablets of codeine into her hand. She filled a glass with water and took them, hoping to continue to control her coughing until Mitch was on his way back to school. She thought that she may have taken more than she should have, but she did not want to have the hacking fits she was prone to while her son was home. The pain was becoming worse, but she had lied about it to avoid additionally upsetting Mitch. She placed the bottle back into the cupboard, and opened the icebox to take out the ham and began to prepare sandwiches.

Viola stood on the porch and waved and blew kisses to Mitch as he drove away. Her chest hurt, and the last time she had coughed, her lovely embroidered handkerchief came away with flecks of blood showing. She was tired and planned on an early bedtime tonight. She also wondered if two more tablets would hurt, and she thought it was time to call Doctor Grenville for something stronger. She would ask for a morphine prescription tomorrow.

Mitch drove away thinking about his mother. He had heard her coughing during the night and noticed how thin she was. He also saw the bottle of codeine she had placed in the kitchen cabinet. As he passed the Wells' cabin, he glanced at the lighted window, but did not stop. There was no interest in discussing ancient stories tonight. None at all.

May 1, 1952

Dear Mitch,

I was so glad to get your last letter, and I'm sorry for taking almost a month to answer. It's been a bit crazy here, and I've been busy. My roommate moved out two months ago. She's living with her parents to save money for her wedding in the fall, and I have picked up a couple more shifts. Having the apartment to myself is great, but all the costs are doubled.

You asked about my family. Maddy is at Indiana University, and Jess is working on Clyde's farm which is doing well. Hazel married a man who raises horses and moved to Tennessee in April. I thought you might know this, but Daddy says you haven't been by for a while. Everyone else is fine. Leon and Elizabeth are having a baby in the fall, and Beatrice and Josh are expecting their third. Mama and Daddy are thrilled, and the cabin is unbelievably full when everyone is home for the holidays.

So sorry we couldn't get together then. I know there was a lot of snow and the roads were almost impossible, but I couldn't stay more than a couple of nights. The hospital is busy and there is a shortage of R.N.'s, so there is always a chance to pick up a few more shifts.

Anyway, to answer your question, no, I am sorry I won't be able to make your graduation. I would love to be there, but that falls on a work day for me, and I can't get the time off. I want you to know that I am proud of all you accomplished and hope the best for you. I love hearing about your student teaching experiences. It sounds like you are a great teacher and the kids really like you. I hope you will be able to get a full-time teaching job in South Bend, but I hear there are plenty of jobs available in the Chicago schools. Just a thought.

I will be thinking of you as you graduate. Send me a program so I can see what went on. Really, Mitch, I miss our times together. Say "hello" to your family.

Affectionately,

Hattie

P.S. I hope to get a telephone soon. I'll send you the number when I do.

Peppermint Tea

Viola stood up and clapped loudly as Mitch crossed the stage at his college graduation. She yelled his name, and he looked up to see her and waved and smiled at her and his Uncle Nathan and Aunt Edna. Mitch did not see that Nathan helped Viola to stand, and kept his arm around her to prevent her from falling into her seat covered with the soft blanket Edna had brought along so that the pain from the hard surface would be minimized. Once the ceremony was over and the family found each other, Mitch could see how pale and thin Viola was. But, the happiness of the day overcame the brutality of the disease embracing her.

There were reservations for a celebration at Robertson's Tea Room, and Nathan drove the family there. He stopped in front of the building so Viola and Edna could get out and wait inside where the newly air-conditioned building would present some respite from the heat. Nathan and Mitch drove away to park the car.

"Your mother is really proud of your accomplishments, you know. In fact, we all are."

Mitch nodded. "Thanks, Uncle Nate. And thanks for coming and bringing Ma. She doesn't look well. How bad is she?"

"Well, Mitch, your mother is a pretty strong woman in her own way. Edna and I check on her daily, and she still walks to the Emporium most days for a while. I've even seen her in the backyard garden puttering around. Doctor Grenville is good to her, and comes to the house every week to check on her. We are all watching out for her."

"I wanted to come home and be with her, but she insisted I stay here. Now I have commitments with the drug store and the summer school class I am teaching, so I will. But, will you promise me that you'll call if I'm needed? You have the Benson's telephone number, don't you? Good. They know who you are and can get in touch with me. You know the drug store's number and I'll give you the school's number. I told Ma I would be home every weekend, but she is afraid I won't be able to keep up my duties here."

"I know Vi wants you to go on and start your life, but I'll get the numbers. O.K., let's get back to the restaurant. I can use a cool drink."

***

The graduation, the round-trip to South Bend and the heat were too much for Viola. She was in bed all weekend, and when Monday came, she was not well enough for work. She called Eva to explain what needed to be done and then went back to bed. *Eva will be a great manager*, she thought, *and I know she's able to correctly complete all the paperwork She's smart. I need to talk to Mr. Melworth this week.*

Viola knew she was getting to the point that work would no longer be possible, but she hoped to last through the summer. She and Doctor Grenville had spoken about increasing the dosages of her medicines, but once that happened, she would not be able to work or drive or do much of anything else. Her pain and cough were worsening.

Edna and Nathan wanted her to move in with them, but she treasured her independence and was reluctant to burden family members. Besides, Edna was watching over her mother, Millie who was frail and going deaf. Viola would stay in the house and tend to herself. She had made decisions months ago.

***

Summer was gone. It was early fall, a Sunday afternoon, and Mitch had been home for the weekend. He regaled his mother and family with stories about his substitute teaching, and while he had not been offered a full-time position, he was sure there would be one soon. In the meantime, he worked as a substitute and at the drug store.

When Mitch left, he hugged his mother for a long time. She was weak, and her glazed eyes told him how the drugs were affecting her. Edna had brought over the Sunday dinner, and the family ate at Viola's dining table so that she would not have to struggle to walk across the street and down three houses to her childhood home.

After Mitch had left to go back to South Bend, Viola readied herself for an early bedtime. She checked the doors and turned out the lights, and the phone rang. It was a collect call.

"Hello?" she asked, after accepting the charges.

"Hi, Ma, it's me."

"Mitch, are you alright? Is something wrong? I just saw you a couple hours ago."

"I am fine. I asked the Bensons if I could use their phone. I just wanted to tell you something."

"Are you sure everything is fine? What is it? Did you forget something?"

"No, don't worry, everything is good. Ma, I just wanted to tell you again that I love you. I just felt I wanted to say it again."

Viola was quiet for a moment. She covered the phone so Mitch would not hear the cough she struggled to hold noiseless.

"Mitch, I love you too. I could not have a better son."

There was a quiet on both ends. Contemplations, considerations, and certainties became tangled in the wires

"Take care, Ma. I'll see you next weekend."

"Thanks, Mitch. You be safe now. Good-night."

Viola hung up the telephone and as she did so, she felt a pain so intense, she needed to grab onto the wall to stay upright. Once she caught a breath, she eased herself down into a chair. It was getting worse. She was certain Mitch could tell, and that was why he called. Tears rose in her eyes, and she tried to take some deep breaths again. *The time is coming*, she thought.

***

She had carefully picked the weeds early in the summer so that the flowers and leaves would dry out. There were plenty to choose from in the dormant Victory garden. She took the dried parts into the kitchen to grind into a powder. The morning was pleasant and sunny, and the sky was going to be clear by noon. The day would be perfect.

Out of the back-kitchen window, she saw the wild peppermint growing alongside the fence. She walked slowly out the door, and down the steps, and over to the fence when a coughing fit overtook her. After it was over, she stood and tried to take some breaths. They were shallow. It was never possible to get enough air. Stooping low, she picked the wild peppermint certain it would make a strong tea. Before entering the house, Viola stood still and looked up to the window at Mitch's bedroom and the one at Mike's. She remembered when the boys were young and laughing and happy. She felt her eyes cloud with tears and blinked quickly. Determined to remain resolute and not become maudlin, she went into the house, into the kitchen, and began to prepare the tea.

Filling the teapot with water and washing out her cups kept her busy. Her pain was at bay for now, and she was thankful for that. While the water boiled, she made one more round of the house. The rooms were clean and straight, but she readjusted a pillow, and in the front room, she opened the window drapery so the morning sunshine hit her favorite chair. She was not frightened, but was concerned that she would be sick before the preparation had a chance to work.

She came back into the kitchen and reached up into the cabinet to take out the bottle of morphine tablets. She poured them out on the counter and counted them. There were twenty. She moved them to the kitchen table and lined them up. She had thought this out carefully. The peppermint should settle her stomach, and to ensure that her empty stomach did not reject her preparation, she opened the yellow breadbox and took out a slice of bread and chewed it slowly. She had two clean cups ready. A strong peppermint tea was seeping with the powder from the plants. She was thorough. As the tea readied, she cleaned the kitchen, removing all remains of plants. Opening the back door, she threw the remnants out to the yard.

She sat down at the kitchen table with her cups of tea and the little white pills. Sipping the first cup, she thought *Not bad, but a bit of sugar will help.* She took a spoon from the silverware drawer and as she came back to the table, the sharp pain she dreaded crossed her chest and ribs, and she doubled over and held on to the shiny clean table until it left her. *Not much more,* she thought, *not much more.* After the pain subsided, she sat on the chair and removed the top of the much-loved pink flowered sugar bowl. A small spoon of sugar went into the first cup, and she tasted it. *Better,* she thought. She took a handful of the small pills, placed them into her mouth. and drank the remainder of the tea.

She waited to see if her body would reject the tea and pills, but apparently it accepted them. Again, something to be grateful for. She then mixed some sugar with the second cup and drank it down with the remaining pills. She sat for a while, hoping to keep everything down. She did.

Picking up the cups and spoon, she took them over to the sink, and washed and dried them, and put them away. The telephone rang, and she automatically reached over to pick it up, but stopped herself. *I almost forgot,* she thought, *it is only Edna with her morning check. She will probably think I am still in bed.* Coughing shook her body, and she held onto the counter until she could take a breath. She stood for a few minutes thinking she might be sick, but it passed.

Viola made sure the back and front doors were unlocked. There was no sense in making it more difficult than it would be. *I suppose it will be Edna who will find me; she will be over once I don't answer another call,* she thought. *That's good. She is strong and sensible and will know what to do. Better her than Nathan.*

She walked to the front room and looked around once more. Everything was ordered. She had not left a note. There was no need. Viola began to feel a bit sleepy, and she sat down in her chair and arranged herself so that the morning sun streaming through the front window warmed her. She pulled the light throw upon which she had embroidered a garden of poppies over her lap and tucked it into her sides. She settled back and took some deep breathes and felt a sense of completion. There would be no more pain or coughing. No more sadness. No more regrets or guilt or remorse. She wondered if the preparation had been enough because she would hate to wake up in a hospital. *Perhaps I should make one more cup,* she thought, but realized she was too tired to get up and smiled faintly. *I must have done it correctly this time.*

The sun was shining on her face, warming, and comforting her. She took what she thought were deep breathes, but they were shallow, and somehow, she could not pull in the air. Her head was heavy and she leaned it back on the chair and closed her eyes. Thoughts wandered through her mind, but she could not hang on to any of them except the one about Mike. *I wonder if I will see him? I hope so.* Holding on to her son's face, Viola smiled and took a few small intakes of air before she stopped trying. Her head shifted to the side, and her right arm fell downward. Her entire body relaxed and slipped a little, but she stayed on her favorite chair. The sun shone fully on her face warming it as it chilled, until there were no more shallow breaths, no more thoughts, no more pains.

Questions

After everyone had left, Mitch sat down on one of the chairs in the larger parlor and sighed loudly. Nathan sat in the other one, and Edna leaned against the wall. It had been a long, sad day, and they were all tired. Millie was upstairs in her room taking a nap, and Edie was stacking the cups and plates in the kitchen, while Ned had taken little Mary out for a walk before putting her down for a nap.

"I can't thank you enough for everything," Mitch looked at his aunt and uncle, and even though he thought there were no more tears left, his eyes clouded over.

Edna walked over to her nephew and leaned down and kissed his cheek. She patted his hand and then stood up and stretched back to relieve the backache.

"Mitch, we're family. There is nothing we wouldn't do for you and for Viola. I know this week has been difficult for all of us. We probably should all take a nap with Mother and Little Mary. How about if I put on a fresh pot of coffee for us?"

"Sounds good, Edna. Is there any cake left? I didn't eat much and could go for a piece."

"Yes, Nate, I am sure there is. Let me help Edie with those dishes and put the coffee on. I'll let you know when everything is ready."

Edna walked out to the kitchen but stopped and kicked off her shoes first. Nathan and Mitch sat back and were silent for a while. Nathan looked sideways at Mitch. He had some questions to ask, but wasn't sure this was the right time to do so. He waited another minute before just blurting them out.

"Mitch, did you know what Viola intended to do? Did she tell you? She never said a thing to us, but apparently Mr. Jamison was in on it. He said there was nothing to pay; that Viola had taken care of it all. I have to say, we were surprised."

"Yes, Uncle Nate. She told me a few months ago, and, asked my permission. She said if I did not think it would be suitable that she would cancel the plans. But I didn't care, and I wanted her to do what she wanted. Ma always had her own thoughts and beliefs, and frankly, the stuff with Pa happened so long ago, it seems like another life. I think both Mike and I had a great childhood, no matter what happened. I wasn't sure if she had said anything to you, but I just figured it was her doing, so I kept quiet. I suppose the town was gossiping about it all."

"Well, they will be after today. It's done, and Viola is at rest the way she wants to be. I am glad you agreed to stay here with us. Being in that big house by yourself would be too lonely. We don't get a chance to see you often, and I know Edie and Ned have enjoyed your company."

There was a noise at the front door, and Ned came in carrying an almost asleep Mary.

"Going to put her down. Will be right back," he said in a partial whisper as he carried her up the stairs to the crib.

Edie came into the room wiping her hands on her apron.

"Was that Ned? Good. Mary needs a long nap today. Come on in the kitchen. Coffee is ready and we put out some sandwiches, and food, and the rest of the cake. I think we all need to relax for a bit."

They went into the kitchen and sat down at the table that had hosted the Mitchell Sunday suppers. Ned joined them, and they passed the food and filled their plates with the leftover salads, and sandwiches, and cake. As Mitch stirred his coffee and watched his family chew he thought, *Mike, and Tillie, and now Ma. They should all be here.*

***

Edie and Mitch sat on the porch swing at Viola's house and pushed back and forth. They finished cleaning and doing some packing and sorting in the house. Mitch was leaving in the morning to go back to South Bend and resume his jobs.

"So, do you think you will ever move back here?"

"Probably not, Edie. There are no teaching positions available at the high school, and that is what I want to do. I'll have better luck finding something in a bigger place like South Bend or maybe even Chicago."

Edie glanced at him and smiled.

"Chicago? Isn't that where Hattie lives and works? Is there something you aren't telling me?"

Mitch grinned and shook his head.

"No, Edie. Hattie and I are still in touch but not as often as we were. I would like there to be something between us, but I don't know. I'm just not sure how she feels, and we haven't seen each other too much during the past few years. I don't think she is seeing anyone in Chicago, but then, I don't know. She hasn't told me, but then she might not. With Ma so sick over the past year, and the two jobs I have, I've been busy too."

"Well, there's lots you don't seem to know. Maybe you should find out. Can you?"

"I guess. Mr. Wells asked me to stop and see him before I drive back tomorrow. He and his wife were at the funeral and spoke to me for a long time, but it was about Ma and how kind she was to the family. They told me stuff I never knew about how she helped them out. Don't know exactly what good luck happened to them, but they seem to be a lot better off now than they were. I used to stop and visit with Mr. Wells when I was traveling back and forth to college. I like him. He's really smart."

"All you can do is try and find out about Hattie. It's too late for me to fix you up with Janet Lynn, now that she is Mrs. Everett!"

"Guess so. Sorry I missed that wedding, but those college years were busy. I did call and wish Tom good luck. Hope they are happy. I never thought those two would get together. Were you responsible for that?"

"Nope, not that one. They met on their own. Will you be substitute teaching next week?"

"I think so. I never really know until the night before when I call in to the school. If not, Mr. Krepple at the drug store has been great to me, letting me work extra hours if I don't have any teaching jobs. So far, I've been lucky. The Bensons are also kind people, and I do like the apartment. Been there almost five years now."

"Got a girlfriend, Mitch? I'll bet you have met some nice girls there."

"No girlfriend. I do have some friends, male and female, and sometimes we get together, but not lately. Right now, I just need to get back to work and figure some things out."

"When will we see you again?"

"I guess your parents are going to arrange for an estate sale of the furniture and stuff I don't want. And, really, I don't have any room for it. I packed up the rest of my stuff and took a few things of Mike's, and I'll be back for the sale. I guess it will take a couple of months to get it together. Thanks for your help today, Edie. This was tough to do, and I am glad you were here."

"Anytime, Mitch. Let's go back to the house. Mary should be up from her nap now, and I told Mother I would help with dinner."

They got up from the swing and walked down the steps and across the street. Suddenly Mitch stopped and turned around. He told Edie to go on ahead, and he would be there in a minute. He forgot something. He turned and strode back to the house and into the backyard where he searched around until he saw what he wanted. He picked it up, went to his car, opened the passenger side door, and placed the basketball he and Mike used to play with on the car floor.

***

"Come on in, Mitch. Bob is out in the back and will be right in. Sit down in the front room, and I'll let him know you are here."

Emma ushered Mitch into the room with the fireplace and motioned him to a chair.

When she left, Mitch looked at the line of books stacked on the sturdy, homemade book shelves. He recognized a few of them, but many more had Latin and Greek titles, and he wasn't sure his high school Latin would be good enough to read them. He turned when he heard a noise and smiled as Bob Wells came into the room. Bob smiled back at him and held out his hand.

"Happy to see you, Mitch, and thanks for stopping. I know you're busy and have a lot on your mind. It was good to see your family, and again, I am so sorry about Viola. Your mother was a generous and helpful woman. But I have already spoken about that. I just want you to understand that Emma and I will always be grateful for the things your mother did for our family when times were really tough."

"I am glad you told me the things you did. Ma was a special person. She was stronger and more resilient than even I knew. I heard lots of stories about her from people at the funeral. Things I was never aware of."

Emma came in carrying two tall glasses of apple cider and placed them down on the table before them. Bob and Mitch thanked her and took a swallow of the cider.

"Um, really good, Thank you, Em. This is the first of the season, and it's always tasty. So, Mitch, I have missed our discussions. You are teaching now?"

"Right now, there is not a position open, but I am substitute teaching and have kept the drug store job. I am hoping something will become available soon. My best bet is a larger city, and I have even considered going to Chicago. That is a large school system, and I suspect positions will be available."

Bob took another swallow of the cider and put down the glass. He sat back and moved the book that was behind him on his chair to the floor. He crossed one leg over the other and looked at Mitch.

"Chicago. That's an interesting thought. Hattie would be pleased to see you again."

Mitch set his cider glass down and leaned forward in his chair. He looked down for a second as though to gather his thoughts and then sat up and looked at Bob.

"Speaking of Hattie, Mr. Wells, I would like to talk about her. I have some questions."

Bob Wells sat back, prepared to listen.

Here to Stay

Hattie ran down the stairs and then ran down another flight. There was someone chasing her, and she needed to get away. She turned a corner and was startled because she did not recognize where she was. There were large trees all around her, and enormous red-winged birds nesting in them, and a large stream in front of her. How did she get here? The person was getting closer, and she did not know where to go. She decided to stand her ground, and when she turned, she saw the person was Mitch. She was so glad to see him that she began to laugh, and Mitch laughed with her. He came towards her, holding out his hand and...

The alarm squawked, waking Hattie. She reached over and shut it off and then fell back against the sheets. Time to get to work. She was exhausted, but all she needed to do was to get through this day. Tomorrow she had a well-deserved day off, and she would sleep late, and then do some of the chores she had been putting off because there simply was no time. Working all these shifts was getting to her, and she determined not to agree to take so many. She figured out last night that by working just four extra shifts a month, she could pay her bills and rent without a roommate. Although, she was still thinking about looking for another one.

She rolled out of the bed, pulled up the sheet and covers in a hasty attempt at making it, and walked into the bathroom. As she got ready for the early morning shift, she tried to remember the last dream she had. Mitch was in it, and then she remembered that she needed to answer his last letter. She sent him a short note when his mother died, but she owed him a longer letter. Tomorrow she would write one. Perhaps at the laundromat, as she caught up with her laundry.

She smoothed cream on her face and brushed her hair allowing the auburn curls to bounce into place. Her hair was much easier to handle since she had it cut, but she needed another haircut. Maybe tomorrow. She slipped her white uniform over her head and pulled on her white hose. Stepping into her shoes, she realized they needed polishing. Taking the white shoe polish out of the tall cabinet, she bent to wipe the front of them so they looked cleaner. Tomorrow she would clean and polish all her shoes.

Hattie spent ten minutes hanging things up and placing things back. *This place really needs a good cleaning too*, she thought. *Maybe tomorrow...* From the small front closet, she took out her heavy black cardigan and pulled it on. Her purse was on the chair and she grabbed it, checking to make sure her wallet, keys, and hospital ID were there. *I need to stop and pick up a few groceries after work. I need some bread and apples and oatmeal, and milk, and maybe lettuce, and I should see what kind of prices the store is asking for hamburger meat. And THAT,* she reminded herself, *can't wait until tomorrow if I want to eat tonight.*

She picked up her wristwatch from the table and put it on, Giving one quick look around, she left, locked the door, and walked down the flight of stairs. Striding to the corner where the streetcar would be stopping in about five minutes, she glanced again at her wrist. *I'll have some time to get coffee and toast when I get to work, and I need to get my toaster repaired. Tomorrow...*

***

As he drove back to South Bend, he decided to take a chance, to change some things. When Mitch got to his apartment, he began the necessary alterations. He told the Bensons he would be leaving in a month and offered to help them find a replacement for him. Young men were always looking for a place, and it did not take long. Within a week, a teacher at the high school knew someone who agreed to take over the apartment. He met the Bensons who approved of him, and Mitch was able to sell most of his furniture to him at a decent price for them both.

Leaving the substitute teacher job was not hard. Telling Mr. Krepple he would no longer be working there was more difficult. He liked the man, and appreciated the opportunities for working he had been given. But it was time to move on.

On the day of his move, Mitch packed his belongings in the car. His trunk was full and the back seat loaded. He went in to the Bensons to say a final good-bye, and Mr. Benson shook his hand hardily while Mrs. Benson hugged him and handed him a large wrapped package of chocolate chip cookies she had baked for him. He handed them the keys and told them that their new tenant would be over in the afternoon to pick them up and pay his rent. Yes, he promised, he would let them know how he was doing as soon as he could. More handshakes and hugs, and finally, Mitch was on his way.

He drove his car to the gas station to fill up and check the tires and oil. He did not want anything to go wrong. Not on this trip. He would stop somewhere for a quick lunch and more gas, and before he started the car, he pulled out the map and checked his route and the hand-written directions once more. He removed his hat and placed it on the basketball which was still on the passenger side floor. Then Mitch began his journey to Chicago.

***

Mitch got out of the car and walked around to the sidewalk. He looked up at the windows in the apartments above the shoe shop. One of them was Hattie's, according to her parents. He checked his watch and rechecked the cross street and the numbers on the building. This was correct. He leaned against his car and crossed his arms as he watched the streetcars go by. One. Two. They stopped at the diagonal corner across the street named *Archer*, but there was no one for him. The third street-car came by and stopped, and there she was. She had her purse over her shoulder and was holding a grocery bag and got off with some other people. They all waited until the sizeable vehicle passed, the traffic light changed, and then crossed Archer Avenue together.

Hattie walked next to an older woman, and they conversed until they parted ways. The older woman continued straight down the cross street while Hattie turned right, crossed another street, and stepped up on the curb. She moved closer to the apartment, but suddenly stopped and looked directly at Mitch who stood up straight and uncrossed his arms placing them at his side. Standing at attention, just as he had learned in the army, Mitch looked steadfastly at Hattie. They were about fifteen feet apart. As Hattie stood still, a couple brushed past, almost bumping into her, and another woman looked at her with annoyance and said loudly, "Well, excuse me!" as she walked around her.

The two of them stared at each other for what seemed like hours. Hattie moved forward cautiously as though she were approaching a specter. She moved directly in front of Mitch, looked into his eyes, and said, "I dreamed about you last night."

Mitch looked at her curled auburn hair, now shorter than he had ever seen it, and replied, "I think about you every day."

Hattie questioned, "Are you here for a visit?"

Mitch leaned forward and took the bag of groceries from her arms and shifted them into his.

"No," he replied, "No. I'm here to stay."

Hattie stood totally still for a few seconds and then opened her purse and took out her key. Reaching her arm out and linking it through Mitch's free one, she pulled him forward, closer to her, and quietly observing him said, "Well then, we should go up to the apartment."

And they did.

Endings

Mitch and Hattie were married on a Wednesday one month later in a quiet mid-morning ceremony at the First Baptist Church in Everstille. The small wedding included just their families. Of course, *small* described quite a large group since all the Wells, except for Hazel and her husband who could not get in from Tennessee, were there. As Bob walked Hattie down the aisle, he grinned at Mitch who grinned back at him, and a hug followed their handshake. After the brief ceremony, the united families shared a luncheon at the newly updated and expanded Mazie's Restaurant, and Mazie herself offered bottles of her best beer for the group to toast the newlyweds. Afterwards, the couple left for a brief stay in the Bridal Suite of Elkhart's newest hotel.

Mr. and Mrs. Mitchell Jasper were back in Everstille early Saturday morning to attend the estate sale of Viola Mitchell Jasper's furniture, household goods and sundries. It was a sadder day than Mitch thought it would be, even though the cash outcome from the sale was more than he expected. The money was going to come in handy since Mitch did not yet have a job in Chicago although he had filed his paperwork with the Chicago Board of Education. He was informed by the woman who grumpily accepted his portfolio *that these things take six to eight weeks at least, and you can check back then.* Speediness was not a hallmark of the Board of Education.

Mitch and Hattie settled into her apartment. They decided to stay there because it was convenient. And cheap. And now, teased Hattie, no roommate was necessary. Upon the couple's return Mitch would begin a part-time job at a grocery store only a few blocks away. The job would not provide much money, but at least there would be something coming in while Mitch waited out his six to eight weeks or more. The store was close enough that Mitch could walk to work. He said not only would the walking save the car, but he would get to know the neighborhood, get to familiarize himself with his new surroundings. It was all an adventure. Hattie and Mitch were happy.

After the estate sale, they stayed overnight at the Mitchell house. The following morning, the family gathered for breakfast. Edie and Hattie set the table while Edna and Millie worked at scrambling the eggs and making the biscuits. Ned had little Mary in the front room surrounded by her toys, and he and Mitch and Nathan were talking and sipping the freshly made coffee.

"So, Mitch, are you and Hattie going to stay in Chicago? Have any plans to return here?"

"For now, Uncle Nate, we are committed to the city. Hattie's job is a good one, and I really think that once I get a position in the city schools, we will do well there. Honestly, I don't see that we'll be returning here any time soon. Of course, our families are here, and we'll be back to visit."

"That's good," said Ned taking a wooden block out of Mary's mouth and placing it on top of three other wooden blocks, "You know you are welcome to stay with us any time. Did you know that we will be moving into Millie's house?"

"Yes, Edie mentioned it. That's a good idea. I am glad that house will stay in the family. I want to thank you for helping with Ma's sale. There is no way I could have done that."

"You're welcome, Mitch," and Nathan yelled into the kitchen, "Is breakfast ready?"

Edie came into the room and leaned down to pick up Mary and said, "Ready. Come on and eat."

The family trooped into the dining room and sat down. Millie and Hattie brought in platters of food while Edna refilled the coffee cups. Edie strapped Mary into her highchair and placed some soft eggs and bits of biscuit on her little plate, and everyone began to eat. Once chewing commenced and talking diminished, Edie clinked her spoon on her orange juice glass.

"Ned and I want to share our good news with you, now that we are positive. We are expecting a brother or sister for Mary next spring!"

There were claps and laughter, and they all agreed that a move into the larger house would happen just in time. Everyone raised their coffee cup or juice glass and toasted the happy news while little Mary, not realizing that she would soon be dethroned, continued to bang her spoon against her high chair and throw scrambled eggs on the floor.

***

The car packed and goodbyes said, Mitch and Hattie headed out of town to visit with her parents before proceeding back to Chicago. They drove past the Emporium, and Banter's Drugs, and the high school, and turned down old Smokehouse Road leading to the cabin. The fall day was cool, and the leaves were beginning their autumn transformation. Mitch turned to Hattie and asked:

"Before we go to your parents, would you mind if we stopped at the cemetery? Mr. Jamison told me that Ma's stone is in place, and I would like to check it out."

"That's a good idea. I want to pay my respects, and I can see Rebecca's and Vernon's too."

Mitch drove slowly into the narrow lane and parked the car. When he and Hattie got out, Mitch motioned for her to follow him up to the top row of graves. He stopped in front of three and pointed.

"Here is where Tillie is. Her mother-in-law and husband and baby son are there. She was the only grandmother I even knew. Mike and I would fight over the last piece of her pie, and she would divide it up evenly and then make another one for us. I have good memories of her. When Tillie died, Ma really missed her. So did Joseph."

"Where are your real grandparents?"

"They are over here," and Mitch and Hattie moved to their graves on the next row. "I never knew them. Grandma died when Ma was about thirteen. Tillie helped to raise her and Uncle Nate."

"I wish I had known Tillie. I do remember how kind your mother was to Rebecca and me. Those sugar cookies she would make were the best. We rarely got treats like that when we were little. Where is your mother buried?"

Mitch looked at Hattie for a minute before he motioned, "Over there."

They moved down one more row, walked to the left, and stood in front of two graves and two headstones, one much newer than the other. Mitch stepped back to get a better view of them both and nodded.

"It looks good. Mr. Jamison did a great job."

Hattie stood still for a moment. She looked puzzled. She turned to Mitch and raised her hand and pointed at the two stones.

"Mitch, what happened? The last time we were here, this was where your father and Mike were. Now your mother is here alongside

Mike. Am I wrong? What happened? Where is your father?"

Mitch's mouth formed into something between a smile and a frown. He sighed and then spoke.

"When Ma knew she was dying, she went to Mr. Jamison and paid him for another plot up there," and Mitch pointed towards the upper part of the cemetery, the newer part, the part that was far away from where they were standing.

"She said she would not be buried for eternity next to a man she had come to despise, and she wanted to be close to her son that she loved. So, she bought that plot and had Mr. Jamison arrange for Pa to be reburied up there...away from her and the rest of the family. She said Pa was always an outsider and should remain one."

"Did you know about this?"

"Yes. In fact, Ma talked to me about it and said that if I didn't think it was proper then she wouldn't do it. I didn't care. Really, Pa was gone so much of the time, we barely knew him, and there are only a few good memories about him. Anyway, I always knew Mike was her favorite. I wanted her to rest easy, and if this made her happy, it was fine with me."

Mitch brushed a leaf that had just fallen onto the top of Viola's stone. He leaned down and pulled some weeds from in front of Mike's. Then he looked at Hattie.

"How do you know Mike was her favorite? I'm sure she loved you both the same."

"She did. Ma was loving and fair to both of us, but I always knew Mike was special to her in a way I wasn't. It's fine, Hattie. When Mike died, I know part of Ma did too. And, frankly, part of me died with Mike. He saved my life, you know. I'll tell you about it soon. Anyway, this whole thing will give the town something to discuss for a while," and now Mitch did laugh.

Hattie reached over and hugged her husband. They stood there silently for a while, looking at the graves and watching as additional foliage fell.

"I want to see Rebecca and Vernon. They are up there."

They left Viola and Mike and walked upwards towards the grave of Rebecca and the Memory Stone for Vernon, and when they got to the place, they both stopped.

"Look at that," remarked Hattie, "Here is Rebecca, and right across the lane, practically next to her is your father. Isn't that strange? Did your mother know where his new grave was going to be?"

"I don't think so. In fact, I remember her saying that she told Mr. Jamison just to put him up and away from the rest. That is weird that they are so close to each other."

Hattie and Mitch walked over and reread the stones of Vernon and Rebecca, and Hattie removed a few leaves and weeds from around them. They stayed still with their arms around each other until a wind kicked up and blew some of Hattie's curls into her face. Mitch pushed them back, leaned down and kissed her ear.

"Think we should get to your parents now?"

"Yes, we should go. They are expecting us, and we have a long trip home too. I'm anxious to get back to our apartment and check the mail. Maybe you got something from the Board of Education. That would be great! Hey, did I mention that the toaster needs to be fixed?"

They glanced once again at the graves and walked to the car discussing the unimportant items married people talk about. Mitch backed the car down the path and pulled out onto the road. They traveled towards the Wells' cabin leaving the cemetery. Leaving their families resting: Tillie and her long-gone husband and baby son; Mary and Michael Mitchell; Viola Mitchell Jasper and her son Michael John Jasper; the memory stone for Vernon Alexander Wells and little Rebecca Wells. And of course, just across the narrow lane from Rebecca, in a newly created grave, in eternal, cruel irony, John Joshua Jasper.

Beginnings

Edie cuddled her new daughter closely. Ned smiled as he watched Mary lean against her mother's knees and glare at her new little sister's head. Margaret, called *Maggie,* was one week old, and Mary did not like her.

"No!" she said to her mother, "Go 'way, baby!"

"Now, Mary, you will need to be kind. This is your little sister, and you will need to help take care of her." Edie attempted to describe her duties, but Mary had already lost interest and was chasing their dog around.

"Ned, did you read the letter from Mitch? I left it on the counter for you."

Ned, almost falling over the dog who was attempting to get away from Mary, went over to the counter, took the envelope, and pulled out the sheets which he scanned rapidly.

"That's great. He is at least subbing in the schools, and said he is sure of a full-time position in the fall. Hattie is still working, he writes, although she is beginning to show. I wonder if she will be able to work until the baby comes?"

"I'm not sure. We'll find out when they visit. I think they are coming down in about three weeks. Ned, quick, get the dog away from Mary! She has its tail in her mouth!"

***

Emma sat back in the chair on the front porch and watched two of her youngest grandchildren roll around the front yard. She was keeping them for Beatrice who had an appointment with Doctor Grenville to find out if she was pregnant with her fourth child. She was.

It was a warm spring day, and the window was open. Emma could see Bob as he sat at the desk and worked on his book. She leaned back to glance in and speak to him.

"I think I might go to Chicago when Hattie has the baby. She and Mitch can use my help for a while. What do you think? Will you be O.K. here by yourself?"

"I think that's a good idea. I'll be fine, and you know we are rarely alone here. Someone is always stopping by."

"Well, when I talk to Hattie again, I'll mention it," Emma turned and settled a struggle between the two children then came back to the porch and sat down. She watched for a minute then turned to the open window again.

"How's it coming, Bob?"

"It's coming, Emma. It would be faster if you didn't ask me every five minutes."

Emma laughed. "Just checking on you. It must be almost finished. You been working on it for years. Will you read it to me when it's finished?"

"If you want me to, but you might not be interested. I am writing about the Roman conquest of Britain. I've had some thoughts over the years, and I think I might have some new ideas about it."

Emma was silent for a second. "Do you will think it will get published?"

"Probably not…won't exactly be a best seller."

"So why are you writing it?"

"I suppose because I want to, Em, my love; I just want to."

***

Edna and Millie were just finishing up the evening dishes as Nathan came in from emptying the trash. The women took off their aprons, and the three of them went in to the front room to relax. Nathan grabbed the evening paper while Edna took her copy of *McCall's*. Millie took out her knitting and continued to work on a baby blanket for Hattie and Mitch.

"Nate, when Mitch and Hattie come down for a visit in a couple of weeks, we should ask the Wells over for dinner. What do you think?"

"Fine with me Edna. I enjoy talking to Bob. Maybe you should call and arrange it tomorrow."

"Mother, could you make a pie or two then? That strawberry ice-box pie you made was delicious."

"My eye? Why it's fine, Edna."

"PIE, MOTHER. COULD YOU MAKE A PIE WHEN THE WELLS COME FOR DINNER?"

"Oh, of course. What kind do you want?"

"Millie, Edna is talking about the strawberry ice-box pie that was so good. Right, Edna?"

"Call Harry? Harry who?"

"STRAWBERRY PIE, MOTHER. THAT IS WHAT NATE SAID. THE NEW ONE YOU MADE THAT WE ALL LIKED."

"Oh, that was a delicious one. Yes, I can. Will there be any strawberries this early?"

"Mother, I think you used strawberry Jell-O for the recipe. Didn't you?"

"Fellow? Is Harry the fellow you are talking about?"

Edna just shook her head and went back to her reading. Millie did not look up from her knitting because she began to count stitches and conversation stopped. Nathan waited a few minutes and then turned to his wife and quietly said:

"Why don't I just order a nice cake from Peterson's Bakery for then? They have some delicious cakes."

Edna looked at him and sighed. She nodded her head and turned the page of the magazine. Outside, the streetlights flickered on, and when a cold breeze came through the open window, Nathan got up and closed it, then sat back down to finish his paper.

Millie looked up and said, "Seems like it might rain."

Edna and Nathan just looked up from their reading and nodded their heads in agreement. The rest of the night passed quietly except for the gentle evening rain that fell.

***

Sherriff Samms leaned against the counter and tipped up the bottle of Coca-Cola for another swallow. Jim Banter came from behind the aisle and stood next to him. It was a quiet night, and the two men stood in silence staring out the pharmacy window. The sheriff was on his rounds, but felt the need for a sweet drink and some talk.

"Any news, Ed? Been quiet around here for a while. Course, I guess that's great from a lawman's viewpoint."

"Yep, quiet is good Jim. 'Bout the only thing I am hearing is the talk about the reburial of John Jasper. A bunch of folks are still chewing it around, and don't want to spit it out. I guess people have a right to be buried where they want to be, and that includes Viola. You hearing about it?"

"There are plenty who come into the store and ask me if I know about it because of Nate working here. But he didn't know 'till it happened. He said he was just as surprised as anyone else. Then there was all that talk about Jasper's doings when he was traveling years ago. You know about it…right?"

"Yep. Jasper was always a slick sort of man. Never understood Viola marrying him."

"That's because you were sweet on her, right?"

"That was a long time ago, Jim. Long ago. Viola was a catch around here, you know that. Her family owning the Emporium and all. But things happen. Sometimes you just can't figure a person out. Couldn't figure John Jasper out. Had a bad feeling about him, but nothing I could put my finger on. Guess we're just as bad as the town gossips…still hashing it all over. Right?'

"Yessirreebob, Ed, guess we are. Yessirreebob."

***

"Where's Andy?"

"He should be back soon. Went into town to pick up a few things and to get the mail. How about some coffee? Just made some fresh, and the bread should be cool enough to cut. I can offer you a slice of that with it."

"Sounds great. Thanks, Tess. You're a great baker. Hope you know how much I appreciate this."

"You are absolutely welcome. It's a pleasure having you here. Come on into the kitchen. I could use a cup of coffee too."

They went into the kitchen where Tess poured coffee and cut bread and then sat down at the table. They had just started eating when Andy walked in.

"Umm, smells like fresh-baked bread!"

"Sit down, and I'll get you some," and Tess got another cup. "Any mail?"

"Nothing for us. You have a letter here," and Andy passed the letter over the table.

The coffee was sipped and the bread was chewed, and after a while, Andy looked over and asked, "What's the news?"

Francis Frank Joseph folded the letter, looked at his brother, and with a pleased grin said, "Well, looks like I'm going to be a great-grand-father!"

***

Mitch put the coins into the pay phone which was down at the end of the maternity ward and dialed. When Emma answered, he tried to keep his voice down, but his excitement took over.

"No, not yet. The doctor said they are both fine, and I can see them in a little while. Would you? That's great. And could you also call Edie and Ned? Tell everyone I will call them later, but I really want to get back and see the baby. O.K. No, no name yet, but as soon as we decide, you will know. I will. Thanks. I'll call again later."

He hung up the phone and walked quickly back to the waiting room where there was no chance he was going to sit down and wait. He headed up to the main desk to ask when he could go into the room when a nurse came out and called him.

"Mr. Jasper? Your wife and baby are ready for you now. Come this way."

Mitch walked behind the nurse, and she smiled as he opened the door to see Hattie holding the baby who was swaddled in a blue blanket with his head peeking out. Hattie looked up at Mitch.

"Come here," and Hattie smiled, "Come here, and hold your son."

Mitch walked over to the bed, leaned down and kissed his wife. He sat on the side of the bed and held out his arms for the baby. Hattie carefully placed him in his father's arms, and he looked down at his sleeping son.

"He's perfect," said Mitch in awe.

He unwrapped the blanket and did the thing all new parents did...counted his small toes and fingers. The numbers were correct. As he began to wrap him up again, the baby's head shifted to the left and there, under his right ear, on his neck was a brown splotch. Mitch looked up at Hattie who was watching him.

"Oh, that's nothing. The nurse said it was just a small birth mark. Nothing to worry about."

Mitch looked down at the boy and then at Hattie.

"Michael," he said, "We'll call him Mike."

Hattie reached over to draw her son close to her and leaned down to his small sleeping face. She pulled the blanket around him and kissed his forehead as small eyelids fluttered.

"Hello, Mike," she whispered.

She looked up at her husband who was watching. Hattie's dimples showed as she reached out with her free hand to grasp his, and as he looked at his sleeping son and his wife, Mitch smiled.

The *Everstille* stories continue.

Following is the first chapter of the second book in the series.

Names

Names are strange things. Some names are obvious and under-standable. For example, *Jenson's Hardware and Agricultural Needs* is owned and run by the Jenson family. *Jamison's Livery Stable and Funeral Services* is handled by Mr. Jamison and his sons and has been forever. Likewise, *Clampet's Groceries* and *Peterson's Bakery* are managed by those families. Even *Mitchell's Emporium and Dry Goods* has the family name in its elegant title. And all those establishments are on or near Main Street, which is the main street in the town. Easy.

Other names are not so clear and logical. The town's name, *Everstille* was either named by one of the founding families who came from some place in France (or maybe Germany, depending upon who is telling the story) called the same, or it was a nod to the moonshiners whose stills may be easily found if you know exactly where to look. Some think that the final *e* of the name lends credence to the founding family from France (or Germany) story. But Sheriff Samms, who knows where most of the stills were and are, just nods his head and allows others to continue the discussion, which, on a warm, late summer day drinking some lemonade at Mazie's, is as good a discussion as any. By the way, *Mazie's* is dubbed that after the owner, Mazie.

And then there are those places which have names with no easy explanation, like North Cemetery which is a couple miles down the west road out of town. Of course, it is on the north side of the road which may account for the name. There was some talk for a while, of renaming it *Jamison Cemetery* after the man whose family owns the gloomy business and administers the sad activities there, but even Mr. Jamison did not want it named after his family. It remains North Cemetery, and most of Everstille's departed citizens have found an eternal home in its expanding boundaries. The Jamison family does have the monopoly on the burial business.

The road west of town was renamed when the Indiana County Board decided to make the country roads easy and logical to locate. The road is officially *County Road 8*. But many Everstille citizens, especially those who have lived in the area most of their lives, still call it by its original appellation, *Smokehouse Road*. The reason for the original name is undetermined and is no more apparent than the reason for the town's name. It had been suggested that there was a smokehouse somewhere in the area where meat from various animals, both wild and domesticated, was smoked. This sounds rational, but no one knows for sure.

Smokehouse Road (or County Road 8) runs east and west and the eastward path verves off to several smaller lanes while the main road continues into Everstille where it is renamed *Main Street* and runs through the town. If you start at the far end of North Cemetery and work eastward toward the town's Main Street, down County Road 8 (or Smokehouse Road), you will pass a quite a few wooded areas and farmlands and paths. One path travels through a copse and ends up in a clearing where a cabin stands. For years the cabin was inhabited by a Mr. Harvey, who under strange circumstances, abandoned the property. His cabin was eventually bought by a man named George Winter, and then inhabited by the Wells family who were in some way related to George. Then farther eastward was a small house with a shed and out-building which was the home of Ethel and Samuel Pinkerton and their children: Ernestine, Gladys, and Tobias. Eventually that house was sold to the Jaspers. East of the cemetery and set back from the main road was the Martin farm, and next to it, the Rivens farm. East of the Rivens farm, down an oak-lined path and into the woods just outside the main town was a shack. Shack is the term for it, although it was still habitable and two older brothers, fraternal twins lived there. Nowhere is there any evidence of a smokehouse.

My own name, Anne Olivia Rivens, also has a story. Both my great-grandmothers were named Anne, or at least a form of the name. One was *Anna* and the other was *Annette*, so I guess my parents thought that Anne with an *e* was a good compromise. I know the history of Everstille because I grew up there. My parents are Jena and David Rivens, and I grew up on the farm with my siblings: David Jr., Raymond, Elizabeth, and Joshua. The older fraternal twins who lived in that shack were my great-uncles, Jake and Lem, and I knew most of the families; the Wells, the Jaspers, the Pinkertons, who lived in the area. I am the youngest child in the Rivens family; Everstille is my hometown; Smokehouse Road is where I spent my youth; and the first part of this story is mine.